KERRY WILKINSON

BEHIND
CLOSED DOORS

PAN BOOKS

First published 2014 by Pan Books
an imprint of Pan Macmillan, a division of Macmillan Publishers Limited
Pan Macmillan, 20 New Wharf Road, London N1 9RR
Basingstoke and Oxford
Associated companies throughout the world
www.panmacmillan.com

ISBN 978-1-4472-4785-2

3 5 7 9 8 6 4 2

A CIP catalogue record for this book is available from the British Library.

Typeset by Ellipsis Digital Limited, Glasgow
Printed and bound by CPI Group (UK) Ltd, Croydon, CR0 4YY

Visit www.panmacmillan.com to read more about all our books
and to buy them. You will also find features, author interviews and
news of any author events, and you can sign up for e-newsletters
so that you're always first to hear about our new releases.

BEHIND CLOSED DOORS

Despite two national newspaper reports to the contrary, Kerry Wilkinson is male. Honestly.

His debut, *Locked In*, the first title in the detective Jessica Daniel series, was written as a challenge to himself but became a UK Number One Kindle bestseller within three months of release.

His three initial Jessica Daniel books made him Amazon UK's top-selling author for the final quarter of 2011. When *Think of the Children* followed in 2013, he became the first formerly self-published British author to have an ebook Number One and reach the top twenty of the UK paperback chart.

Following *Playing with Fire* and *Thicker Than Water*, *Behind Closed Doors* is the seventh title in the Jessica Daniel series.

Kerry has a degree in journalism, plays cricket badly and complains about the weather a lot. He was born in Somerset but now lives in Lancashire, thus explaining the climate gripes.

For more information about Kerry and his books visit:

Website: www.kerrywilkinson.com

or www.panmacmillan.com

Twitter: http://twitter.com/kerrywk

Facebook: http://www.facebook.com/JessicaDanielBooks

Or you can email Kerry at

kerryawilkinson@googlemail.com

By Kerry Wilkinson

LOCKED IN

VIGILANTE

THE WOMAN IN BLACK

THINK OF THE CHILDREN

PLAYING WITH FIRE

THICKER THAN WATER

BEHIND CLOSED DOORS

BEHIND CLOSED DOORS

PROLOGUE

Liam followed the sound of the footsteps ahead that were cracking and crunching a path through the woods. There was more clamour from behind too, the man so close Liam could smell his aftershave carrying on the breeze.

As he stared into the darkness of the blindfold, he tried to figure out if the sensation surging along his leg was the normal type of pins and needles he often experienced after waking up, or if he was actually in pain. He remembered one morning when he was a kid, hearing a banging on the cupboard next to his bed, only to realise it was his foot tapping against the wood. He had been resting on it the whole night and couldn't feel a thing. Now the sensation was similar, the stinging he knew he should be feeling replaced by a numbness that made his legs heavy.

Liam felt a hand at the bottom of his back, pushing him along, his feet catching the twigs on the floor, sending him stumbling. The man behind reached forward, grabbing the scruff of his collar roughly, stopping him from falling and then shoving him again.

'Keep walking straight,' he ordered, as if Liam had any thoughts of running away. He knew he was getting what he deserved.

Liam's shoes scuffed across a loose stone, making him trip. He steadied himself, fumbling in the dark until his hand found a tree trunk that he used to haul his body up quickly before the man could shove him again.

Behind, he heard a grunt of amusement.

There was a wet patch on his knees from the fall, the first definite sensation he had felt in his legs since being dragged into the woods. The rest of his body seemed unlike his own, his arms floppy and unresponsive despite the bark chips on his hands, his eyelids heavy and tired. He knew there must have been something in the water he had been given that made him like this but it was all part of his punishment.

Liam focused on the dampness through his trousers, trying to savour more or less the only thing he could feel. Underfoot, the land began to slope gently downwards. The footsteps in front of him were moving quickly away but the man was still close behind as a gust of wind howled ominously, swirling and curving through the trees. It chilled Liam's ears, making him shiver, unbalanced. With his vision blocked and his limbs sluggish, Liam's sense of hearing was his only steadying influence and he lurched to the side, skidding on a patch of leaves and getting his foot caught in something that felt like a rope.

This time there was nothing to use to stop his fall. Liam hit the ground face-first, his head cannoning off a loose rock. He tried to breathe in but inhaled a mouthful of grass, spluttering painfully as the taste of coppery blood filled his mouth. Jolts rocketed through his hip and it felt as if he had been punched in the chest, the pins and needles firmly replaced by agony. The worst sting was from where he had bitten his tongue. Blood flowed down his windpipe, making him cough again. He tried to breathe through his nose, only to find more blood there.

Abruptly Liam felt himself being hauled up. The collar was tight around his neck, throttling into his throat. Flecks of blood splattered from his mouth, his chest tight and sore. He wanted to bend over to compose himself but the man now had both hands on him, one gripping his windpipe, the other wrenching his arm. He yelped in pain, wishing he could feel the pins and needles again, but there was more to come as his assailant punched him hard across the face, still grasping his throat. Liam was struggling to breathe as a second blow came, smashing across his ear and sending him sprawling to the ground again.

He heard the hard thud of the man's boot on his back and legs before he felt it, each crunch punctuated by a tirade of abuse shouting about what a disgrace he was. Liam lay on the floor hugging himself. He knew that each word the man spat was the truth, each kick a necessary part of his penance.

Finally, he heard the second voice, telling the man to stop and that Liam had had enough. Liam felt one final boot to the back of his neck before he was hauled to his feet. The blindfold had slipped slightly but he could see only stars anyway. Blood poured from his mouth and nose, dribbling across his chin and dripping to the ground. The man grabbed his arm, hauling him down the rest of the slope until Liam felt water sloshing around his ankles.

'Keep walking,' he was told as his arms were released.

Liam daren't refuse, staggering forward as the water gradually reached his knees, the icy chill making him gasp in surprise. He was back to not knowing if he was hurting, the water freezing and boiling at the same time, suppressing the pain of the blows, new and old.

He continued walking until the water was above his waist and then he heard the voice of his saviour. 'Come to me, Liam.'

The soothing way his name was spoken made him feel as if he was the only person in the world and he took two more steps forward before he felt hands on his neck, untying the blindfold.

Liam blinked rapidly, the searing white of the moon reflecting from the surface of the water and making his eyelids flutter so quickly that the strobing flashes of light and dark reminded him of being in a nightclub in his younger days.

'Are you ready?'

Liam nodded, still gasping for breath as his eyes adjusted to the scene. The gentle black of the rippling water was serenely beautiful, a calming, fitting way for him to be cleansed.

'Kneel.'

He was shivering uncontrollably but Liam did as he was told, the water lapping his chin.

'Do you know why you're here?' he was asked.

'Yes.'

'What do you have to say for yourself?'

'That I'm sorry. I wish I hadn't gone back to my old ways.'

Liam felt the waves brimming around him, splashing over the top of his lips as their presence closed.

4

'That's good of you,' the voice cooed. 'But now it's time to wash those sins away.'

Liam felt one hand pressing on his forehead, another on his back as he was rocked backwards into the water. He hadn't taken a breath quickly enough and water flooded into his nostrils and mouth. His instincts made him want to cough, to gasp for breath, but the hands held him under.

He flailed his legs, trying to squirm towards the surface, but the grip was firm, pushing him down deeper until Liam could feel nothing but the frosty water enveloping him in a final, decisive baptism.

1

Detective Sergeant Jessica Daniel stared at the muted television screen as the stream of adverts flittered past. With little else to do and no inclination to turn up the volume, she made up her own version of what the actors would be saying to each other. A man had taken a gulp of some luminous pink juice and was now running around like a lunatic, women falling at his feet.

'Just like real life,' Jessica said out loud to the empty room as her thoughts were interrupted by the sound of the doorbell.

Quickly, she switched off the television with the remote control and moved around the room until she was sitting underneath the window. There was a knock on the door and then the bell rang a second time. Jessica held her breath, wondering if the uninvited visitor would be peering through the crack between the curtains above her, looking to see if there was anyone in.

Sometimes the postman came around but Jessica always ignored him, letting her neighbour take in the parcel and then picking it up later. As the door rattled again, Jessica knew it couldn't be him. He would never ring the bell more than once, let alone knock twice as well.

The letterbox clanged and then Jessica heard Detective Chief Inspector Jack Cole's voice echoing through the hallway, calling her name. She tried to work out the last time she had spoken to him. It was definitely months, with her ignoring his phone calls until they stopped completely.

'Jess, I know you're there . . .'

Her name reverberated a second time, not a 'sergeant', 'detective', or even 'Jessica'; instead he was letting her know that he wasn't there as her boss but as something else.

A friend.

Jessica knew she had abandoned her mates over recent months, not the other way around.

'Jess, please let me in . . .'

Another knock, another ring of the bell and then a tap on the glass above her.

'I'll wait here all day if I have to.'

'Go away!'

Jessica's reply had escaped before she had a chance to stop it, ending any pretence that she wasn't in. The letterbox banged closed and Jessica stood, turning to see Jack's face watching through the gap in the curtains. Perhaps it was because of the dim light or silvery skies but his skin seemed greyer than the last time she had seen him. His forehead was crinkled with worry but he was sporting a kindly half-smile. She couldn't help but make eye contact as he mouthed 'Hello'.

She wanted to close the curtains, to tell him to leave her be, but something drew her towards the hallway until she found herself turning the key and pulling the door open.

Jack was standing there, hands in pockets. Rain had welded his thinning hair to his scalp, drops cascading over him, dripping to the floor.

Jessica hadn't noticed it was raining.

'Can I come in?' he asked, glancing towards the sky.

'Why are you here?'

'To see you.'

'You've done that now.'

The DCI brushed a flurry of water away from his face. 'Okay, to talk then.'

'We're talking now.'

He snorted a mix of laughter and rain. 'I'm guessing this is what it feels like to be on the opposite side of an interview room to you.'

Jessica shrugged, not wanting to think about anything from the station.

'So can I come in?'

Pulling the door open, Jessica stood to the side, not saying anything. Cole offered a 'thank you', stepping inside and wiping his feet before she closed the door.

'I didn't know you'd moved,' he said, taking off his coat. 'HR still have you in a flat in Salford Quays. I had to put a few calls in to find out where you were living. It was like being a proper police officer again, before all the form-filling came in.'

Jessica took his coat and hung it over the banister of the stairs, leading the way through to the living room.

'Nice place you've got here,' Cole said. 'One of the constables before your time used to live in Swinton too.

He once told me that the name comes from Old English, where it meant pig farm.'

Jessica pulled the curtains open, letting the fading grey of the Manchester skies fill the room. She moved to the sofa as the DCI sat opposite her in an armchair.

'Being called a pig is part of the job, so it's probably fair enough,' Jessica replied.

Cole smiled. 'What was wrong with the flat?'

Jessica wasn't in the mood for chit-chat but figured she didn't want to go out of her way to be rude. 'It wasn't ours. We were only staying there because of the fire at Adam's house.'

Cole nodded. 'Ah yes, it was your friend's as I recall.'

Jessica knew he was trying to draw her into a conversation, fishing for information, wondering if they owned this new house together, or if it was just her. She could feel him watching her but didn't want to make eye contact. 'It's good to see you,' he eventually said.

Jessica tucked her long, unwashed dark blonde hair behind her ears, suddenly feeling self-conscious about her appearance. She was wearing tracksuit bottoms and a vest-top with loose straps that kept slipping over her shoulder from where she had lost weight.

'Why are you here?'

'Because it's time we had a chat. I know you've been through a lot.'

Jessica felt the lump in her throat that had been all too close recently. She glanced towards the window, not wanting her boss to see the wetness around her eyes.

'You don't know what I've been through.'

'I didn't mean it like that.' He paused, hunting for the right words. 'We all miss you. I know it's a workplace and we get paid for being there but it's like a little family too. I've watched you grow up.'

Jessica didn't reply.

'I was out with my daughter at the weekend, it was my turn for custody. She's a right bundle of energy. We went to the park with one of her friends and she spent hours racing around, climbing, running, swinging, but most of all laughing. I probably only have a few months of that left before she doesn't want to be seen with her dad any more. I was on a bench overlooking everything and she came over every half an hour, saying, "Did you see me, Dad?" Me and her mother have had such problems but I've never been happier than I was seeing that grin on her face.'

Jessica swallowed hard. 'Why are you telling me this?'

'Because on the way home, they were both in the back seat of the car. Someone had been to their school talking about careers and they were full of it. My daughter said firmly, "I want to be a policeman just like Daddy". I didn't have time to tell her not to bother because of the hours, pay and everything else we deal with because her friend cut in. She said, "Only men can be police officers". I don't know where she got that from but my daughter asked if it was true. I told her that not only could girls be police officers but they were often the best ones.'

The lump in Jessica's throat was so large that she could barely breathe and she struggled to reply. 'What do you want me to say?'

'Nothing, I just wanted you to know that we're thinking of you. Isobel and Dave are lost.'

'I'm not ready yet.'

'And there's no pressure for you to be . . .'

Cole tailed off, the only noise being the gentle clatter of rain on concrete outside and the faint sound of traffic from the main road. Jessica tried to think of the last time she had been out by herself, other than to collect a parcel from next door or to visit the shop at the end of the road to pick up some bread or milk. The house had become her prison as much as a home.

She could still feel his eyes on her but continued staring at the blank television screen.

'How are things with—?'

Jessica interrupted before Cole could finish. 'Why are you really here?'

He took a deep breath. 'Something's happened—'

'I told you I'm not ready yet.'

'It's not what you think. We've been asked for assistance by a different district.'

'That happens all the time. We tell them we've got no officers free and they move on.'

'This is different. They're looking for a certain type of person.'

'And you think that's me?'

'I think most things could be you if you wanted them to be . . .'

Jessica didn't respond at first, letting the rain fill the gap before eventually replying. 'You're not going to make me do anything just by being nice.'

Cole laughed. 'Would you rather I was nasty?'

'Just tell me what it is.'

The DCI cleared his throat, any pretence gone. 'We pulled a man's body out of the canal a few weeks ago. He was only wearing his underwear, no wallet, no ID. His head had been shaved, so had his eyebrows, chest, armpits – everything. He had been badly beaten and was covered in bruises.'

'What killed him?'

'He had been drowned. You know what it's like, no free officers, waiting on forensics. It's the same every time. Isobel was a star as ever, working her way through the lists of missing people until we only had a dozen or so to check. We eventually got it down to one name.'

'Anyone I'd know?'

Cole shook his head, raising his voice slightly as the sound of the rain increased. 'It was someone named Liam Renton. He had a very minor criminal record with a couple of drunk and disorderlies, theft from a shop and a threatening behaviour charge that was dropped.'

Jessica didn't want to appear interested but she could feel herself being drawn in. 'How old was he?'

'Twenty-four. He's a native Manc.'

'How does that connect to a different district?'

'We visited his family. Unlike what you might expect, his parents are still together. He's got two younger sisters and a younger brother. They come from a respectable area.'

'That doesn't mean much.'

'Quite – but I visited myself. You know what it's like when you have a feeling about people but there was none of that. None of them had spoken to him in a year or so. His mum said he had big problems with alcohol and drugs but it was his younger brother who knew the most.'

'How young?'

'He's eighteen but he'd heard things from around the estate about what his brother was up to. At first it was all drink and drugs and that was why he had been ostracised by the family but around six months ago, Liam cleaned himself up – at least according to his brother.'

'What then?'

Cole shuffled nervously in the seat, glancing away from Jessica towards the window and then back again. 'Then he disappeared. The rest of his family hadn't seen him in a year but his brother knew what he'd been up to from the mutual people they knew. Then it all stopped.'

'But he only turned up dead recently?'

'The brother said he'd heard Liam had been recruited.'

'What for? The army?'

Cole shook his head, reaching into his back pocket for a notebook. The fact he was completely prepared wasn't lost on Jessica. So much for only wanting a chat.

'How well do you know the Bible?' he asked, not looking at the pad.

'A bit. I went to Sunday School as a kid. Basically we're not allowed to be gay but we are allowed to keep slaves. We're supposed to love one another but an eye for an eye is fair game too. It's all very confusing.'

Cole looked down at his pad. 'There's a group up on the Lancashire–Yorkshire border that live in a massive stately home. They've been on the local watch list for a little while. Once a week or so, they visit the centres of the bigger cities, Manchester, Leeds, and so on, recruiting.'

The penny dropped for Jessica. 'They're a religious cult?'

Cole shrugged. 'That's the point, no one really knows what they are. To all intents and purposes, they are simply a group of friendly people trying to help. On the streets, they preach that drugs and alcohol are sins. They say they can help cure people of their addictions.'

'And that's where Liam ended up?'

'Yes.'

'So why hasn't the local force gone in and sorted things?'

Cole glanced at his pad again before putting it back on the arm of the chair. 'There's a lot of money involved. I don't know the exact details of the house and the people inside but they have expensive lawyers. Police have been to interview the people in charge, who even admitted that Liam lived there.'

'But . . .'

'They said he simply left and that they haven't seen him in weeks. Officers spoke to everyone there but the story was identical: he had started drinking again, so they asked him to leave. That was the last they saw of him.'

Jessica stayed silent for a moment, knowing exactly where the conversation was headed. She even knew why Cole had come to her. A year ago, she would have jumped at the chance but things were different now.

It was as if he had read her mind. 'They're asking neighbouring forces for a certain type of person: someone tough and streetwise, female if possible. Someone not known in their local district. A person who can blend in, get on with people if need be but generally poke around and find out what's going on. The key is that it has to be someone who can look after themselves. They'll be on their own.'

'You want to send me in?'

'I don't want to do anything. Nobody knows I'm here. I know what's happened to you over the past nine months and I'm not trying to say I understand because I don't. I'm simply saying I know. If you want to stay here doing whatever it is you're doing then that's fine. You're on indefinite leave and we'll wait for you – I'll wait. But if you want to return, this is a way of coming back without actually having to.'

Jessica shook her head. 'What if I don't want to?'

'Then we'll move on. They'll find someone else. The crucial part is that if you're going to do it, then you have to have a sense of self-preservation. It could be dangerous, they need someone who's sharp and resilient. Someone who can get themselves out at a moment's notice if necessary.'

'You think that's me?'

Cole's reaction surprised her. Jessica had been expecting him to lay a guilt trip on her, offering her a way to return to work, even though she wasn't ready. Instead he started to stand. 'Actually, now I've seen you, no, I don't.'

Jessica remained sitting, aware of him standing over her. She wasn't sure why but his words felt like a rebuke, a questioning of everything she had ever done.

'Is this about what happened with Scott and the gun going off?'

A poor piece of judgement by Jessica had led to her trying to make an arrest with her friend and colleague, Detective Constable David Rowlands. Their target pulled out a gun and fired. The fact they had so badly misjudged what could have happened led to an official inquiry.

'We were all cleared of that,' Cole replied. 'It was no one's fault but the person who brought weapons onto the premises and the one who pulled the trigger. Besides, we both know there's far more to it than that.'

Jessica stood quickly, aggrieved. She glared into her boss's eyes but he had none of the anger she was suddenly feeling. 'Is this some reverse psychology thing? You say I'm not up to it, so I change my mind to try to prove you wrong?'

Cole shook his head. 'Even if it was, you'd see through it instantly, in much the way you just have.'

'So what is it then?'

He sighed, turning up the collar on his shirt and moving through the house to the hallway where he took his coat from the banister and put it on. Jessica followed him, furious he wasn't replying.

'Come on,' she demanded, tears close. 'What is it?'

As soon as he met her eyes, she knew. 'I already told you – it's about self-preservation. If the volunteer gets into trouble, they need to have the sense to get themselves out. They have to look after themselves first. You can only do that if you're bothered what happens to you.'

'You don't think I care what happens to me?'

Jessica could hear the whimper in her voice. She wanted to deny it, to shout that she *did* care, but she knew it would be a lie.

Cole watched her carefully.

'I'm broken,' she whispered.

He stepped forward, putting a protective arm around her. Jessica embraced him, cradling her head into his shoulder and barely hanging onto the tears.

His reply was firm and fatherly. 'If you want things to change, sometimes you have to help yourself.'

SATURDAY

2

Jessica gasped as she walked into the pub, the chill of the air outside replaced by the warm orange glow and crackling of the fire next to the bar. Her footsteps creaked on the hard wooden floor and Jessica felt people turning to face her, wondering who the stranger was. She made her snap judgements, as she always did.

There was the farmer on his own at the bar, dried mud on his wellington boots and a heavy dark green waxed jacket, ready to head out again. In a booth to her right was a middle-aged man and a woman, refusing to acknowledge anyone else. They were no doubt having an affair and had sneaked off to this countryside hideaway, safe from the accusing eyes of their partners.

In the back corner was a couple staring at plates of half-eaten food, not talking, not doing anything other than wallowing in the broken remains of their unhappy marriage. Behind the bar, a bored young bar girl in a too-tight T-shirt was wiping a glass with a tea towel, wiggling her pert bottom for the customers as she turned and reached to put it onto a shelf. She would no doubt be out of this back end of nowhere and off to see the real world as soon as she had some money.

Jessica scanned the rest of the bar, looking for the person she was supposed to be meeting. She only had a

name but had arrogantly assumed it couldn't be that difficult to find one person in such a small place.

'Can I help you?'

The girl behind the bar had finished putting the glass
on the shelf and was eyeing Jessica.

'I'm fine,' Jessica replied, although she had now attracted
the attention of the lone farmer at the bar. She walked past
him, looking from side to side and checking each booth
until she had done a full lap of the pub. When she was by
the door again, Jessica took out her phone, noting that she
was on time, and then called the person she was due to
meet.

Her phone beeped an instant rejection.

'You won't get a signal around here, love,' the farmer at
the bar said, scratching the greying stubble on his chin
and grinning crookedly. He had yellow teeth, with a gap
at the front where one was missing. 'Are you looking for
someone?'

'Someone named Charlie. I'm supposed to be meeting
him here . . .'

He grinned, gaze scanning across her body. 'I can be
Charlie if you want me to be.'

Jessica ignored him, starting another lap of the pub.
The only men there were either in groups with other
blokes, or with a female.

As she finished her second circuit, Jessica took out the
note from Cole with the name, time and place written on
it and checked the name of the pub over the top of the
bar, just to make sure she was in the right place. The

farmer was grinning at her, patting the empty seat next to him, but Jessica ignored him, starting a third lap.

In the back corner was a woman sitting by herself reading a book. Jessica's lack of interaction with people over the past few months made her nervous about approaching a stranger but she didn't have many other options as everyone else seemed to be in groups or pairs.

'Excuse me,' Jessica said, approaching the table. 'Do you live around here?'

The woman looked up from her book. She was a little older than Jessica, in her late thirties, with long brown hair tied into a ponytail. She had long eyelashes and a small button nose. Considering she was the prettiest woman in the pub, it was a surprise she was the only one by herself.

'I do but I've not been here for too long,' she replied. 'If you're looking for directions, I'm probably not the best person to ask.'

Jessica peered down at Cole's note. 'I'm looking for Charlie Bailey. Do you know him?'

The woman grinned as she closed her book, putting it on the table and stretching out a hand. 'Charlotte Bailey, pleased to meet you. You must be Jessica.'

Jessica shook her hand awkwardly, unsure what to say and feeling even more self-conscious. 'Sorry, my DCI left me a note saying "Charlie" and I assumed . . .'

Charley took the note, reading it with a smile and handing it back. Her voice was posh, each word perfectly pronounced. 'It's the way he's spelled it. I go for an E-Y at the end. I'm guessing you tried calling but there's no reception out here.'

Jessica slid into the booth opposite her. 'I tried when I got off the train, then from the taxi, then when I arrived at the pub.'

Charley shook her head. 'It's pretty remote here. You get patches where everything works perfectly, then five steps away, you'll lose reception entirely. The locals spent years campaigning against a phone mast being put in, so they can't really complain.'

'You're not local then?'

It was an obvious question given the accent but Charley answered anyway. 'No, I'm from Jersey.'

'The island?'

'Unless you know another one.'

Charley continued smiling and Jessica could tell she had been asked these questions many times before. Jessica figured that if she was going to end up working with someone, then she may as well find out all she could about them.

'How did you end up here?'

Charley raised a hand, catching the attention of a barman who was picking up glasses. She ordered a glass of wine for herself and a soft drink for Jessica.

'I studied medieval history at Cambridge. When I finished, I wasn't sure what I wanted to do but applied to the police on a whim. I did a bit of time in uniform down south and did the usual swap over to CID, working my way up. One day, I saw a job advertised on our internal system for a DCI position up here. One thing led to another and here I am.'

Charley's eyes were bright blue, brimming with enthusiasm and a charm Jessica could only wish for.

'So you come from the Channel Islands?'

'Yes.'

'And you went to Cambridge? *The* Cambridge, not some satellite polytechnic where you have a load of dropouts studying fashion and the media, or something like that?'

'Yes.'

'But you joined the police?'

'Yes.'

'And now you're up living on the Lancs–Yorks border in the middle of nowhere?'

'Exactly.'

Jessica paused for a moment, wondering if there was a polite way to phrase her next question. When she realised there wasn't, she simply went for it.

'*Why*?'

Charley laughed, a girly giggle that Jessica guessed could have snared many men over the years. She flicked her hair away from her face, grinning. 'I suppose I figured, "Why not?". It felt like something different to do.'

'But you studied history at Cambridge. Surely that opens a few doors?'

Charley shrugged. 'Yes but boring doors. I wanted to go and work with real people.'

'Do you know anyone around here?'

'Not before I came.'

'So you moved halfway across the country by yourself, even though you didn't know anyone?'

'I suppose it sounds a bit strange when you put it like that. For me it was a new experience.'

Jessica's own definition of a new experience within the policing world would be a transfer to a Caribbean island to work in the sun for a few years. Some village in the middle of nowhere would certainly provide a new experience – but it wasn't one she would go out of her way to choose.

Before she could say anything, the barman returned with a tray and their drinks. Charley knew him by name, patting him on the arm and saying she hoped his mother was feeling better. He was only eighteen or nineteen and blushed at the attention of an attractive woman twice his age, stumbling over a reply before tripping over his own feet as he turned to walk away. Jessica could see that Charley had already made her presence felt in the area, although being a DCI meant she must have responsibility for more than simply this village.

As he walked out of earshot, Charley raised her eyebrows. 'You've got to keep them on their toes,' she winked.

Jessica wanted to dislike her but couldn't resist being charmed. Despite this being somewhere that she struggled to find on a map, there was something almost romantic about the notion of dropping everything and anyone you had ever known and creating a new life for yourself. She could sense the appeal.

Charley took a sip of her wine. 'So, you're Jessica,' she said. 'I've heard a bit about you.'

Jessica fought not to squirm, wondering if someone had

been talking out of turn about what had happened in the last nine months. 'What have you heard?'

'Well, mainly read. I looked your name up. You've been involved in some interesting cases in the past. You're quite the star. I'm surprised you're still a sergeant . . .'

Charley might have been fishing for answers but Jessica ignored the unasked question anyway. 'It's not just me.'

The other woman took another sip of her wine, smiling knowingly. 'No "I" in team. I get it. Unfortunately, this is very much an "I"-type of job. Are you good at working on your own?'

Jessica always felt she was better by herself, figuring things out, getting on people's nerves and generally making things happen. She nodded, unwilling to talk herself up.

Charley turned, pointing directly behind her towards a window. 'About two miles that way is an enormous old stately home. It's one of these places that has been handed down through generations of families for hundreds of years. It's never been open to the public, so we can only guess at what it's like on the inside, but outside it is beautiful. It's made of this stunning honey-coloured stone, with huge windows and lush green lawns. To see it is like stepping back in time. You can imagine Victorians in their flowing gowns and top hats playing croquet in the front garden.'

'And this is where things are based?'

'"Things" indeed. I know your lot fished Liam Renton out of the canal but he's not the only person connected to that place who has gone missing. The force around here have been watching them for eight or nine years, long before I arrived, but there's never anything concrete. When you sent through the ID on Liam's body, I went with a team of my own. They invited us in, shunted us into the closest room so we couldn't see much and then we did interview after interview getting the same useless information. With Liam they admitted he'd been there but said he had been expelled weeks previously. Everyone repeated it, no inconsistencies, no one to say any differently. With their big, expensive lawyers there, there's little else we can do.'

'So you want me to get myself into their group?'

Charley took a larger swig of her drink but her eyes didn't leave Jessica. 'We want someone who would fit the right criteria. Young, vulnerable-looking, steely on the inside. We don't know what they might be getting up to.'

'Who are the people you know about?'

Charley didn't seem to mind Jessica steering the subject away from herself. She pushed back into her chair. 'The person who owns the house – at least according to the deeds – is Sophie Lewis. She's married to Jan Lewis. Sophie's father was a very wealthy landowner but she was his only heir and is now the only remaining member of that family.'

'I've never heard of her.'

'There's no reason you should have done but neither of them use their real names anyway. Jan calls himself "Moses", Sophie is "Zipporah".'

Jessica scrunched her face in confusion but Charley continued. 'In the Bible, Zipporah is Moses's wife.'

'Is it a religious sect?'

Charley shook her head. 'We're not sure. In the city centres when they are recruiting, they don't really talk about God or the Bible. They talk about getting past the addiction of drugs, alcohol and other things. They speak about depression and how it can be cured. When they get people back to the house, we have no idea what happens. Moses never seems to leave, instead sending his followers out to do his work for him. In fairness, for the most part, people seem okay there but there's obviously something going on because of Liam and the ones before him.'

Jessica finally took a sip of her own drink. 'What do you need me to do?'

The other officer didn't point out that Jessica hadn't been accepted to do anything yet – she was simply here for a chat. 'The first thing would be to get yourself in. From what we can tell, they go to four different city centres on alternate Sundays. They do Leeds, Bradford, Sheffield and Manchester. Assuming they don't change the pattern, tomorrow will be Manchester.'

'So I should visit them?'

'We're not really sure how tough the recruitment policy is – assuming there's anything formal at all. It might be a case of talking to them and being invited, or there could be something far more disturbing. Whoever it is would be on their own. One of the things we do know from the recruiting sessions is that electronics are banned within the house. No phones, no way to communicate. Everything would have to be weighed from the need to find out what's going on compared to the individual's own personal safety. We need someone who has good judge-ment, someone who might have to cross a line or two but knows where to stop.'

Jessica nodded, her heart beating faster. If it wasn't for the 'good judgement' instruction, Charley might as well have said they needed her.

'If there are no communications, how would I report back?'

Charley again ignored the 'I'. 'Whoever it was would have to remember everything. Don't write it down, don't talk to anyone else there. When the time came and there was enough to report, they would have to sneak out as and when they could. There may be slight changes to the plan depending on what we can clear but that would basically be it. We need to know if they have weapons. Does Moses have everyone enraptured? For instance, would the other residents do something like kill themselves if he told them to? Would they attack others? Who is his right-hand man? What about Zipporah? She's one of the recruiters but we know he changed his name first, so we're assuming she's in his thrall too. Then of course, we want to know where the people are going – and why someone like Liam Renton is dead.'

'How high is this going?'

Charley finished her wine in one. 'Let's just say there are people above me who know. This way, I act as the face of whatever goes on. If it goes wrong, guess who gets it in the neck. If it goes well, guess who gets the credit. We both know what it's like. In essence, this is my thing, at least for now.'

'And you want me?'

Jessica knew it was a direct question that needed an answer. Without a drink to hide behind, Charley had to reply. 'Perhaps. Your record is good. What are things like away from the station? Are you single?'

Jessica stumbled over the start of a reply but Charley was firm. 'I'm not asking because I need your personal life story, I'm asking because we need a certain type of person. Are you single?'

'It's complicated . . . I'm not married.'

Charley narrowed her eyes. 'If this goes badly it will be someone's career down the pan at the absolute least. At worst . . .' She tailed off, before adding: 'We can't have someone who's worrying about their home life. It has to be someone who can become a part of whatever community it is they have inside the house. You might be there for a few days, perhaps months. We need someone who has nothing to lose.'

Jessica couldn't meet Charley's eyes, staring out of the window and feeling the lump in her throat again. 'I've already lost.'

SUNDAY

3

Jessica could not remember the last time she felt nervous walking around Manchester city centre. The scroats with their hooded tops, backsides hanging out of their jeans and skewed baseball caps were a constant annoyance, even when she was on the job, but they never made her nervous. As she passed a group of lads resting at the corner of the shopping centre smoking, one of them whistled.

'Y'all right, sexy?' someone called.

Jessica didn't know if they were shouting after her or some other unfortunate girl behind her but she didn't stop to find out. Is that what courtship had come to? What did the lads think would happen? That some attractive young woman would throw her heels aside and dash across the path, desperate to copulate because some too-thin rake of a boy called her 'sexy'?

She kept walking, thinking how she would have had the lot of them emptying their pockets in an impromptu stop and search if she had been a couple of years younger.

A couple of years angrier.

It wasn't them making her nervous, it was being outside. The endless blanket of grey sky overhead, the smell of drizzle in the air, the hum of the trams, the number of people hurrying from shop to shop, desperate to snap up a bargain. The setting and sounds were familiar and yet it felt alien, as if she had stumbled into the wrong city that looked the same but was somehow subtly different. The confidence she once had around people felt like a distant memory too, replaced by an edginess whenever anyone with a pushchair came too close, or if a child skipped across her path.

Jessica wondered if she had made a mistake. She didn't know if Cole had used reverse psychology on her but she had gone for it anyway, determined to prove she still had it. With Charley, it was more a fascination that this talented, attractive woman would ditch everything she knew to move to the middle of nowhere for a new experience. It felt so appealing, so close, that Jessica found herself wanting to do her best for Charley, to show the other woman that taking such a brave punt wasn't a silly thing to do. If a change of life worked out for Charley then perhaps . . .

Jessica didn't get a chance to finish the thought as she looked up to see the group of people standing in a semicircle under the covered area at the front of the Arndale shopping centre. Charley had shown her a photograph of Zipporah, who was standing in the middle. On the edges were the younger women; attractive and thin, perfect for recruiting vulnerable young people.

After watching them for a few moments, she crossed to the other side of the path, walking towards the group with her head down, hands in pockets.

'Hello,' one of the younger girls said as Jessica approached.

Her first instinct was to keep walking, as she did when any of those idiot charity collectors came anywhere near her with a clipboard. Instead, she glanced up at the smiling girl and returned the smile with a weak one of her own.

'Morning.'

'I was wondering if you might have a few minutes free. My name's Heather and—'

'I'm not buying anything.'

Heather had long blonde hair tied loosely into a ponytail, with high cheekbones that curved prettily as she smiled. Her face should have been beautiful but her eyes didn't match the expression; they looked through Jessica, sad and longing.

'I'm not trying to sell anything,' she replied, taking a few steps away from the rest of the group until she and Jessica were by themselves next to a pillar. 'We're here to help people who need it.'

'What makes you think I need helping?'

Heather couldn't have been any older than twenty-one or twenty-two. She narrowed her eyes. 'Do you?'

Jessica wanted to be slightly awkward, thinking most people approached by the group wouldn't automatically want to be a part of it. They would expect an initial hostility. Heather's question took her by surprise, largely because it was so direct.

'I . . . don't know,' she stumbled, truthfully.

Heather nodded slowly, her smile gentler this time. 'Let me introduce you to Zip.'

She touched Jessica gently on the arm, leading her

towards the semicircle. There were murmurs of approval as Heather directed her towards the centre.

There was one man in his early twenties but everyone else was female, all a similar age with one exception – Zipporah. From the few details they had on her, Jessica knew the woman was thirty-nine, although she looked younger. Her hair was long, straight and black, her eyes a piercing brown. She was looking at Jessica with a motherly sense of concern, even though there were only a few years between them.

Jessica doubted it was impromptu but the younger people, including Heather, drifted away into twos and threes, clutching leaflets, ready to talk to anyone else nearby.

'What's your name, dear?' Zipporah asked. It was easy to forget how close they were in age because everything about the woman with the exception of her flawless skin exuded experience.

'Jessica.'

The woman offered her hand and they shook. 'I'm Zipporah but many call me Zip. I know you're probably uneasy about being accosted on the street but I can assure you we mean no harm to anyone. We're simply looking for lost souls . . .'

Jessica couldn't maintain eye contact, glancing awkwardly towards the floor. She wondered if the reason Cole had come to her wasn't because he thought she was perfect for it from a policing point of view but because the only way they could truly place someone on the inside was if they found someone dead enough on the inside to fit in. She suddenly felt teary again, giving herself the perfect cover by actually being the lost soul both sides wanted, a pawn in other people's games, and she had wandered straight into it.

'I'm sorry,' Jessica said, wiping her eye with her sleeve, her voice cracking.

Zipporah rubbed her back softly. 'There's nothing to be ashamed of, sweetie, sometimes things don't work out in our lives.'

Unable to stop herself, Jessica opened up. 'It all started with my dad . . .'

Before she knew it, she had told the story of the past few months, leaving out the part that she was actually a police officer but giving almost everything else away. She didn't have to lie or embellish because this was the life she found herself with.

Shoppers continued to hurry past and she could feel their eyes upon her, wondering who the crazy woman in tears was. If this had been a year ago, she would have been wondering why there was a group of nutters handing out leaflets and thinking it was strange that someone had been taken in by it. But there was something maternal about Zipporah. She stroked Jessica's hair and back, she knew when to speak and when to stay silent. When she did talk, it was with a perfect mix of sympathy and concern.

'We've had many people through our doors with circumstances like your own,' she said, nodding towards Heather. 'She's been through unimaginable things but look at her now. She's smiling and talking to strangers.'

'What is it you do?'

Zipporah smiled kindly. 'We have a community of our own a little north of here. We believe that much of what goes wrong in people's lives is down to the expectations and stresses of the modern world. We are largely self-sufficient and work together to make each other's lives better. We have people with drug problems, alcohol problems, all coming to stay with us as an alternative to society's traditional methods. There are people like yourself who have had a tough time and want to escape from everything. We welcome anyone who is happy to fit in.'

'How many of you are there?'

The woman smiled again, keeping eye contact as if trying to read Jessica. 'There are a few of us.'

'Are you the person in charge?'

This time Zipporah laughed, although it was clearly forced. 'Oh no, my husband Moses is the person who helps to keep everything running smoothly. We come out to the city centres to recruit and he makes sure everything is fine at the house. He may be my husband, so you might think me biased, but he truly is a great man.'

'If I wanted to join, what would I have to do?'

Zipporah lowered her voice, breaking eye contact and stepping closer to Jessica so no one could overhear. 'We're not an exclusive community but we do need to make sure everyone is suitable and will fit in. You would have to be assessed.'

'What does that mean?'

'Nothing serious but you have to understand we are private people. Our success is due to the fact we don't embrace modern society. One of our few concessions is a minibus which we need to get around. We will be leaving from outside of Piccadilly Station at two if you would like to come with us. Of course I understand that people have various commitments and sometimes cannot make such a quick decision.'

She reached into her pocket and took out a card, handing it to Jessica. On it was printed the address of the house.

'If you want to come and find us, subject to the assessment, you would be welcome to do so. Obviously you would not be permitted to bring a vehicle, so you would have to rely on a different form of transport if you chose not to come on our bus. We realise it is a large commitment but you would also not be permitted to bring anything except for the clothes you have on. Our entire philosophy is based upon building something new and different. Having things from your old life wouldn't fit with that.'

Zipporah stepped away again, clearing her throat. It was dawning on Jessica quite how far she was going to have to go. This could be weeks, months, away from everyone. She hadn't been spending time with people anyway but at least the option had been there. Here, she would be on her own with no idea of what the 'assessment' might mean, let alone anything beyond that.

Jessica knew she was going to accept but that she could not be on the bus. At the very least, she had to speak to Charley.

Before she could say anything, a man began shouting nearby. Zipporah and Jessica turned at the same time to see a figure with thinning dark hair grabbing at Heather. The other members of the group surged forward at the same time, putting themselves between the two.

'She's my daughter!' the man yelled. 'I've got a right to see my daughter.'

Heather shrunk away, staying behind the wall of people as Zipporah stepped through them, standing in front of the man.

'If she wants to see you, she will.'

He jabbed a finger in her face. 'It's you, isn't it? You're the one who stole her away, filling her head with lies and nonsense. Making her think she was better off without her family.'

Zipporah was unmoved, even though the man towered over her. Her features were fixed as his finger waved centimetres from her nose. The man was shaking with rage, his large belly bulging under the bottom of his shirt, long tattoos on both of his forearms. He was glancing over the tops of the people towards his daughter.

'Heather, honey. Come on, love. We miss you.'

He sounded heartbroken. Heather was next to Jessica, shivering.

'Are you okay?' Jessica asked quietly, unsure if she should be taking sides.

'Just keep him away,' the young woman replied tearfully.

'He seems really concerned. I think he just wants to talk.'

'You don't understand . . .'

Zipporah continued to stand firm. 'I think you should leave,' she said calmly.

'How can I leave? She's my daughter. I watched her grow up. I wiped her nose, cleaned the scuffs when she fell off her bike. I picked her up at night, dropped her off in the mornings. She's my little girl . . .'

He was close to tears but no one moved and Heather continued to cower, edging slightly behind Jessica so she was out of sight. Shoppers were stopping and staring.

As the stand-off continued, three security guards came out of the shopping centre. Two of them were young and fit, the other was as wide as his colleagues put together. He seemed to be the one in charge, approaching slowly, one hand on the radio clipped to his belt.

'We're going to have to ask you to move on,' he said, trying to sound firm but clearly out of his depth. Jessica knew the type, a security guard more used to watching monitors and sending juniors out to do the real work. Somehow he had got himself promoted one rung too far, meaning he had to deal with anything remotely serious. His voice was wobbling more than his stomach.

Zipporah didn't take her eyes from Heather's father. 'We have a right to be here. We're here every month.'

The security guard held back, letting his colleagues come between the two parties. 'I'm afraid you're going to have to move on, Sir,' he said.

The man turned away from Zipporah and the two guards to face the one in charge. 'But she's my daughter. Don't you have kids? What would you do if she was stolen away from you?'

Jessica watched the guard looking nervously from one

side to the other. 'You're still going to have to move along. The police are on their way.'

She doubted it would be anyone she knew but the last thing Jessica wanted was someone in uniform recognising her, not now she had set things in motion.

'I'm going to go,' Jessica said, turning to Heather, her back to the commotion behind them.

'Were you happy with what Zip said to you?'

Jessica didn't have to lie. 'Yes.'

'Are you going to come to the house?'

'Do you think I should?'

Heather's gaze flickered briefly over Jessica's shoulder towards where her father was still shouting. She suddenly seemed like a young girl, instead of the confident woman of before. When she focused back on Jessica, she nodded. Jessica didn't know what she had gone through, or what the issue was with her dad, but the emptiness in Heather's eyes told her all she needed to know.

'I'll see you soon,' Jessica said softly, before turning and walking quickly away before her colleagues arrived.

NINE MONTHS AGO

'It's always like this,' Jessica said, turning to Adam. 'They've been going deaf for years. I could stand here all day ringing the doorbell and they'll never hear it.'

'Don't you have a key to your parents' house?'

Jessica pressed on the plastic, making sure it wasn't already open. 'They got new doors and windows put in a couple of months ago.'

'Specifically to keep you out?'

Jessica turned, slapping Adam on the arm. 'Cheeky. I'm the apple of their eyes; their only child off in the big city defending people's freedoms.'

'Really?'

'Well, no. I am in the big city but spend most of my time in an office. I am the apple of their eyes though.'

'I can't believe we've been going out all this time and now I finally get to see the house.'

Jessica turned back to the front door and knocked again. 'When I'm rich and famous, there'll be a blue plaque here, celebrating where I grew up.'

'What are you going to do to become either rich or famous?'

'I quite fancy inventing something. Perhaps a stupidity detector? The minute someone's about to do something dumb, an alarm goes off. It would save me so much work.'

'What are you going to use to invent it?'

'Some pieces of wire, a light bulb and a bloody great big mallet. If people start to associate stupid behaviour with being clobbered by a mallet, they'd soon stop.'

Jessica felt Adam's hands around her hips and shivered, tingles racing along her spine. 'Come on, let's go around the back. We'll be out here all day otherwise,' she added.

Adam and Jessica moved around the small detached house until they reached a side gate.

'This is really nice,' Adam said. 'I'm not sure what I expected but it wasn't this.'

'You've met my parents when they've been down to Manchester, where did you think they lived? In an igloo?'

Adam laughed, tucking a longish strand of hair behind his ears. Jessica's subtle hints that he should have it trimmed were falling on deaf ears and she was days away from ordering him to do it.

'I'm not sure,' he said. 'I suppose it's because of you. You're a city girl, all noise and action. You never stop. I've never even been to Cumbria before but it's all so . . . quiet.'

'Unlike me . . .'

Jessica tried to look stern but couldn't manage it, cracking and breaking into a grin.

Adam was smiling too. 'Yes, unlike you. Everyone's got flower beds, you can drive from one end of the village to the other in five minutes, there are no big supermarkets, two primary schools, fields everywhere. It's so different.'

'It's a nice place to retire to but it's so boring. Nowhere to eat, nothing to do, everyone knows what everyone else is up to—'

'Nowhere to get into trouble, you mean.'

Jessica laughed. 'Exactly. Come on, give me a hand.'

Since the catch was on the opposite side, she pressed her foot on the horizontal metal rung across the low gate, shushing Adam as he told her to be careful. 'I'm not an invalid,' she said irritably, as he helped to lift her up and over the gate. 'If you wanted to feel up my arse, all you had to do was ask,' Jessica added, landing on the other side with more of a thump than she wanted to admit. This type of climbing, or anything similar, was soon going to be a thing of the past.

Adam had his hands on his hips. 'In my defence, it's so big, there wasn't anywhere else to put my hand.'

Jessica snorted in playful annoyance. 'Just for that, you can stay out there.'

'Okay, but I've got the car keys, remember. If you want to stay up here for a few days then feel free. I'll drive back down to the big city.'

'Fine.'

Jessica unclipped the gate and waved Adam through, taking his hand in hers as they strolled through to the back garden. At the far end, Jessica's father was walking away from them, pushing a lawnmower.

'How old is he?' Adam asked.

'Sixty-seven this year. Now he's retired, he does more work than he did when he was actually working. He's off playing bowls three times a week, then he gets up and goes for a walk every morning. If it's not raining, he's in the garden every evening. Mum's never had so much peace.'

'How long have they been married?'

'Forty-three years.'

'Wow.'

'I know.'

'And they've had to put up with you for most of that time.'

'Oi!'

Before Jessica could scold Adam any further, her father turned the corner with the lawnmower and noticed them. The loud moaning of the engine cut out instantly as he stepped away, waving and hurrying towards them, a huge grin on his face.

Jessica stood clutching Adam's hand as her father neared. Age had treated him kindly. Despite the increase in wrinkles and the odd wince when he stood, he had the same boyish sparkle to his eyes he'd always had, coupled with the astuteness that could only come with age.

'Daddy,' Jessica said, releasing Adam and reaching out as her father wrapped his arms around her.

'Why didn't you say you were coming up? Your mum could have put something on especially.'

'We didn't want to cause a fuss.' She nodded towards the lawnmower. 'You should get someone in to help you with this.'

'What, mowing the lawn? I'm not decrepit yet.'

'I didn't mean that but you do too much.'

He released her, throwing his arms in the air. 'Bah, it keeps me young.' He reached forward, shaking Adam's hand. 'Good to see you again, son,' he said, winking in the way Jessica knew was just to tease. Adam was always a little edgy around her dad, in the way she guessed most men were around fathers-in-law. She knew Adam was uncomfortable at being called 'son', not because his own parents were dead, simply because it made him feel a little *too* much like part of the family.

'How much is it for you to take her permanently?' Jessica's dad asked, raising his eyebrows and looking at Adam.

'How come every time I bring a lad home, you try to sell me off?' Jessica complained.

Her father turned to her, grinning. 'Because I've had forty years of looking after you. It's someone else's turn. If that costs me a few grand, then fair enough.'

Jessica hugged into his arm. 'I'm not that old.'

'Not long now until the big four-oh though, is it?'

'Long enough – when do you think I was born?! Anyway, where's Mum?'

Her father nodded towards the house. 'Inside. She was reading the last I saw.'

'No one answered the front door.'

'Her hearing's been going for years. I stood out there for twenty minutes myself the other week when I forgot my key.'

'That's what you get for changing the locks on me.'

Her dad threw his head back, roaring with laughter. 'I told your mother that would annoy you more than anything. Still, she's yours now, son.'

He nodded towards Adam again, making him squirm, before turning back to the garden.

'Anyway, I've got work to do before it gets dark. You go and say hello to your mother. I'll be in soon.'

He leant forward, kissing her on the forehead. 'It's good to see you again.'

As he turned, walking away, Jessica could hear his chuckles carrying on the breeze.

'He's only winding you up,' she said, taking Adam's hand and leading him towards the house.

'I wouldn't mind so much if he'd actually paid me the money promised. Last time, he reckoned he'd pay five grand for me to take you off his hands.'

'I'm only worth five thousand?'

'Well, I'd hope to negotiate him up to five and a half, maybe six.'

The back door was unlocked and Jessica led the way into the house.

'Mum?'

There was a shuffling from the living room and then Jessica's mother walked through the doorway, seeming confused as she glanced from Adam to Jessica. 'Why didn't you say you were coming up?'

She yawned as Jessica stepped forward to hug her. 'Because we knew you'd make a big fuss if we said we were coming. I wanted it to be low-key.'

Her mother was looking tired, her short grey hair stuck to the side of her head as if she had just been sleeping on it. She reached forward and hugged Adam.

'Nice to meet you again, Mrs Daniel,' he said.

'I've told you before, it's Lydia.'

'We tried the front door,' Jessica said. 'But you've changed the locks.'

Jessica's mother turned, leading them into the living room.

'Sorry, love,' she said over her shoulder. 'I've got a spare key for you somewhere. I'll sort it out later. I've been having problems sleeping recently. One minute I'm in my chair reading, the next it's three hours later. Then I can't sleep at night. You know what doctors are like – they say it's one thing, then it's another. You may as well ask the wall for its opinion for the amount of good it does. I must have dropped off when you were at the front.'

She relaxed into a rocking chair, leaning backwards and making it sway gently. Adam and Jessica sat on the sofa across from her.

'How's the new house?' she asked.

'It's good,' Jessica replied. 'It needs a bit of work but it's nice to be somewhere that belongs to us. It all happened really quickly.'

There was a short silence as Lydia fixed her daughter with a knowing stare. 'So why are you really here?'

She was used to having her mum one step ahead of her, but Jessica hadn't expected such directness. 'Who says we're here for anything other than to say hello?'

Lydia tilted her head to the side, grinning. 'I've known you way too long to think you've driven all of this way to pop in and say hello . . .'

Jessica shrugged, the game up. 'I was going to break it gently.'

'What?'

Jessica leant back into the sofa, lifting her top and using both hands to cradle the area underneath her stomach

51

where there was a small bump, noticeable now it wasn't concealed by the loose-fitting piece of clothing.

She thought her mother would be pleased but didn't expect the shriek of enjoyment coupled with the beaming grin. 'You're . . .'

Jessica couldn't stop herself from smiling, running her fingers across the taut skin. 'Yes.'

Her mother crossed the room, kissing them both on the head, beaming. 'How long?'

'Not very. I'm still figuring things out. I climbed over your gate at the back, forgetting I'm supposed to be looking after myself. I'm so used to simply doing things that it's going to take a bit of getting used to.'

'You're still working?'

'For now. They want to promote me.'

Lydia returned to her rocking chair. 'They don't know yet?'

'My friend Izzy does. Other than her it's just us.'

Jessica's mother breathed out deeply, looking from her daughter to Adam and back again. 'I'm so pleased for you both, after everything that happened to you in America. What are you going to do about that?'

Jessica exchanged a glance with Adam, having predicted this would be one of her mother's first questions. They had flown to Las Vegas to get married but the chapel they had used did not have the correct licence, meaning the ceremony was invalid. Jessica still wore the wedding band she had been given that day but there was nothing official.

'We're not going to rush into getting married, not after last time. We're happy.'

There was a flicker of disapproval but Jessica knew her mum would keep her feelings quiet. Trying to talk her into or out of something over the years had rarely got either of her parents anywhere.

Her mother's eyes narrowed. 'Are you happy with this too?'

Jessica nodded. 'I think so. It wasn't planned but if we'd left it at that, it never would have happened because I would never have given myself time away from work. I didn't think I'd ever want children. Now, it feels right. I can't wait.'

Lydia smiled knowingly. 'You won't be saying that when you're flat on your back, legs splayed, screaming in agony.'

Jessica shook her head, determined to keep hold of the picture she had painted for herself of what childbirth would be like. 'Thanks for sharing,' she said sarcastically.

'Adam?' her mum asked.

He sat up a little straighter, squeezing Jessica's hand. 'I've never been happier. It wasn't that long ago I found out I've got a sister. Now I'm going to have a son too.'

Jessica pulled her hand free. 'How do you know it's going to be a boy?'

'I just do. Perhaps he'll be an inventor and you'll get your blue plaque by default.'

He didn't say it but Jessica knew what he was thinking. For the first time in a long time, he was going to have a proper family. Both of his parents had died when he was a baby. His grandmother had brought him up but she had passed away a few years ago. His sister, Georgia, was the product of an affair between their mother and a man Adam had never met. Despite that, they shared a bond and spoke regularly on the phone. There was even talk she might move back to Manchester. With Georgia, the baby and her, he had something he had craved his entire life.

Lydia set her chair rocking again. 'I'm really pleased for you both. Have you told your father?'

Jessica stood. 'No, we were going to wait for him to come in. I'll go and see how he is.'

She walked through to the kitchen, listening for the hum of the lawnmower. Instead, she could hear nothing but the chirping of birds. Jessica could feel her heart beating quicker, knowing instinctively something wasn't right.

As she reached the door, it was as if the birds realised, their cheeps rising to a deafening peak. Jessica pulled down the handle and stepped onto the patio, ice breezing through her unrelated to the temperature. At the far end of the garden, the lawnmower was collapsed on its side, next to the face-down unmoving body of her father.

MONDAY

4

Jessica had never been to Colne before and from the initial impression leaving the train station, she didn't think she would be back any time soon. There was nothing particularly wrong with the place, rolling lush hills in the background and tidy sandstone buildings along the side of the road, but there was a dread in her stomach that she had yet again made the wrong decision. Her life seemed to be peppered with them. Now she found herself on her own again, leaping head-first into something she wasn't sure about.

As Jessica stood on the side of the road outside the train station looking both ways, she rubbed the area below her stomach absent-mindedly before realising what she was doing and snatching the hand away. At least once a day she found herself doing it, seemingly unable to control her subconscious.

'You looking for a taxi, love?' Jessica turned to see a man leaning against a cab eating a chocolate bar. 'You look a little lost,' he added, smiling.

Jessica usually bristled at the use of the word 'love' but wasn't in the mood to argue with anyone. She told him the address of the house, which made him choke on the final piece of his snack.

'Are you sure?' he asked.

'Why?'

'That place has a reputation.'

'What reputation?'

He looked both ways, as if worried someone would overhear him, and lowered his voice. 'Just that there's lots of people there. Hardly anyone ever sees them but there's this bloke who runs everything. He's called Noah or something like that.'

'Do you think he's building an ark?'

'A what?'

Jessica shook her head. 'Never mind. Can you take me anyway?'

In all the taxis she had been in, Jessica had never known a driver be so quiet. Usually they talked about everything and anything. She'd once been in a cab taking her from one side of Manchester to the other where the driver listed everyone famous he'd ever had in the back. By the time he named a Hollywood film star, she suspected there was a slight distortion of the truth going on. One other driver had practically been in tears, telling her how he was a law graduate struggling to find a job and that this was the worst thing he had ever done. The night before he had been called out to a notorious estate and mugged. She'd felt so sorry for him, she'd given him twenty quid for a five-pound fare, telling him to call her personally if he ever got assaulted again. She'd never heard from him since but it had given her a new appreciation of what drivers actually did. Either that, or he told the same story to everyone, cleaning up in tips along the way.

She guessed this driver's silence was because he was

wary of anyone going to the house. He even seemed reluctant to take her money after dropping her off outside a set of wide metal gates. Jessica had brought just enough to pay for a train and taxi fare, knowing Zipporah had told her nothing else was permitted in the house. She presumed that included money.

Next to the gate was a large stone pillar with a speaker, push-button and round hole in which Jessica could make out the lens of a camera. The gate only came up to her chest and she could have climbed it if she wanted to but figured that if she was going to go through with this, she should do things as properly as possible.

As the taxi roared away into the distance, sputtering cloudy exhaust fumes into the otherwise fresh air, the twittering of the birds overhead sent Jessica spiralling back to that day at her parents' house where her father collapsed.

The first tile to tumble in what had become a crescendo of dominos falling.

Jessica blinked rapidly, sensing this was her crossroads. Behind her there was the life she had; on the other side of the gates, a chance to start putting things back together. She was alone but then she had to be; as Cole had told her, sometimes the only person who can help you is yourself.

She reached forward and pressed the button. At first nothing happened but then she heard a gentle whirr of the camera. She stepped backwards, ensuring she would be completely in shot, and then the gate made a loud clunking sound, swinging open a fraction.

She stepped through, closing the gate behind her and

began walking along the wide driveway. On either side there were huge patches of lawn, trimmed in tidy straight lines with the smell of fresh grass drifting on the breeze. The drive arched up and it was only when Jessica reached the peak that she could see the majesty of the house far in front of her. It was everything Charley had said but more: a massive stately home carved from butterscotch-coloured stone set among beautiful green meadows, two ponds at the front and a long driveway so straight that it could have been laid with a set-square. The symmetry was perfect, as if whoever planned it had created one half and then held a mirror to it, telling the builders to copy what was already there.

Jessica continued walking, guessing the driveway was at least half a mile long. In the distance off to the side was a wooded area, on the other a tall wooden fence on the far side of the lawn. The nearer she got to the house, the quieter it became until it was as close to silence as she could imagine. In an instant, the serenity was broken by the gentle tinkling of rain.

Jessica stood still for a moment, enjoying it washing over her as the drops bounced into the pools on either side. She noticed the raised fountains weren't running but most of the clatter came from the raindrops bouncing from the large circle of tarmac in front of the house for cars to turn around. Not that there were any vehicles in sight; even the minibus Zipporah had spoken about was nowhere to be seen.

There were three storeys of windows, ten on either side of a towering wooden front door at least three times

Jessica's height. Gargoyles clung to the roof ledge, with each window frame decorated with delicately created stone flowers. Jessica stood in front of the door, trying to take everything in as water dribbled down her back. Whatever horrors people believed might be happening inside, there was still something indelibly beautiful about the outside, even with gathering dark clouds overhead.

As the door remained closed, Jessica glanced from side to side for a knocker, doorbell or anything that might help her to attract the attention of someone inside. From a distance the windows seemed normal but up close, they were tinted in such a way that they mirrored the outside. She felt watched but Jessica couldn't see anything or anyone on the inside.

She climbed the three stone steps until she was up against the door. She ran her palm across the sanded wood, sensing the thickness of it. She tried knocking but it was as if the door absorbed the sound, muffling and killing it. There was no way anyone inside would have noticed unless they were specifically listening. After getting no response from what she assumed was a doorbell, Jessica tried peering through the closest window. The tint reflected nothing but her own face and yet she still had a sense that someone was watching her, examining the way she moved and judging the choices she made. Perhaps waiting to see if she was going to turn and walk away? Maybe this was the first of the assessments Zipporah had spoken of; a test to see if she actually wanted to be there, or if she would turn and leave at the first sign of adversity.

Jessica retreated until she was in the centre of the

turning circle and sat on the damp ground, letting the rain flow over her. The tempo of the drops increased in an instant, a cacophony of sound echoing around her as Jessica sat unmoving, staring at the front door. She started to shiver as the rain soaked through her clothing. Her hair stuck to her scalp and each time she blinked, water dribbled into her eyes.

Puddles were forming on either side. She rarely wore a watch anyway but with anything external banned, Jessica had no way of knowing how long she had been there.

Eventually the door creaked open a sliver, held in place for a few moments before being pulled open fully. Zipporah was standing there, one hand on her hip.

Her words were barely audible over the rain. 'I'm glad you came, Jessica.'

Jessica stood slowly, weighed down by the water drenching her clothes. Zipporah was staring at her, a gentle smile on her face as she held the door open.

Inside the house, Jessica struggled to take everything in. The ceiling was so high, she felt dizzy looking up. The hard marble floor echoed from her footsteps and the sound of water dripping from her. Behind, Zipporah closed the door with a loud bang, sliding a heavy bolt into place.

Directly in front of Jessica was an enormous painting showing a man with a curly brown beard and bushy eyebrows. Sitting cross-legged on what looked like a throne, he was staring thoughtfully into the distance.

'That's Moses,' Zipporah said softly, standing next to Jessica. 'You'll meet him soon. He will change your life.'

The painting was roughly double life size, making

Moses look like a giant. Jessica had read the small amount they had on him in their files and knew he was also in his late thirties, barely older than her, the same age as Zipporah. He seemed young and old at the same time, the beard implying wisdom, his green eyes sparkling with youth. Even from his image, Jessica could sense a magnetism, a natural charisma that you either had or you didn't.

'Come, let's get you dry.'

Zipporah strode away quickly leading Jessica through the house. The corridors were lined with wooden panels that reached halfway up. Paintings and photographs were placed at regular intervals. Jessica wanted to stop and look but Zipporah was moving so quickly that she practically had to run to keep up. She could sense other people nearby, footsteps around corners, the low murmuring of voices, but she didn't see anyone.

The further she moved into the house, the darker it became. The overhead light was dim, with no windows opening onto the corridors. Eventually, Zipporah stopped, holding a door open and beckoning Jessica inside.

'This is our clothes store,' Zipporah said as Jessica entered to see rails of dresses, skirts, trousers and tops. 'We make everything on site. We do have to buy the material but one of the things we aim to do is teach people to be as self-sufficient as they can. We have some incredibly skilled craftspeople on site, almost everyone learning from scratch to be able to create things like this.'

Many of the colours were plain, perhaps even un-inspiring, but that was the type of thing Jessica chose to wear usually anyway. The dresses were cut sensibly, no bottom-hugging hemlines, no plunging necklines. The other clothes were similar too; old-fashioned designs, straightforward colours.

'You can take your pick,' Zipporah said, handing Jessica a towel.

She closed the door behind them, watching Jessica carefully. She didn't say it but there was a clear instruction for Jessica to get changed now, in front of her where she could see if she was trying to smuggle in something she shouldn't.

Jessica unclipped her jeans but had to yank them down as they were stuck to her skin. She dropped her thin jumper next to them on the ground, forcing herself not to shiver as she stood in her underwear and began to towel her body, all under Zipporah's unmoving eye. As she rubbed the area below her stomach, she couldn't help but shudder, hoping the other woman had not noticed.

Deliberately not looking towards the door, Jessica took a knee-length skirt from the rail and a light blue shirt made of thick cotton, finishing off with a wide leather belt to keep the clothes tight to her thinning body. She swapped her flat shoes for a pair that was almost identical.

When she was fully dressed, Zipporah picked up her old clothes and shoes from the floor, bundling them under her arm without a word.

She reopened the door. 'We eat together every morning and evening. You'll be able to meet people then. I'll take you to your room for now.'

Zipporah moved quickly again, up two wide flights of

stairs that were lined with thick, luxurious ruby carpet, with more paintings and framed photographs placed around the walls. Jessica continued towelling her hair as they went along until she felt almost dry. More corridors, more darkness until eventually they stopped outside an oak-panelled door.

Jessica handed Zipporah the towel.

'If you ever have any sort of problem with anything, please come and see me. Moses is a father to everyone, which I suppose makes me the mother.'

'Okay.'

'I know we spoke out on the streets but I should remind you about the few rules we have here. No electrical goods are permitted – including phones. We keep this house as secure as we can, not to imprison anyone as it were, but to keep out those who may wish to cause us harm.'

'Who might want to hurt anyone here?'

Jessica thought of the heavy bolt across the front door. So far, she hadn't seen any other way out. Zipporah narrowed her eyes, weighing Jessica up. Just as Jessica was thinking she should have stayed silent, the woman answered. 'There are many people in the outside world who do not understand what we are trying to do here. Our only commitment is to you as people; to help make you better individuals and to keep you safe.'

Jessica still didn't know exactly what they were trying to achieve there but didn't want to push her luck. She nodded in acceptance.

'We also do not allow drugs or alcohol within these walls,' Zipporah continued. 'Any breach of these policies will automatically lead to you being expelled. We expect everybody to respect each other. Aside from if you come with us for recruitment days, we also do not permit our residents to mix with outsiders.'

Her tone was steady but not overbearing, like a teacher laying down ground rules, as opposed to a headmaster telling off a naughty child. She smiled again. 'Is all of that acceptable to you? It's for the good of everyone.'

Jessica nodded.

'Okay, let's introduce you to your roommate.'

Zipporah pushed open the door. Even though it was still grey outside, the bedroom was bathed in light, a tall, wide pane of glass overlooking the driveway she had walked down. Sitting on a four-poster bed in front of her was Heather, reading a Bible.

She glanced towards Jessica, smiling and putting the book down before standing and opening her arms to offer a hug. 'It's so good to see you,' she said.

Jessica embraced her but the woman was even thinner than she was. Heather held her so tightly, clawing at her back, that it quickly became uncomfortable. Jessica patted her gently, wanting to be released. When she eventually was, she saw a wetness around Heather's eyes.

'I hoped you would join us,' she added.

In the doorway, Zipporah was smiling approvingly. She indicated a second four-poster bed and then a second door. 'This is yours,' she added. 'There is a private bathroom you both share through there. We'll bring you up some more clothes and a change of underwear sometime soon.'

Jessica was genuinely impressed. She had never seen

such luxury, let alone had a chance to live in it. Heather was on her own bed again, still beaming. Jessica stepped towards the window, peering down at the drenched landscape.

'I'll leave you to get to know each other. Heather will give you the tour,' Zipporah said, before adding ominously: 'But please remember we must all submit to Moses's rules.'

As she left, the door clicked into place, leaving Jessica to notice there was no lock.

5

The bathroom was as big as Jessica's living room, with a vast spacious tub that could fit three or four people comfortably, a full-length mirror and gleaming porcelain taps, all on top of a speckled, spotless marble floor. As with the main bedroom door, there was no lock, leaving Jessica uneasy at the lack of privacy.

'We're expected to keep everything clean and tidy,' Heather explained.

'What else do you do?'

Heather smiled but she seemed tired. Her eyes didn't have the same sense of longing as before but there was something not right about her, something Jessica couldn't place. 'I'll show you. I'm sure Moses will assign you somewhere to work after he has spoken to you.'

'What do you mean?'

'Everyone who comes here meets with Moses at some point early on. Zip might have invited you but the final say on who stays and goes always comes down to Moses.'

'Are many people asked to leave?'

'I don't think so but then Zip wouldn't invite someone to join us if she didn't feel they were going to fit in.'

'How long have you been here?'

Heather's features, so pretty when she smiled, curled into outrage. Although it disappeared as quickly as it had appeared, Jessica knew she had asked the wrong thing.

'Sorry,' she added.

Heather shook her head dismissively. 'Come on, I'll show you around.'

As Heather led her down the stairs, Jessica noticed large crosses above the overhangs. Heather had been reading a Bible but Zipporah had never mentioned anything religious to her, instead focusing on Moses and his own teachings. Their own names were biblical, of course, but Jessica was struggling to see the link.

On the ground floor, Heather took her along a darkened corridor, grinning as she opened a door. 'You're going to like this,' she said. 'This is our games room. It's where some of us relax in the evenings. At the moment it's empty because everyone is working.'

Jessica allowed herself a slight smile, knowing the contents of the room were like something DC Rowlands could only have dreamed about. There was a full-size snooker table, two table football games, a darts board at the far end and four long sofas.

'It beats watching television, doesn't it?' Heather said.

Except for her late-night talk-show vice, Jessica had never been a big viewer anyway. 'Does that mean there are no TVs or radios in the entire house?'

Heather nodded, apparently enjoying being Jessica's guide. 'Absolutely not. It's one of Moses's main rules. Who needs them anyway? We have more than enough here to entertain us.' She turned back towards the door. 'Come on.'

Across the corridor from the games room, Jessica

noticed a door built into the underside of a staircase but Heather had already moved past before she could ask about it. The stairs didn't actually seem to go anywhere, they were more decorative. Even if you walked to the top, there was no opening to the next floor. Heather stopped, pointing to a door on the other side of the stairs. 'That's Moses's office,' she said. 'It's the only place I know about which is out of bounds.'

'Why?'

Heather crossed her arms, frowning. 'Because those are the rules.'

'Okay, I'm sorry.'

Heather nodded sharply, but it was clear that any form of insolence was not tolerated. Not only that but Jessica could see in Heather's expression that the thought of doing something untoward had not crossed her mind. She knew she was going to have to be careful.

They moved on through the house, Heather showing Jessica into a large open hall. Lines of people sat at workbenches, talking quietly to each other. As Heather led Jessica into the room, none of them acknowledged their presence, continuing to focus on what they were doing.

'This is our work hall,' Heather said. 'Here we make clothes and crafts. We help each other to become better. If Moses thinks this is where you are best suited, you might end up here.'

'I'm not very good with a needle and thread.'

Heather laughed. 'Neither was I before I came here. Usually I'd be working but Zip said I could finish early to show you around.'

That was interesting to Jessica because she hadn't told Zipporah if or when she would be arriving. Perhaps she had been watched as she was sitting in the rain, and that was when Zipporah had sent for Heather?

Although everyone generally appeared to be young, it was hard for Jessica to judge who they were as they were largely working with their heads down, talking to each other without looking up. It could appear rude but Jessica sensed it was more because they were focused on what they were doing, as opposed to deliberately wanting to ignore her.

'What do you do with the crafts?' Jessica asked.

'Zip and a few of the girls go to market once a week. We sell some of the clothes we make, plus the crafts. It's nothing over the top but it shows us how we have to work for what we've got. Everything is provided – our food, our drink, our roof. Nobody gets anything for free. Plus it teaches us new skills. Everyone wins because we all have a purpose.'

Her words sounded genuine, if rehearsed, and Jessica couldn't fault too much of the logic. Perhaps if people struggling with alcohol and drug dependency were taught new skills and given somewhere to develop their talents, they wouldn't need to return to their vices? The issue of punishment and rehabilitation was something that raged far above her place in the criminal justice system.

As they were leaving, Jessica had to remind herself she was here investigating a murder and potentially a string of missing people. Her natural suspicion of anything that seemed too perfect on the surface was almost lacking, as if she too had been taken in by the stunning surroundings and the pleasantness of the people.

Heather led Jessica towards the front door, unbolting it and leading the way outside. The rain had stopped and faint rays of sunshine were beginning to peek through the thinning clouds.

'Is this the only door out?' Jessica asked as Heather made her way across the front of the house, turning along the side.

'It's the only one we use.'

At the rear of the house, a long patch of grass had been ploughed into long troughs. Half-a-dozen men were doing a mixture of jobs from planting, to raking, to clipping.

'This is where we grow our food,' Heather said. 'We sell some of it but most of it is eaten by us. We only buy a few things, such as meat, because we don't keep animals here.'

On the edge of the patch, a thick-set man was standing, scowling at them. Heather lowered her voice.

'That's Glenn,' Heather said without prompting. 'He's in charge of outdoor operations and he's close to Moses.'

Glenn continued to stare at them. He was too far away for Jessica to see any of his features in depth, but he had broad, strong shoulders and greying hair.

'Come on, let's go inside,' Heather added, sharing Jessica's unease.

In the house, Heather showed Jessica the kitchen and laundry room, each filled by people working. A couple of them even said hello, before instantly getting back to what they were doing.

She couldn't be exact but Jessica counted around thirty

people working in the various places – far fewer than she would have guessed. Judging by the apparent size of the house, they could have a room each and still have plenty of space left over. Aside from Glenn outdoors, none of the departments seemed to have anyone in charge, they simply all got on with what they were supposed to be doing.

'Do you get paid?' Jessica asked as they reached the staircase again.

'What would we need money for? Everything we need is provided. We are paid through being able to live comfortably and safely. What more could you want than that?'

There was an implication that something in Heather's past meant that there was a time when she hadn't felt safe but Jessica didn't want to push things, at least not so soon after arriving.

Heather led the way back to the clothes store, entering behind Jessica. 'If you want to choose a few things, we'll take them back to the room now.'

Jessica began walking along the rails, paying more attention now she wasn't dripping wet. 'Are you allowed to take anything you want?'

'It's not about want, it's about need. These clothes belong to all of us. We are a check upon each other.'

She pulled a long, flowing cream dress from the rack, holding it up for Jessica to see.

'I made this one.'

Jessica took it from her, running her fingers along the soft, smooth material. 'It's really nice.'

'Why don't you take it? I'm sure it would fit you.'

Jessica rarely wore dresses but even when she did, it was never something that reached her ankles. She was far from fashion-conscious but knew what she liked. She associated long dresses with people much older than her.

Despite her talk of the items belonging to everyone, Jessica could tell that Heather was proud of what she had created. She suspected the girl would have taken it for herself if it was the done thing.

Jessica placed the hanger around her neck, checking to see if the dress would fit.

'It's beautiful,' she said. 'If no one else minds, I'd love to take it.'

Heather beamed with pride, bobbing up and down on the spot, unable to contain herself.

'It's the first dress I made. I've done smaller things but it was something new.'

Jessica chose a few more items from the racks, trying to pick things that wouldn't make her stand out, not that there was much risk of that.

Back in the room, Heather helped Jessica to hang the clothes. They shared a wardrobe that was so wide, it would have satisfied even Jessica's friend and former housemate, Caroline. They had lived together for years, with Caroline constantly complaining about the lack of space for her clothes and shoes. Heather had around a dozen items hanging up and two pairs of shoes: a pair of low heels she said was for dinner and the trainers she had on. Jessica had the same amount of clothes, leaving a gaping hole in the centre of the wardrobe wide enough to fit three people side-by-side.

'Dinner will be soon,' Heather said. 'We all eat together and are expected to change after a day at work.'

Without any obvious self-consciousness, Heather slipped off her clothes, placing them onto her bed and folding them.

Jessica moved across to the window, staring out towards the gate in the distance. The sun was winning the battle with the clouds, a hazy orange glow spreading across the sky. She tried pulling down the handle but it was rigidly fixed in place.

'It's locked,' Heather said.

Jessica turned to see her roommate wearing only her underwear. She could see her ribs pressing into her skin but Heather had no apparent embarrassment or concern at being so exposed in front of a relative stranger.

'Why? We're three floors up.'

'All of the windows are locked. It's for our own protection.'

Zipporah had said something similar, that one of the main aims was to keep them safe. Jessica had been a police officer long enough to know that most places like this were kept secure not to keep strangers out, but to stop people getting out. Already she had only one way to leave – through the front door – and she suspected that would not be so easy if it came to it. One of the first rules of heading into somewhere new and unscouted was to know where the exits were; the more the better. Charley's hints about Jessica getting herself to safety if need be were proving unerringly disconcerting given the apparent prison she found herself in.

Jessica remained calm, knowing there were still areas of the house she hadn't seen yet. There must be at least one other door somewhere, even if it was blocked or hidden. One of her first priorities when she had some time alone would be to plot an exit strategy.

Heather flicked through her wardrobe, pulling out a dress that came to just below her knee. She pressed it against herself. 'I'm too thin for everything,' she muttered, barely loud enough for Jessica to hear. As the young woman took out a skirt and twisted it around in her hand, tutting, Jessica thought it was a strange attitude for someone apparently unconcerned that the style of the clothes they wore was chosen by someone else.

In Jessica's experience, for all the talk of equal rights, liberation and feminism, the biggest reason most people got dressed up – male or female – was to impress the opposite sex. It might not be so in every case but Jessica could see from the way Heather was prodding at her own skin that there was someone she wanted to make an impact on.

'That looks nice,' Jessica said as Heather held up a second dress, this one green and slightly shorter.

The younger woman didn't seem so sure, making a humming sound before eventually taking Jessica's word for it.

'I'm glad you stopped me in the city,' Jessica said, as she started to rummage through her own selection of clothes.

Heather giggled slightly. 'You're the first person I've ever recruited. Most people don't stop. They're so rude but you get used to it. I think that's why Zip put you in a room with me.'

'Did you have a roommate before?'

'I was with one of the other girls but I think Zip sensed you might come, so I moved into here last night. That's when I tidied everything up.'

'How did you come here?' Jessica asked as breezily as she could, head still in the wardrobe, skimming hangers from one side to the other.

At first there was a silence but then came the slow reply. 'I had a big falling out with my dad about an old boyfriend. Things got a bit out of hand and then I fell out with my boyfriend too. In the end I was left with neither of them.'

Jessica pulled out the dress that Heather had made and took it off the hanger, still not turning around. 'But your father must care for you if he comes all the way into the city to talk to you?'

Slipping off her clothes, Jessica stood in her underwear, exposed and vulnerable when Heather replied with the worst thing she could have said. 'I could turn it around onto you. If I'm trying to get away from my father and ex-boyfriend, then who are you escaping from?'

6

Jessica turned to face Heather, who was staring at her calmly but defiantly.

She had a point.

If Jessica was going to go around asking such personal questions, she would have to expect them herself. Opening up to Zipporah on the street was necessary – her only way in. Exposing her darkest secrets to someone who had barely been born when Jessica was leaving school felt more personal. She would happily confide in one of her colleagues. DC Izzy Diamond was a little younger than Jessica but married with a child. She felt older, more mature; Heather was still a child in comparison – even if her question was perfectly reasonable.

Jessica licked her lips, wondering what she should say. Could Heather ever understand the things that had happened to her since her father collapsed? The girl was in her early twenties but Zipporah had hinted that she had been through a lot herself.

Before Jessica could say anything, a loud siren sound blared through the building. Heather's eyes shot towards the ceiling. 'It's dinner time,' she said, turning around and asking Jessica to zip her up.

Jessica put the cream dress on, much to the approval of her roommate, who squealed in delight. 'It's perfect on you,' she added. Although she might not have gone for the colour, Jessica had to admit that it clung to her in all the right places.

Heather practically skipped down the staircase, a giddy schoolkid in the ultimate playhouse. Jessica could hear a general bustle around the hallways as people she vaguely recognised from earlier poured out of the nearby bedrooms, dressed in smart trousers, shirts and dresses. Everyone moved downstairs without fuss, following Heather to what Jessica had earlier been told was the work hall.

The smaller desks had been cleared away, replaced by long banquet tables in a U-shape covered with embroidered white tablecloths. Each place setting had matching fine silver cutlery, with a crystal wine glass, and jugs of water spaced around. Heather tugged on Jessica's wrist, leading her along one of the rows and standing behind a chair roughly in the centre.

Around them, the others followed, each standing until the only free seats were the three at the end that formed the middle part of the U.

Jessica counted quickly, being careful not to seem too obvious. There were twenty-eight people standing, with three free seats. Opposite her, Jessica spotted Glenn, who was staring across the table towards her and Heather. When Jessica caught his eye, he looked away quickly. He was shorter close up but, if anything, that made him more intimidating. His shoulders and arms were brutish, his chest bulging against his blue shirt. Jessica did not want to risk standing out, so she looked away herself, staring at the place setting in front of her.

She wondered how many of the thirty-one people knew what had happened to Liam Renton. Had someone around her drowned him and then dumped him in the Manchester canal?

Jessica glanced up as the doors at the far end of the room creaked open. Zipporah entered, wearing a long dress similar to the one Jessica had on. Behind her was a younger girl with long, straight dark hair and unblemished skin that almost glowed in the fading sunlight streaming through the tall windows. She was perhaps nineteen or twenty, and looked around the room nervously, not making eye contact with anyone. Her dress was shorter, clinging to her attractively in a way that again had Jessica thinking the rules about everyone having similar clothing didn't necessarily apply to all. Even though she would be the centre of attention in any room, the girl appeared far more self-conscious than Heather had done, traipsing behind Zipporah, staring at the floor.

After they had taken their spots behind two chairs, there was a pause. Heather was gripping the top of the chair tightly, and Jessica could sense the anticipation in the room.

Finally, the door opened a second time and the man from the painting in the hallway walked in, beaming. The art was unerringly accurate in every way other than its size. Moses was wearing sandals and a light brown robe. His beard and eyebrows were perhaps a little greyer but he looked as if he had just stepped out of the past, a walking cliché of every assumption ever made about what people looked like in biblical times.

Moses held his arms out wide and bowed slightly before padding his way to the table and standing in between Zipporah and the younger woman. With a gentle nod, everyone took the cue to sit, a thunderous scraping of chairs roaring around the room until everyone except Moses was seated.

He bowed his head, everyone following instinctively, and then started to pray. Jessica had been taken by surprise, noticing too late that everybody seemed to have their eyes closed. She leant forward, double-checking she had the right number of people, only to accidentally lock eyes with Glenn across the table. His hands were clenched together but his eyes blazed, fixed on her accusingly. She could understand why Heather felt uneasy earlier; there was little that was friendly about his manner.

Jessica snapped her eyes closed, listening to the final words as Moses thanked the Lord for providing the food, shelter and safety, before he said 'Amen'. The word was repeated around the room and then there was a second scraping of chairs as four people at the other end of the table stood, scurrying out of the room.

'What's going on?' Jessica whispered.

'They're the cooks,' Heather replied.

Jessica could feel Glenn still staring at her but ignored him, picking up one of the jugs of water and filling her and Heather's glasses.

She lowered her voice as much as she could, nodding slightly towards the head of the table. 'Who's the girl next to Moses?'

Jessica put the jug down and leant back into her

chair as Heather angled towards her, whispering. 'That's Katie.'

'Is she their daughter?'

Heather shook her head gently.

'Some other family member?'

Another shake.

Heather was staring directly ahead towards Glenn, who Jessica knew would still be watching them.

As the cooks re-entered carrying platters of food, it dawned on Jessica what she had missed. Of the people around the table, there were twice as many women as men. Not only that but the men were almost entirely Glenn's age – middle-aged and greying. The women were all younger, with Jessica one of the oldest. Moses had surrounded himself with men older than him and women who were younger. Given the natural charisma he exuded, plus the lack of alternatives, any of the vulnerable girls looking for a father figure to protect them had one natural choice. Jessica glanced up to see Katie gazing sideways towards Moses, awestruck, killing any doubt that she was anything other than his mistress. Zipporah had entered with her, apparently unconcerned. Either that, or she had no choice.

Jessica didn't get a chance to ask anything else as a large metal plate of steaming vegetables was placed between her and Heather, with a smaller bowl of sauce-soaked meat on the other side. It was as if everyone around the table had been brought up by Jessica's mother, taking small amounts and eating in near silence, exactly as Jessica had been taught to do when she was younger. It hadn't taken long for habits her mother wouldn't approve of to develop after she left home.

The meat casserole was straightforward but tasty nonetheless. Jessica couldn't quite figure out whether it was pork or beef but wasn't hungry anyway. She rarely was nowadays, but followed everyone else's lead while trying to take a closer look at the people around her. There was only one non-white face, an Asian man who was likely the youngest male there. He was certainly the only one who looked under thirty. Liam Renton had been twenty-four when he was killed, so he would have stood out as well.

Just as they were finishing, a chair scraped opposite Jessica. She looked up to see the woman sitting next to Glenn pulling her arm away from him, muttering a 'no' loud enough for everyone to hear. She folded her arms but Glenn fixed her with a glare of such fury that she cowered under it, sliding back towards the table, head bowed. Everyone carried on as if it had not happened.

'Is that his wife?' Jessica whispered.

'Yes, Naomi,' Heather replied softly.

'What's going on?'

This time the reply didn't come. Jessica swayed towards Heather in case it was because she wanted to speak more quietly but Heather whispered a snippy: 'You've got to stop asking questions.'

Soon, the cooks returned, clearing the plates and glasses until the table was empty of everything but the table-cloth. Nobody stood, or spoke, sitting in silence until they returned and the table was full again.

Moses stood, arms wide and welcoming. He looked

along the lines of people smiling gently, focusing on Jessica for a second or two longer than the others.

'It has been another lovely meal,' he said, his voice reassuringly firm. He named the four cooks and thanked them for their efforts. Jessica joined in as everyone clapped politely.

'We do have some new faces this week,' Moses added. 'I thank our recruitment team for their efforts.'

Another round of applause.

As soon as Moses stopped clapping, everyone else did too. 'Come now,' he said, stepping backwards until he was in front of a wide fireplace surrounded by a thick marble step.

At first nobody moved but then Jessica realised she was being watched by everyone around her.

'Go on,' Heather whispered, as if Jessica should have known she was being summoned.

Jessica stood slowly, glancing from side to side as two men rose at the same time. They were both older than her, one with a bright red face, the other thinner than she was. They both had untidy mops of grey hair and were wearing identical black trousers and white shirts, like waiters.

When the three of them reached the front, Moses organised them into a line, facing away from the fireplace towards the table. There was more movement of chairs as the other residents shunted themselves into position so everyone could see what was going on. Jessica felt the same hum of anticipation that had been there when Moses had entered.

She was between the two men, with Moses in front, walking the line. Jessica did not risk meeting his gaze, instead staring at a spot on the far wall as she felt him running his eyes up and down her.

'It's time for your assessment,' he said, moving behind the thinnest man, asking for his name, date of birth, previous occupation and why he was there.

Jessica felt him side-step behind her. 'Name?'

'Jessica Compton.'

'Date of birth?'

With everything pre-planned with Charley in case it came down to this, Jessica told him the truth.

'Previous occupation?'

'I worked in a post office.'

Her parents' former jobs; safe and away from what she actually did.

'Why are you here?'

Jessica gulped. She had known she was going to be asked this at some point, but hadn't expected it quite so soon – let alone in front of a room of people. She felt more exposed than she had when forced to change in front of Zipporah.

'I've had a few problems in the past year.'

'With what?'

'Everything. My career, my family, my father . . .'

Jessica could not stop her voice cracking. She knew she had to be as truthful as she could. Giving a slightly false name and occupation was one thing but the more lies you told, the more likely you were to trip yourself up eventually. She thought Moses was going to press her for more but instead she felt him moving on, until he was asking the final man the same questions.

His reason for being there, perhaps unsurprisingly given the red blotchiness of his skin, was because he wanted to escape alcohol.

There was a ripple of applause as Moses walked around them until he was again at the front. He nodded his approval, striding casually from side to side as he spoke. 'Thank you very much for sharing. One of the things we try to instil here is that we must trust each other. This is a different place from the world you may know on the outside. There it is full of drugs, alcohol, degradation. A place where you cannot trust your neighbours, your own family. Here we work together to overcome our problems.'

He stopped to squeeze Zipporah's shoulder before continuing. 'You already know the rules for staying here and I expect you all to abide by them. We cannot allow people to break them because of the catastrophic knock-on effect it could have on others who have been doing so well.'

He spun on the spot, turning to face the three of them. He scanned across them, nodding slightly. 'I sense you are all ready to commit but first you must learn what trust is.'

Again he walked behind them, standing behind the thin man.

'When I ask you to fall, I want you to trust me. Allow yourself to drop backwards. Do not put your hands down, do not try to cushion your fall. Trust.'

Jessica felt sure she had seen something similar as part

of some dreadful training day but she couldn't quite remember.

'Fall.'

The man next to her flopped backwards awkwardly. Jessica didn't turn to see but she heard Moses grunt slightly as he caught the man's weight, lowering him to the floor as another gentle wave of applause went around the room.

'Thank you for trusting me,' Moses said, pulling the man to his feet and inviting him to take his seat again. As he sat, the people around him patted him on the back and shook his hand, inviting him into whatever strange family Jessica had found herself in.

'It is the same for you, Jessica,' Moses said, side-stepping behind her. She felt uneasy that he knew her name, even though she had told him only minutes before.

'Fall.'

Jessica closed her eyes and dropped backwards. For a fraction of a second, she thought she was going to hit the floor but then she felt Moses's hands slipping under her armpits, catching her as air swished past her ears.

As he lowered her to the floor, his fingers cupped her breasts, squeezing them gently. In an instant, they were gone but Jessica was so shocked, she couldn't speak as he took her hand and pulled her up.

'Thank you for trusting me,' he said, stroking the base of her back before sending her over to her chair.

Heather patted Jessica on the shoulder, whispering, 'Well done', as everyone around her reached to either shake her hand or pat some part of her. She tried not to wince, suddenly conscious of anyone touching her. Naomi even reached across the table, nodding approvingly as they shook hands. Glenn was unmoving.

Jessica still felt speechless. The last time she remembered being groped in such a way without her permission was at school by some boy who was too immature to know what he was doing. That hadn't stopped her kneeing him somewhere painful and telling him that if he ever tried it again, she would chop his hands off. Moses's actions had happened so quickly that she doubted anyone had noticed. She could still feel his fingers upon her, that gentle squeeze telling her more about him than his words ever would.

At the front, Moses was standing behind the final man. 'Fall.'

Jessica was still feeling short of breath, threatened and violated. As she turned towards the front, it was as if she was dreaming, everything happening in slow motion as Moses stepped deliberately to the side. The sickening crunch of the man's head connecting with the sharp edge of the marble step reverberated terrifyingly around the room. Jessica had witnessed violence first-hand, she had heard that splintering of someone's skull in the past. As everyone gasped together, Jessica leant backwards, peering around the row of people to see a steady pool of dark red blood trickling along the floor.

7

Despite the gasps, nobody moved until Moses nodded towards one of the women on the opposite side of the table from Jessica. She stood calmly, approaching the crumpled body and rocking him gently to the side. Glenn and the Asian man stood too, picking the victim up and carrying him through the door they had all entered by, leaving a trail of blood as the woman followed.

After another nod from Moses, two more people got up, hurrying through the other door before returning moments later with a mop and bucket.

In under five minutes everything had been moved or washed away, as if it had never happened. The scent of bleach hung in the air as the cleaners returned to their seats. Moses had stood unmoving through the entire incident. When he spoke, his tone was slightly lower but firmer and full of authority.

'Sometimes we all have hard lessons to learn. I did not do this lightly but certain people here have perhaps become a little too comfortable. We should trust each other but we must be wary of others – outsiders.'

While he had been speaking, Moses had not singled out anyone specifically, staring into the distance. As he paused, he glanced down, focusing on Heather.

'I heard of the incident with our dear Heather's father. Many of us know the things she has been through and we have all seen the progress she has made.'

He bowed his head slightly, acknowledging her.

'I want you all to know that I was proud of the way you acted; sticking up for each other, acting calmly, without malice, without aggression. Outside of these walls, that is exactly the type of behaviour we will attract simply because of who we are and what we stand for. We learn to be self-sufficient, to act outside of their rules.'

He paused for breath, letting his words sink in, even though Jessica was pretty sure he had not said anything of any substance.

She was used to the methods because of the number of solicitors and lawyers she dealt with; people who could waffle for five minutes at a time without making a single point. Not long after she had become a detective constable, she had been in court testifying against a burglar she'd arrested. He had been caught in possession of goods stolen from a house but claimed he'd found them in a hedge and was on the way to the police station to hand them in. Somehow, his solicitor had managed to get the jury to acquit him. Outside the court, both the client and solicitor were beaming, high-fiving, unable to believe their luck. Jessica asked the solicitor if he was proud of himself and the sneering response was something she had never forgotten: 'Listen, love, you've either got the gift of the gab, or you ain't.'

Moses had the gift of the gab. It wasn't what he said, it was how he said it – with conviction and utter belief. It didn't matter that he spoke in generalisations – because he said it so earnestly, people believed in him.

The room was enthralled, hanging on his every word as he explained why he had let a stranger crack his head open to make the point that they should trust each other, not the outside world. It didn't even make sense, because he was the person who had shown he couldn't be trusted by betraying the faith put in him.

Jessica could see how it worked: vulnerable people taken away from their families, fed ideological nonsense by a father figure, something many of them either hadn't previously had or hadn't been able to rely on.

At worst, he ended up with a group of young women he could manipulate into his bed. At best, he had an army at his disposal.

Whether it was because of her age, life experience or even that she was a cynical copper, Jessica could see the danger within him.

She had switched off but heard Moses's final sentence: 'We should continue to spread the word, despite the persecution. Trust each other, trust me, and together we will build a better life for ourselves.'

As he sat, the room erupted into spontaneous applause. Jessica joined in, making sure she didn't stand out. Moses turned and kissed Zipporah first and then Katie. Both women seemed as happy as everyone else. The atmosphere was so electric that Jessica felt herself being drawn in. Everyone was trying to outdo the person next to them, clapping louder until somebody whooped. Soon, everyone was doing the same, the noise rising ever louder until Moses stood again, holding his hands out and bowing.

Slowly the reception ebbed away until there were one or two people clapping, competing to be the last to stop.

Jessica had never seen anything like it but her heart was beating quickly, caught up in the moment too.

The hour after the meal was spent split into smaller groups around the ground floor for evening worship. The starting point was the Bible but there was little that was religious about it. Zipporah led Jessica's group, reading a passage and then inviting people to share their own similar life experiences. There wasn't a single person who didn't collapse into tears as they told their story: sexual abuse, drugs, violence, dead and injured family members, plus everything in between. On and on it went until it was Jessica's turn. She spoke about the shock of seeing her father collapse, getting away without expanding because everyone was drowning in their own emotions by the time it was her turn.

Jessica had no idea how often this happened but if it was every night, then it was no wonder everyone present was conditioned to be scared of the outside world. Putting their stories together, anyone could have deduced that society was full of bad people just waiting to prey on them.

They finished with a reading and hymn, which Jessica mimed to, before everyone was dismissed. They all moved into the hallways but Heather was in a different group and Jessica had no idea where to go. One of the other women slowed until she was at Jessica's side. She was older than Heather and Katie but probably still not thirty.

'I'm Abigail,' she said, offering her hand for Jessica to shake. 'It was very moving what you said in there,' she added as Jessica tried to remember what Abigail's story had been.

'Yours was very thought-provoking too,' Jessica replied, thinking that sounded plausible enough.

'What are you doing now?'

'I don't know. Heather told me people often go to the games room in the evening but I'm not sure where I am.'

Abigail giggled girlishly. 'I'm sure you'll pick it up quickly enough. I remember my first week here. I was walking in circles trying to find the work hall. I passed the door three times before Zip helped me.'

'What's Zip like?'

'Oh, she's lovely. She's like everyone's mum. I'd say you can go to her if you ever have a problem but no one ever has an issue here – at least nobody I know.'

The others began to separate, but Jessica stayed close to Abigail as she led them into the room with the snooker table. The Asian man who had helped Glenn with the injured recruit and another man were playing darts at the far end but it was otherwise empty.

'Do you play snooker?' Abigail asked.

'I'm too short.'

Abigail laughed loudly but it didn't sound forced. 'Me too. We can just sit and chat if you want?'

Jessica agreed, wanting to try to get a feel for the other people who lived there. So far she had little Charley could be interested in. Being charismatic and encouraging others to be suspicious of the outside world wasn't a crime.

Allowing the man to crack his head was ultimately too small an incident by itself.

As soon as they sat, Heather entered with a couple of other girls. She instantly headed towards Jessica, sitting next to her and squeezing her hand.

'How was your study session?' she asked.

'Good,' Jessica replied, wondering what else she could say.

'Let me introduce you to a few people.'

Everyone Jessica met was keen to tell her the story of what they had left behind to be there. It was only her first evening and thanks to the study session, she had already heard some of the tales twice. The openness was particularly disturbing, not least because Jessica didn't want to tell anyone what had happened to her unless she really had to.

The Asian man finished playing darts and joined her on the sofa, with Heather on the other side.

'I'm Ali,' he said, offering Jessica his hand. His skin was smooth and he had large black eyes with long eyelashes some girls would spend years trying to perfect.

'Jessica.'

'It's always nice when we have new people.'

'Can I ask what happened to the man who hit his head? You helped to move him.'

Heather tensed but Ali seemed happy to oblige. 'He's absolutely fine – it looked a lot worse than it was. Moses has been to see him and he understands what happened. He feels honoured that Moses chose him to be part of the lesson.'

Jessica knew that Moses was good with words – but

convincing someone that splitting his head open was a good thing was impressive by anyone's standards.

'At least he's okay.'

'Moses would never do anything to deliberately hurt any of us. This was a lesson to us all.'

Jessica thought it was time to change the subject, leaning back as casually as she could, closer to Heather. 'Apart from this, what do you usually do in the evenings?'

'Some of us play cards,' Ali replied. 'Obviously not for money but I suppose there's a bit of a competitive edge. We play other games too: dominoes and dice.'

'I often just read in my room,' Heather added. Jessica assumed that meant she read the Bible, seeing as she hadn't noticed any other books in the house.

Ali continued: 'We all mingle and mix, getting to know each other and our backgrounds. We consider it an honour when people share their life stories. It helps us all to grow. You can probably guess that I don't come from a Christian background. My parents were Muslim. I fell in with a bad crowd after leaving college. Drinking and doing drugs. Then there were the girls . . . I kept it a secret for long enough but one of my parents' friends spotted me one night. They disowned me and I ended up living on the streets for a while.'

'In Manchester?'

'Glasgow.'

'You don't have an accent.'

Ali shrugged. 'I used to stow away on trains, hiding in the toilets and stealing leftover bits of food from the tables when people got off. One time I was caught and thrown off in Bradford. The guards wanted to prosecute me, or at least make me pay. When they realised I was homeless, they sent me on my way after taking my picture and saying they'd send it to all the train stations around the country so people would be on the lookout for me.'

Jessica almost cut in, telling him that wouldn't have happened in practice, but she stopped herself in time.

'Anyway, I had never been to Bradford before. I only knew that's where I was because of the big sign on the way out of the station. I'd never seen so many people who looked like me. It was nice in some ways but I think people sensed I was different. I had been sleeping on streets and trains for weeks, so it's no surprise. I found myself in the centre, stumbling around, and that's when someone introduced me to Zipporah. I got on the minibus that evening and I've never looked back.'

Jessica paused, letting his words sink in. She'd heard similar tales that evening but never told with such relish. He was as committed as anyone.

'What exactly was it here that turned you around?'

Ali bit on his bottom lip, before breaking into a smile. 'It's everything. Some of it is simply being away from everything that used to be around me. I work with Glenn outside, so it's nice being in that fresh air.'

'What do you do?'

'We plant crops and harvest them according to the time of year. We grow as much as we can here.'

'Is it only the men who work with Glenn?'

Ali stopped, biting his lip again, thinking. 'I suppose so. I've never thought of it like that. Everything we do is assigned by Moses. If he thought a female was suited to being outside, I'm sure he'd put them there.'

'Don't you ever want to see your parents again?'

Ali began answering and then stopped, correcting himself. 'It's not a question of that. Here, we are given a chance at redemption.'

'Couldn't you visit them and come back?'

Ali glanced at Heather, who was out of Jessica's eye line. 'Have you met one on one with Moses yet?'

'No.'

Another awkward glance.

'There aren't many rules for living here but one of them is that when you're here, you're here. Anyone is free to leave but you have to stick to that decision.'

'So if you leave you can't return?'

'We are taught to take responsibility for our actions and decisions. If you choose to go, that's a decision you have to deal with.'

'Do many people leave?'

This time Ali was emphatic. 'Hardly anyone. Every now and then someone will stop coming to dinner because they have chosen to go.'

'Has anyone ever told you they were opting to leave?'

'No, people just do – or don't.'

Ali's answer was an honest one but he didn't catch the implication of Jessica's question. She was thinking that if people stopped coming to dinner, it could be because something more sinister had happened, as when Liam drowned. Just because everyone else was told that person had chosen to leave, that didn't make it true.

She wanted to push the point, asking who exactly told them that a person had left, but there was no way of doing so without appearing too interested. She could guess it was Moses or possibly Glenn in any case. She had got somewhere though – hardly anyone left, but when they did, it was without fanfare or seemingly without the knowledge of the others.

Jessica stopped there, even though Ali was hinting that she could open up to him if she wanted. Very politely, she told him that she would see him another time, before turning to Heather and saying truthfully she was feeling tired.

They went upstairs together, Heather talking enthusiastically about what a nice day she'd had. There had been other days in her life when Jessica had heard a skull crack, but she didn't think she could count any of them as 'nice'.

As soon as they were in the room, Heather pulled the curtains, the only light coming from separate lamps next to each of their beds. She asked Jessica to unzip her dress, unclothing fully before climbing under her sheets. Jessica removed her own dress, complimenting Heather on its quality, before sliding into the bed still in her underwear. The sheets were crisp and cool, making Jessica shiver with pleasure. There were very few things in the world that could match the wonderful feeling of new sheets tucked in tightly. They were smooth and soft on her skin, so taut that she could barely move.

Jessica freed an arm to click off the lamp, leaving only a faint light coming from Heather's side of the room. She was partially sitting up, reading her Bible.

'Everyone's so friendly here,' Jessica said.

Heather peered over the top of the book. 'I'm really glad you think so. It's so good to have you here.'

Jessica paused for a second, thinking how to phrase her questions. 'It's such a big house, I suppose there's always an occasion where people fall out or something happens but it's great that everyone's so kind about things.'

Heather didn't answer instantly but she hadn't looked back down to the Bible. 'How do you mean?' she replied eventually.

'Nothing really, just that we all know what it's like at school or work, where there's a lot of people in a small area. Eventually people end up arguing over something or another. It might not mean anything but that's just what happens.'

Another pause.

'Everyone's very happy here.'

'Of course they are, that's not what I'm saying. It's like with Naomi at dinner. Sometimes there are little niggles between people. It doesn't mean anything but it's really great that you all get along and get over things.'

Jessica was pushing her luck but hoped she was careful enough how she worded things not to be too obvious.

'I suppose you're right. Perhaps that's what makes things different here.'

Jessica lay still, listening to the stillness of the night. It was only her first night. Should she risk it?

'Someone mentioned something about a person named Liam who upset a few people . . .'

Silence.

Jessica could hear Heather breathing. 'Where did you hear that name?'

'When I was being introduced to everyone downstairs, someone spoke about a Liam who had upset them.'

'Who?'

Jessica laughed, trying to make light. 'I don't remember the name. I've met so many new people today that it's difficult to keep up.'

'Liam caused trouble here – he broke the rules. We all know what they were but he couldn't abide by them. We tried to help him.'

'So he was asked to leave?'

'He ran away.'

Jessica knew Heather would have been told that by either Glenn or Moses, possibly even Zipporah. She did at least now know that Liam had encountered problems while here.

'Do many people run away?'

'Of course not. We're all one big family.'

Jessica didn't reply, closing her eyes and turning to face the wall. There weren't many families where people disappeared and ended up dead in a canal forty miles away.

8

Jessica had struggled with sleeping for most of her life. Sometimes she would lie awake through the night, staring at the ceiling, worrying about cases she was working on. Other times, she could sleep through entire days if she didn't have someone to wake her. With no watch and no alarm clock, she had no choice but to force herself to stay awake, listening for the rest of the house to go quiet. At first there was the padding of feet as people headed off to their bedrooms, then there were the clunks and clangs that come with any house. They were even louder in something as old as this.

Water pipes squeaked as people took showers; outside, owls hooted to each other until, eventually, there was nothing but the sound of Heather's deep breathing.

Jessica hadn't realised it until now but there was very little more disorientating than not knowing what time it was. She tried to think if there was anywhere in the house where she had seen a clock. There were many paintings, portraits and photographs. The call to dinner had come via a bell and Jessica assumed all meals and probably their wake-up call would be signalled in the same way.

There was no single thing that made the house particularly sinister; it was a combination of lots of small details. Having no reference point for the time, other than whether it was daylight, left them completely at the mercy of whoever sounded the bell. The way everyone so willingly opened up about the horrors in their lives might work in small doses but it simply became a way for them to constantly wallow in their pasts, rather than focusing on the life in front of them. Mixed with the way Moses could so easily manipulate them, it made for a potentially dangerous combination.

When they were utterly reliant on one person, it wouldn't take much before they became unable to picture life any differently. Day after day, Moses would be drumming into them how dangerous outsiders could be. Jessica had seen it with Heather's father – the moment he began shouting, they all acted together, creating a wall of people between him and his daughter. That happened when Moses wasn't even there.

Jessica's eyes were tired but she continued waiting, turning things over in her mind.

Eventually, when she couldn't wait any longer, she slid the covers away, untucking them as quietly as she could, reaching under the mattress for the mobile phone she had hidden. In the negotiations between her district and Charley's, it was the one concession that had been made. She wasn't happy at the method of bringing it in but, given she had to strip to her underwear in front of Zipporah, it had proved to be the only way – exactly as Charley had suggested might happen.

Under the covers, she poked at the buttons, unfamiliar with a device that wasn't hers, trying to find the right one to make the screen flash to life. Having the phone was one thing but there was no way to charge it, meaning she couldn't be wasteful. They had provided her with an old model with nothing but the bare minimum of functions. She could send a text message and make a phone call but nothing else. This way, the battery would last far longer. Slowly it came to life, flashing up the time as 03.18 and then connecting to the network. How there was signal here but only an intermittent one in the village a few miles away, Jessica didn't know.

She crept through to the bathroom, closing the door behind her. She lay in the bath, wrapping a towel around the phone and her mouth, hoping it would make her voice quiet enough not to disturb Heather.

There was only one number programmed into the phone. Charley answered on the second ring, sounding as awake as if it were the middle of the afternoon. 'What time do you call this?'

'I'm in.'

'Good. Are you safe?'

Her tone was clipped and short but it was good to hear someone's voice from the outside.

'I think so.'

'Anything to report?'

'Liam was definitely here. Someone says he ran away but they all believe whatever they're told. As well as Moses, there's another man called Glenn who I'll try to keep an eye on.'

'Weapons?'

'Not that I've seen.'

'Anything else strange?'

'One of the new recruits was hurt. It was in this trust exercise but Moses let him fall and he cracked his head.'

'Is he all right?'

'I'm not sure. He wasn't dead. These people would do anything for Moses if he asked them to. Almost all of the girls are in their early twenties. I'm pretty sure he's got a mistress, who's maybe nineteen or twenty. There's something under the surface but I'm not there yet.'

There was a humming sound from the other end of the line. 'Thanks for the call. You know what we said; emergencies and updates only to keep the battery. I should go.'

'Charley . . .'

'What?'

'It's nice to hear someone else's voice. Everyone here has a tone to them, like a robot, as if it's rehearsed.'

There was no emotion to Charley's reply. 'Okay.'

'There was one other thing you said I could call you for . . .'

'I remember.'

'Please tell Adam that I love him and miss him.'

A pause and a sigh. 'Will do.'

The line went dead.

Jessica sat in the hospital waiting room staring at the floor. The last time she had been in a similar position was when Dave Rowlands had broken his arm. She also remembered the day she'd found out her colleague Carrie had died, in a room just like the one she was in. Hospitals meant death and devastation.

Today was going to eclipse any of that.

'Are you okay?' Adam asked.

He had been absent-mindedly tapping his foot on the hard floor for the past five minutes. It was annoying but Jessica did not have the anger to tell him to stop. She just felt empty.

'I'm fine.'

'Would you like a drink?'

'No.'

'Something to eat?'

'No.'

'Would you—?'

'I'm fine!'

Jessica couldn't stop herself shouting, attracting the attention of a woman with two young children on the far side of the waiting room. Adam went silent, even stopping tapping his foot.

A few moments later, a door swung open noisily,

clattering against the frame with a bang. Jessica didn't look up, even when the person asked for 'Miss Daniel'.

She could feel Adam nodding towards her but the floor still seemed like the best option, the gentle brown zigzags on the cream surface offering her something to look at which wasn't the white imposing walls of the hospital.

Jessica felt someone sitting next to her.

'Miss Daniel?'

'Yes.'

'Your mother's in there now.'

'Okay.'

'Has someone explained things to you?'

'Sort of.'

She assumed the voice belonged to a doctor but continued to stare at the floor, sensing him exchanging a look with Adam.

'Do you mind if I talk you through it? Even if it's only for a minute?'

Jessica breathed in through her nose, the faint smell of disinfectant creeping through her.

'Is he in pain?' she asked.

The doctor cleared his throat. 'He's comfortable and he's able to speak with full awareness.'

'Tell me why you can't save him. All this equipment, all this technology. Tell me why.'

Jessica's voice was calm but angry. She heard the doctor gulp. It wasn't his fault but she wanted a reason.

'Your father had a brain aneurysm. We operated and did everything we could to stabilise him. Unfortunately, it was too big and had done too much damage. Every time we bring him back to consciousness, the pressure increases on his brain to such a degree that we find ourselves in the situation we are now. The only way he can live any sort of life is if he remains unconscious.'

He didn't say it but he might as well have added: 'And what sort of life is that?'

'So how long has he got?' Jessica asked.

'We can't say for sure, perhaps ninety minutes, perhaps two hours. He's been with your mother for around ten minutes since we brought him back to consciousness. All I can say is that he will be mostly himself during that time and that he shouldn't be able to feel the pain.'

'And then he'll die?'

'I'm sorry.'

The doctor continued sitting for a few seconds, wondering if Jessica had any further questions. Instead, she continued staring at the floor. He muttered something consoling to Adam, but Jessica wasn't listening, then he stood and walked away.

Half of Jessica wanted to turn and run, not knowing if she could see her father in such a position. He was the person who had taught her to ride a bicycle, took her blackberry-picking in the summers, buried her in sand at the beach.

One night when she was young she'd had a nightmare and gone downstairs, curling up on the sofa, shivering. He had followed her down, tickling and joking with her, before carrying her back to bed and kissing her on the forehead. 'Don't worry about the monsters, Jess,' he'd said. 'If they want to get to you, they'll have to come through me first.' She believed him then as she did now, that strong, soothing voice teasing and reassuring in the way only a father's could.

Adam's hand was on her back, rubbing gently, but she shrugged him away.

Time passed, doors opening and closing until eventually her mother entered. Jessica could tell from the weight of the footsteps they were hers, even before she heard the voice. 'He'd like to see you now, Jess.'

Did she want to see him? That great man who had helped make her the person she had become was now in a bed wasting away as the clock ticked away on his life. Who did she want to remember him as: the person with the tanned arms who used to push her higher on the swings, or the man he was now, dying in a hospital?

Slowly Jessica rose, unable to meet her mother's eyes.

'I want to go on my own,' she told Adam, voice cracking, as he started to stand. 'Sorry,' she croaked, but he told her he understood.

Her mum told her which room and then Jessica trudged her way through the corridors. The bright white overhead lights dazzled her, the disinfectant stench becoming stronger. Jessica felt woozy herself, unsure how to cope as she stood in front of a door, staring at the numbers.

With a deep breath, she pushed it inwards, stepping forward into the dimmer light, focusing on the figure in the bed. He was half-sitting up, her father but not her father. Thinner, frailer, no trace of that playful grin he so often had.

Jessica sat on the chair next to the bed, taking his hand

in hers. He tried to smile but his lips simply twitched. It wasn't the same.

'Jess.'

'Daddy.'

'Your mother told me you had something exciting to share.'

Jessica shrugged, unable to stop the tears forming around her eyes. She stood again, pulling up her top and pressing her father's hand to the area under her stomach.

'It's a little boy.'

She felt her father's fingers twitch on her skin and, with that, she was gone. He rolled over as much as he could, using both hands to touch her but Jessica could do nothing but cry. Within seconds, he was soothing her, shushing and reaching for her hand again.

Jessica sat, rolling her top down and trying to calm herself; she was supposed to be the strong one.

'My little girl all grown up,' he said, his voice wavering but still undoubtedly her father's.

'I'm so sorry you're not going to meet him.'

He chuckled slightly but it might have been a cough. 'Are you happy?'

'Yes.'

'Is Adam happy?'

'Yes.'

'And he looks after you?'

'He's the best.'

'Well then, what would you like me to say? What more could a father want than to see his daughter happy?'

Jessica swallowed hard. 'We're going to name him Marcus.'

This time, there were tears around her father's eyes. 'You shouldn't name him after a silly old man like me.'

Jessica continued gripping his hand, wanting him to squeeze her hard, to show he was fighting whatever was killing him. There was little resistance, the only sign of life in his greying body his bright blue eyes.

She couldn't speak, not knowing what to say, but her father seemed to sense it, breaking the silence instead.

'Have I ever told you the story about what happened the night you told your mother and me that you and Caroline were moving to Manchester?'

'No.'

Her father shuffled lower in the bed, closing his eyes. 'It wasn't long after the pair of you got back from your gap year. Your mother thought you were going to get home and then settle down in one of the local villages and do something like become a teacher. Throughout that year, she was saying she couldn't wait to get you back and that perhaps you'd meet some nice young man when you returned.'

Jessica spluttered a mixture of tears and amusement.

'Exactly,' her father croaked. 'I think she probably knew but she wanted to believe that was going to happen. The day we took you both to the airport, I knew you might not come back and that, if you did, you'd go off to find your own place in the world.'

'I didn't get far.'

'Maybe not but Manchester's a big place compared to our village. All those people, different races and religions, knives, guns – it's a far cry from where you grew up.'

'People are people.'

Her father opened his eyes again, smiling. 'Your mother and me see those things about you in the paper, even when you don't tell us it's going in. She'll go on the computer and print all these things off, asking if I think we should call you to see if you're okay. I say what I always say – she'll come to us if she needs to. But that's exactly why you're special, Jessica. Because people *are* people and you see that. Some are nicer than others, some have different coloured skin, some believe things which might seem crazy to the rest of us. But people are people and the fact you can do the job you do, see everything you must have seen, and still come out the other side saying that makes me so proud to know you're my daughter.'

With that he closed his eyes again, fingers twitching against Jessica's as she held him, unable to speak, unable to do anything other than cry.

More time passed until Jessica heard a gentle knocking at the door.

She took another deep breath, sitting up straighter and squeezing her father's wrinkled fingers. 'I have to go, Daddy.'

'I know, sweetie. Can I ask you one last thing?'

'What?'

'Did anyone finish mowing the lawn?'

Jessica gasped with surprise and laughter. Her father was sniggering too, before collapsing into a cough. She released his hand, knowing it was time to let her mother return. She couldn't bring herself to see his final moments.

'I love you, Jessica,' he said, in the way only he could.

'I love you too, Daddy.'

TUESDAY

9

Breakfast was much the same as dinner, the house's residents sitting around the U-shaped table eating in relative silence until the cooks cleared everyone's plates away. The man who had cracked his head the night before was there, bandages wrapped around his skull, sitting closest to Katie, who was at Moses's side. Jessica watched him closely at first, intrigued at how he was smiling. Ali had been speaking the truth when he'd said the man hadn't minded. People were people but some of them were very strange.

The meal finished with Moses standing and reading a passage from the Bible, before sending them out to their various jobs. The two other new recruits had apparently already been assigned roles but Jessica didn't know what she was doing. As she stood, a little confused, Moses beckoned her with a casual wave of his hand. Heather said she would see her later and then joined some of the others, packing away the tables ready to turn the hall back into somewhere they could work.

Jessica followed Moses out of the room, running to keep up as he didn't stop to wait, or turn to see where she was. She slowed as she got nearer and he led her along the corridors until they reached the room Heather had told her was Moses's office.

Out of his pocket, he look a large metal ring with at least thirty keys looped onto it. Flicking through them, he found the correct one and unlocked the door, holding it open for Jessica. As she stepped inside, he moved too, standing so close that his chest was pressing into her back before she could get away.

He brushed past her, hand sliding along her back, before he sat behind a desk, inviting Jessica to sit opposite him.

He hadn't locked the door but Jessica still felt uncomfortable being alone with Moses in a room out of sight of everyone else. His appearance was kindly but he was bigger than her, almost certainly stronger and she already knew what his hands were capable of.

Jessica did a quick scan of the room. There were filing cabinets lining one wall, broken up by a large cupboard which was almost as tall as the room.

'I figured it was about time we had a one-to-one chat,' Moses said, leaning back into the chair. Jessica didn't reply at first but she heard a gentle ticking sound from the desk, her eyes flitting across the back of a small clock before moving on, not wanting him to think she believed it was significant.

'It's nice to be here,' Jessica replied.

'First, I feel I should apologise for what happened last night. I know it must have been a shock for you to see the blood of a stranger. I hope you understand the point I was trying to make. He was absolutely fine and is already recovering well.'

Moses's green eyes were fixed on her, youthful yet

holding a wisdom too. Perhaps a hint of danger? Jessica maintained eye contact, not wanting to be the vulnerable girl who looked away first.

'I understand.'

'My wife has filled me in on a few of the details of what has happened to you, with your father dying and so on. I know you've had a horrible time over these past few months. Grief can do terrible things to us. It is truly wonderful that you have chosen to confront that and be here with us. I hope our family will help you to overcome what has happened in your life.'

'I hope so too.'

'You will find all sorts of people here: alcoholics, drug abusers, people who have been abused by others. I hope you are able to deal with such things.'

'I've already met some people. I've taken strength from them.'

Moses smiled, the crinkles around his mouth folding into a dimple. 'That's wonderful, Jessica. It's terrific you are making progress already.'

She hated the way he said her name. It wasn't in the loving way her father or Adam might have, it was as if she was a possession of his. How could no one else see through him?

'Thank you.'

'So tell me about your former life. Where was it you worked?'

'I helped to run a post office.'

'Where?'

'In one of the larger villages out in the lakes.'

'How long did you do that for?'

'My whole adult life. After I left school, I was helping my parents out. Gradually, I was doing more and more. As they got older, it eventually fell into my hands.'

'So it was a family business?'

'Yes.'

'Passed down from father to daughter?'

Jessica wanted to tell him not to talk about her dad. The life she had described was the life she could have had: away from the city, away from the murders, the assaults, the knives, the guns. Away from Adam and what had followed after her father died. None of that would have happened; she could have been happy.

'Yes.'

Moses nodded, satisfied. He ran a hand through the long strands of his beard, bringing them together and then separating them. 'How nice,' he concluded.

'It was.'

'But you're aware of our rules about contact with the outside world?'

Jessica thought of the mobile phone wedged under her mattress. She had made her bed herself, doing it as tidily as she possibly could, just in case Heather was tempted to try to help out.

'I am.'

'I'm sorry about that. A lot of the newer people do find it hard but it is for the benefit of everyone. Every society has to have its rules. Outside, they have theirs, here we have ours. Outside, people get away with breaking theirs if they have enough money, or know people in the right places. In here everyone is equal. We all live by the same code.'

'I understand.'

Moses hadn't taken his eyes from her but Jessica felt a minor victory as he looked away. It was instantly replaced by unease as he stood, walking around the desk until he was behind her. At first she could just hear his breathing, but then his hands were on her shoulders, massaging them gently.

'Relax,' he cooed.

Jessica wanted to flinch away but forced herself to stay where she was. Charley's warning raced through her mind: *'It has to be someone who can become a part of whatever community it is they have inside the house.'*

She knew she was walking into the unknown but then this was a community where Moses could sit openly with someone probably still a teenager as his mistress and no one batted an eyelid. How far could she let this go?

Jessica pressed back into the seat, forcing her shoulder muscles to loosen as his fingers rubbed through the thin material of her top.

'Do you have any sort of boyfriend on the outside world?'

Jessica closed her eyes, knowing Moses couldn't see her from behind. 'No.'

'Husband?'

'No.'

'Even after everything that happened with—'

Jessica cut him off before he could say it. 'No.'

'A pretty thing like you hasn't got a man pining for them?'

'No.'

'That's almost a shame . . .'

Jessica hadn't liked anyone touching her in recent months but this was worse than anything. She had to fight to stay still, keeping her eyes locked closed to block it out.

His voice was soft but Jessica had been in enough bars to know when someone was trying it on. 'That feels better, doesn't it?'

No.

'Yes.'

His fingers moved around until they were on the back of her neck, gently massaging. He was so close, she could feel his breath.

'You're older than many of the girls here, Jessica.'

Stop saying my name.

'I hadn't realised.'

'Many of the females who come to us are in their late teens or early twenties. Perhaps it's something about the female mindset? For the men, it's alcohol or drugs. For the women, it's men.'

'Okay.'

'You're different though. For you, there are deeper problems. I know what you've been through.'

You don't.

'I feel better around all the people here. Everyone's really accommodating. Heather's great.'

Moses's fingers stopped rubbing and Jessica felt him moving. She opened her eyes as he moved in front of her, sitting on the edge of the table, staring into her eyes. He reached forward, cupping her chin with his fingers.

'I want you to know that you can come to me with anything,' he said. 'Some of the girls here see Zip as their mother-type figure but you're older, more mature, than them. I want you to think of me as the father you lost.'

You're nothing like him.

'Where can I find you?'

Moses released her chin, smiling. 'Oh, I'm always around. I'd say my door is always open but that's not strictly true. That said, I'm often here in my office, so you can knock. Sometimes I am out strolling the gardens. Other times, I'm just around the house. Have you met Glenn who works outside? He'll know where I am.'

It was at least interesting to know that Glenn and Moses did have the relationship she suspected.

His hand slipped down until it was resting on the top of her thigh. Instinctively, Jessica sat up straighter, closing her legs together.

Moses didn't flinch. 'I'm not sure how much Zip has told you about things but you should know that when you commit to stay here, then that's it. We will not stop you leaving at any point but if you do, you cannot return.'

His fingers slipped towards the inner part of her thigh. Although they weren't pressing hard into her skin, there was a clear indication that she should open her legs.

Jessica held firm.

'I understand.'

He held his fingers there for a few seconds more but

Jessica continued to resist, not by forcing anything, simply by not moving. With no flicker of emotion, Moses removed his hand, shuffling back onto the edge of the desk, nodding.

He didn't speak for a few seconds, leaving Jessica wondering what she should do. She didn't want to leave – to fail – but there was no way she was going to allow things to go any further.

His demeanour changed in an instant. 'Okay then, Jessica, I suppose we should figure out what types of things you're good at. What sort of things do you do at the post office?'

'It's a lot of sorting and organisation; mainly money.'

'Hmmm . . .'

Moses ran his eyes across her and Jessica could not resist the shiver that ran along her back. She could still feel his fingers on her, feel his breath.

'We don't really deal with money. When we go out to sell our wares at market anything we make is immediately re-spent on materials to produce more, or on meat to bring back for the cooks.'

'Okay.'

'Do you cook?'

Despite the situation, Jessica almost laughed. Of everything she could do, cooking was almost at the bottom of the list.

'Not very well.'

'We have people who could teach you.'

'It's not really for me.'

Moses nodded. 'Not many people aspire to be cleaners

but you'd be surprised by the pride some people can take in their work.'

'I'm not sure that's for me, either.'

Another nod.

'There are other things. We have our crafters, of course. The people who make the clothes, bedding, tablecloths and most of the other things you see around here. That's one of Zip's things. It's where Heather works too. If not that, we have the team that works outdoors. They help to keep the gardens tidy and grow our food. It's hard manual work but I'm sure Glenn wouldn't mind another body to help out. We also have our recruiting team; people who write our flyers ahead of the weekends.'

'Why do you recruit?'

Moses blinked quickly, the question taking him by surprise. His thick eyebrows arched downwards but quickly returned to normal. 'We're always looking for lost souls. We think we have something special here.'

'But after dinner, you told us all to be wary of the outside world and yet people here go out there, where it's dangerous.'

Moses nodded, apparently enjoying the challenge, however gentle. 'You're absolutely right. It is why I only permit certain people to go with Zip on those afternoons. People have to be strong, to be able to face what may happen out there. I believe you saw an example of that the other day.'

'With Heather's dad?'

'Exactly. I'm told that our people were calm and worked together to defuse the situation. It's that type of thing that makes me proud of what we have achieved here – but not everyone would be able to cope with such confrontation. That's not even talking about the sheer number of people who cannot cope with us being on the street. We are shouted at, sworn at, spat at. Persecuted. It takes a strong mind.'

'Not me?'

Moses leant forward again, touching Jessica's knee. 'Not yet, Jessica. Maybe at a later time if that's what you wanted to do. For now I can see how unhappy and unfulfilled you are. You're crying out for a figure to take the place of your father.'

I'm not.

'How about we place you outside for now? The weather's still holding up, except for that rain yesterday, and I sense it would be useful to have a female influence in such a male-dominated area. It is physical though.' He ran his hand up Jessica's leg, then her stomach, brushing her breast, before putting it back by his side. 'Do you think you're up to it?'

'Yes.'

'Okay then, let's introduce you.'

Jessica breathed a sigh of relief as he crossed the room, opening the door. It may have been a perfectly normal thing to do but it signalled the end of her ordeal, at least for now. His back was to her, his wandering hands by his side.

Jessica followed him to the door but he didn't turn. She knew enough about how to look after herself that she could do him some serious damage before he touched another vulnerable girl again. He wouldn't even know it had happened.

In the fraction of a second that she flirted with the idea, the moment was lost. Moses ushered her out of his office, locking the door behind them, as she suspected he would.

He led her through the corridors, which were slowly becoming familiar, until they reached the front door. He unbolted it and led her around to the rear of the house.

Glenn was on the far side of the patch of land, his stocky figure unmistakeable, even from a distance. Closer there were two men digging enthusiastically, tossing mounds of dirt to the side.

'Good morning,' Moses called as they neared. Both workers stopped, looking up as Jessica glanced from one to the other. It was only when the second man continued staring that Jessica gave him a second look, realising with a horrifying sinking feeling that she knew him.

10

Jessica felt her stomach lurch. All of the effort that had been put in, Charley's plans, Cole coming to see her, was all going to come crashing down because of something they couldn't have envisaged. Out in the middle of no-where, the now-recognisable face stared at Jessica as she tried quickly to look away.

It wasn't fast enough to escape Moses's attention as he glanced from Jessica to the man and back again.

'What's wrong?'

'Nothing.'

'Do you know each other?'

Jessica shook her head.

Moses turned back to the man. 'What's wrong, Wayne?'

His words slurred slightly into each other. 'Nothing, Sir.'

'I've told you before, you don't have to call me "Sir". I'm Moses, please use my name.'

'Yes, Sir . . . Moses.'

He turned away from Jessica, concentrating on digging as the second man followed suit.

Moses led Jessica away, heading across the field towards Glenn. 'I'm sorry about that,' he said. 'Wayne is one of the more complicated characters we've taken in.'

Jessica thought he didn't know the half of it. She must

have missed Wayne at dinner and breakfast, most likely because they sat in lines. If he was on the same side of the table as her, the only way she'd have spotted him other than as a head to count would have been by crossing the room. He hadn't said anything about recognising her either at her assessment, or now. The way he had looked at her was with familiarity but perhaps not recognition of exactly who she was.

Wayne Howson was a well-known drug user from the streets of Manchester. When she was in uniform, she would pick him up once or twice a fortnight, usually for begging or causing a public disturbance. One time, someone had reported him for urinating outside a pub on Deansgate in the middle of the afternoon. That brought him a public indecency charge. He'd also been caught for theft a dozen times and any number of other public nuisance incidents. He had been in and out of prison, living on and off the streets, over and over. One of the benefits of moving into CID was that the day-in, day-out pain in the necks were passed onto someone else. Of course, you lumbered yourself with far more dangerous characters too but Jessica hadn't missed Wayne Howson.

The last time she had seen him was in court. He had tried defending himself against a shoplifting charge, even though it was captured on CCTV. His argument had been that it must have been someone who looked like him. When he was asked if he had a twin, he answered, 'Possibly'. Proceedings had been adjourned for an hour as the prosecution frantically scrambled to get a copy of the records to prove he was an only child.

Unsurprisingly, he had been found guilty, with the magistrate particularly unhappy at the amount of time wasted. Because of his lengthy record, he'd been given three months in prison. As far as Jessica knew, he'd been released after half of his sentence. She hadn't bothered to follow his progress since then but now, years later, here he was staring, not quite able to place her.

For now, she'd have to hope things stayed that way.

Glenn didn't exactly seem pleased to see her, a scowl apparently a permanent feature of his face. Moses introduced them, waiting expectantly as they shook hands. Glenn's hands were rough and dirty, the skin of someone familiar with manual labour.

'What are you good for?' Glenn asked Jessica abruptly.

'I'm stronger than I look.'

'You're not going to be stronger than the six men I already have.'

Moses stepped in. 'Glenn . . .'

Glenn shook his head, obviously not happy at being talked down to in front of her. 'Do you know much about the seasons and planting?'

'I can learn.'

'Fine.'

Glenn turned to Moses, lowering his voice. 'Is everything else in hand?'

'Yes.'

'Good. I'll visit you later.'

Moses turned to leave, resting a hand on Jessica's shoulder. 'Remember what I told you. I'm always available if you need me – for anything.'

'I'll remember.'

Jessica had no intention of going to him about anything, other than to pin him to the floor and tell him he was nicked when the time came.

Moses walked away, waving to the other workers as he headed back to the house.

'Whose idea was it for you to come out here?' Glenn asked as Jessica was facing away from him.

'Moses said it might help to have me out here for a while.'

Glenn snorted, showing he might be Moses's right-hand man but that they certainly didn't agree on everything.

'It's going to be hard work, sometimes in the rain and wind, sometimes in the blazing sun.'

'I know.'

'And you're happy being out here?'

'I come from the north – rain is like a family member.'

Another snort and a mumbled, 'We'll see', which Jessica wasn't sure she was meant to hear.

'We'll start you off with something simple,' Glenn added, hurrying past her towards the house.

For someone with short legs, he certainly moved quickly, his thick shoulders and hunched frame bustling away so fast that Jessica again had to run to keep up. He stopped when he reached a spot just past where Wayne had been digging.

'What do you know about potatoes?' he asked. 'And I don't mean that's where chips come from.'

'I'm not sure . . . they grow in the ground?'

'Exactly. And now's the time of year to put them there.' He twisted around, showing Jessica a long line of soil. 'I need you to dig a trench along there. Go down about a foot. You do know what a foot is, don't you?'

'Yes.'

'Good, all this metric stuff nowadays just confuses everyone. Anyway, once you've dug the full trench, come and find me.'

'Are you going to still be out here?'

'Where else would I be?'

Glenn was standing with his legs apart, knees slightly bent as if about to launch into a scrap, even though Jessica didn't realise she'd said anything wrong. 'Nowhere, I don't know. Sorry.'

He shook his head dismissively. 'Just get on with it. It shouldn't take you much past lunchtime.'

As Jessica reached for the nearby spade, Glenn stomped away. She wondered which part of what had just happened would inspire anyone who had come to the house to escape their demons. Glenn certainly didn't have the soft exterior that Zipporah did, let alone the charisma of Moses. Still, he hadn't tried to touch her either, which immediately placed him above Moses in Jessica's estimation.

She began to dig, the first manual labour she had done in a long while. Running the vacuum around the house once or twice wasn't in the same league as digging a long trench. She had thought that a foot didn't sound like much but the ground was like clay, thick and sludgy and hard to remove. She didn't know the time but it felt as if she had barely moved a dozen steps before her shoulders and back ached from the work.

She paused for a few moments, leaning on the spade and staring towards the house. It was the first time she had properly seen the rear. There was definitely a door off to the left, although she had no idea where it led into, let alone if it was unlocked. The faint tint of the glass made it impossible to see anything inside but then Jessica noticed one of the windows was a slightly different shade. It was only when she stepped to the side that she realised it was because it was open and was reflecting the sun at a different angle to the others.

Jessica dug a little more, making sure not to attract attention, as she tried to work out which part of the house it must be. She eventually deduced that the wider windows next to it were beside the staircase and that the open window was in Moses's office. Inside, she had been so disconcerted by the way he was touching her that she hadn't noticed. She hadn't even felt cool in there, the way his fingers scraped along her skin making her hot, but not in a good way.

With every other window locked, Jessica did at least have a second way to get out if necessary, assuming there was a time that the office was left open. She tried to think of a reason why it had to be locked. Aside from the clock, there was nothing obvious but then she didn't know what was in the row of cabinets, or the cupboard. Sooner or later, she was going to have to find a way into that room.

'Do you need a hand?'

Jessica had been so lost in trying to figure out which

room the window belonged to that she'd failed to notice Wayne sidling close to her. His words sounded pained and merged into one another.

'I'm fine,' she replied, not necessarily to keep up appearances, but more because she wanted to prove to Glenn that she was capable. It was then it dawned on her that perhaps his aggressive brand of motivation did work. Whereas Zip killed you with kindness, he made you want to prove him wrong.

What a dick.

Wayne sounded hesitant. 'Are you sure? It's a lot of hard work for one . . . person . . . by themselves.'

'You can say "girl".'

Jessica tried not to face him, hoping he wouldn't recognise her. Wayne mumbled something under his breath which she didn't catch as she continued digging, facing the house, away from him.

'I said I know who you are.'

Jessica breathed in sharply, continuing to dig. 'I think you must have me mistaken for someone else.'

'I remember you from the streets. You were younger then but I wouldn't forget that uniform you used to wear. Whenever they came for me, I always hoped it was you who was going to be there. It was always disappointing when they sent the men, or one of the fat ones.'

Jessica sighed, turning. 'I don't know what you're talking about. I worked in a post office.'

Wayne screwed up his eyes, looking at her closely but Jessica couldn't hold his gaze, returning to digging with a grunt of exertion. She could hear him shuffling nervously behind her. Then the breeze changed and she could smell the alcohol on his breath. It was only faint but explained why his words were slurred. She wondered how he had possibly got it into the house. She didn't know how long he had been staying there but it seemed unlikely he would have smuggled something in weeks or months earlier and drunk it only now. Besides, she had struggled to get a phone in. If he had got some alcohol in, it couldn't have been very much.

'I think you should return to work, Wayne,' Jessica said, hoping he would listen. He had seemingly been working without a problem, despite his state. The more he talked, the more likely he was to get himself found out.

When nothing happened for a few moments, Jessica turned to see Wayne rocking from side to side unsteadily.

'I know who you are.'

'Sorry?'

'I know who you are!' He was shouting now, pointing and turning towards the others. Ali moved first, standing and walking towards them. Jessica gripped her spade tighter, her only line of defence.

'I know who you are!'

'Shush.'

'I know who you are!'

Each cry was louder than the last until Wayne was bellowing at the top of his voice. Ali was too close not to have heard. Over his shoulder, Jessica saw Glenn running. He moved quickly anyway but now his speed was like an athlete's.

'Wayne, stop,' Jessica hissed but it did no good.

'Is there a problem?' Ali asked, nearing them.

Jessica shook her head but Wayne had lost whatever grip he'd had on himself. His eyes were rolling back into his head and there was saliva around his mouth as he shouted one more time.

In an instant, Glenn was there. He didn't bother asking questions, or listening to whatever either of them had to say; instead he barrelled into Wayne, shoulder-charging him to the floor and back-handing him viciously. A smear of blood flew across the grass.

'Druggie, smackhead scum,' Glenn spat, fists flashing again.

Wayne rolled over to his side, groaning, as Glenn got to his feet, turning to Ali. 'I told you earlier there was something not right.'

'He was slurring his words a little but he often does that. I thought he'd just had a bad night's sleep. He was still digging fine.'

Glenn turned to Jessica. 'What did he say to you?'

She felt caught, unable to tell the truth but not wanting to see Wayne hurt any further. 'I'm not sure, he was asking if I wanted help.'

'What was he shouting?'

'I don't—'

'It was something about knowing who she was,' Ali interrupted.

'What do you mean?'

'I don't know, he was shouting it at the top of his voice.'

Glenn nodded to Jessica again. 'Does that mean anything to you?'

She had to lie. 'No.'

'That's what you get when you can't control yourself.'

Glenn hauled Wayne roughly to his feet, forcefully cupping his chin between his fingers. 'Where's your stash?'

Wayne's eyes were still back in his head and his answer was a faint grumble.

'Useless,' Glenn said, tossing him back to the ground.

Jessica's disapproval must have been apparent as he turned to her, lip curled, pointing towards the driveway. 'If you don't like the rules, you can leave any time you like. The gate's that way.'

Without waiting for a reply, he grabbed Ali's arm. 'Moses is going to have to deal with this. Come on, let's get him inside.'

The two men dragged Wayne for a short distance before Ali helped pull him up and Glenn hoisted him over his shoulder in an almost unbelievable feat of strength. The final word Jessica heard was a perfectly clear 'sorry' from Wayne as he was carried away.

11

Glenn returned with Ali not long after but there was no sign of Wayne. The rest of the afternoon passed with little interruption other than a break for water and some fruit. Jessica finished her trench, although it took longer than the time Glenn had predicted. She suspected he had only told her that knowing she would fail.

Just as she was about to ask Glenn what she should do next, Jessica heard him shouting, 'It's time' from the other side of the allotment.

The choice of words wasn't lost on her. She hadn't noticed if he wore a watch but he must have some way of telling the time, which she doubted was anything to do with the fact that the sun was dipping over the top of the house. As the other workers began carrying their tools towards the building, Jessica followed them around to the front and through the door, which had been unlocked for them. She had wondered if there was some sort of shed or other outside place where things might be left but the tools were placed in a large, locked cupboard in one of the rooms close to the entrance. There were plenty of other supplies there too: mops, buckets, fold-down tables and chairs. Before Jessica could look any closer, Glenn was ushering her away, fixing a large padlock through the metal hoops. She noticed a selection of keys clipped to his belt. Unlike Moses, they weren't all fixed to one large ring; instead they were separated into twos or threes, running the entire way around his waist.

'What?' he asked aggressively, noticing Jessica's wandering eyes.

'Nothing, sorry . . .'

Jessica turned to see Zipporah nearby with a half-smile on her face. She beckoned Jessica over with a nod of her head.

'How was your first day working here, dear?' she asked as they began walking along the corridor.

'Hard.'

Zipporah laughed. '"Those who work their land will have abundant food, but those who chase fantasies have no sense."'

'Is that—?'

'It's from Proverbs.'

'I'm afraid I don't know the Bible very well.'

Zipporah led her through another corridor until they reached the base of the stairs. She sat on the second step, patting the space next to her. Jessica felt her back crack as she sat.

'Being here isn't really about the Bible. We use the stories and verses to help us have a framework but some of us believe more than others. Galatians talks about 'the fruits of the Spirit, one of those fruits being kindness'. In Leviticus, Matthew, Mark, Luke, Romans, Galatians and James, it says to love your neighbour as yourself. Principles like that are more important than exact knowledge of scripture.'

Jessica wanted to ask how that could tally with the way she had seen Wayne beaten outside, simply because he had given into temptation at some point. She didn't have to speak because Zipporah answered anyway, as if reading her mind. 'I don't necessarily approve of everything my husband and people like Glenn might get up to but the important thing is keeping the majority of people safe and away from their demons. Sometimes things might happen in strange ways because of that. We just have to trust that people are acting in our best interests.'

Jessica didn't speak for a while, slightly disconcerted by the fact Zipporah appeared to know what had happened. It perhaps wasn't a surprise, she was married to Moses after all, but Jessica was now wondering if the woman had deliberately sought her out after she returned inside.

'Don't forget you can always come to me if you have a problem or want to ask a question.'

'I will.'

Jessica wondered if there were any other family members lining up to tell her the same thing. Perhaps Katie could offer her a shoulder to cry on too, meaning the trio would have something to chat about whenever they got together in whatever bizarre relationship it was they had.

Zipporah started to say something but stopped herself as Glenn walked past, doing a double-take when he saw them on the stairs. 'What are you doing, Zip?'

'Just talking.'

He nodded sharply. 'Time to go.'

Without looking backwards, he strode away, Zipporah running to catch him up.

12

The top Jessica had chosen for the evening meal was larger than the dress Heather had made. As she ate, she found herself constantly tugging at the loose material around her hips, trying to make it fit. Everyone seemed to have the same seats, with Naomi diagonally across from her eating in silence and Glenn constantly scanning the people opposite him, making sure everything was as it should be. The meal itself was more or less the same as it had been the previous day, except that the meat had been prepared in a different way.

When the tables had been cleared, Moses rose, holding his hands out for a silence he already had. 'Tomorrow is market day,' he said, 'and it has been another bumper week. I thank you all for your wonderful efforts. Zip has already approached the people she is taking with her. Please do not be offended if you are not included. We all have our roles to play.'

Jessica hadn't been told anything, even though she'd had a conversation with Zipporah, so assumed she was staying in the house the following day.

Moses continued, reading a passage from the Bible about forgiveness. Jessica found it hard to concentrate but remembered the final line: 'If you forgive men when they sin against you, your heavenly Father will also forgive you.

But if you do not forgive men their sins, your Father will not forgive your sins.'

'With that,' Moses continued, 'I have some grave news. Our brother Wayne has left these premises.'

There were gasps at the far end of the table. Moses nodded, waiting for everyone to quieten again.

'I know. I am as disappointed as the rest of you. Unfortunately Wayne lost his battle with the demons that had been haunting him. He asked for the forgiveness of us all which was, of course, granted. Unfortunately, we all know what the penalties have to be for such lapses. It is not because we don't forgive him, nor because we do not wish him well, it is for the good of everyone still present. Many of you are still fighting those same demons that Wayne has been dealing with and it wouldn't be fair to any of you to see what he has to go through. If any of you would like to speak to either Zip or myself, we will be here for you.'

Afterwards, they all headed off to their study session. Jessica was in the same group as the evening before but instead of talking about themselves, in the wake of Wayne leaving everyone was invited to share a memory of how alcohol or drugs had affected their lives. Jessica was asked to go first and she told the story of how a former colleague had been stabbed in a bar after leaving himself vulnerable through alcohol. She didn't tell them it was the person who helped her become the police officer that she was, instead allowing everyone to believe it was someone she worked with at the post office. There was applause and tears, even though Jessica didn't feel that emotional. She couldn't think of Harry Thomas without remembering the bad thing too. The ghost of that still hung over everything in Jessica's life, even all these years later.

As they went around the circle, it was more of the same. More misery, more heartbreak, more bad decisions and many more tears. Jessica didn't know how many evenings of this she could take. It was too hard to take yourself out of the room, to switch off and pretend human beings weren't pouring out their souls to one another.

People are people.

It was no wonder the residents seemed to be such emotional wrecks. After another few weeks of this, Jessica would be the same as everyone else. As she heard one of the younger girls say her mother had been killed by a drink-driver, leaving her an orphan in a children's home where she was abused, Jessica felt the lump in her throat building again. Despite her suspicions about Moses and Glenn, she had to remember that there were a lot of vulnerable people here too, who deserved to be looked after. Whatever happened, whatever she found out, it had to include getting them to safety.

After the session, people began to drift off to do their own things. Heather was outside the games room waiting for her but Jessica said she was feeling tired from working in the gardens and that they could catch up later.

Leaving Heather behind, Jessica went to the bedroom, closing the door behind her and grabbing the phone from under the mattress. In the bathroom, she shut the door and sat on the toilet before calling Charley.

She answered before it could ring a second time. 'What have you got?'

'Don't you ever say "hello"?'

'Hello. Now what have you got?'

Jessica spoke quickly, telling her about the assault on Wayne.

'Where has he gone?'

'I don't know, Moses said he'd left the house.'

'He didn't elaborate?'

'No.'

'And you didn't see him leave?'

'No.'

'All right, I'll get some of our people on it. If he did leave, he might have got a taxi or a train. Do you know where he's from?'

'He knew me. He's from Manchester.'

Charley had a moment of panic that Jessica had been recognised, but she finally accepted that her colleague was still safe.

'We'll get a few people out talking to homeless people in Manchester in that case,' she said. 'If that's where he's returned then somebody should know. If Moses was telling the truth and he's out, then he might be willing to talk.'

'Do you think he's telling the truth?'

Charley paused for a moment, clearing her throat. 'The very fact you're asking tells me you have your doubts. If he's not left the house or the grounds that means he's still somewhere there. If that's the case, then that's why you're there.'

'I'm doing my best!'

Jessica had inadvertently raised her voice but checked

herself, repeating it more quietly to prove to no one in particular that she could.

She stood, walking to the centre of the bathroom, hunching over and resting her forehead on the sink. The coolness of the hard material was reassuring.

'What else is going on?' Charley asked.

'Moses keeps his office locked. I was in there earlier.'

'Why's it locked?'

'I don't know.'

'You've got to find out.'

'I know! I know what I'm doing.'

She was shouting again.

Another pause. When she spoke again, Charley's tone was lighter, friendlier. 'Jessica.'

'What?'

'Are you okay?'

She thought of the way Moses had touched her, the endless manipulation of her emotions by hearing story after story of people's suffering. She definitely wasn't.

'I'm fine.'

'I'm only pushing you on these things because I want you out. I want you safe but I want this to end without anyone being hurt.'

Charley's voice was calm, reassuring.

'I know.'

'Good, what else? Is there anywhere else you can't go?'

'I don't think so but there's so much to see and I can't check everywhere because there are people around. Glenn is involved in something. He's a brute, so strong. There's a store cupboard where they keep all sorts of tools and things.'

'Weapons?'

'Not specifically but there are axes and machetes in there. Things that could be used as weapons. It's locked.'

'Who has the keys?'

'Glenn definitely, probably Moses too. They both carry keys around.'

'That's really good, Jessica, you're doing so well.'

Jessica knew Charley had used her name as a way to reassure her. That was one of the first lessons when you wanted to calm someone – say the person's name, keep saying it. It was why 999 operators asked for your name first and then kept saying it. The problem was that they were tricks Jessica was entirely familiar with. The fact Charley was praising her, trying to keep her composed, must be because she hadn't sounded sensible in the first place. That only made Jessica worry more. She had barely been here two days; was she really starting to fall apart already?

The surface of the sink was beginning to warm, so Jessica adjusted her position, resting her forehead further around the bowl. The coldness made her think clearly.

Charley spoke slower, the over-pronounced syllables of her accent more precise than ever. 'Jessica, unless you have anything else to say, I should really go. You know that once that phone battery is dead, then that's the end.'

'I know.'

'You can leave any time you want. Either walk away or call.'

'I know.'

'Okay then, I'm going to hang up.'

'Adam . . .'

Charley cleared her throat again. Jessica could tell she was thinking that they had sent in the wrong person. They wanted someone single, a person who didn't have ties to the outside. If their positions were reversed, she would have never sent in someone like herself.

'I gave him your message.'

'Did he say anything?'

'No.' Charley paused for a moment, before adding: 'I really should go.'

Jessica didn't reply, unable to press the button herself. She wanted someone to talk to; someone away from the house, someone like her. It was only when she heard the click of the bathroom door and the padding footsteps that Jessica stood up rigidly, spinning on the spot in one movement to see Heather standing in front of her, eyes narrow, hands on her hips.

'Who were you talking to?'

13

Jessica's heartbeat jumped from normal to racing so quickly that she felt a pain in her chest. Somehow she had known the lack of locks on the doors would catch her out at some point but she hadn't expected it to happen like this. She was about to say she had found the phone when she realised that Heather hadn't seen it. If she had, she would have been staring at Jessica's hand; instead she was looking her in the eye. Carefully, Jessica reached behind her, sliding the phone into the back of her trousers, hoping Charley had followed through with her promise by hanging up.

'I was just feeling a little upset,' Jessica said.

One of Heather's eyebrows was raised. 'It looked like you were talking to the sink.'

'I sort of was,' Jessica replied, thinking quickly. 'When I was a little girl, I had a pet goldfish. One morning, I found him floating on his side, dead. My dad flushed him down the toilet. He said that the fish had gone off to fish heaven. One of my friends at school told me they talked to their dead fish through the toilet but I didn't want to do that. I used to sit on a stool and talk to him through the sink. I was only about five or six.'

She giggled, trying to play it down but Heather, un-surprisingly, seemed even more confused. 'So you were talking to your fish?'

Jessica shook her head as the phone slipped lower in the trousers, lodging in her underwear. She straightened her back, tightening the muscles, trying to make sure it didn't slide any further and fall out of the leg. She was relieved when it didn't move.

'No . . . I suppose . . . It's complicated. I wasn't talking to my fish, I was thinking of my dad and I suppose that moment was in my mind. I was only at the sink for a few seconds. I didn't hear you come in. I can't really explain it.'

They stood staring at each other for a few moments until Heather's face fell. 'I've been missing my dad too.'

At first Heather sat on the edge of the bath but then Jessica rested an understanding hand on her shoulder and led her back into the bedroom. As soon as the young woman's back was turned, Jessica slipped the phone under her mattress, pulling a flap of sheet down to cover it, before crossing the room and sitting next to Heather on her bed. It was slightly softer than her own and Heather lay back, feet still on the floor, staring at the ceiling.

'I know all the rules about leaving and not being able to come back but it doesn't stop you thinking of people on the outside, does it?'

Only when she allowed herself to flop backwards on the bed too did Jessica's heartbeat begin to slow down. She took Heather's shaking hand in hers, gripping it tightly.

'Sometimes these thoughts will just pop into your head. It's up to you what you choose to do with them.'

'I wish he hadn't come to the centre at the weekend.'

'What happened between you?'

Heather sighed and Jessica knew she was about to tell her everything. 'It's as I told you before – it was all about an ex-boyfriend. I was doing my A-levels at the time but me and some of my friends could look old enough to get into the clubs if we wanted to. We'd tell our parents we were sleeping over at each other's houses and then get dressed up and go into the centre. Most of the bouncers wouldn't think twice about letting you in but even if they did, you'd just hoist your bra up a bit and try again and they'd wave you through. There was this one night we were out and this group of lads all came in together, sharp, shiny suits, bright white smiles. We found you in the city; you know the type.'

Jessica squeezed her hand. 'I know.'

The dickhead type.

'I was only seventeen but, for whatever reason, this one guy came straight to me. His friends were all off with older women, which made me feel even more special – simply because he'd picked me. Even now, I remember that night perfectly because it was the first one where I really felt like a woman, instead of a girl. It's strange but the one thing that sticks in my mind is his cufflinks.'

Jessica couldn't stop herself interrupting. 'Really?'

Heather laughed slightly, although she sounded close to tears. 'I know. They were these big square things with some sort of stone in, a diamond I think. It wasn't glittery like all the fake ones you see, it was duller, but that's how you can tell it's real, isn't it? I couldn't stop staring at them, thinking how expensive they must have been. He was saying such nice things . . .'

'What was his name?'

'Dan.'

'And what happened?'

Heather unlinked her fingers from Jessica's, wiping her face. 'It's not what you think, well, it wasn't at first. Everyone thought the same – some hotshot guy with loads of money preying on a teenager. I wasn't naive, well, I didn't think I was. Each time we met up, I kept thinking that he was going to break up with me. I couldn't believe my luck. It wasn't just about . . . y'know . . . either. He'd take me places. We went to the zoo once on a Saturday when it was packed with people, just because I said I liked snakes.'

'You like snakes?'

'Yes.'

'I don't think I've ever met anyone that likes snakes. Do you like spiders too?'

Heather giggled again, sitting up and wiping her eyes with her finger. Jessica sat up too, resting against one of the four posts and crossing her legs. 'Who likes spiders?'

'I don't know. Who likes snakes?'

Heather shrugged. 'Anyway, you wouldn't do that for someone unless you actually cared for them, would you?'

'Probably not.'

'Exactly, but my dad never saw it like that. At first, I kept it secret because I knew how he would react. When he found out, he was annoyed that I hadn't told him. They'd not even met but my dad said we had to break up because my exams were coming up.'

The talk of fathers left Jessica blinking rapidly, trying to halt her own sobs. 'Dads are like that. They're protective over their little girls.'

Heather nodded, tears now flowing fully. Jessica went to the bathroom, returning with tissues and handing the box to the other woman.

'It was more than that though. As soon as he found out Dan was a lawyer, he was furious. He'd say things like: "He's only after you because you're young". "I'll get the police onto him, he must be some paedo". I was almost eighteen, so there was nothing illegal. I was never forced . . .'

'I get it.'

'When it was clear I wasn't listening, he'd move onto even worse things, saying Dan was only buying me things so that I'd sleep with him and that made me the same as a whore.'

Jessica shuffled across the bed, putting an arm around Heather. She could never imagine her own father saying anything like that to her. He certainly would not have approved of Jessica having a boyfriend when her exams were on, but would have simply explained that life lasted a long time and that those couple of years would count for very little in terms of relationships. Jessica could hear his voice in her head, soothing but firm. She would have ignored him, of course, as many teenage girls did when their fathers tried to speak to them. But she would have appreciated it years after, when it was too late to matter.

'I'm so sorry,' Jessica said, as Heather rested her head on her shoulder.

Heather snivelled loudly. 'I think he was trying to be hard on purpose, to try to make me concentrate, but that only made me go the other way. I started skipping school, even though Dan was at work anyway. Then the teachers began getting involved. I'd been predicted straight As and they were concerned, so they'd write letters. I'd try to intercept them before my parents read any, so then the school started to call. Eventually Dad told me I had to stop seeing him or move out.'

'What did you do?'

'What do you think? I was in love with him, well, I thought I was. It was only a few years ago. He let me stay at his flat.'

'What happened?'

'I got pregnant.'

Before she knew what she was doing, Jessica found her hand creeping down to her own abdomen, catching herself before Heather noticed.

'Did you have . . . ?'

'No . . . It was a difficult time. Dan had been promoted at work and made new friends at other law firms. There were some evenings when he didn't come home and he wasn't answering my calls. I'd be all alone in his flat, unable to leave because I didn't have a key to get back in. He'd come home the next day as if nothing had happened.'

'Was he doing that because you were pregnant?'

'No, it was more than that – he didn't even know at that point. The new people he met changed him. He had more money but nothing to spend it on. I was so blind at first. We were at this party in this amazing apartment overlooking the city that belonged to one of his friends. It was a few days after I'd found out I was pregnant and I hadn't told anyone. At first he was annoyed because I wasn't drinking but then he drifted away with his other friends. There were all these women there – tall, blonde, thin – in these amazing dresses. It was like he had outgrown me. I was some eighteen-year-old about to take my exams, they were like models.'

Heather stopped to dry her eyes and blow her nose before continuing. 'I've never told anyone all of this, not even in the evening sessions.'

'I won't tell anyone anything you don't want them to know.'

'I know, it's just we're supposed to share with each other and I've been holding back this whole time, giving away bits and pieces. Everyone else is so honest.'

Jessica had to be careful, seeming loyal to Moses but at the same time sympathetic to Heather. 'Everyone deals with things in their own way. I'm sure there are others who have taken their time.'

Heather snivelled again, pulling away from Jessica and puffing up a pillow to rest on. Her eyes were red and swollen and she started playing with her hair, tugging it tightly and tying it, before undoing it and starting again. 'At that party, things started getting out of hand as the night wore on. It began with people drinking bottles of beer and a few hours later, they were downing bottles of vodka and all sorts. I already felt out of place because I was sober but then the guy who owned the flat pulled out this bag of white powder. They were cutting it up into lines on the table in front of everyone, taking it in turns and cheering. I'd always been a good girl at school – I didn't even smoke – and suddenly that was happening.'

'Did Dan get involved?'

Heather shrugged. 'He was one of the worst. It was only then I realised he'd been acting differently because he'd been doing drugs with his new friends. He was pestering me, going on about how I was spoiling everyone's fun by not joining in. We had a massive row in front of everyone and I ended up running out. I couldn't go home because I'd been thrown out and I couldn't go back to Dan's because I didn't have a key to get in.'

'So you slept rough?'

'Underneath this stairwell in a tower block where the door was left hanging open. It was warm at least.'

'But you were pregnant at the time?'

Heather looked away towards the window, blinking rapidly, rubbing her nose. 'Yes.'

'What about the next day?'

'I didn't have any money so ended up walking across the city in between rain showers. There was no one at Dan's flat, so I sat against his door for hours. I tried calling him but there was no answer. When it started to get dark, I eventually phoned my dad.'

'Was he pleased to hear from you?'

'Sort of. He picked me up and drove me home. I cried the whole way and he didn't say anything. Most of my stuff was at Dan's but he wouldn't answer his phone. Eventually that night, I ended up telling my parents that I was pregnant.'

Jessica could tell from the way Heather gulped that she

was about to recall the most important event of her life. She couldn't blink back the tears quickly enough and her nose was running but she didn't bother trying to clear her face.

'I'd gone up to my old bedroom. There was no bedding, so I called out to see if someone could help. My mum stayed downstairs but my dad came up. They'd been rowing about me. He stormed into their bedroom and came out with some pillows. He looked at me and said: "You know you've thrown your life away, don't you?" He wasn't even angry, it was just disappointment. I could see it in his eyes that he'd had all these plans, wanting me to go off to university and have the type of life that he and Mum had never had. I wanted it too at some point but I'd been drawn into everything with Dan.'

Jessica thought of the final conversation she'd had with her father, when he'd told her he was proud of her. She tried to think how devastated she would have been if those eyes had been full of disappointment. She would never have got over it.

'What happened then?'

'It's hard to describe because I only see it in flashes. He thrust the pillows out towards me but I was right next to the stairs. I remember falling and rolling, banging my head and my shoulders and then the worst pain I've ever had below my stomach.'

'Did he push you?'

Heather took a deep breath, continuing to tug at her hair but harder than before. 'I don't know. I really don't remember. I was close to the edge anyway but I'm not sure if I stumbled backwards, or if he touched me.'

'But you lost the baby?'

'Yes, well, whatever it was at that stage. People spend all their time arguing over what's a baby and what's a collection of cells. You go over it in school but it was gone before I'd even got used to the idea of having it.'

'Dan never knew?'

'I didn't see him again. I never even collected my things. I left that night and didn't go back to my parents' either. I met a few people on the streets and there's this refuge thing in the centre. One day I was on the streets and Zip was there with the others. I got talking and was invited onto their bus. I've been here ever since.'

'How long ago was that?'

Heather shook her head. 'I don't know. Maybe a year? Maybe longer. It's hard to keep track of the days. I'm not even sure if I've had a birthday.'

Jessica realised how disorientating it would be for anyone staying long-term. Only the length of the days and the change in the seasons would give them any indication of what time of year it was.

'What about your father finding you the other day?'

'When we were in Manchester the month before, I spotted one of our old neighbours. I didn't think they'd seen me but I suppose they must have gone and told my dad. It was the first time I'd seen him since that night.'

Jessica didn't reply for a few moments, letting it all sink in.

'It's better here,' Heather added.

Despite everything that might be going on in the house, Jessica couldn't disagree. A life with a coke-head boyfriend, a child lost – possibly through her father's actions. If Heather felt safe and secure here, then at least it was some respite from what had become a nightmarish life. Either that, or she had left one bad dream, only to stumble into another.

'What's better about it?' Jessica asked.

Heather's voice cracked but she had almost composed herself, wiping her eyes with another tissue and dropping it onto the pile next to her. 'The people . . .'

Jessica suddenly realised what she had missed. 'Moses?'

'Yes.'

'Have the pair of you . . . ?'

Heather looked away and Jessica didn't have to finish the question. The way she had fussed over her appearance the previous evening now made sense. Presumably at some point she had been replaced in Moses's affections by Katie. A younger version.

'Was it just you?' Jessica asked.

Heather shook her head, still unable to look at Jessica. 'A lot of the girls have. It'll be your turn soon. He shares his wisdom with all of us.'

He certainly shared something with the women but Jessica wouldn't have described it as 'wisdom'. It definitely wouldn't be her turn any time soon either.

'Doesn't Zip mind?'

Heather's only reply was a shrug. From what Jessica had seen, it wasn't as if Moses's wife had much choice, even if the house did belong to her.

'What now?' Jessica asked, meaning how long did Heather think she was going to stay at the house for.

Her reply of 'I suppose I wait until Moses calls for me again' told Jessica that Heather was never going to leave. She was irrevocably in love with him and this was where she would wait until he came back for her.

14

Wayne Howson opened his eyes, struggling to see through the dark. After fighting to focus on whatever was in front of him, he closed them again. It felt more comfortable that way. He could sense the once-familiar dizziness around his eyes, that indescribable feeling of waking up after an evening spent drinking. Or a morning and afternoon. Those were the days.

He was sitting, resting against something solid but soft. He couldn't remember putting himself into the position. Had he been sleeping sitting up? It wouldn't be the first time.

He tried to remember what had happened, vaguely recalling being in the house, then in the gardens, but not much more. There must have been alcohol somewhere because he could taste it. The foul aftertaste mixed with that sweet flavour of the first drop.

It had been a while.

Wayne tried opening his eyes again but could see only vague, hazy outlines of grey shapes within the black. Spikes of pain fizzed through his shoulderblades as he reached to rub his eyes, the jolt awakening the rest of the pain in his body. In an instant, his back ached, his stomach felt strained, as if someone had stretched him. The throb around his eyes was spreading to the rest of his face. Even his teeth hurt.

He'd had hangovers when he was younger but this eclipsed any of them. Besides, he'd almost become immune to the effect of drink as time had gone on.

Wayne placed his hands on the floor, running them along the cold, hard surface and trying to figure out where he was. It didn't feel like the house and it certainly wasn't the garden. There was a distinct aroma in the air too, something with a hint of rusting iron but he couldn't place it, even though it seemed familiar.

'Wayne . . .'

The stranger's voice echoed slightly, giving Wayne the impression that the room must be large.

'Who's there?'

Wayne listened to his words reverberating around the room. They sounded husky, hardened, as if they hadn't come from him.

'It's me, Wayne.'

'Who?'

'You know who it is . . . think about it.'

The words continued to bounce around the walls but Wayne's mind felt heavy and he was struggling to understand what was being said, let alone who was saying it.

'Would you like a drink, Wayne?'

Alcohol.

It was the source of everything good that had happened to him over the years. Nothing could beat that feeling of light-headedness, that gentle warmth of his skin and the laughs. It had given him so many good times.

But then it had caused everything bad too; those freezing-cold nights on the streets, the waking up in the middle of the night, sweating and disorientated. All those nights in police cells, all the people he'd known who had forgotten him over the years.

Wayne heard footsteps echoing around the room, although something he couldn't quite figure out didn't sound right. Someone was coming close to him – and then he could smell the booze. It wasn't even the cheap cider he used to content himself with, it was some sort of vodka. Subtle but unmistakeable.

The bottle was placed on the ground, the solid clank of the glass hitting the hard floor enticingly.

'It's all yours, Wayne . . .'

'I don't want it.'

'Are you sure?'

Wayne had known the answer the moment he had smelled it. He would never escape the hold it had on him. He scrabbled forward in the dark, reaching out until his fingers closed around the cool glass. He held it under his nose, breathing it in, feeling the fumes drifting through his nose. That other smell was still there too, somewhere in the background. Soon the smell was not enough as he raised the container to his lips, taking a long drink. It burned the back of his throat, making him wince, but he instantly felt that wonderful woozy sensation spiralling through him.

'Is that good, Wayne?'

He answered by taking another swig. Then another. The aches and pains that had been racking his body were evaporating in a mist of satisfaction.

At first they were small mouthfuls, then larger gulps.

His tongue was on fire, the back of his mouth raging. He stopped for a rest, giggling.

The voice had gone silent and Wayne had no idea how long he had been awake. He could feel himself being watched, eyes somewhere peering through the dark.

'Hello?' he called, one hand still grasping the bottle.

No reply.

Wayne pulled himself up, grunting with a mixture of effort and pain. His head was spinning, his legs like jelly. There was some sort of post nearby which he grabbed on to, trying to get his balance.

'Hello?'

His voice echoed around the darkness, a dozen hellos bouncing back and forth as if he was calling to himself.

A sound of something smashing made him jump. He spun around, trying to figure out where it had come from but it was as if his body had moved quicker than his mind. Still the room turned until he found himself hugging the post to stop himself falling.

It was only when he heard the crunch under his feet that he realised his hands were empty. The smashing had come from the bottle hitting the floor. He must have dropped it without noticing. Wayne thought about trying to clean up but then remembered he didn't know where he was.

'Hello? Sorry about the bottle.'

He wasn't sure if the words had come out correctly. Something about the word 'sorry' was sticking to his tongue so he tried again, slobbering and swearing as he struggled to speak.

'You don't have to apologise, Wayne.'

The voice sounded soothing but he still couldn't place it. There was something familiar, even reassuring about it.

'I can help tidy up.'

'You don't need to do that.'

Wayne was already bending over, fumbling around the floor for the broken pieces. His eyes had adjusted slightly to the dimness and he could see the vague shapes. As he ran his hand along the floor, he gasped in shock as a sharp piece of glass sliced along the side of it. As he pulled his hand away, he overbalanced, toppling backwards onto a large shard.

He shrieked in pain, rolling over but only making it worse as another fragment stabbed into his leg.

'Help me,' he whimpered.

Silence.

Wayne tried to push himself up but another piece ravaged his skin. He could feel the blood dripping, the splinter twisting in his hand.

'Please . . .'

'Wayne.'

'Yes.'

'Why did you drink the vodka?'

Wayne reached across with his free hand, trying to pull the glass clear from the other. More pieces were lodged in his leg and he could feel the spilled liquid seeping through his trousers. He pinched the slice between his thumb and forefinger but only succeeded in twisting it further, making him howl in agony.

'Wayne.'

'What?'

'I asked you a question.'

The tone of the voice was level, questioning, not accusing. At first he thought it was coming from somewhere in front of him but then he wasn't so sure. It was above him, behind him, everywhere. Wayne started to answer but stopped himself, trying to remove the glass again. The pain made him feel good. He knew he deserved it. 'I don't know.'

'Louder, please, Wayne.'

'I don't know.'

'What about the other stuff you drank earlier?'

'I don't know.'

'I thought you were getting better, helping yourself?'

'I don't know.'

'Wayne.'

'Yes.'

'You do know you have to be punished, don't you?'

The words billowed around the room like a breeze, making Wayne shiver.

'I'm sorry.'

'I know you are but our actions must have consequences. You know that, don't you?'

'Yes.'

'Thank you, Wayne. Will you stand for me now?'

Wayne's head was still cloudy but it was as if the pain from the glass was cancelling it out. He used the pole to haul himself up again, swaying slightly but resting against it to keep himself steady.

'That's very good of you, Wayne. Do you know what's going to happen now?'

'No . . .'

For a moment there was silence. Wayne glanced from side to side, feeling someone's presence but unable to see or hear anything. All at once, lights blazed overhead. They had come on so suddenly that Wayne jammed his eyes closed, the bright white stinging too much for him to take. He heard feet shuffling and then something cannoned into his cheek. Before he knew what was happening, he was falling again, feeling the glass cutting into his hands and legs.

As he moaned, he remembered what had happened in the gardens. He had been hit then.

'Glenn?'

The voice didn't reply but he felt something crashing into his ribs and heard the crack. He tried opening his eyes but it was still too bright. All he could see was the vague outline of someone coming towards him. They lashed out at him with a boot. Once, twice, three times, each kick harder than the last.

As liquid choked up into his mouth, Wayne realised what the metallic smell had been. It was only faint but it was unmistakeably blood, the remnants of whatever had gone on in this room. He coughed violently, sending a spray of blood, snot and saliva across the floor, adding his to whoever's had gone before.

'Wayne.'

He rolled onto his back, panting for breath and trying to shuffle away from his attacker.

'Can you see what I have in my hand, Wayne?'

He squinted into the light, which still made his eyes tingle. There were stars at the edge of his vision but a clear silhouette in the centre.

'Are they scissors?' Wayne asked, moving backwards until he was pressed against a wall.

'Close. Look again.'

The figure stepped nearer but that only made Wayne's vision blur further. He squinted harder, trying to see what the object was.

'Is it a pair of pliers?'

'Very good. How about this?'

The attacker reached across to some sort of bench out of Wayne's gaze and held something else in front of him.

'A saw?'

'Good.'

The attacker showed him two different types of hammer – one with a heavy claw on the back, a pair of garden shears, a machete, a spade. One after the other. Each time Wayne got the answer wrong, there was a delay until he identified it correctly.

Finally the last item was put down. 'Do you know why I was showing you those things, Wayne?'

He cowered under the shadow, shivering and gasping, blood dripping from his chin. 'No.'

'It's because you're going to become very well acquainted with them over the next hour or so.'

Wayne tried to slide away but the figure reached down and pulled him forwards, dragging him along the floor and then kicking him in the back.

'Look, Wayne, someone's dropped in to enjoy the moment.'

Wayne stared ahead, wondering what he was looking at. It took him a few seconds to realise it was a mirror that ran the entire length of the wall.

'It's me,' he said.

'Yes, Wayne. Yes it is.'

He felt another kick in his back, lurching forwards before thrashing backwards as his throat was squeezed and he was pinned to the ground.

Wayne's eyes darted sideways in terror as he saw a hand reaching towards him, the jaws of the pliers wide and ready to bite.

SEVEN MONTHS AGO

Although she had never been particularly religious, Jessica had always liked hymns. At primary school, they used to sing every morning before assembly, the entire school as one belting out 'All Things Bright and Beautiful', 'What a Friend We Have In Jesus', 'Thine Be the Glory', 'Onward, Christian Soldiers', or Jessica's favourite, 'Amazing Grace'.

Sometimes she would catch the last part of a programme on television with a hymn at the end and she would be transported back to being six years old, singing at the top of her voice without a care in the world.

All these years later and they were still embedded in her mind; everything from the tempo to the lyrics. She knew where the organ should pause, where she could breathe. It was as if she was that little girl again – except that now her daddy was gone.

Jessica stood in the church, not even bothering to mime the words. Around her, people sang out of tune; an apt tribute to her father who would have been sitting at the back hoping his wife didn't catch him laughing at how ridiculous it all was. Jessica would have been there with him, smiling out of sight of her mother.

As it was, she had to sit at the front, watching everything from close up. The vicar was the same one who had christened her all those years ago in the beautiful old church that was the centrepiece of the village. Whether you were religious or not, there was a majesty about this place, the towering steeple, the ancient stained glass, even the way the voices echoed around the inside.

Jessica hadn't lived in the village for over fifteen years and yet it would always be home. There might be a few extra houses on the edges, perhaps a field or two which had been sold off for ugly out-of-place homes, but all the back streets and tight alleyways were the same. In Manchester, there were still times where she struggled to figure out how all the main roads connected together; here she could get from one side of the village to the other in no time at all, skimming through the maze of cut-throughs without having to think.

She used to skim across the graveyard when she was late for school, dashing across people's resting places and not worrying.

Now one of them would belong to her father.

The hymn came to an end and Jessica heard the shuffling behind her as the village sat as one. Everyone had turned out because if there was one person they all knew, it was the man who had run the only post office in the area for the best part of three decades. The village hadn't even had a cashpoint installed until after Jessica had left, meaning the only way the residents could get their money was via her father.

The vicar said something about him being a 'lynchpin of the community' but to Jessica he was simply her daddy.

'Jess.'

It took Jessica a few moments to realise it was Adam

who was speaking, his whispers lost among the vicar's voice reverberating around the ancient walls. She felt his hand on top of hers but didn't look around.

'Jess. Are you all right?'

She nodded but couldn't speak, an emptiness rippling through her.

Soon there was more movement and Jessica's mother was on her feet, sliding along the pew and walking carefully towards the front, shuffling papers in her hand. In the few weeks since they had been in the hospital, it was as if she had become a different person: older, greyer, quieter. Before she'd had a vibrancy to her but that had been replaced by aching hips and stick-thin legs that could barely take her weight.

Jessica knew she wasn't looking after herself too well, either, sometimes going entire days forgetting to eat. Still, at least she had Adam to harangue and remind her that it wasn't just herself she had to look after. As the days went by, she could feel Marcus growing inside her, each small grumble of her tummy filling her with the hope that perhaps he was about to kick for the first time. The nurse had told her it would probably be around four to five months until she felt anything and then, wonderfully, it had happened.

Now she was beginning to show properly, having to wear bigger clothes, noticing those looks from colleagues who didn't know yet, wondering if she was getting fat or if she was actually pregnant. It was her little game, ignoring the way people stared at the gentle bulge around her midriff and waiting for them to ask, pausing for an awkward few seconds and making them think they had insulted her before revealing that she was indeed pregnant and hadn't simply been attacking the doughnuts for the past few months.

They were perhaps her only moments of enjoyment she had around the station but even they had worn thin as pretty much everyone knew now. Instead they gossiped about whether she would ever return to work and who the new DI would be if she didn't get the job.

Jessica cupped a hand around her abdomen, more for her own reassurance than anything else. At the front of the church, her mother had taken her place behind the lectern, still shuffling her papers and clearing her throat.

'Thank you, everybody,' she said unsteadily, her eyes not leaving the papers. She went on to speak about how she and Marcus had met at a dance in a neighbouring village. She laughed gently through her tears, admitting she had been there with another boy when her future husband had caught her eye across the room, winking at her and then promptly being ejected for smuggling in alcohol. A week later, she had received a letter in the post signed by 'that idiot from the dance' asking if they could meet up some time. Within a year, they were married.

'I never did find out how he discovered my name and address,' Jessica's mother added tearfully.

Jessica thought that was that but then her mum moved on to the next sheet. Without trying, she had the church in the palm of her hand.

'. . . And then our little miracle came along,' she added.

Jessica gulped away a sob, realising what was coming as Adam's hand closed around hers.

'I wasn't supposed to be able to have children,' her mother said. 'The doctors said there was something wrong but then, one day, I just knew and along came our little Jessica.'

Jessica felt the hairs on the back of her neck stand up, knowing all eyes were upon her. She wanted her mum to stop speaking but she had finally composed herself, talking more clearly than she had done before.

'Many of you here knew Jess as a child; some of you taught her, some of you grew up with her. Most of you were probably pestered by her at some point.' She stopped to laugh, which was matched a little disconcertingly by others around the church. Jessica even saw the vicar smiling.

'Jessica was always the apple of her father's eye but that's because they were so alike. He would take her out in the car, driving deliberately quickly to make her shout and scream when he thought I didn't know. He'd push her high on the swings, he would cheat at Monopoly to make sure she never beat him—'

Jessica interrupted, unable to stop herself snorting a mixture of laughter and tears. She'd always known he was doing something to stop her winning but had never worked out what. The fact she consistently cheated to ensure Adam rarely beat her at board games simply meant it was another thing they shared.

Her mother smoothed a loose strand of hair behind her ear, composing herself again, blinking quickly and staring upwards. 'When Jessica was a little girl, we were redecorating our spare bedroom. I say "we" but it was mainly Marcus, fitting new cupboards and painting. My only job was to keep Jessica away. I took her to the park but it started to rain so we had to go home. I was trying to get her to sit and watch television but every time there was a bump or a bang from upstairs, her eyes would shoot upwards, wanting to join in the fun she thought she was missing.'

It was one of Jessica's earliest memories, wanting to be with her father and help him out.

Lydia Daniel peered down towards Jessica, a gentle smile on her face, her eyes red and puffy. 'Eventually I couldn't take her whining any longer.' Her lips twitched. 'I took her upstairs and told Marcus he'd have to look after her because she was driving me crazy. He tilted his head to the side, and with that special grin of his, he handed Jess a paintbrush saying that he had a job for her. I went back downstairs and got on with whatever I was doing but then I realised how quiet it was. I crept up the stairs and opened the door only to see Jess sat on her father's lap, making hand prints on the wall.'

She stopped to wipe her eyes but she wasn't the only one. Jessica could hear people shuffling behind her, quietly blowing their noses and choking back their own emotions.

'They hadn't heard me and I stood there for ages just watching them talk and play until there was an entire patch of the wall covered in her little hand prints. And that's how I'll always remember Marcus, sitting on the floor with our Jess on his lap covered in paint as if they were the only people on earth.'

She paused, glancing up to the sky, whispering 'I love you, Marc', before stepping down and walking slowly back to her seat. The people around her patted her on the back and put their arms around her. Jessica could do nothing but stare towards the front.

The vicar had no chance of following it, rushing through a reading before finishing with a hymn. Jessica stood and listened but didn't feel herself. As everyone turned and started to file out, Adam took her hand, walking in silence as everyone consoled her. She hugged her mum, thanking her for the story, but she felt removed from the scene, as if she was watching herself. The words were meaningless, an endless stream of people saying they had missed her around the village and that it was a shame they had to see her again in these circumstances. 'Thank you' became a catchphrase, as if she could say anything else when people kept telling her what a wonderful father she'd had.

It was Caroline who saw it first.

The wake was taking place in the village hall and it was as packed as Jessica had ever seen it. She had spent the evening failing to avoid people, sitting in the corner with Adam and then by herself as he got called away to do family things on her behalf.

'Are you all right?' Caroline asked, sliding behind the table next to Jessica.

'It's just been a long day.'

Caroline rested an arm around Jessica's shoulders, pulling her closer. 'You look tired.'

'I've not been sleeping. With everything here, the baby and work . . . it's just hard.'

'When do you go off on maternity?'

'I don't know. A few months yet. I'm trying not to think about it.'

Caroline paused but Jessica knew what she was thinking. There were only so many ways and so many times you could ask a person if they were okay. Caroline was her best friend, someone she'd known her entire adult life. They both knew this village as home. She could tell as well as anyone when something wasn't right.

'How's Hugo?' Jessica asked, deliberately changing the subject.

'He's fine. He wanted to come but I didn't know if it was best. You know what he's like.'

'He'd have been fine. I took him to your wedding, remember?'

'I remember.'

Jessica realised she shouldn't have brought it up. Caroline's marriage had fallen apart in less time than it had taken them to get together in the first place. Jessica didn't know if she was formally seeing Hugo now and didn't want to be nosey enough to ask. She and Caroline didn't have the relationship they once did, plus she doubted Hugo could ever entirely commit to anyone given the chaotic nature of his life. His combined act of comedy, magic, puppetry and who knows what else was beginning to catch on more than just locally.

Jessica had watched him on television a couple of weeks ago. He seemed utterly oblivious to the cameras being there, mooching onto set in the same scruffy clothes he always wore before dazzling the presenter, the audience and most likely everyone at home by pulling off some sort of trick which resulted in the presenter's tie and watch disappearing without him noticing. By the time he reeled off the first names of everyone in the front row, despite not having met any of them before, there was almost a riot as a cackling band of middle-aged women shouted their approval.

Jessica had seen it all before.

'He's doing something in Edinburgh this weekend,' Caroline added. 'He was going to come back but I told him not to.'

'It's fine. I'm glad you came.'

'As if I was going to be anywhere else. We should do something soon, before you have too many other things going on.'

'You mean before I'm too fat to leave the house.'

Caroline grinned, shuffling away to give Jessica some space. 'That too.'

'Caz . . .'

'What?'

Jessica rubbed her stomach. 'I don't feel very well.'

'What's wrong?'

'I'm not sure. I've not been eating or sleeping well. It's been building.' She pointed towards the bump. 'It hurts here.'

Jessica tried to keep herself calm, knowing that twinges were perfectly normal – her doctor had said as much. It had been a stressful day and she had been struggling to look after herself.

'What would you like me to do?' The slightly panicked tone of Caroline's voice didn't help.

Jessica breathed in deeply, remembering the way she had been taught. She could feel the discomfort jabbing into her. It wasn't what she would call pain but it definitely wasn't right.

'I'm not sure,' Jessica said. 'It might be something I've eaten.'

WEDNESDAY

15

After Heather's outpouring from the night before, Jessica had spent over an hour lying next to her on the bed, waiting until she had sobbed herself to sleep. She had seen more tears in the past nine months than at any point during her life. Jessica could feel it weighing on her. Cole might have thought this would be the perfect way for her to get back into the job again but it was simply pouring more hurt on top of everything she had already experienced. Yet Heather was more damaged than she was, not just hurt by what she had been through but pining for a man she would never have to herself and who showed none of the women any respect.

Jessica had slept surprisingly well after that. She didn't know what Moses was trying to achieve, or how deeply Glenn was involved, let alone how much Zipporah knew, but one of the things she couldn't fault them for was the comfort of the beds.

She jumped as the alarm woke her up, rolling over and reaching for the spot where her phone would be if she was at home. She would usually jab and smack the screen until it stopped making a noise. It was only when her arms flapped against an empty space that Jessica remembered where she was.

Heather was up quickly, washing and dressing as if the

previous night had not happened. Jessica stayed in bed, rolling over to face away from the light.

'Breakfast is soon,' Heather said as she passed Jessica's bed.

'I don't feel well.'

'What's wrong?'

'Something in my stomach doesn't feel right.'

'We all ate the same.'

'I know, perhaps I strained something being outside yesterday? It just hurts.'

Jessica had her eyes closed but she could sense Heather nearby, watching her.

'Okay, I'll tell Zip.'

Not long after Heather had left, the door opened and Zipporah entered. She seemed weary, bags under her eyes, her lips tight and thin. Jessica knew the signs of exhaustion well. Even though it didn't look like a cold day, she was bundled up in a turtleneck jumper and thick jeans.

'How are you, my dear?' Zipporah asked, crouching by the bed.

Jessica repeated her story, clutching her stomach and groaning as Zipporah ran her fingers along it, before stroking Jessica's hair away from her face.

'It's going to be a quiet day around here anyway because it's market day.'

'How many of you go?'

'We have a few sites to visit, so today it will be around a dozen of us. You could have come if you were feeling well – it's not the same as recruitment.'

Jessica rubbed her stomach again, groaning. 'Sorry.'

'No matter, perhaps next week? I'll tell Moses that you're going to be here. It's important that we keep track of everyone. If you're feeling any better later, I'm sure they'll be able to find some food for you. We're always back for dinner in any case.'

She stroked Jessica's cheek with the back of her hand but it felt different to the times when Moses had run his fingers across her skin. This was more motherly, protective. It was so easy to forget how young she was.

'I don't know what you're used to,' Zipporah added, 'but we do not allow any sort of pain medication here.'

Jessica didn't want any but it left an obvious question: 'What if someone is really ill?'

'We have a medical professional here.'

Jessica assumed she meant the woman who had assisted after the new recruit had smashed his head.

'What if someone is really, seriously injured, though? If they were dying?'

Zipporah paused, licking her lips nervously. 'We would make sure they were well looked after.'

'But would they be allowed to return if they had been taken to a hospital?'

The other woman's eyes darted from side to side. 'We've never been in that situation.' Before Jessica could reply, she added: 'Get well soon. We're all better for having you here.'

She started to stand but Jessica sensed now was the time to ask one of the questions stuck in her mind. 'You seem tired today.'

Zipporah shifted around until she was sitting on the

edge of Jessica's bed, rubbing her eyes. 'Some days it's harder to carry around our burdens than others.'

'Can I ask you something?'

'Of course. You can always come to me.'

'It's about Moses and Katie.'

Zipporah nodded, smiling gently. 'I realise it might seem a little different at first for people who are used to things being a certain way on the outside.'

'But you don't mind?'

Zipporah swallowed, glancing towards the window. 'It would be unfair of me to try to keep him to myself. He is a great man. Of course others should enjoy the wisdom he has to share.'

That word again.

Jessica wondered how well it would go down in a packed Manchester bar on a Friday evening. 'All right, love, I'm just wondering if I can share some wisdom with you?' Depending on which bar, he would either end up having a stiletto jabbed in his eye, or he'd be 'invited' into a back alleyway by a pair of bouncers and 'encouraged' to stop harassing the customers. Actually, Jessica knew of a bar or two where he'd probably end up in that back alleyway with a middle-aged divorcee.

Either way, it sounded as if Zipporah and Heather had taken their cues from the same person. Jessica could almost hear Moses saying it himself as justification.

Jessica wasn't sure how to reply. The way Zipporah had looked away hardly convinced her the woman was pleased with her husband's infidelity. 'I just—'

Zipporah's demeanour suddenly changed. 'Listen,' she

snapped. 'If you want to be with him, you don't need to ask my permission.'

Jessica was stuck with her mouth open. That wasn't what she had meant at all. 'I'm sorry, I—'

Zipporah dismissively waved a hand, instantly calm again. 'No, it's me who should apologise. I'm sorry for raising my voice. Sometimes we should practise what we preach. I have no objections to any interest you may have in my husband. I cannot blame you. He is truly special.'

Before Jessica could reply, Zipporah was on her feet again, heading towards the door. 'I have to go now. I do hope you feel better soon.'

Jessica stayed in bed for a while, listening to the scraping of plates and the clatter of cutlery floors below her. She didn't have the best choice of clothes but picked a pair of trousers she knew she could move easily in, as well as the most practical, warmest top she had taken from the store.

From the window, she watched as the minibus was brought around to the front of the building. Ali got out of the driver's seat and began loading various goods into the back with Glenn, who turned around, peering up towards Jessica, sensing he was being watched. Jessica was just out of sight, knowing she could view them clearly with the angle and probably the tint of the glass making it impossible for them to see her.

She saw trays of vegetables, plus crates that were easily hoisted, meaning they likely contained clothes or crafts. Jessica realised she didn't even know which market it was they went to. Charley hadn't mentioned anything but she couldn't believe their surveillance had somehow missed it.

Ali and Glenn waited next to the bus as Heather left the house along with Zipporah and eleven others. Glenn stood in the centre of the turning circle, watching the van roar away. With Moses and Glenn remaining, and Wayne having left, that meant half the number of residents had gone to the market.

As the van disappeared over the ridge out of sight, Glenn turned towards the house, hands on hips, scanning from side to side, looking for anything out of place. Jessica didn't dare move, just in case he was somehow able to peer through the tinted glass.

Of everyone she had met in the house, he was the coldest. The others at least made an effort to appear friendly, regardless of whether it was their true nature. But she had not seen him heading off to the after-dinner sessions where everyone shared their stories and she had no idea what had drawn him to the house in the first place. He had the apparent trust of Moses and there was something between him and Zipporah too, given the way she had scurried after him when he told her it was 'time to go'.

After a few minutes of pacing, Glenn walked around the side of the house, heading towards the allotments. Jessica waited for a few minutes before making her way onto the landing. She rested against the bedroom door, listening for any hints of noise in the house. The high ceilings and wide corridors were empty, echoless, leaving an eerie calm hanging over the property. Jessica padded forward, the luxurious carpet absorbing the sounds, making it easier to sneak around but more likely someone could get close without her realising.

From the journeys down to mealtimes, Jessica knew the bedrooms were split between the top and middle floors. For the first time since arriving, she did a full loop of the top floor. She didn't risk opening any of the doors but the view from the windows gave her a first proper sight of the land at the rear of the house. From ground level where she had been working, she had seen the lawns and the woods but the central window allowed her to see into the distance.

The garden stretched a lot further than the one at the front, meaning the area owned by Zipporah and Moses was vast. A fence encircled the whole patch, with the woods Jessica had noticed first time around dipping into a valley after a few hundred metres. The morning sun reflected off the surface of a small lake just over the tops of the trees. From the ground there was no way she would have seen it. Liam Renton had been found in the Manchester canal, drowned, but it was unclear if the death had happened elsewhere and then his body had been dumped, or if he had died in the canal itself. He had been dead for a few weeks, his decomposed body hiding the clues they needed to tell them more. If he had been attacked here, then the lake would seem an obvious place. She assumed Charley's team knew about it but it was hard to judge the size, let alone the depth, from where she was.

Not for the first time, Jessica was entranced by the sheer beauty of the view. At the far end of the gardens, there was farmland that dipped away, brown, yellow, orange and green fields interspersed with hamlets and villages far into the distance. It was so different to what she was used to in Manchester. She had become so accustomed to the towering buildings, lashing rain, grey skies and depressing sink estates that she had almost forgotten what it was like to live anywhere else. The view was a reminder of the type of place where she had grown up. When she was younger, the fact everyone knew everyone else had been frustrating as it was hard to do much without her mother finding out. Away from the constant outpouring of emotion and influence Moses had on everyone, the family-like atmosphere was something that suddenly appealed to her. It had been like that at the station at one point but staff cuts, fall-outs and DI Jason Reynolds leaving had diluted things.

Glenn was pottering around the allotment area with a couple of the other people who hadn't gone to market. Zipporah would surely have told him that Jessica was ill and he hadn't come looking for her. Jessica couldn't remember the exact numbers but there couldn't be more than ten people in the house, including Moses.

She already suspected it, but there was only one staircase to the middle floor. The second one, which had the door underneath, had either been blocked at some point, or was there for decoration.

She did a quicker lap, only stopping to take in a wide double doorway, which she suspected led into Moses and Zipporah's bedroom – assuming they shared the same room.

As she reached the bottom of the stairs, Jessica heard at least three male voices. She pressed against the wall, moving slowly until she realised they were coming from the games room. Inching along, Jessica reached the open doorway, waiting until all three were talking at the same time before risking a peek around the frame. The cooks were there, standing around the snooker table, chatting and laughing as if down their local with a round of bitter on the go. The biggest difference was the subject of their conversation. Jessica had no idea what lads talked about when they were in a group but if Dave Rowlands was anything to go by, it was likely to be football, girls, beer, robots, or why some Star Wars film she hadn't seen was better than another Star Wars film she hadn't seen. She doubted it would be how pleasant the gardens looked and how they were looking forward to trying a slightly different recipe that evening. She certainly didn't believe they would be standing around talking about their admiration for a man who had changed his name to match a biblical figure.

Jessica stood with her back to the wall, listening. Even with everything she had seen and heard since arriving, this felt like the strangest because they were in a near-empty house with no one around to overhear. They could have talked about which of the females they most fancied, how the lush gardens were ripe for conversion into a sports pitch, or whatever else took their fancy. Instead, they were still conforming to the ideals expected.

'When's the delivery this week?' one of them asked.

'Friday morning.'

There was a slight pause before the reply came: 'Two days?'

'Exactly. I'll get the back door unlocked last thing Thursday so we can get straight onto it. No one wants to be messing around at that time of the morning.'

Jessica thought of the door she had seen when she had been outside looking towards the back of the house. On the tour, Heather had shown her where the kitchen was but she hadn't been inside. Now the floorplan added up in her mind. The fact the door was locked for most of the time was no surprise. From what she had seen from a distance, it didn't look as sturdy as the front door but it was something to bear in mind as an additional way to get out of the house if she really needed to. Doors were weak points and although she wasn't as strong as she used to be, she might have more success putting something hard through it, as opposed to attacking the reinforced, locked windows.

Jessica waited until she heard a clatter of snooker balls and then darted past the open doorway, walking briskly until she was outside Moses's office. She stood next to the door, listening for any hint of movement inside. The fact she was apparently ill would give her an excuse for trying to find him. She pressed down on the door handle but it didn't budge. From what she had seen, Moses wasn't the type of person to leave the office unlocked and it wasn't as if she had a good way of stealing the giant bundle of keys from his belt.

Remembering the open window, Jessica rushed through the empty corridors to the front door, which was bolted closed, even though Glenn and a couple of the others were still outside. Because it had been unlocked when they re-entered the previous day, Jessica assumed it was only opened at certain times. She tried the nearby windows, which were locked, but knew she would not get many better opportunities when the house was this empty and she could come and go without being noticed.

With the excuse that she was looking for either Glenn or Moses, Jessica acted instinctively, feeling that buzz of being at work that she hadn't had in far too long. She opened the bolts as quietly as she could and then slotted the door back into place after exiting. Knowing she would appear ridiculous if anyone was watching from a distance, Jessica ducked under the windows, hurrying in a hunched position around the building, deliberately heading in the opposite direction to the path that Glenn and the other outdoor workers took to get to the back.

When she reached the rear corner, Jessica quickly glanced around to see Glenn strolling back towards the house with a pickaxe in his hand. She waited until he was out of sight and then dashed to the window of Moses's office, which was still open a crack.

Jessica poked her head up, peeking through the space into the empty room. After one final check behind her, she reached inside, unhooking the handle, and climbed in.

Her heart pounding, Jessica re-latched the window and started to look around the office. She was drawn to the clock on Moses's desk, feeling strangely satisfied at seeing the digits '10.42'. It gave her a sense of self, knowing that if she'd been at the station, on a bad day, she would have just emerged from a multitude of morning meetings. On a good one, she might have got through two cups of tea from the machine, spent twenty minutes chatting to Izzy and winding up Dave and, if they were really lucky, actually got some work done. She felt a little lower when she realised she knew exactly what would be on daytime television, having done little but watch it over the past few months.

She was about to reach for the stack of papers on the desk when she heard voices in the corridor. At first she thought it might be the cooks heading away from the games room but she froze as she heard the distinctive sound of Moses outside the door followed by a jangle of keys.

His tone was crisp but it was the scratch at the door that most filled her with dread. 'Have you got your key? Mine's stuck somewhere on here and I can never find the right one.'

16

As she heard a key scraping around the lock, Jessica tried holding her breath but realised she would make more noise breathing out deeply than if she simply took lots of short, shallow breaths in the first place. She pressed against the wood at the back of the cupboard she had spotted the first time she'd been in the office. Above her were shelves that could only be reached with a ladder. Around her feet were boxes and plastic containers full of items she hadn't had time to check before squeezing herself in. A jagged corner of one box was digging into her thigh but the wood was so creaky that every slight movement would be heard.

The office door was finally pushed inwards and Jessica bit her bottom lip, trying to ignore the jabbing pain in her leg. She had heard Moses outside but now it was Glenn speaking, waiting until the door was closed before complaining about how he couldn't get anything done with everyone at the market.

'You know why it's necessary,' Moses replied calmly.

Through the slit in the centre of the doors, Jessica could see them sitting on opposite sides of the desk.

'What time is it?' Glenn asked – a clear violation of the rules if anyone else had said it.

'Quarter to eleven,' Moses said, unperturbed. 'What are the weekly numbers?'

Glenn reeled off a list of what they had planted and harvested that week. Jessica could hear the gentle scratch of a pen.

'Will you need more people later in the year?' Moses asked.

'Yes but only send blokes my way. That new girl's distracting.'

'She's not strong enough?'

'That's not it. Yesterday she dug a trench an hour quicker than I expected her to, even though I gave her a ridiculous timeframe. Some of the lads could learn from the way she just got on with it. The problem was that every time I glanced her way, she was bent over with the spade. You know what men are like. Even with everything that goes on around here, they were still stopping to peek in her direction. I'm pretty sure that's what brought on the incident with Wayne.'

Jessica hadn't thought of herself in those terms for a little while. The fact a group of the men had been admiring her from a distance was worrying in that she was living with them all, although she couldn't resist feeling a tiny twinge of relief that she wasn't a complete turn-off.

'What do you want to do?' Moses asked.

'Nothing for now. Zip said she's not feeling well today but we couldn't have got much done in any case. I'll see what happens tomorrow. It might pass if they all start seeing her as one of the lads. If not, you can always swap her out.'

'Zip's keen on getting her involved a little down the line. She says she's got something about her.'

'What do you reckon?'

Moses laughed as he replied. 'Oh, there's *definitely* something about her.'

Jessica assumed they were initially talking about Zip wanting her to be part of the recruitment team but shuddered as Glenn joined in with the amusement. Moses repulsed her and Glenn was so unpredictable, she wouldn't put anything past him.

'Seriously,' Glenn said eventually. 'Are we thinking long-term about her?'

Jessica heard Moses exhaling loudly, mulling things over. 'We'll have to see. I've heard good reports about the evening sessions but I don't know about the other things. She looks the right type.'

'So is it wise to keep using her outside? We don't want her getting hurt.'

It felt strange hearing Glenn show what sounded like concern for her. Jessica wondered if it was because he thought she was causing a disturbance outside and trying to find a way to get rid. The way he glared across the table at mealtimes certainly didn't make her feel welcome and yet his question had sounded genuine.

'For now,' Moses replied. 'We've got to give her something that keeps her interested. The whole point is for people to want to stay here.'

Glenn was drumming his fingers and didn't reply instantly. When he did, it was a short: 'Fine.' After another pause, he changed the subject: 'Does Zip have a shopping list for later?'

'Nothing special. A few bits of food and material. We

have enough equipment for now plus people get suspicious of the cash. Everyone wants cards nowadays but that leaves a trail. We'll have to look into another supplier.'

Jessica had no idea what he was talking about but Glenn clearly did.

'Is there any rush?'

'You'd know more than me – it's your area.'

'In that case we're fine, at least for now. We might have to have a rethink in a couple of months. Does Zip know how much cash to keep to the side?'

'She should do by now. She's the one always talking about money anyway, especially with things the way they are with the house. Those lawyers are expensive too.'

'Okay, I'll deal with it when the time comes.'

'Good, I don't want anything to do with it. This is your thing.'

Glenn laughed but the dynamic was different, as if he was the one in charge. 'You can't keep saying that. You're a part of it the same as anyone else.'

'I'm certainly not.'

Glenn stopped drumming his fingers and there was an awkward pause before he said sarcastically: 'You keep telling yourself that.'

There was more silence before Moses eventually responded. 'What about the rest of the greenhouse?'

'It seems fine. There's been a fair bit going on recently but I'm on top of it.'

'And you don't need anything for that either?'

'Not at the moment.'

'Good. How's Naomi?'

Even hidden away, Jessica could sense an atmosphere. Moses was rattling through the queries but Glenn was taking more time to reply. This time Jessica could practically feel the force of his voice.

'What's with all the questions?'

'We don't get to talk about these things very often.'

'What's your point? I'm not in here asking you about Zip . . . or Katie . . . or any of the others for that matter.'

Now Moses's voice had an edge to it as well. 'Careful. This isn't your house and they're not your rules.'

'It's not your house either.'

'Shall we ask Zip about it?'

She couldn't see his face but Jessica knew Glenn was smiling. 'Maybe we should – perhaps she's got tired of all the girls?'

Moses sighed but he still didn't sound outright angry. 'I'm not getting into this and I'm not being spoken to like that. I'm simply pointing out that there can't be any further incidents like the one with Naomi at dinner the other evening.'

'She knows. We spoke.'

Jessica didn't think Glenn was the type to do much speaking when he had a problem.

'She didn't sound very happy,' Moses said, not sounding particularly concerned.

'Oh, she's not,' Glenn replied, with little concern either. 'But it's not as if she's going anywhere. Zip's taken her to market today, which will probably cheer her up somewhat. She just wants to be outdoors now and then. When she was young, her dad was in the army and she moved around a lot. I don't think she's ever been in a place as long as she's been here.'

'But she's—?'

'Yes, I told you – she's not going anywhere.'

'Anything else I should know about? Did our problem get away okay?'

'Wayne?'

'Of course Wayne. Who else would I be talking about?'

Involuntarily, Jessica shifted her leg, unable to take the pain of the box digging into it any longer. She winced, trying to straighten without making a sound, missing Glenn's reply before she finally managed to twist her body into a position that didn't feel as if it was going to make her crumple forward.

'Well, that's one thing,' Moses replied, answering something Jessica had missed.

'He's another on the list, like that Liam kid.'

'Well, if they go around causing trouble, what do they expect?'

Jessica was poised, waiting for either of them to admit to killing Liam, perhaps even Wayne since no one had seen him after the assault in the gardens, but the reply she wanted didn't come.

'That's down to recruitment,' Glenn said. 'We should be more picky.'

'Do you mean we should get more girls?'

Glenn laughed. 'You'd like that, wouldn't you?'

'All right, I told you that's enough. It's not about whether they're male or female, it's about what they bring.'

'I thought you didn't want anything to do with it?'

'I don't but we're both affected if Zip's not finding the right people.'

Glenn shot straight back: 'She's your wife.'

'Yes but she probably listens to you more than she does me. If you tell her to stop bringing back middle-aged men then she will.'

Jessica had no idea what they were talking about. The confirmation that Glenn had as much influence on Zipporah as Moses only enforced what she had seen with her own eyes but Jessica was slightly surprised that Moses seemed fine with it. There was something between them, though, but Jessica couldn't figure out if that meant they were killers. Even if they were, what could be the motive?

Glenn muttered something about having a word with Zip but didn't sound particularly keen. He seemed annoyed enough at having to deal with his own wife, so it was little surprise he didn't jump at the chance to sort out a problem with someone else's.

'Any more word from the police about that Liam kid?' Glenn asked.

'Why would there be? Everyone told them he had left. It's not as if there's anything else for them to work from.'

Jessica waited for a 'we took care of that', but again it didn't come. Glenn started drumming his fingers on the desk instead.

'Why haven't I got an office?' he asked. 'There are enough free rooms in this place.'

'What would you do with it?'

'I'm not sure but it would be nice to have a clock and a calendar to keep track of things.'

'You've got a key for here.'

'It's not the same.'

'You know the house rules about electronics and gadgets. It won't work if you're walking around with a watch on.'

'I know, I was just saying.'

Another pause as Glenn stopped drumming his fingers. Jessica's back was beginning to seize up again. She scrunched her eyes tightly closed and clenched her teeth, trying not to move.

Much to her relief, she heard the scraping of a chair and then Moses's voice. 'Come on, let's go. I've got your inventory numbers and we'll check the cash with Zip tonight. If she's made what she should have done, then we'll be fine.'

The second seat creaked along the floor and the two men left, locking the door behind them. Jessica counted to fifteen and then allowed her body to flop to the floor. She was sweating and panting from the strain. When she had calmed herself, she gently pushed open the cupboard door, peering around it, even though if anyone had remained in the room they would have heard her anyway.

She returned to the stack of papers on the desk, hunting through each one carefully. It was a mixture of the obscure and the ridiculous, with most of the instructions being notes from Moses to himself, saying things such as, 'Ask Zip to get shoe shiner', and a list of everyone's names. Jessica skimmed through looking for either

Liam's or Wayne's, but neither of them were present. She was on there – 'Jessica Compton' – the J of her name written in an elaborate calligraphy she could never have managed herself. Seeing it written down made her situation all the more real, even if it wasn't her actual name.

Seeing the surname reminded her of Adam.

How much more could she put him through? How many times could she completely mess up?

Trying to focus on the present, Jessica kept searching through the papers until she was satisfied there was nothing of use there. She started going through the drawers, which were largely full of stationery and more papers. When she reached the bottom one, she found a lever arch file, with a sheaf of plastic wallets inside. Each one was numbered and contained a receipt for goods apparently paid for with cash. The top few were from a year ago for paint, carpets and a few other general household items. It was only when Jessica reached ones from six months previously that they began to look out of the ordinary.

Someone had paid for a computer, plus a selection of accessories, such as external hard drives. Across the top, someone had written 'upgrade'. Jessica looked around the room, wondering if she had somehow missed the device, but it was nowhere in sight. The next receipt appeared to be for some sort of computer networking equipment, the following three all for additional computing items.

For a group that supposedly lived without access to modern technology, it was a strange set of items to be buying – especially as Jessica had seen nothing like it anywhere in the house.

Knowing she wasn't going to solve the mystery just through the receipts, Jessica placed the folder back in the drawer and returned to the cupboard, this time having a proper look at the items. The boxes were full of reams of paper and ink cartridges for a printer.

In the first of the filing cabinets were plans for the house. They had been created years ago and didn't show the turning circle but they were still fascinating, showing the woods as part of the house's land, even though there was now a fence in place.

She checked the clock on the desk again to see that a little over an hour had passed since she had first gone into the room. She had nothing concrete to take to Charley, instead picking up lots of little pieces of information she hoped would be useful.

Before she left, Jessica thought she would try the final filing cabinets. She wasn't hopeful of discovering anything considering the sheer amount of papers that were in the others, but was intrigued when she opened the top drawer to find a folded blanket across the top. She had to push herself onto tiptoes to reach in enough to pull it out but she was left open-mouthed at the contents underneath.

Sitting on its side was a half-full bottle of whisky, lined up neatly next to bottles of vodka, rum and wine. Jessica reached in, removing the ones that weren't full, unscrewing the lids and sniffing.

They certainly smelled of alcohol.

She replaced the bottles and blanket as tidily as she could before opening the bottom drawer.

As she stood staring, Jessica knew she had no easy way

of testing the authenticity of her find this time. Placed in the centre of the drawer, sagging slightly to one side, was a large clear bag full of white powder. Jessica didn't have to pick it up to see the slightly smaller bag of round tablets sitting next to it.

17

Jessica's biggest worry was that Glenn would have bolted the front door behind him after re-entering. It was always going to be a calculated risk getting into Moses's office from the outside but she figured the door would have to be unbolted for when the group who had gone to the market returned. As she hoped, the door was unlatched and she crept inside without anyone noticing.

Back in the bedroom, Jessica took out the phone and called Charley, sitting in the window sill, half-watching the driveway but also ready to move if there was any sound close to the bedroom door.

Charley answered before it could ring a second time. 'You're going to wear the battery out.'

Regardless of the time of day, she had the same tone of voice: efficient but ready to launch into full sarcastic mode at any moment.

'Do you ever say good morning?'

'As of forty-one seconds ago, it's the afternoon.'

'Fine, how about a "good afternoon"?'

After a pause and a sigh, Charley asked Jessica what she had.

'I got into Moses's office.'

'And?'

'And you don't sound very grateful.'

Jessica was trying to stop herself getting annoyed at the lack of enthusiasm. Perhaps the thing that frustrated her most was that she knew she would be the same if the roles were reversed.

Charley's tone didn't improve. 'Let's just assume I'm grateful, respectful, happy, not overworked and not being shat on from above. What have you got?'

'I found a bag of white powder in there, pills too. They were hidden away at the bottom of a filing cabinet.'

'How much?'

'Enough coke to wipe out a nasal septum.'

'Are you sure that's what it is?'

'Well, I've not got my full drug-testing kit with me and I only snorted two lines, so I can't say a hundred per cent.'

Finally Charley cracked, laughing gently. 'You're hilarious. Seriously, though, we can't raid on the basis of that. What if it's plaster of Paris or talcum powder? Or if it goes missing between now and us raiding? The tablets could be paracetamol.'

'No drugs or alcohol are allowed on the inside, not even painkillers.'

'Perhaps they've been confiscated from people entering the house? We need more.'

'I found receipts for computer equipment, networking stuff too, but all technology is banned in the house.'

'Where is the equipment being kept?'

'I don't know.'

'What is it being used for?'

'I don't know.'

'It's still not enough. What about Liam? Or Wayne?'

Jessica knew the stresses Charley would be under and the expectations from above. She knew the burden of proof required, but she also wanted to get out of the house.

'They said Wayne was another in the list, like Liam.'

'Who said?'

'Moses and Glenn.'

'What was that in relation to?'

'Nothing in particular, that's all they said. I didn't understand everything they were talking about.'

Charley paused for a moment, making a humming noise. 'They could have been talking about them being on the list of people who had left the house.'

'They weren't though.'

'How do you know if they weren't talking about a specific subject?'

Jessica sighed, staring out of the window at the empty gardens. 'I just know. It was the way they said it.'

Charley paused. 'Jessica . . . you know this isn't enough.'

'Well, what about you? What are you doing at your end? I thought you were going to look into Wayne?'

'We have been but CCTV is a lot sparser out here. There's nothing of him near the train station and we've made discreet inquiries with local taxi firms, who say they've not picked anyone up. If he did leave then we have no record of it.'

Jessica wasn't surprised. Whatever had become of Wayne, she doubted he had simply walked out of the gates as Moses had suggested.

'Have you heard anything about a greenhouse?' Jessica asked.

'As in somewhere you grow flowers and plants?'

'I assume so. Moses mentioned something to Glenn, asking if the greenhouse was running okay but I've not seen anything like that in the grounds. From the top windows, you can see for miles and there's nothing.'

'And there's nothing indoors?'

'Not that I've seen.'

'Bear with me a moment.'

Jessica listened to the tapping of computer keys. It made her feel strangely nostalgic, missing the mundane parts of her job that involved sitting behind a desk.

'It doesn't seem to be slang for anything,' Charley said. 'I've just got lots of sites offering me deals on buying one. I have no idea which types of people spend all their time hanging around in these things.'

'Now, now,' Jessica replied. 'Those in glass houses . . .'

Charley started to reply before clocking what Jessica had said, chuckling to herself. 'You're on one today, aren't you?'

'Jokes don't go down well in this place so I've got to test my material somewhere.'

Charley composed herself, adding: 'I'll put someone on it to find out if there are any obscure religious references to a greenhouse or something else. It could be drugs slang, I suppose, but nothing I've ever heard.'

'Me either. I've not heard anyone else referring to it around the house.'

'Tell me about this Glenn character.'

Jessica barely knew where to begin. 'He's this little guy

but he's well built, strong and solid. He's calling the shots around here at least as much as Moses.'

'Really?'

'He was even making jokes at Moses's expense. He runs the outdoor section and it was him Moses was asking about the greenhouse. Whatever's going on around here, he's at the centre of it.'

Jessica heard a shuffling of papers before Charley replied. 'We've got nothing on him. It doesn't look like he's a relation of either Moses or Zipporah. Could he be a recruit?'

Jessica paused, thinking she'd heard a creak outside. When she was confident it was her imagination, she replied. 'Perhaps but I doubt it. I was listening to the cooks in the games room and everyone has a way of speaking that's complimentary to each other. Moses is passive but Glenn has none of that tact. He speaks about people with contempt and disdain, like if you were down the pub taking the piss out of your colleagues. If he is a recruit then he must have been here a long while.'

'You wouldn't rule it out, though?'

'No, he's got a wife here too but she seems scared of him. I think they've been having problems but I've not seen her anywhere other than at mealtimes.'

'Anything else?'

'They were talking about something to do with a "new supplier" and using cash because card payments could be traced.'

'We've looked into their bank accounts but everything is above board, with things such as electricity bills being paid for. There's actually not as much money there as you might think, so we've been checking off-shore. If they have an inkling they could be under scrutiny, then cash would make sense.'

'Do you know they go to the market once a week?'

'We've had plain-clothes people down there but there's not much we can do. It all seems legit. If they're using the cash to reinvest, then it would explain a few things.'

'Do you have any idea what they're buying? All the receipts for the computer equipment were cash payments.'

Charley made a humming sound again. 'They're obviously not talking about buying drugs if they were talking about card payments. Perhaps it's that they're after more computer equipment but people get suspicious with too many cash payments? Or newer equipment?'

'It did say "upgrade" on the receipt but what would they be using it for?' Charley didn't reply. Jessica wished she had written herself a list of everything she had to mention, before she remembered one more thing. 'There are woodlands over the top of the fence. I think there's a pond or a lake or something in there too but I can't see properly. I saw some plans for the land and it looks like the whole lot is owned by Zipporah's family.'

'It is,' Charley replied, obviously familiar with the situation. 'When you look at those top-down satellite maps, you can see it there. We checked the deeds but it's private land.'

'If Liam was drowned—'

'We know, we're on it but we'd need a warrant the same as for anything else.'

'What about everything I've given you?'

Jessica tried not to let her frustration show but it was hard.

Charley clearly detected an attitude. 'Are you ready to come out?'

'No, I—'

'Look, we knew it was going to be hard getting someone in, let alone being able to keep them there. We all know it's dangerous, we all know the sacrifices you're making.'

'I just wonder how much more you need. You've got one dead body, somebody potentially missing. There are drugs here. We've raided places for far less in Manchester.'

Jessica could hear Charley clucking her tongue into the top of her mouth. 'Yes, but it's not quite the same, is it? Despite what their accounts say, these people have money – they can afford lawyers far bigger than any of ours. All it will take are the words "religious persecution" and we'll get nailed. People will lose their careers.'

'So what do you need?'

'More. We'll do all we can at this end to see if we can find out anything about Wayne. Find me this greenhouse if you think it's important. Could it be in the woods?'

'If it is, there's no way I can get out and back without being noticed.'

'Okay . . .'

Jessica waited to see if Charley had anything else to add, hoping she had some sort of inspiration she'd missed. Her eventual response wasn't unexpected: 'Anything else?'

'I don't think so.'

'All right – you should really hang up. Look after that phone battery.'

Jessica waited until Charley had ended the call and then checked the battery indicator. In just three days, she had already drained over a quarter of it. She slipped it under the mattress, before returning to the window, staring at the emptiness of the gardens and wanting to go home.

18

Jessica spent the rest of the afternoon in the bedroom, cleaning. When she first arrived, she couldn't figure out why Heather had seemed so pleased to do it, now she reckoned it was because there wasn't much else to do. She realised early on she was only cleaning areas that were already spotless, wondering what Adam, Izzy, Dave or any of her other colleagues would think if they could see her.

Not long after she had finished, Heather arrived back, slightly rosy-cheeked from being out all day. She seemed pleased that Jessica was back on her feet, pressing her palm to her roommate's forehead in the way a mother would check for a temperature, and then telling her they'd sold everything they'd taken.

'How much money did you make?' Jessica asked, thinking it was a reasonable question.

Heather shook her head. 'I don't know, Zip deals with everything like that. Why does it matter?'

Jessica shrugged. 'I suppose it doesn't. I was just wondering how good today was for us all compared to a normal day.'

Heather seemed to accept the explanation, smiling. 'Oh, it was more than usual. Zip had us working extra hard this week to get things finished.'

That was interesting considering what Jessica had overheard in Moses's office and the fact Charley said there was less money than expected in the bank accounts they knew about. Was there some great need to get their hands on cash?

The pair got changed for dinner and filed down the stairs with everyone else when the bell sounded. Zipporah and Katie were already waiting at the end of the table as everyone took their places, Zipporah nodding and smiling at Jessica, who returned the acknowledgement to indicate she was feeling better.

It was only when she got to her seat and looked closer that Jessica realised Zipporah's neck and arms were covered in bruises. Some people's turned black or purple, but hers were yellow, not that dissimilar to her natural skintone. From a distance it was barely noticeable but Jessica wondered if she had gone out of her way to cover it up with the turtleneck jumper that morning. Now, in her evening dress and from close up, they were clear. Jessica thought of the way Glenn had summoned her away when they had been sitting on the stairs, plus the brutal injuries suffered when Moses had let the new recruit fall and crack his head open. Either of them could have been responsible for the marks.

She had assumed Glenn was unlikely to simply talk Naomi into submission but hadn't considered that Zipporah could be in the same position. It might also explain why Zipporah seemed so annoyed that morning, telling her she could sleep with Moses if she wanted. Perhaps that was one of the things they argued about?

Jessica had to look away from Zipporah, unnerved by the marks. Across from her, Naomi was deliberately avoiding eye contact too, staring at the table. Jessica's eyes flickered across the other woman's features but she couldn't see any bruises. Either way, she didn't know how much longer she could sit and say nothing as people were harmed around her. She knew what the longer game was but keeping quiet went against everything she believed in.

Moses soon entered and everyone sat as the cooks brought in the food. From overhearing their conversation, Jessica already knew it was some sort of chicken dish but she found it hard to eat, wondering if there was a safe way she could approach Zipporah to ask if she was all right. Or if there was someone she could ask about the greenhouse.

She picked at her food, moving things from side to side and mashing everything together, trying not to draw too much attention to the fact that she wasn't eating.

Jessica noticed a slight edge at this meal that she hadn't felt before. Moses ate his food without talking to either of the women around him, with others seated at the table sensing the unease and staying quiet too.

The scraping of cutlery on plates was unnerving in the silence, grating, grinding and scratching until the din was interrupted by a sound far more worrying.

Somewhere in the far reaches of the house, a phone began to ring.

19

Everyone around the table stopped moving, staring at each other, first in confusion and then in the realisation that somebody had broken one of the strictest rules going.

Jessica avoided everyone's eyes but looked from side to side aimlessly, matching the others. The ringtone wasn't a piece of music, it was the tinny type of annoyance that came pre-programmed with older mobile phones – such as the one Jessica had under her mattress.

She tried to remember if she had turned off the phone after talking to Charley. Surely she had? She remembered checking the battery and then tucking it under the mattress but had she pressed the off button? If so, had she held it in for long enough? She couldn't remember. Even if it was on, Charley would have known better than to call. It couldn't be her phone . . . could it?

Then she realised it could be a wrong number, anyone dialling a single incorrect digit. She had no idea what the default ringtone was for the phone she had been given but would bet it sounded exactly like the one echoing through the house.

Glenn was on his feet before anyone else had the chance. Without a word, he ran for the door, heading towards the stairs.

Moses stood, glancing from person to person as if he

was trying to read their minds. Nobody spoke but Jessica could feel eyes staring into her accusingly. Or was it in her mind?

The ringtone stopped and the house was silent.

'Would anybody like to confess?' Moses asked, his tone level and calm, even though his eyes were boring into each of them. He didn't appear angry, more hurt at the rejection of one of his core rules.

Silence.

Jessica felt a bead of sweat slide down the back of her neck and fought to suppress the shiver. Across the table, Naomi was finally looking up from the table but this time it was Jessica who could not make eye contact. She felt as if everyone was looking at her.

She was the new girl, so the phone was most likely to be hers – unless someone was being even more devious than her.

What was going to happen to the person responsible? She hadn't even been here a day when she had seen one man crack his head open. Wayne had been attacked in front of her and had now apparently left. Liam had been killed, perhaps here, perhaps not, but the fact remained that violence was only ever a wrong word away. She couldn't imagine what the punishment would be for such a blatant breach of the rules.

She tried to judge the distance to the door. If she slid her chair back now and made a dash for it, could she get out of the room to the front door and unbolt everything before anyone got to her? If so, would she be able to get all the way up the drive to safety before someone caught her?

Perhaps they would be able to get to the minibus in time – there was no way she could outrun that. She had been away from the force for so long that she was out of shape and had lost weight and muscle definition. Now she wasn't even confident she could beat Dave Rowlands in a race – and that was saying something.

If she stayed, she needed an excuse. Could she get away with saying the phone wasn't hers if it was found under her mattress? It seemed unlikely, especially as someone – probably Heather – had made the bed for her before she had arrived. She couldn't get Heather into trouble, especially when it wasn't her fault.

She couldn't even feign confusion over the rules as both Zipporah and Moses had gone through them with her, not to mention Heather bringing it up too. Zipporah had watched her undress, so there was no way she could even claim that it had accidentally been stuck in her clothing.

With no realistic way of being able to escape, plus nothing she could think of that would allow her to talk herself out of trouble, Jessica sat in the silence of the room trying not to catch anyone's eye.

In the distance, the ringtone began again.

Seconds passed, perhaps minutes, perhaps lots of minutes. Jessica had no idea.

Eventually Glenn returned, his fist clenched around what Jessica assumed was a phone. Considering the speed with which he had torn out of the room and apparently raced up the stairs and around the bedrooms to find it, he didn't seem out of breath in the slightest.

He strode across the room towards Moses, whispering something into his ear and then passing him the object. Jessica's heart was hammering so loudly that she felt sure Heather next to her must be able to hear it. People were now shuffling nervously in their seats and Naomi had returned to staring at the table.

Jessica was trying to see what was in Moses's hand but his fingers were clamped too tightly around it.

'Would anyone like to confess?' Moses asked, glancing from one person to the next.

Jessica thought about it: would it be better to confess and get it out of the way, or would the inevitable punishment be worse if she remained silent?

Moses stood straighter, loosening his fingers and holding out the phone for them all to see. 'I said, would anyone like to confess?'

Jessica felt so relieved to see that the device wasn't hers that she almost forgot where she was, starting to breathe out deeply before stopping herself and controlling things.

This time, she felt as free as everyone else to look around the table. Assuming it had been discovered in a bedroom, the person who owned it must know they had been found out.

'Last chance,' Moses said, more firmly this time.

To Jessica's left there was a scraping of a chair as a man stood. He was the youngest male in the group, apart from Ali. He was shorter than Jessica and very slight, with none of Glenn's build or presence. His thin shoulders twitched nervously as he peered towards the front, avoiding Moses's gaze.

'It's mine,' he said.

Moses's eyes narrowed but he didn't move, uttering a single word: 'Kevin.'

Glenn hurried across the room, grabbing Kevin's upper arm and pulling him towards the front.

Kevin was in Jessica's evening group but she hadn't had a proper conversation with him since arriving. She didn't know exactly where he worked but it wasn't outside and it wasn't with the craft team.

Moses seemed genuinely sad as Kevin was thrust in front of him. Moses breathed out loudly, shaking his head as Glenn waited nearby.

'Oh, Kevin,' Moses said. 'Why would you do this? Everyone knows the rules.'

Kevin hadn't stopped staring at the ground. Out in the open, he seemed even thinner than he had when he first stood. His clothes were too big for him, but his wrists were narrow and his face was so lean that his cheekbones jutted out.

'I'm sorry,' he replied, still not looking up.

Jessica didn't see Moses move but Glenn stepped forward anyway, standing between them and cupping his fingers underneath Kevin's chin, forcing him to look up. 'It's polite to look at someone when they're speaking to you,' he said harshly.

They were almost the exact same height but incomparable in every other way, Kevin like a child, Glenn a thuggish man.

Glenn stepped away but Kevin was now trembling as he peered into Moses's face. The fact Moses hadn't done anything to stop Glenn said everything about their relationship.

'What have you got to say for yourself?' Moses asked, his voice still level.

'I'm sorry,' Kevin repeated. 'I've been feeling a little lonely. I called my girlfriend but there was no answer. She must have called back.'

'Are there not enough people here to confide in?'

'Of course, I'm really sorry. It was a moment of madness.'

'Where did the phone come from?'

Kevin gulped, glancing away towards the fireplace and the step that had been drenched with blood days before. Realising he was disobeying Glenn's instructions, he quickly corrected himself, looking back to meet Moses's stare. The rest of the residents were hushed, waiting for the reply.

'I brought it in with me. I hid it.'

Around the table there were a few gasps but Jessica didn't get the sense that anyone was really surprised. More people than Kevin had surely considered it when they were told the only way to join the community was if they left everything at the doorstep. Despite that, with Glenn hanging around menacingly, it was probably sensible to seem outraged.

Moses nodded slowly. 'But you knew the regulations?'

'Yes.'

'You knew there was to be no contact with the outside world?'

'Yes.'

'And that no technology was to be brought here?'

'Yes.'

'But you broke not one but two of our most critical rules?'

'I'm sorry . . .'

Moses began pacing, walking along the length of the fireplace, the echo of his shoes the only noise.

'What did your girlfriend say?'

'Nothing, I couldn't get through.'

'You expect us to believe that?'

Jessica had seen this type of behaviour from lawyers in the past, grandstanding and playing up to the public gallery in a courtroom. Moses not only had a presence and a way with words but he had a sense of showmanship too. The more he talked, the more questions he asked, the longer he drew things out, the edgier Kevin was becoming.

'It's true,' Kevin protested but it didn't particularly matter. This was all for show.

Moses went back and forward asking variations of the same questions over and over, sometimes looking to the table and asking if they believed certain parts of the story. Jessica believed all of it but it was hard to do anything differently when the people around her were being whipped into a frenzy.

'You've let everyone down,' Moses brayed, to howls of outrage from the table.

Kevin nodded meekly.

'You've let me down.'

Fists banged the table.

Moses turned to the table. 'You've let your brothers and sisters down.'

More baying.

'Most of all, you've let yourself down.'

More thumping of the table, more shrieks, and finally Moses had what he had been trying for as Kevin collapsed to his knees in tears. All the while, Glenn stood watching impassively.

If it hadn't involved real emotions, Jessica would have been impressed. In a packed room, Moses knew what to say, when to say it and – perhaps most importantly – how to phrase things. In just a few minutes, he had wound up over twenty people, simultaneously breaking one person's spirit.

Now he paused, breathing in the atmosphere, in his element.

In his own way, he was as dangerous as Glenn and Jessica suddenly realised why the smaller man felt he could be insolent. It was because he offered the operation something completely different. He was the brawn, the muscle, but Moses would always hold something over him because he could make a room turn with just a few words.

Jessica fixed her eyes on Glenn, who was standing with his knees slightly bent, ready for Moses to say the word. He hadn't stopped looking at Kevin.

'We all know what you've been through, Kevin,' Moses said softly. The change in tack was something Jessica sometimes used herself in interviews. Using somebody's name was a way of bringing them back into a conversation or interrogation if you thought you were losing them – either that or a way of letting them know that you were one of them.

Kevin glanced up from the floor, face drenched with tears to meet Moses's eyes again.

'You've been doing so well,' Moses cooed. 'All your past problems were behind you. You were mixing well with everyone, making friends, becoming the person you once were again.'

'I know.'

'But all the time, you were hiding this secret.'

'I'm sorry.'

Moses paused, breathing in the room again. He ran his fingers through his beard, separating a few strands and then clumping them together.

'Do you wish to stay here, Kevin?'

'Yes.'

'I'm sorry, I didn't catch that.'

Jessica knew he couldn't possibly have missed it because she had heard the reply perfectly, despite Kevin's tears and blocked nose.

'Yes,' he repeated.

'Then you realise that you must face the consequences of your actions?'

'I know.'

Moses stood tall, finally nodding to Glenn. 'Take him downstairs.'

The first part of the meal had happened almost in silence but no one apparently felt like finishing their food after Kevin had been led away by Glenn. He hadn't even fought.

Afterwards, they all went off to their various study sessions. The subject of Jessica's was what they thought of rule-breaking. Jessica went along with everyone else, saying how much it disgusted her. That was despite the fact that at various points in her career, she had broken and entered, burgled a house, lied, and many other smaller things that she guessed probably wouldn't be approved of by the group. More than any of that, of course, was that the core things they thought they knew about her identity were false.

Still, what was one more white lie in among a group of people so brainwashed that they couldn't see the madness of everything around them?

Jessica was looking for an opportunity to ask the one question she had but it didn't come during the session. She didn't particularly want to mix but it was the only way she might get her answer, so she headed to the games room when they were finished. Heather was already there, trying to play darts.

Jessica crossed the room to stand next to her.

'Do you want a go?' Heather giggled. 'I'm rubbish.'

In the canteen at Longsight station, there used to be a dartboard set up that featured photos of various local lawyers, or printouts from the police website of whoever had pissed them off that week. It had been taken down ahead of an inspection and no one had ever seen it again. For a group of people who were supposed to investigate thefts for a living, the fact the culprit had never been identified was a stain on everyone's character.

Jessica took the darts from Heather, trying to match her enthusiasm as she nailed three into the twenties.

'Good shot,' Heather said.

'Beginner's luck,' Jessica replied dismissively.

Heather took the darts back, launching the first one into the wall above the board.

'Where does Kevin work?' Jessica asked, trying to sound casual.

Heather's second dart landed in the black circle around the board.

'He's a handyman, he fixes things around and about the house.'

Jessica thought that could explain why he hadn't simply been exiled in the same way as Wayne. If he was actually useful, it was no surprise Moses and Glenn would want to keep him around. This way, they also had him even more in their debt for letting him stay.

'There was one thing that puzzled me at dinner,' Jessica said.

Heather's final dart pinged into the centre of the treble-twenty.

'Well done,' Jessica added.

Heather sounded disappointed. 'I was aiming for the bullseye.'

As they walked to the board, Jessica lowered her voice. 'Do you mind if I ask you something?'

Heather plucked the three darts from the board and handed them over. Playing the friend card had worked and she stepped closer to Jessica, whispering: 'What do you want to know?'

'With Kevin, Moses told Glenn to take him downstairs but I didn't know there was anything under here.'

'Oh, is that all?' Heather replied, walking back to the end of the makeshift oche. 'There's a basement. I thought I'd shown you it on the tour.'

'Where is it?'

'Do you remember the door underneath the stairs? The ones that don't go anywhere.'

'That's it? What goes on there?'

Heather raised her eyebrows, looking Jessica in the eyes. 'I'm not sure but if I were you, I wouldn't go out of your way to find out.'

20

Jessica didn't want to push by asking too much more. She hung around the games room, putting on a show of fitting in without doing too much to actually engage. Nobody seemed particularly concerned that Kevin had been taken to the basement, probably meaning it had happened before and that they expected to see him again.

The entrance under the stairs was almost directly opposite the doorway to the games room. Jessica remembered seeing it on the tour with Heather, thinking it was simply a storage cupboard. She had walked past it time and again without knowing what it contained. Given the size of the rest of the house, the basement could potentially be enormous.

For some reason, the door to the games room always seemed to be left open. Jessica positioned herself close to it, playing cards with Abigail, Heather and one of the men. Lunchtime and after-work card games around Longsight station might as well have been a contest between the men to see who had the biggest genitals given the competitiveness involved. In her younger days, Jessica had learned to play poker but hadn't joined in for years, the male-driven atmosphere a little too much for her.

Playing cards in the house was an altogether more serene affair. The only game Heather knew was rummy, so

Jessica spent hand after hand bored senseless, keeping an eye on the door.

Eventually, there was a clunk and a clang and the door underneath the stairs opened. Jessica didn't want to appear overly interested but didn't have to worry because everyone moved towards the door of the games room anyway.

Glenn was standing in the hallway, hands on hips. Kevin crawled out from the doorway under the stairs with a groan. His face was speckled with cuts and bruises, parts of his neck and throat already turning purple. At first Jessica wondered why Glenn wasn't telling them all to leave, or at least close the door. 'Move along, nothing to see here,' was something everyone had said in the force at some point. There could be a mid-air plane crash, debris landing across a motorway causing a hundred-car pile-up with untold carnage and flames shooting far into the sky, yet there would still be a constable somewhere with a roll of blue tape telling everyone there was nothing to see.

Glenn didn't even face them, though he must have known he was being watched. He waited for Kevin to haul himself to his feet and then waved towards someone out of view. From the other side of the stairs, the woman who had attended to the man who hit his head on the marble step came over. She peered at Kevin's injuries, muttering something too low for Jessica to hear, then, wrapping an arm around his waist, she led him away.

As he turned, Jessica expected Glenn to be angry at the undue attention, but he simply nodded towards everyone standing in the doorway. Calmly, he relocked the door under the stairs, slipping a thick key into a slot two-thirds of the way around his belt, and then headed up the stairs.

Gradually, everyone returned to what they were doing but there was definitely less of an appetite to have fun. Jessica knew the reason Glenn hadn't minded people watching was because it suited his and Moses's aims if everyone knew exactly what could happen to them if they broke the rules. If they were useful, they would be taken to the basement and punished. If they weren't, it was banishment. Anyone who had been fully indoctrinated into the ways of the house and who couldn't remember what it used to be like in the outside world would willingly take the beating.

Jessica hadn't seen anyone except Glenn leave the basement with Kevin, so could only assume he was responsible for enforcing discipline. No surprise but one other thing she could tell Charley.

As Heather drifted away to talk to someone else, Jessica caught Abigail's eye. 'Is that normal?' she asked, nodding her head towards the basement.

Abigail shrugged, unconcerned. 'If you want to stay, you live by the rules.'

Jessica was weighing up whether she should drop a hint about the greenhouse, wondering if Abigail might have an idea of what or where it was, when the alarm that usually signified wake-up and dinner started to ring. Perhaps it was because she was downstairs, as opposed to in the bedroom, but it sounded louder to Jessica. She pressed her palms to her ears, trying to shield herself from the noise.

She looked around, confused, but all the others had

stopped what they were doing and were now moving towards the door.

'What's going on?' Jessica shouted to Heather.

She couldn't hear the reply over the din but the single word wasn't difficult to lip-read: 'Trouble.'

It was hard to describe the atmosphere in the hallways. Not only was there the small group leaving the games room but other people were emerging from various parts of the house. It felt calm and panicked at the same time, people walking, not running, all heading steadily up the stairs. Yet each person's face was a mixture of bemusement and worry, betraying the composed nature of the way they were moving.

On the middle floor, the alarm was even louder and everyone Jessica saw had their fingers fully in their ears. Jessica had initially assumed there was a fire, or a drill for one, because that was what she usually associated with such a noise, especially at this time of the night.

Instead of going outside and away from it, people were heading back to their rooms, meaning it had to be something else. Jessica followed until she and Heather were in the bedroom. She lay on her bed, unable to focus on anything. The piercing wail sizzled through her so fiercely that she could feel it as much as she could hear it, even with her fingers firmly pressing on her ears to try to block it out.

When it eventually stopped, it took Jessica a few moments to realise the sound had gone. She could still hear a faint ringing, removing her fingers and glancing around the room to see Heather sitting on the edge of her own bed, hands by her side.

'It's stopped,' Heather said, stating the obvious.

'Why was it so loud?'

'I'm not sure. We've had these alarms before – it means something is happening.'

Heather's voice sounded faint, almost tinny, as if Jessica was hearing it through an old battered speaker.

'Like what?' Jessica asked.

'I'm not sure.'

'What was going on the last time it went off like that?'

Heather shrugged. 'If we needed to know, we would have been told.'

That was the type of reasoning that meant Heather probably wasn't cut out for policing when they eventually got out of there.

Feeling a little unbalanced as she stood, Jessica tapped her ears to try to make them feel normal again. Even though the noise had stopped, she could still hear a faint buzzing. She wobbled slightly, using one of the bedposts to hold herself up. It had been one of the most disconcerting moments of her life.

Jessica moved across to the window, nudging the curtain aside to try to get some sense of where she was. It was dark but the moon was high and the skies clear, casting a bluey-white glow across the gardens. She stared into the distance, towards the ridge of the driveway and the far side where the gate was out of view. Gradually, her balance began to return until she felt more like herself.

It was only then that she noticed a flicker of movement directly below. She had to press against the glass to be able to see anything as the angle was too steep but there were undoubtedly people on the turning circle, directly in front of the house.

'There's someone out there,' Jessica said, gazing at all the activity.

'You should move away from the window,' Heather replied firmly.

Jessica didn't want to be seen to be directly ignoring what might well be house rules but she had no intention of stepping away either.

'Moses and Glenn are outside,' she added, shuffling slightly to the side to try to peer around the impossible angle. There was a gentle glow of yellow light spilling from the inside of the house, where the front door must be open a fraction.

She could see only the tops of their heads and they were very close to the doorway. A few metres ahead of them, there was a group of five or six people, all wearing dark clothing. It hadn't been a particularly cold day and Jessica doubted it was that cool an evening, but the figures were all wearing hats or what could even be balaclavas.

Whatever was happening didn't appear to be too friendly, with Glenn jabbing a finger. There were clearly words exchanged before the yellow light disappeared, signalling that the door had been closed.

'There's a whole gang out there,' Jessica said.

'We've had problems with kids in the past,' Heather replied, still not moving from her bed but sounding a little annoyed. 'You shouldn't be by the window. When the alarm goes, we're supposed to return to our rooms and not get involved with anything.'

'I'm not getting involved, I'm watching. They don't look like kids to me.'

Below, the group turned and started to walk away. As they moved from the shadow of the house into the clear light of the moon, Jessica could see from their builds that they were all young men. They walked freely, without the burden that came from years of hard work. As they reached the start of the garden, one of them crouched, picking something up before turning and throwing it towards the house. Jessica couldn't hear it but she could sense the laughter as the six of them bolted up the driveway.

'I think one of them threw a rock at the house,' Jessica said.

'I told you, we've had a few problems with kids. Moses and Glenn deal with it. They look after us in all ways.'

'Why doesn't someone contact the police?'

Jessica turned to see Heather staring at her, scowling. 'Because it's our business.'

As the young men disappeared over the brow of the driveway, Jessica moved back to her bed, feeling Heather's eyes watching her in silent disapproval.

Jessica burst through the front door and threw her keys towards the basket Adam had placed in the hallway to try to ensure she never lost them again. She didn't bother to see where they landed, hurling her coat at the peg and bounding through to the back room where they still had all the boxes that hadn't yet been unpacked.

Behind her, she could hear Adam closing the door, doing whatever it was he did but she couldn't care less. She reached across the first stack of boxes, pulling the largest one towards her and running a fingernail across the tape to open it. Pulling the flaps open, she began hunting through the items, wondering how they had managed to amass so much junk in such a short period of time. Empty picture frames, plant pots, extension leads, ornaments, coasters, empty boxes within boxes, books she'd never read, Christmas cards from years ago.

So much crap.

Jessica shoved the box back onto the pile and opened the one next to it.

'What are you looking for?' Adam asked behind her.

She didn't bother to acknowledge him, continuing to hunt through more piles of scrap that she couldn't remember buying. Most had probably been Christmas and birthday presents. No one ever knew what to buy, so they invested in some sort of tat in one big merry-go-round of rubbish nobody actually wanted.

'Jess?'

'What?'

'What are you looking for?'

'Something.'

'What?'

'Just something.'

Soft toys, a board game she knew for a fact was missing pieces, a cracked, empty CD case, cushion covers with no cushions, tea towels, a remote control for a television she'd had in her bedroom when she lived with Caroline.

Why had she even kept all of this stuff, let alone moved it around with her?

'Can I help?' Adam asked softly.

'No.'

'I might know where whatever it is that you're looking for is.'

Jessica didn't look up, shoving the second box back into place and starting on a third. 'Do you know the number for a skip company?' she asked.

'Should I?'

'I don't know, that's why I'm asking.'

Adam sighed. 'You don't have to take it out on me.'

Jessica kept her tone level, knowing it would annoy him more if she wasn't shouting. 'I'm not taking anything out on you, I'm asking a perfectly reasonable question about whether you know the phone number for a skip company.'

A pause.

An old telephone which probably didn't work, a manual for a lawnmower Jessica had never owned, a bag of random buttons, batteries, some old keys for something Jessica couldn't identify, rawl plugs, sink plugs, dishcloths, a pack of scouring pads, more soft toys, a wooden frog she'd carved at primary school.

'I don't know the number for a skip company,' Adam eventually replied, calmly. 'But we can find one if that's what you want. What do you need it for?'

'All of this. I don't know why we bothered moving it, let alone put it in storage in the first place.' She turned, thrusting a candle holder into the air. 'What are we going to do with this? It's just shit. You can't even give this type of stuff away. If I took it to a charity shop, they'd turn me away for taking the piss.'

Jessica threw it into the corner of the room, enjoying the clang it made and hoping it had broken.

Adam said nothing as she reached for the next box, ripping the top open and continuing her search.

'We should talk about things,' Adam said.

Jessica ignored him, having found the box she was after. She dropped paintbrushes and a roller on the floor, pulling out a steamer to remove wallpaper and a scraper.

She turned, barging past Adam, heading into the kitchen. Jessica could sense him behind her as she set the tap running, allowing the water to flow into the hole at the top of the steamer.

'What are you doing?' Adam asked from somewhere behind her.

'What does it look like I'm doing?'

'Jess, please don't do this.'

'You don't even know what I'm doing, so how can you tell me to stop?'

'I know what you're thinking.'

Jessica shook her head as the water overflowed out of the spout. She wrenched the tap off, sealing the steamer.

'Well, aren't you the clever one. Reading my mind, knowing what I'm thinking. You should go on television if you're that clever.'

'You know that's not what I meant.'

Finally it was the reaction she wanted, his tone short, his patience tested.

Good.

She wanted him to be wound up, to feel what she was feeling. That calmness he always had was so frustrating that it made her want to antagonise him as much as she could. To push him, wind him up, make him grit his teeth and shout, to want to punch the wall in the way she did.

Jessica pushed past him, heading up the stairs towards the spare bedroom. She shoved the door open, kicking the plastic box of soft toys to the side. Where did they all come from? Were they breeding or something? It was ridiculous, they were both in their thirties and yet there were cuddly things everywhere.

She shoved the cot to one side, fumbling the plug into the socket and waiting for the steamer to heat up.

Adam was behind her again, waiting in the doorway, watching.

'Please don't do this,' he said, calm again, which only made Jessica more determined.

She ignored him, facing the wall as a steady mist seeped out of the end. Jessica pressed it to the wall, counting to ten in her head and then removing it, slicing the scraper through the soggy yellow paper and slashing it away from the surface.

'Jess.'

'What.'

'Please stop.'

'No.'

'You don't have to do this.'

Jessica didn't reply, pressing the steamer to the wall again.

'Jess . . .'

'Just leave me alone.'

Jessica stripped away another patch of wallpaper, scraping hard against the wall until a trickle of plaster dropped onto the brand-new carpet.

Adam hadn't moved. Jessica could sense him, still in the doorway, still composed, not shouting, not angry, not wanting to throw things. She hated him.

'Do you remember what you said when we decorated this room in the first place?' Adam asked quietly.

'No.'

'It was a Friday and you'd had a long week at work – as if you ever have anything else – and I'd got stuck in the city centre because there was an accident on the roads and everywhere was gridlocked. We got home and looked at each other, hungry, tired and generally just annoyed at our lot. But we still had this house of ours and we still had each other. We ended up eating breakfast cereal for tea because we didn't have a freezer and then we came up here. The floorboards were exposed, the walls were bare and crumbling in places, then covered with this awful paper in others. You said it was like the worst hotel ever.'

Jessica tried to stop herself, but couldn't hold back a gentle laugh. Of course she remembered, she would never forget that weekend. She tried to turn the laugh into a cough, turning away from Adam and pressing the steamer to the wall even harder, stripping away another layer. Wanting to be angry.

'We stayed up until the early hours, stripping paper and clearing every last thing out of here,' Adam continued. 'We had to open the window because the room was full of steam from that thing and it was so smoggy. Outside it was cold but it somehow made everything in here all right. When we were done, your hair was full of little pieces of wallpaper, there were bits stuck to your cheeks, your ears, your arms, everywhere. It looked like you had the worst acne scars going.'

Jessica closed her eyes, trying to blank him out.

'We slept for a few hours, covered in shite, and then we got up and carried on working. I was supposed to be hanging the wallpaper but it was impossible because you'd made such a mess with the paste. It was too thick, then you tried to water it down but it was too runny. When you finally had it sorted, you got it everywhere. We could barely walk around because the floor had more paste on it than the walls and our shoes kept sticking. You'd already ruined one set of clothes, so we stood in here for eleven hours, in our underwear, trying to get the wallpaper on the wall. The whole time, I was trying to stay quiet because you'd been going on about how we didn't know what we were doing and that we should pay someone to do it. You never brought it up but I could see it in your face the whole time: that smug "I was right" look that you've been working on for years.'

Adam paused for breath as Jessica switched off the steamer, resting her forehead against the wall, listening.

'You were right, obviously,' he added. 'We'd spent the best part of twenty-four hours getting rid of a bit of old wallpaper, covering ourselves in paper and paste, wrecking our clothes and generally making a massive mess. By the time it was dark, we'd only just started painting. Then you changed your mind about the colour, saying blue was too boyish, so you wanted yellow instead. There was only one roller, which you insisted you wanted, so I was stuck with this puny little brush doing the edges as you went crazy with the paint. You were going up and down, side to side, diagonally, whatever took your fancy and it was beginning to dry strangely. Because we'd been at it all day, we left it for the night and went back to bed.'

'I slept amazingly that night,' Jessica whispered to herself.

Adam must have overheard, replying, 'So did I,' as he crossed the room, hugging himself into her back. Jessica closed her eyes, desperate to be angry but feeling his calming influence spreading.

'The next morning,' he continued, 'you kept going on and on about how hungry you were, bullying me into going to that burger place's twenty-four-hour drive-through to get us muffins, coffee and hash browns. You ate all of yours, half of mine, and then we started all over again, this time painting properly. By the time it was finished, it was dark again, we'd spent over two days sorting out one room, and you were covered in a crusty mess of paper, paste, paint, dust, plaster and God knows what else. We stood in here looking at each other and I couldn't stop laughing. You didn't even realise how ridiculous you looked. You were in the shower for forty-five minutes before you were satisfied it was all gone. Then we came in here, sat on the floor and had a cup of tea looking at the room we'd created for our son.'

Jessica pressed her forehead harder into the wall, feeling the coolness as she remembered the feeling she'd had that day.

'When we'd finished drinking, we knew it was time for bed. We'd barely slept in two days, we'd eaten nothing but junk, drunk nothing but tea and we each had to be at work in a few hours. But neither of us wanted to move. I don't know about you but for me it was the sense of what this was going to be. We'd not only made something inside of you but we were creating this place too – just the two of us. You were right that we could have hired someone to strip the walls and paper the room but this was something just for us, even though we were rubbish at making it. I sensed that as we sat and stared at these plain walls. I was knackered but I've rarely had such a fun time because it was two days with you. Two days of messing around, joking, laughing, being shit at something but not caring.'

Jessica could feel Adam's breath on her ear. She wanted him to stop speaking because she didn't want to hear about the good times. She wanted to embrace the fury within her. To pound the walls, to hammer his chest, to shout at him, to have someone to blame.

Instead, he carried on, as smoothly as before. 'Finally you stood and you pulled me to my feet. You hugged me and I could have held onto you all night. You looked around the walls and said: "Look at what we've made."'

'You touched my belly and said: "We've made this too."'

She felt Adam choke slightly but wanted to feel him hurting as much as her.

'I did,' he said. 'And then you started laughing and said that any kid we ever had was not going to be allowed to grow up because you had no intention of ever redecorating this room again.'

Jessica opened her eyes, staring at the yellow of the walls directly in front of her. That weekend was as special to her as it apparently was to him. So much mess, so much fun. She remembered the paint and the paste in the same way he did but she remembered the laughter more. No cross words, no arguing, just two days of enjoying being with each other. If she could lock that weekend away, she would return to it every chance she got.

She turned, resting on his breastbone but keeping her hands by her sides, not allowing him to hold her properly.

'It's not the same in here any more,' she said, staring at the floor. The soaked strips of paper were mashing into the previously pristine carpet, creating an ugly, thick creamy pulp. She dropped the steamer onto the ground with a clatter.

'We don't know what went wrong,' Adam said. 'You heard what they said; we'll have to return to the doctor's for the test results. Then we'll know.'

'It's still not the same in here.'

Jessica felt Adam gulp. 'I know. If you want to start again, then we can. We'll tear everything out until it's as empty as it was before and then we'll have another go. But you shouldn't do things like this when you're angry. You might regret it tomorrow.'

'Why aren't you angry?'

'Who says I'm not?'

Jessica balled up her fists, pulling away from him and leaning against the wall. 'You should be furious. You should be doing this, not me. After everything that happened with your parents, you should be screaming, shouting, tearing your hair out, telling everyone how unfair it is.'

Adam glanced away and Jessica knew she'd gone too far. It wasn't fair to bring up his parents. He'd never known them, his mother dying when he was two, his father killing himself at the prospect of not having his wife around. She wanted to say sorry but couldn't; the only pity she felt was for herself.

She saw the hurt in his eyes but he shook his head, letting it go. 'We're not all the same, Jess.'

'We are for things like this.'

'We're not. Just because I've not said things out loud, it doesn't mean I'm not as upset as you.'

He reached out to stroke her abdomen, but Jessica stepped away, not wanting anyone else to touch her there. Not today.

'You think it's my fault, don't you?' Jessica said, her anger returning, stronger than before.

Adam pushed back, resting against the crib. 'No I don't.'

'That's why you were nodding and taking notes when they were talking about going to the doctor's to find out what went wrong.'

'No it wasn't. It was because I was worried about you – I *am* worried about you – I want you to have all their tests so we know you're safe and well.'

'It could be you – perhaps you're the one who's got something wrong and you're the reason this happened.'

Adam nodded wearily. 'Maybe it is. If they want to test me, that's fine.'

Still he didn't raise his voice, still he didn't do anything other than look at her, reach for her. Jessica pushed him away, raising her voice. 'Stop being so fucking nice.'

'Jess . . .'

'Just be angry. Shout at me. Tell me it's my fault. Scream. Do something. Don't just stand there looking dimwitted.'

'Jess . . .'

'Come on, say something. I know you want to. Call Georgia and tell her what's happened. Call my mum and tell her. Why don't you just—'

Jessica didn't get a chance to finish raging before Adam

interrupted, his words soft, his eyes fixed on the floor. 'It was my baby too.'

'What?' she snapped.

'It was my baby too. You may have lost it but it was both of ours.'

'You didn't have to see what came out.'

'I know.'

'You didn't have them poking, prodding, scraping—'

'I know.'

Jessica stopped speaking, raising her fists in frustration at not having the words. She wanted to hit him, to make him feel the pain. 'You can never understand what it feels like.'

'But I can be here and it was still my baby.'

'Then why aren't you angry too?'

'I am but I'm not the same as you. We deal with things in different ways and we have to find a way to get over this. I know it's too soon but I want you to be happy in the end and the only way that's going to happen is if you can find a way to not be angry at the world.'

Jessica took a deep breath but the rage was ebbing away. She willed it to return, wanting to feel something other than the emptiness she was left with. Adam stepped towards her and this time she didn't fight, allowing him to cup her head under his chin.

'It's just so unfair,' she whispered.

'I know it is,' he cooed into her ear. 'But at least we have each other.'

THURSDAY

21

When the alarm went off to wake them the next morning, Jessica found herself flashing back to the din of the previous evening. It was a lot quieter now but she could still feel the far reaches of her inner ear hurting.

She tried to work out which day it was, working backwards until she remembered it had been market day – Wednesday – meaning today was Thursday. She had only been in the house for a short while and yet she was utterly disorientated by it. Everyone's weeks were defined by recruitment day on a Sunday and market on the Wednesday. Without those, it really would be complete confusion.

At breakfast, it was as if the previous evening had not happened. Kevin was already standing behind his chair, the wider cuts on his face stitched up with neat zigzags and a bandage around one of his arms. As everyone entered, he bowed to them, whispering an apology over and over until they had all heard it.

Nobody mentioned what had happened to him, the same as nobody acknowledged the alarm and the people outside – that was if they had even noticed them.

Moses walked in behind his two women and then read a passage from Hebrews which Jessica completely tuned out. The meal began as usual but they were disturbed midway

249

through by a faint humming sound. Without checking with Moses, Zipporah stood, striding out of the room.

'What was that?' Jessica asked Heather.

'There's a buzzer at the front gate for people wanting to come down the driveway.'

Jessica remembered ringing it herself and thought it was strange being on the other end, knowing someone else was trying to get in. It occurred to her that the gang last night must have jumped the fence, something she had missed at the time.

A few minutes later, Zipporah rushed back into the room, worry etched across her face. Glenn noticed it too, dropping his fork and crossing to Moses, where Zipporah crouched and whispered something low enough that only he could hear. Moses must have known all eyes were on him but he couldn't stop his eyebrows arching downwards in annoyance. Glenn leant in closer, whispering something which Moses nodded at, before standing.

Zipporah and Glenn returned to their seats and this time Moses left the room, although he was walking noticeably slower than Zipporah had, trying to maintain an air of calm, even though it was clear to everyone that something had happened.

Glenn picked up his fork and continued to eat, followed quickly by Naomi. Everyone else took the hint that they should continue as normal. Jessica risked a few glances towards Zipporah, who was angling herself away from Katie, watching the door.

When Moses returned, Jessica could tell something wasn't right. He was trying to adopt his usual serene attitude but there was something lacking. His eyes kept darting towards Glenn as he walked around the table until he was in front of the fireplace. He opened his arms out wide, embracing the room, and then began to speak.

'Brothers, sisters, it is a grave day. Our dear friend Wayne left us a short time ago and I regret to tell you that this morning he was found dead.'

There were gasps around the table and even Jessica was shocked. She didn't believe that Wayne had simply left but the fact his dead body had now been found confirmed her worst fears.

Moses held his hands higher, silently and successfully demanding quiet.

'The police are here and they wish to talk to everyone one by one.'

More gasps of horror. This time Moses let them continue a little longer before raising his hands.

'I know. You have every right to be concerned about this but they assure me they simply want to ask what you may know about Wayne.'

He glanced over the table towards the door where there was someone in a suit standing, one hand on her hip. The sight of an outsider within the house brought more gasps and the people at the far end of the table started shuffling their seats away in horror.

The officer in the doorway remained still but was clearly taken aback by the obvious shock reverberating around the room. Jessica glanced towards Moses, who stayed silent, not exactly enjoying the spectacle but doing nothing to stop it, or allay anyone's fears.

'I have been assured that the police officers mean you no harm whatsoever,' Moses said, emphasising the words, even though the statement was utterly unnecessary. By saying the police meant them no harm, he was only putting into people's minds that it could be a possibility.

People were still moving their seats away from the door, the scrapes and screeches creating such a din that Moses stopped himself midway through a sentence, knowing he couldn't be heard.

Shouting wasn't his way, so he raised his arms, demanding silence again.

'Because the police have asked to see everyone individually, they have requested that we do not remain in here. They suggested that everyone returns to their bedrooms and I will then come for you when they are ready.'

Jessica knew the reason was to prevent people conferring. There was no way they would be able to control everyone's movements in such a large, unfamiliar setting, so this provided the next best solution.

'I would ask you all to cooperate,' Moses added, now looking from person to person, rather than focusing on the whole room. He concentrated on her and the other new people, as if they needed telling in particular. The officer at the far end of the room might not have noticed the significance but Jessica did: 'Don't say anything stupid'.

Things were already bad enough with two dead bodies connected to the house, plus Kevin and the man from Jessica's initiation looking as if they had been in a battle.

Unsurprisingly, given his stitches, the officer indicated

towards Kevin, saying they would like to speak to him first. Moses and Zipporah started to lead everyone else out of the room. Glenn and Naomi got into line behind Jessica and Heather, walking up the stairs at the same pace as everyone else. Jessica clocked it straight away – if it wasn't for her tipping Charley off, no one would know he had any central involvement. Zipporah was known because she owned the house; Moses because they were married. Glenn was an unknown and doing his best to fit in under the watching eyes of the officer, meaning the illusion would be kept.

Moses stayed with them the entire journey up the stairs, promising: 'I'll return soon,' as Jessica and Heather entered the bedroom.

Jessica moved across to the window, looking down to where three police cars and two unmarked vehicles were parked across the turning circle.

Heather was sitting on her bed, knees tight to her chest, arms wrapped around herself. 'What do you reckon they're going to do?'

'Who? The police?'

'Yes.'

'I guess they'll ask us what we know about Wayne.'

'But we don't know anything.'

'We know he was here.'

'But he left!'

Heather was getting louder, rocking herself back and forth. At first Jessica had thought she was simply toeing the official line Moses and everyone else would no doubt be spouting but now she realised the young woman was genuinely scared. It was similar to the spontaneous reaction downstairs, with residents moving their chairs away from the door. Moses had spent so long telling everyone to be fearful of outsiders that they all were.

Being on the streets recruiting was different because it was on their terms. Actually having outsiders in the house was the thing they had all been told to be scared of. Even Jessica felt it a little; seeing the officer in the suit standing in the doorway felt unnatural, an invasion.

Jessica tried to sound as reassuring as she could. 'All you have to do is tell them what you saw.'

'I didn't see anything.'

'So tell them that.'

Heather was tugging at her hair, eyes wide. Jessica moved across to the bed and sat next to her, placing a hand on her shoulder.

'It's going to be just me and them, in a room on our own,' Heather said.

'There will be people outside,' Jessica replied. 'If there is anything you're uncomfortable with, you can say that. If they keep on, you can call for help.'

Heather stopped pulling at her hair but was clinging onto Jessica's arm so hard that it was hurting. Jessica clenched her teeth, wriggling until she was free, placing her arm around the younger woman instead.

'What if they try to corrupt us?' Heather whispered.

Jessica didn't know how to respond at first but the chilling way Heather had said the word made it sound utterly terrifying.

'Why would they try to corrupt you?'

'Because that's what they do. You haven't been here long enough to know what it's like yet. You haven't sat in the sessions where they tell us what it's like beyond the gates. They bring in newspapers. You must know what it's like out there.'

Jessica knew that you could make most things seem scary if you were selective enough in the elements you chose. If they had been picking newspaper reports of the worst possible crimes with the most graphic images and discussing only them, then it was no wonder Heather was so worried.

'Just remember to call for help if there is anything you are unhappy about,' Jessica said. 'I'm sure they'll just want to talk about Wayne. If you tell them the things you know, there isn't anything else they can do to you.'

Heather struggled to compose herself, running through a whole host of increasingly unlikely scenarios of what might happen if she was left alone in a room with the police officers. Jessica stopped trying to shoot down her theories for fear of seeming too much like the outsider that she was. In the end, all she could do was try to comfort the other woman.

When there was a knock at the door, Heather jumped so much that she and Jessica banged heads. Neither of them had a chance to say 'Come in' before Moses entered.

'It's your turn, Heather,' he said.

It took a little persuasion but he eventually convinced her that he would do everything he could to ensure that she would be safe. Heather dried her eyes and washed her face before following him out of the room.

Jessica was about to return to her own bed when the door swung back open. Moses was standing there, offering his most kindly and charismatic smile.

'Do you think we can have a chat?' he asked, not waiting for a reply and closing the door behind him.

Jessica knew she couldn't refuse but she certainly didn't want to be alone in a bedroom with him.

'I did my best to calm her down,' she said, starting to stand.

Moses ran a hand through his beard, nodding. 'I know you did.'

Jessica moved across to the window, using the police cars as a reminder to herself that there were people downstairs she could cry out for if she needed to.

Moses crossed to Jessica's bed, running a hand along the smooth sheets and sitting within touching distance of where her phone was hidden under the mattress. He patted the spot next to him. 'Come.'

On a list of things Jessica wanted to do, sitting next to Moses on anyone's bed, let alone hers, was very low but she knew she could not resist. She took one last glance out of the window towards the cars, hoping Moses recognised that she could scream any time she wanted, and then joined him.

She sat awkwardly with her hands in her lap but he shuffled closer, placing a hand on top of hers.

'It's been so good having you here these past few days, Jessica,' he said.

Jessica hated the way he spoke her name. He made the middle letters sound like a hiss in a poor attempt at being affectionate. She didn't even know what he was talking about. She had been there barely four days and contributed next to nothing.

'Thank you,' she replied.

He moved a little nearer, putting the other arm around her. He was so close, she could feel the lower strands of his beard tickling the top of her head.

'I know you must be anxious about speaking to the officers downstairs but I will ensure that all of you are looked after. They know they are only in this house through the good grace of me and my wife. We haven't even called our lawyers in this time. None of our brothers and sisters will be harmed.'

'That's reassuring,' Jessica replied, trying not to let the cynicism invade her voice.

Moses moved even closer, moving the hand that had been in her lap up her body and stroking her hip.

'I thought we should probably talk about what you saw when you were in the garden.'

Jessica's first thought was that he was referring to the time she had broken into his office, wondering how he knew, before she realised he was talking about Wayne being assaulted.

'What you saw happening to our brother Wayne was perhaps a little misleading,' he added, his hand sliding higher. 'I think it would be unfair to mention that, especially in relation to Glenn.'

There he was again. Moses was doing this to cover for him. Downstairs, Glenn had filed off like everyone else, now Moses was telling her to keep his influence quiet.

'I'm not sure what you mean,' Jessica replied, wondering how much she could get out of him.

She instantly wished she'd said nothing, as Moses's hand slipped further up her body until it was brushing the side of her breast.

'Glenn told me what happened in the gardens when they discovered Wayne had been drinking. He says things got a little out of hand because Wayne was shouting in your direction. He said he was worried about what Wayne might do to you, which is why he stepped in.'

It was such an outrageous rewriting of what had happened that Jessica had to stop herself saying so. As she swallowed the words, Moses's hand moved across to the front of her chest, cupping her breast entirely.

Jessica clamped her jaws together, trying to calm herself.

'I can feel your heart beating quickly,' he added.

It's because I'm being indecently assaulted.

Jessica didn't reply at first, not trusting herself. Two more breaths through her nose and she finally found the words. 'I suppose I'm a little worried about what they might ask me.'

Lies.

'But we're clear now about what you thought you saw in the garden? Glenn only ever has other people's best interests in mind.'

'I know.'

'You have to realise we are trying to create better people here. Sometimes things happen that outsiders would not understand.'

His other hand dropped down from her shoulder as he shuffled sideways, sitting behind her, cupping both of her breasts. Jessica closed her eyes, curling her toes, biting her lip, knowing she could stop this at any moment. She hated Charley for putting her in this position, hated herself for accepting it and, most of all, hated Moses for believing he was entitled to treat people in this way.

Moses leant in, his lips close to her ear. 'If the wrong things get said, bad things could happen.'

He squeezed her roughly as he spoke, leaving her in no doubt about what he meant.

'I understand,' Jessica said, unable to stop herself trembling.

Moses finally released her, standing and smoothing his clothes. 'Good, that's very good, Jessica.'

He reached a hand down to help her up from the bed. 'It's your turn next, so perhaps we should go downstairs.'

Jessica tried to stand but her knees were like jelly. She supported herself on one of the posts around the bed, Moses hooking a hand underneath her armpit. She shook him off, before remembering the role, thanking him for his help but saying she was feeling all right. He wasn't fooled and, for a moment, Jessica saw the real Moses, or Jan, or whatever he called himself. He smiled at her, knowing exactly what he had done. He was manipulative, dangerous and a sexual predator. One way or the other, before she left the house, Jessica was going to make sure he regretted ever laying a hand on her.

22

Jessica pushed open the door to one of the smaller rooms attached to the main entranceway next to the front door. She almost gasped in relief as she saw Charley sitting on her own there, pad of paper on the table in front of her.

Charley shook her head a fraction, telling Jessica not to speak, then extended her hand.

'Good morning, my name is Detective Chief Inspector Charley Bailey. I'm sorry for disturbing you all. Hopefully we will be able to get through this quickly and then get out of your hair.'

The door was pulled closed, leaving just the two of them. Jessica opened her mouth but Charley again shook her head, sitting and writing on the pad before spinning it around for Jessica to read.

They may be listening.

Jessica glanced up to the ceiling. It was something she had never considered. In among the receipts, she hadn't seen anything for monitoring equipment but she hadn't checked everything and it wasn't inconceivable. The bedroom she shared with Heather surely couldn't be bugged, else they would have heard her talking on the phone. That didn't mean the main work room and other areas like this weren't being listened in to. Moses's warning that bad things could happen implied he would know if something was said that he didn't want getting out. Jessica assumed it was bravado but perhaps it was more.

Now she nodded to say she understood.

'What's your name?' Charley asked.

'Jessica Compton.'

'Good, Jessica, and how long have you been here?'

'Four days.'

'Wow, is that all? You're the newest person we've spoken to so far.'

Jessica reached forward, taking the pad and the pen. As she gave some vague description out loud of how she had been recruited by Zipporah, she wrote:

I am going to fucking kill Moses if this isn't over and done with soon.

Charley's eyes widened as she read, writing her reply quickly: *Do you need out?*

No. I'll deal with it.

What happened?

Jessica snatched the pen back, underlining *I'll deal with it* so hard that the paper ripped.

Charley spoke aloud: 'So how have you enjoyed your four days?', at the same time tearing off the top sheet of paper and folding it, putting it in her jacket pocket.

It had been less than a week ago that they had first met but it felt like so much longer. Jessica still couldn't get over her story: moving to the middle of nowhere on a whim, with no friends, no family. She so wanted the other woman's bravery.

'It's been wonderful,' Jessica said, before launching into

a string of reasons why the house was the greatest place she had ever been associated with.

Wayne's body found in Manchester, Charley wrote.

Where?

Under bin bags. Dustmen nearly took him. Horrific injuries.

Jessica took the pen, hovering over the pad, talking slowly about her week for the benefit of anyone who could be listening. That's what someone's life meant – being dumped under bags of rubbish and a second or two away from becoming landfill.

How did you know it was him?

Tattoos on his upper arms matched our records + matched DNA.

Why there?

Charley shook her head, taking back the pen. *Bodies found in woods/rivers, etc = link to here as last place seen. Bodies found in their home city = they returned home.*

Jessica finished talking about how life-changing it was to eat together and read the note, thinking it just about made sense. If you buried or dumped a body, there was always a possibility it could be found and this would be the last known link. Wayne had been homeless before being recruited and had been left in the back streets where he spent years living. Liam was the same – at least twice a year someone drunk and/or high on drugs was pulled out of the canal. There was still a degree of suspicion but this at least gave everyone at the house plausible deniability. If it hadn't have been for Liam's family knowing he had come here, the police would have been none the wiser.

That did give Jessica something to think about: *How did you know Wayne was here?* she wrote.

Charley nodded towards her, mouthing: 'You,' adding out loud: 'And have you seen anything that could be described as untoward since you arrived?'

Jessica frowned, writing: *How did you tell THEM you knew he had been here?*, before insisting that everything was family-orientated and things were just perfect.

Charley shook her head, taking back the pen. *Use your imagination. We made something up.*

Jessica peered at the last line, annoyed. She could have figured it out for herself but she wanted to know exactly what the story was, desperate to feel in control. She reached across, trying to snatch the pen and glaring at Charley, who was busy talking about Wayne's background.

Charley pulled the pen and pad away, widening her eyes as if she was silently scolding a child.

How could they get the body away from here? she wrote, handing back the pad and pen.

Jessica put them down and simulated driving, acting as if someone had cut her up and sticking her middle finger up to the invisible driver.

If someone wanted to treat her like a child, then she'd act like one.

Charley shook her head, saying out loud: 'This is getting us nowhere, Jessica, there must be more to it than that.'

If anyone was listening, it sounded as if she was talking about Jessica's apparent ignorance of anything involving

Wayne but Jessica knew what she really meant, giving her a thin antagonising smile.

Minibus, she wrote.

Who drives it?

Glenn / Ali.

Ali?

Some guy who works outside. Asian.

Charley nodded, tearing off the sheet and folding it tidily into her pocket again.

Jessica was busy talking about Wayne working outside, saying that she had never seen anything strange about him. She kept hold of the pen, pulling the pad back, writing: *People here last night – throwing stones, etc. Dark/hoods.*

Charley read it, nodding again. *Locals.*

Why?

Charley shrugged, holding up her hands to indicate the room. *Jealousy? Something different? It's a bit Wicker Man around here.*

Jessica couldn't stop herself from smiling. Charley winked and suddenly Jessica felt foolish for acting so immaturely.

'You've not been very helpful,' Charley said, flicking her eyes towards the ceiling in case Jessica was in any doubt about who she was saying it for.

'How dare you,' Jessica replied, hoping someone was listening, considering the performance she was putting on. 'You come in here, trampling over our beliefs, with your stupid hair.'

Charley's grin shrunk as she tugged a strand of her hair, pointing at it.

'This is no time for personal insults,' she said, then asked Jessica if she had ever heard anyone mention Liam Renton.

Anything else? Charley wrote.

A basement.

Where?

Jessica pointed to the floor, smiling, and it was Charley's turn to stifle a laugh.

Under stairs, Jessica wrote.

Jessica feigned thinking about whether she had heard of anyone named Liam, making a humming noise for the benefit of the recording device she wasn't even sure was there.

What happens there? Charley wrote.

Some kid Kevin was beaten for having a phone.

Charley's eyes widened, realising what that could have meant for Jessica.

'I spoke to some young man named Kevin in this room,' Charley said. 'He was covered in cuts, bruises, stitches, all sorts of things. He reckons he got them by slipping and falling down the stairs. What do you say about that?'

Jessica nodded towards the word 'basement' on the pad. 'If he says he fell, then he fell.'

'You didn't see anything else?'

'No.'

'I'm going to read off a list of people we know reside here and I want you to tell me what you know about them.'

As she spoke, Charley pointed to the word 'basement', writing next to it: *Can you get in?*

Jessica shook her head, while replying 'yes' to Charley's spoken question and almost confusing herself. All she needed now was to try to pat her head and rub her stomach at the same time and it would be like being in primary school again.

'Jan Lewis,' Charley said.

'Who?'

'You might know him as Moses.'

Jessica started saying how he was a great person, writing one single word on the pad and underlining it. *Shit.*

Charley tore the page off, pocketing it again. 'Sophie Lewis?' she asked.

'Who?'

'Zipporah, Moses's wife.'

'Oh, she's lovely,' Jessica said, writing: *Beaten? Bruises, marks, etc.*

By Moses? Charley wrote.

Jessica shrugged, writing: *Moses / Glenn.*

'We've got someone here named "Glenn",' Charley said. 'We don't have a last name but he's married to someone named Naomi.'

'Who?' Jessica replied again, her stock response. Charley seemed confused, before Jessica added: 'Oh, I think I know who you mean. There's someone who runs the outdoors bit called Glenn but he doesn't seem to be too important.'

'That's what everyone's been saying.'

Jessica took the pad, writing: *Moses + Glenn = ??? He wants you to think Glenn is unimportant.*

Charley nodded to say she understood. 'How about his wife?'

'I've only seen Naomi at mealtimes,' Jessica replied, pointing to the words 'Beaten', then 'Moses / Glenn' on the pad. Aloud, she added: 'His wife is lovely. She sits opposite me at breakfast and dinner. Everyone really likes her.'

Charley was still nodding, slotting the pieces into place. She beckoned for the pen, writing: *Greenhouse?*

Jessica shook her head.

'I'd love to say you've been helpful,' Charley said out loud, 'but I'm not sure that's been the case. Everyone seems to have the exact same thing to say.'

'Perhaps that's because there's nothing for you to be looking into?'

Charley tapped the pen on the pad – pointing at the word 'Beaten', then writing *Zipporah / Naomi* next to it.

'If you have anything else to tell us about this . . .'

Jessica shook her head.

Charley again removed the page, writing at the top of the new one: *We can raid for DV.*

Jessica tried to figure out how they could get a warrant based solely on that but then remembered receiving an email about new legislation for domestic violence protection when she had been in the station. They had updates on a monthly basis and most of them were instantly forgotten, simply because there were so many. Jessica always assumed someone above her would know enough about whichever law it was that had been changed that week but that particular email had stuck in her mind because it was something she felt so strongly about.

She presumed Charley had read it properly and nodded.

No proof, Jessica wrote, indicating towards the long sleeves on Charley's jacket to imply that the women covered up.

Charley clearly understood, leaning forward to pull the pad back but Jessica added to it quickly: *Why not raid now? Wayne's dead.*

She pushed it across the table to Charley, who pointed to the words 'No proof'.

'Well, Miss, Ms, or Mrs Compton, whatever your name may be, you've been thoroughly unhelpful.'

'At least I've got a proper name, Charley, Charlotte, Charles, or whatever your name may be.'

Charley smiled. 'Let me lead you out,' she said, stepping around the table and placing a hand on Jessica's shoulder. She leant in whispering, 'You're doing great', and then opened the door, sending Jessica out into the main hall where Moses was sitting, knees crossed, a fixed, firm stare on his face.

23

'Have you finished harassing enough young women for one day?' Moses asked, addressing Charley, although Jessica thought it was quite something coming from him.

Charley stayed calm in the way Jessica rarely could when someone was aggressive to her. 'I did assure you, Mr Lewis, that we would be utterly respectful to you, your house, and everyone who lives here.'

'This is the second time you've been here recently, upsetting people. I've allowed you in both times even though I have no obligation to do so.'

'We've been here twice because we've found two bodies, each with connections to this community. I am incredibly grateful you have allowed us such freedom, especially without the need of solicitors this time, and know it must be difficult for everyone here. All I can say is that I really hope we are able to get to the bottom of what happened to both Liam and Wayne. I'm sure that is high on your list of priorities too, seeing how valued they were around here.'

Moses acted with the same assured calm he did when he was addressing the residents, opening his arms slightly to indicate how approachable he was. 'Some notice next time would be nice.'

'I would love to do that, Mr Lewis, but we don't seem to

have a phone number on record for you. Without that, I'm not sure how much notice you would like.'

'Outside communications are not permitted here.'

Charley nodded shortly, indicating towards the officer who had been waiting in the doorway of the breakfast room. 'Are you finished?' she asked.

'Yes.'

'In that case, we will leave you be, Mr Lewis. Phone or no phone, feel free to contact us if you think of anything else. We're based in the centre, I'm sure you know where. Normal office hours apply.'

With a final, 'Thank you for your time, Ms Compton,' Charley spun and headed towards the front door, half-a-dozen officers falling in behind her, each glancing back nervously towards Moses.

Jessica could not bring herself to look at Moses again, so she turned, heading through the corridor towards the stairs before he could say anything.

As she reached the first floor, Zipporah was rounding the corner, about to head downstairs. They each took a step back, apologising for nearly bumping into each other. Close up, with the sunlight beaming through the window next to them, Zipporah's bruises looked so much worse. There was a cut above her eye that had only partially healed. She had tried to cover it with make-up but the out-line was clear. The curve of her eye socket was a jaundiced yellow, her earlobe flattened and purple. She was even holding her left arm at a slight angle across herself. Having been in a few rough situations herself and not come off well, Jessica knew it was a sure sign that she was carrying an injury, probably in her upper arm.

'Are you all right?' Jessica asked.

Zipporah pursed her lips, her eyes flicking across Jessica as she weighed up how best to respond. Jessica could see a thin but probably painful split along the centre of Zipporah's top lip. The blood had dried but the mark was still clear.

'It's just a bump,' she replied, glancing away nervously.

Jessica hadn't made it clear she was referring to the injuries, so the fact Zipporah brought it up told her all she needed to know about what was on the woman's mind.

'You can tell me if there's a problem,' Jessica said carefully. She realised it was a risk but Moses's advances and veiled threats made her more determined than ever to get things finished at the house as soon as possible.

Her worst fear that Zipporah would recoil and run to Moses was instantly dispelled as the woman stayed put, first peering listlessly past Jessica out of the window and then making eye contact.

'It's not as simple as you think.'

'It's just talking.'

'Sometimes words can be dangerous, Jessica. We have to be careful about what we say and who we say it to.'

Jessica wondered what she meant. Was it a warning that other people could be listening to this conversation? Or did it come from fear that whatever was happening in her marriage would get worse if she spoke about it?

Before she could reply, Zipporah spoke again: 'If it was simply talking, it would have to be a mutual thing . . .'

Jessica had told Zipporah much of her story about losing the baby and her father – it was how she had got into the house – but she had kept things back too. Was it that obvious?

The thought flashed through her mind that this was the opportunity to tell Zipporah about why she was really there. Perhaps Zipporah herself would reciprocate, giving Jessica and Charley everything they needed to end this operation once and for all.

'What would we talk about?' Jessica asked, knowing she sounded unsure.

'It was your idea.'

Jessica so wanted to pull Zipporah into a side room and tell her everything. She wanted to leave, she didn't want to have to look at Moses, let alone risk him touching her again. Everything that had gone wrong since she'd lost the baby came down to how little she trusted other people. Even Adam was a poor second when it came to backing anyone over herself. Surely the time had come for her to put her faith in someone? She could see it in Zipporah's face: an eagerness to end this, to return to the life she must have once had before her husband poisoned it.

Jessica couldn't continue to hold her eye. 'I should really go back to my room,' she said, hating herself for not being able to put trust above her instincts. The same instinct that had brought her to this house in the first place.

'As you wish.'

Jessica stepped around Zipporah towards the final staircase just as the sun dipped behind a cloud. The landing was flushed by a dim greyness, shadowing the woman's injuries as Jessica walked away wondering if she had just turned her back on a woman in need.

Jessica sat in the bedroom with Heather, watching the empty driveway from the window.

'Do you know what the plan is for the rest of the day?' she asked, not expecting an answer.

'You shouldn't ask questions,' Heather said irritably.

Jessica didn't reply, feeling more and more alienated.

'Sorry,' Heather added after a few moments. 'I hated being in the room with those people. They were talking at me. Talking, talking, talking. Asking about things I don't know, trying to persuade me to leave.'

Jessica doubted that was true. When she turned to face Heather, she sensed something wasn't right. Earlier, Heather had been genuinely scared, cradling her own body and rocking herself. This time, she was saying similar words but her body language was different: perched on the edge of her bed, attentive and carefully watching her.

'You're still here though,' Jessica replied.

'You too.'

Jessica had interviewed enough people to know when a person was unsure how to phrase a leading question. It usually came when someone was denying something but couldn't speak quickly enough to get their words out. Heather was different, starting a sentence, stopping herself in the middle and then stumbling over the words before repeating the exact thing she had tried not to blurt out.

'What was it like for you in there?' Heather eventually asked.

Jessica could hardly tell the truth about her relationship with Charley but what was far more worrying was that it was clear Heather was asking on behalf of someone else. Given her obvious love of Moses, it was most likely him. This room was Jessica's one respite from the rest of the house; now she knew she couldn't even count on that.

'It was fine,' Jessica replied.

'What did they ask you about?'

Heather's eyes flickered all around the room – anywhere except near Jessica. She could not have been a worst choice as a source of information. The only good thing was that it indicated the interview hadn't been bugged after all.

'Just about Wayne,' Jessica said. 'They wanted to know what I'd seen and how much I knew about him.'

'What did you say?'

Jessica thought about inventing something outrageous to see who it would end up getting back to but realised it was a dangerous game to play, seeing as she was almost a prisoner here.

'I said I didn't know very much. That I'd only met him once or twice and then he left. What did you say?'

Jessica couldn't resist turning the question around so she could watch the other woman squirm a little. She didn't appreciate being spied upon and she didn't like having to permanently be on edge, especially in the one room where she was supposed to feel safe.

Heather stumbled over her reply but Jessica knew she couldn't trust her any longer and was relieved she hadn't asked her if she had ever heard of the greenhouse. If she had, it would have got straight back to whoever now had her interrogating Jessica.

As Jessica lay on her bed, feeling tired even though she hadn't done much, she realised that either Moses or Glenn – or both – were suspicious of her. Somehow she had to find out everything Charley needed her to without arousing any more suspicion.

Jessica had the bedroom to herself. Heather had been called away to work in the craft area now the police had left but the call had not come for her. She could have felt paranoid that she was being left out but chose to believe it was because of the teeming rain, keeping the outside workers indoors.

Partly because she was struggling to think her way around the events of the morning, Jessica had barely left her bed. She lay listening to the steady drumbeat of rain against the window, drifting in and out of sleep, trying to think of a way she could get into the basement and wondering what and where the greenhouse could be.

Her muddled mind misheard the knock at the door the first time, confusing it with the rain. It was louder the second time, the thump of fist on wood shaking her out of her daydream back into the present. Her first fear was that it was Moses returning but as she swung her legs off the bed, she quickly realised he wouldn't have bothered knocking.

Ali had half-turned to walk away when Jessica opened

the door. 'Oh, it's you,' he said, before correcting himself. 'Sorry, I was looking for Heather.'

'She was called down to the work room an hour or so ago.'

'Oh right, of course. I assumed because we were off that everyone was.'

Jessica shrugged. 'I thought we were staying inside because it was raining. I've been waiting for someone to come and get me.'

Ali was bobbing awkwardly from one foot to the other. 'How are you, er, doing with it all?' he asked. Unlike Heather, he appeared to be just nervous, rather than trying to cross-examine her.

'Working? I've only had one day. I was ill yesterday, then we've been off today.'

'Sorry, of course. So much has happened this week that everything's blended together. It seems like ages ago that you came along.'

Jessica couldn't argue with that. It was hard to keep track of time. She knew it was only four days that she had been here but it felt like weeks.

'Can I help?' she asked, craving someone to talk to who didn't have an obvious desire to investigate her every word.

'Not really, I was . . .' Ali glanced over Jessica's shoulder and she saw the hopeful gaze he had been sporting dissolve into disappointment. She might not be an expert on relationships but it told her he had a thing for Heather. If they were both off, he had hoped to spend an afternoon with her. Jessica wondered if he knew about Heather's feelings for Moses. She doubted it.

'It's been a hard week with Wayne and everything,' he said.

'I didn't realise you were friends.'

'It's not that, it's because we all end up hearing each other's stories. I always felt drawn to him because we'd been through a lot of the same things.'

Jessica flicked her head, indicating for him to come into the bedroom but he shook his head.

'I think I'll come back to find Heather later,' he said, before turning and heading back towards the stairs.

24

Dinner was another tense affair. Moses's Bible reading was from Isaiah, about traitors and destroyers. He thanked everyone for their cooperation through the day, insisting he would not allow 'outside forces' to corrupt what they had. He seemed edgy, which only fed the uncertain atmosphere in the room. Jessica couldn't figure out if he was doing it on purpose as a way of bringing them together, or if he had genuinely been rattled by the police visit.

'Would anyone like to share their thoughts about today?' he asked, scanning along the table. Jessica wouldn't meet his eye.

He waited in silence to see if anyone would respond but the room stayed eerily silent. As well as Moses at the front, Jessica could sense Glenn glaring across the table too. Something had changed and she didn't know what.

When it was clear no one was going to speak, Moses said a prayer for Wayne, their 'brother who has passed', and then excused them for the evening.

Jessica followed the others through the hallways but the mood was subdued, few people bothering to speak to each other. The games room was similarly quiet, the only sound being the thud of darts into the board and the clatter of snooker balls into each other.

Over the past few months, so many people had told

Jessica she should talk to someone about everything that had happened to her that she had simply stopped speaking to anybody. She had almost forgotten how to interact but this felt like people were going out of their way to avoid talking to her. She would glance up, only to see people quickly look away; try to start a conversation only to have it shot down with a one-word answer.

It wasn't the first time she had been unpopular in a group situation and probably wouldn't be the last – assuming she got out of the house. But in all past situations, she knew why she was in that position, usually because she had spoken out of turn or wound someone up either accidentally or, more likely, on purpose. This time, she wasn't sure but the unease had begun with Moses's advances that morning, continued with Heather's obvious fishing for information, and now culminated in people apparently not talking to her. Was it something she had said or done? Or was this some new sort of test to see how she would react? Worse still, was she becoming paranoid? It wouldn't be the first time she had been accused of thinking everything revolved around her.

Still, this felt real. Heather would usually sit close to her but she was on the opposite side of the room, refusing to acknowledge anything. What little chat there was around the room related solely to the games.

As well as the feeling that she had somehow annoyed the others, Jessica was bored, stuck in the house with pastimes she would usually have no interest in, surrounded by people she had no connection to and couldn't trust.

For the first time in months, she missed her old life: her job, her friends, driving to work, forgetting her coat, the buzz of finding a lead. Most of all, she missed Adam and the way it used to be before things had fallen apart.

Again.

She longed for the weekend they'd spent trying to decorate but mainly making a mess. He was one of the few people who actually understood her, let alone could put up with her. He was in the small minority of people she could tolerate for longer than a few minutes here or there.

Cole might have been manipulative in getting her here, Charley might have been taking advantage by using everything that had happened to her as fuel to get her into the house, but what they had both achieved was to make her appreciate what she had left in her life, as opposed to the things she had lost.

The irony was that it had taken coming to this place for her to realise it. She wanted to return home but knew she couldn't be happy there unless she finished the job here.

How much of her life would still be left standing when she eventually got out, she didn't know.

Jessica felt as depressed as she had done since arriving at the house but that was coupled with a greater sense of purpose to get it all over with. Knowing she wasn't going to get anything done by sitting around being ignored, she left the room without a word, heading into the deserted corridors and going for a walk. She checked each of the paintings to see if any were of the house and could perhaps give a clue to what the greenhouse was. Nothing jumped out but she at least felt like she was doing something.

Jessica did one full lap of the ground floor before heading up the stairs, stopping at the top and staring out of the central window towards the land beyond. The moon was lower but larger, the white so bright that everything across the gardens could be seen clearly.

Lost in the view, Jessica heard movement behind her. Thinking it was someone going up to bed, she didn't turn, assuming they wouldn't want to say anything to her anyway.

It was only when the bag was slipped over her head and the hand covered her mouth that she realised someone in the house was ready to have a word.

25

Jessica knew how to look after herself. She swung her elbows back viciously but her attacker knew what to do, stepping close and wrenching her arms up into a full nelson before yanking them down again as her wrists were clamped together with plastic ties. The ends were pulled tightly, a male voice shushing her as she squealed in pain. Jessica tried to flail her legs but they were kicked out from under her, leaving her writhing on the floor.

The backs of her knees were burning from the force of the blow, the ties cutting so deeply into her wrists that they were already going numb. As she breathed in, Jessica got a mouthful of the harsh hessian material, scratching her lips and leaving her gasping. Instinct told her to panic, to fight and thrash, but she already knew she was beaten. Flashes of every tight situation she had ever been in swirled through her mind: being choked in her own hallway by a mass murderer, paralysed and unable to move after being injected with a drug, almost being caught breaking into a house by the police waiting outside.

The fire.

Smoke seeping into her lungs, clouding her thoughts, making her chest heavy, leaving her at the mercy of the flames.

As she was roughly hauled up, Jessica's feet bounced

limply on the floor but the horrors of what she had been through helped her to compose herself. The bag was tied around her neck, leaving a small gap at the bottom. If she breathed steadily, she would be fine, leaving herself with enough energy to fight if the opportunity came. If she panicked now, she would quickly tire before she had a chance to assess what was going on.

She may have made many mistakes in the past but she at least tried to learn from them.

'Walk,' a male voice ordered, so Jessica obeyed, allowing whoever it was to direct her down the stairs. It didn't sound like Glenn's but she couldn't figure out who else the voice could belong to, her hearing muffled by the bag, judgement clouded by the way her heart was beating so quickly.

Her worst fear was that Moses was involved. If he was bold enough to touch her when she was able to fight back then what might he be like when she was helpless?

Be calm. Concentrate.

The footsteps were soft on the carpeted floors but Jessica was attempting to work out how many people there were. The male voice belonged to the person with a hand on her shoulder but she tried to blank his movements, as well as her own, paying attention to the other sounds.

It was difficult to know for sure as it had happened so quickly but she thought there must be at least two people involved because of how her wrists were tied.

At first Jessica could hear nothing but her own movements but then she caught it: a soft creak of the banister. She was being led one step at a time down the centre of the staircase but, behind her, someone was using the handrail. It was gentle but there was a definite groan from the antique wood, a protest at the years of being shunted back and forth supporting any number of people ascending and descending.

As they reached the bottom, Jessica tried to figure out where she was being taken but there was no attempt to disguise the route to the front door. Whoever was holding her told her to be still and then she heard the clunk of the bolt opening, before being instructed to walk.

Even through the bag, Jessica could feel the change in temperature. The cool night air sent a shiver rippling through her, the bright white of the moon creeping through the small holes in the material and disorientating her even further.

First there was the solid crunch of the concrete and loose stones underneath her feet, then the squelchy, slippery surface of the lawn. Jessica closed her eyes, blocking the dazzling mix of light and dark that was making her dizzy, focusing on the sounds around her.

She listened for the second set of footsteps splashing through the mud, trying to figure out if it sounded like someone with thick, clumping footsteps, or if it was daintier. Jessica was struggling to keep her footing, the way her hands were clamped behind her back making it difficult to balance across the wet, uneven terrain and almost impossible to discern the individual movements of anyone other than herself.

Still she stayed calm, waiting for the persuasive pokes

and prods in her back and shoulder that were directing her further away from the house.

'Wait,' the voice insisted and Jessica again did as she was told. Perhaps it was Glenn, after all. It had the husky roughness she associated with him but was slightly higher in pitch.

A gate squeaked open and a hand snaked around her waist, pulling her forward.

'Wait,' they repeated after she stepped through.

Underfoot, she could feel thin, sodden twigs and knew she had been brought to the woods. Somewhere in the distance, an owl hooted but there were other noises too; creatures scurrying in the undergrowth, snaps and crackles from the far reaches of the darkness.

Jessica's shoulders were beginning to cramp from the harsh angle they had been secured in. She tried to wriggle her fingers but could feel nothing but pins and needles. Her training in how to put on handcuffs had been such a long time ago that she could barely remember it, but it was something hard to get wrong. The biggest mistake people made was putting them on too tightly. The fact she was already feeling numb meant the ties had been pulled far too forcefully. She clenched and unclenched her fists, trying to stimulate the circulation but only making her shoulder pain worse.

She could feel her heart thumping faster, realising that a few more minutes in the restraints meant her hands would be useless if she was ever released.

'They're too tight,' Jessica whimpered, trying to sound as girly and pathetic as she could. She needed whoever it was to underestimate her, perhaps even feel sorry for her.

'Keep moving.' The voice was definitely Glenn's.

'They're hurting me, Glenn.'

Jessica knew it was a risk but she wanted to humanise both herself and him. She still didn't know who the second person was, or if there was even a third or fourth. It was easy to commit acts upon someone whose face was covered. Only true monsters would look into a victim's eyes and still not care what they inflicted upon them.

The base of a hand pressed into the lower part of her back, pushing her forward.

'I can't feel my fingers, Glenn,' Jessica pleaded again.

'Shut up and keep walking.'

'I am walking but my arms are going numb. They're too tight, it's hurting.'

'Not long now.'

'Where are we going?'

This time the shove in her back was more pronounced, Jessica's feet knocking together, making her stagger. Instinctively she tried to move her hands to stop herself falling but that only made the plastic dig in further and it was too late. She slipped, stumbling forward face-first, bracing herself for the impact. Before she felt the blow, she realised someone was holding her up from behind, clenching the waistband of her trousers to stop her falling. They didn't say anything but Jessica's eyes popped open, the gentle haze of moonlight still befuddling her as it seeped through the minuscule holes in the bag.

The person holding her trousers didn't let go, hauling

her up and then pushing her forward. She might have lost weight but she wasn't that small and the display of strength was as impressive as it was worrying. Assuming it was Glenn, he had lifted her one-handed without so much as a grunt of exertion.

Despite her awareness of the situation, knowing she shouldn't panic, Jessica was beginning to feel her body's instincts taking over. She was gasping for deeper breaths even though she knew she shouldn't; she was battling against the harsh ties, even though it was making it worse.

It was only when Jessica felt the patter on her arms that she realised it was raining. She wondered if whoever had brought her out here might change their mind, or at least take her somewhere dry, but they kept their grip firmly on the band of her trousers.

Water began leaking through the canvas, soaking her head, making the material stick to her skin. Breathing was instantly harder, every mouthful offering a taste of the roughness of the sack instead of the air she craved.

Stay calm.

Jessica's foot rattled into something solid and she felt the hand holding her, preventing her from falling over the top of it.

'Sit.'

Jessica had never realised how hard it could be to perform such a simple task without the use of her hands. She turned around, trying to lower herself, but couldn't stabilise her body enough to stop herself falling backwards. Her backside hit the wood hard, her trousers absorbing the wetness of what felt like a tree trunk. Again, she felt the hand on her, gripping her tightly and preventing her tumbling.

She sat, waiting for further instructions, listening to the noises around her, unable to distinguish if the sound of footsteps came from one person or half-a-dozen. It felt as if people were circling her but it was difficult to be sure because the rain was tinkling from all of the surfaces around her. It took her a few moments to realise that whatever additional sounds there had been were now gone.

Still it rained.

'Hello?' Jessica said, unable to fight the panic she had been suppressing. She started to stand but could not get enough leverage through her legs without using her arms. There was still a dull ache at the back of her knees from where she had been kicked at the top of the stairs.

Jessica could hear nothing but drizzle, licking the trees, pounding the bark, soaking the soil. As a shiver tore through her, she gasped in shock as the hood was snatched away in one clean movement. She hadn't felt anyone loosening it at the back, which left her wondering if it was ever as tight as she'd thought.

Crisp, cold air filled her lungs making her cough viciously. She couldn't see anything other than a bright white light. She blinked quickly to try to clear the mixture of pain and confusion. Slowly, the scene drifted into view, silhouetted tree trunks and low-hanging branches encircling a clearing.

Someone walked around the stump she was sitting on, their hazy outline gradually becoming a man: short, thickset, big arms.

Glenn said nothing, standing imposingly over her, waiting.

'My wrists hurt,' Jessica said.

He didn't move.

Jessica tried flexing her fingers again but it felt like somebody was stabbing something sharp into them.

Glenn's eyes flickered over her head before quickly focusing on her again. She could sense a person – or people – behind her.

'What is your name?' Glenn eventually said, his words dissolving away with the rain.

'You know my name.'

He didn't move, arms clamped to his side, eyes fixed. Jessica couldn't stop herself shivering, rain streaming down her back, her clothes and hair sticking to her.

'What is your name?' he repeated.

'Jessica Compton.'

Could he know she was lying?

'Why are you here?'

'I'm not sure. Zipporah invited me.'

A slight shake of the head. 'Why are you here?'

'I've had problems, with my dad, with my life. Zipporah said she could help.'

'You're not answering the question.'

'I am!' Glenn seemed unaffected by the weather but Jessica's teeth were chattering. 'I don't know what you want me to say,' she added, unable to stop the frustration creeping into her voice.

'I want you to tell me why you're here.'

'Because I need help.'

'How?'

'Zipporah listened to me in Manchester when I told her about my dad and my baby. She said there was a safe place I could come where other people like me lived together peacefully and everybody helped everyone else. I thought it sounded right for me.'

'You've still not answered the question.'

'I have!'

Jessica didn't know what he wanted to hear. Her reason for coming had been because Cole and Charley thought she was the person they had been looking for. She couldn't tell Glenn that – but the truth was Zipporah had been persuasive. She listened without making judgements about Jessica's character, without that stupid tilt to her head that everyone seemed to have when they were trying to be sympathetic. Jessica had spent months shying away from talking about her problems and yet, ultimately, that was what had brought her here.

'I wanted to be helped,' Jessica said, suddenly realising it was the answer he wanted. It wasn't even false.

This time Glenn nodded. 'Have you been?'

It sounded like such a ridiculous question considering the situation she was in. She remembered sitting in the rain before being allowed into the house. Since then it had been an endless stream of initiations: the trust exercise by the fireplace, being groped, ignored, given tough manual labour with an impossible target, denied access to the outside world and left unsettled by the lack of a clock or calendar.

This was the final insult, something that apparently built character by breaking you down first.

It dawned on Jessica that it had simply made her more determined to do what she always did: win. If that could be described as helping then so be it.

'Yes,' she replied.

'How?'

'Being with everyone has helped me see things differently.'

It was the truth: mainly she had seen how vulnerable people could be manipulated.

'Why do you think we have brought you out here?'

'I don't know.'

'I asked you why you *thought* we'd brought you here, not if you knew.'

Glenn's relentlessness was so intense that Jessica felt more intimidated by him than ever, especially with her arms still tied behind her. She was at his mercy and yet, so far, all he had done was talk.

'I think it's because you're a bully.'

Jessica wanted a reaction but the one that came wasn't what she expected. Glenn flicked his head upwards, signalling to whoever was behind her.

Jessica heard a shuffling sound, turning to see Ali emerge from the shadows behind, the dim light of the moon glinting a dangerous white from the blade of the knife in his hand.

He crossed to Glenn, handing him the knife and then spinning around to face Jessica. For a moment, he said nothing, his eyes scanning her up and down, before he uttered five words that Jessica had dreaded hearing since the day she had entered the house.

'We know who you are.'

26

Jessica couldn't take her eyes from the blade. Glenn was moving it from one hand back to the other, his attention now on the blade instead of her. As he twisted it around, the light caught the edge, reflecting chillingly through the rain towards her.

'Thank you, Ali,' Glenn said.

Ali couldn't meet her eyes either and Jessica was left staring at them, the only sound being the slowing rain.

How could they know who she was? Charley had suggested she could use a fake name to get into the house but Jessica knew she would never be able to remember to answer to anything other than her own. 'Jessica Compton' was close enough, the name she should have had if it wasn't for an administrative error in Las Vegas. It didn't mean anything to anyone else other than her and Adam. No one at the house had asked for any sort of identification, or taken anything from her with her name on. The only way they could have found out who she was would have been if they somehow knew her real last name. Then they could have discovered pictures of her on the Internet as Jessica Daniel, found out what she did and who she worked for.

'Why are we here, Ali?' Jessica asked, thinking he would be the more approachable of the two. 'Why have you got a knife?'

He glanced towards Glenn, who replied: 'You've been asking too many questions – querying our methods and our ways. It has been noticed.'

Jessica knew it had to have been Heather who had gone to either Moses or Glenn. Strangely, Jessica didn't feel angry with her. She was a young girl who had been through a lot and then ended up being manipulated by Moses. He didn't love her; he probably didn't love anyone except himself. But he was happy to leave that hope hanging for all the girls, presumably to engineer moments where people would come to him and tell him anything untoward they had seen.

She wondered if he was still behind her, waiting in the woods, keeping to the shadows, ready to announce himself. It seemed his way to get other people to do the dirty work for him.

Heather was someone who had never been given a chance to grow up. She wanted to be loved to make up for her loss but she was never going to find that here, even if Ali had a thing for her. If anything ever happened between them, Moses would probably do everything he could to stop it, perhaps even make a new rule that people in the house could not partner with anyone else unless they were married. No doubt he would find a reason why it corrupted the mind.

'Why are you here, Ali?' Jessica asked, trying to speak in a slightly higher tone, sounding girly and vulnerable.

Glenn answered for him. 'He has to learn the ropes.'

As he spoke, Jessica attempted to wriggle her wrists, hoping that by some miracle the plastic ties had been affected by the rain. If anything they felt tighter, cutting and digging into her flesh.

'The ropes for what?'

'How things work around here.'

'How do they work?'

Glenn didn't reply at first, while the sprinkling of rain ended as suddenly as it had begun. For a couple of seconds there was silence and then isolated spots began dribbling from leaves overhead, patting the already sodden ground in a disjointed symphony.

It felt like he was waiting for a silence that didn't come, staring at the blade in his hand as Ali carefully looked on.

'I'm not sure you're in a position to be asking questions,' he eventually replied.

'What are you going to do to me?'

Glenn ignored her query, asking his own. 'Why *have* you been asking questions?'

'Because this place is new to me. I want to fit in but the only way I can do that is by figuring out how everything works.'

Glenn crouched, picking up a piece of wood from the floor and running the blade along its length. 'Why are you really here?'

'I told you, I want to be helped.'

'Who do you work for?'

'I work in a post office. Worked. Now I work with you outdoors in the gardens.'

Jessica thought of Ali's statement – 'we know who you are'. If that was really true, there would be no need for any of this. Surely she'd already be dead?

'You're lying,' Glenn said, not looking up.

'I'm not.'

Three more times he asked variations of the same questions, asking what her name was, where she came from, what she did and why she was there.

Then he came to the question Jessica suspected was the reason why she was there: 'What did you tell the police this morning?'

'I told them I didn't really know Wayne as I had only been here for a few days.'

'Did they ask if you saw him leave?'

'I said that I hadn't. That's the truth, isn't it?'

Jessica didn't expect a reply and she didn't get one. 'Did they offer you anything for information?'

'What information? I don't know anything.'

Glenn peered up from the blade, dropping the wood and stepping closer. Ali was a little behind him but Jessica could tell he was nervous from the way his arms were crossed. He wasn't as ruthless as Glenn in any sense, so if he appeared worried, then she should be.

'That wasn't the question I asked,' Glenn said.

'Sorry, I know. They didn't offer me anything.'

'Did they ask you about individual people within the house?'

'Yes.'

'Who?'

'You.'

Jessica expected a reaction and, although Glenn tried to hide it, he couldn't prevent one of his eyelids from twitching. He passed the knife from one hand to the other and half-turned to look at Ali. Jessica saw the widening of Glenn's eyes, the annoyance. He didn't say anything but the expression said it all: 'I told you so'.

He twisted back to Jessica, trying to seem as calm as before, but he was standing a little straighter, rattled. 'What did you tell them?'

'I said you worked outdoors.'

'What else?'

'That you were married to someone called Naomi. That's it, I don't know anything else.'

'Did you tell them about what happened with Wayne?'

When you assaulted him?

'Moses explained to me what had happened. I didn't say anything.'

A hush fell across the woods as the last few raindrops hit the ground. Jessica was freezing and couldn't stop herself from shivering. There was an itch at the centre of her forehead that she couldn't raise her hands to touch. The best she could do was crinkle up her skin in an effort to make it go away.

'What are you doing?' Glenn asked.

'I need to scratch my head.'

Jessica hoped either of them would show some sort of sympathy by cutting her free or, at the absolute least, scratching it for her. Neither of them moved.

'Who else did they ask about?'

'Moses.'

'What did you say?'

'That he seemed like a good man. That he was well respected and helped a lot of people.'

'Who else?'

'Zipporah – I told them she was a good listener and had brought me here.'

'Anything else?'

'I don't know anything else.'

'What did you tell them about the house?'

'Nothing, they didn't ask.'

This conversation made Jessica even more certain that the room she had been in with Charley wasn't bugged. It would have made things a lot easier if they had known that at the time.

Glenn motioned for Ali to come to him and they turned their backs, facing into the darkness of the woods. Jessica could hear their voices but they were speaking far too quietly for her to catch individual words. When they turned around, the knife was in Ali's hand again.

'You know what to do,' Glenn said reassuringly as Ali started to walk towards her.

Jessica could see how uncomfortable the blade appeared in his grasp. It was long and thick, not quite like a machete but not far off. His arm was trembling as his fingers clenched the handle tightly; the sure sign of someone not used to holding a weapon.

He wouldn't catch Jessica's eye, staring over her head into the woods beyond as he approached. Jessica felt her heart rate increasing, adrenaline starting to flood her body. She tried to stand but her legs were useless, pained from the kick, stiff from sitting too low. All she ended up doing was falling sideways, her ear clattering into the rough bark of the log. Every movement Jessica made seemed to make the ties feel tighter as Ali reached her, stepping behind the log and pulling her back into a sitting position.

'Get on with it,' Glenn said irritably from across the clearing. Jessica glanced up to see that he wasn't even watching properly, standing sideways, tapping his foot as if eager to get into the warm.

'I'm sorry about this,' Ali said softly, regretfully. 'I'm not very good with a knife.'

27

Jessica waited. She had been through many things over the years but through all of that, she had never felt a blade enter her. She'd experienced people using syringes and stun guns on her, she had been punched, kicked and witnessed a young thug pull out a sawn-off shotgun. Knives were scary weapons though, a twist here, a few centimetres too low there, and suddenly your intestines were falling out of your body. In the hands of someone who knew what they were doing, they could kill instantly or lead to a long, painful death. With someone who didn't have a clue, there would simply be pain. Jessica doubted Ali had enough knowledge of anatomy to know what the difference was.

She closed her eyes, knowing there was nothing she could do to stop it as, unexpectedly, her wrists snapped apart, flopping uselessly by her sides.

Ali stepped around to the other side of the log, the neatly clipped plastic ties in his hand.

'Sorry if I was too close to your skin,' he said.

Jessica's hands had been so full of pins and needles that she hadn't even noticed the blade next to them.

'You passed,' Glenn called out, walking closer. 'We know you're a lost soul the same as so many in the house.'

We know who you are.

'I . . . thank you,' Jessica mumbled as a reply, unsure what else to say. She was clenching and unclenching her fists, trying to get some feeling back into them.

Ali sat on the log next to Jessica, passing the knife to Glenn, who clipped it onto his belt.

'I'll be by the gate,' Glenn said, walking away into the shadows.

'What's going on?' Jessica asked.

'Sometimes the group thing in the house gets a bit much,' Ali replied. 'I've wanted to talk to you since we first met in the games room.'

'You didn't have to do all of this!'

Ali apologised, adding: 'It wasn't my idea. That's not what all of this was for.'

'What was it about then?'

Ali opened up his arms to indicate the house. 'It's about everything here. This is the way things are done.'

Jessica didn't understand.

'I've not had a good time of things,' Ali continued. 'It's this place that has helped me overcome everything.'

The combination of her soaked hair and clothes, the shivering and the clipped chatter of her teeth made Jessica think that this wasn't the best place to have a cosy chat, even as it dawned on her that was exactly what Ali wanted. Given everything that had happened over the evening, she figured she might as well oblige.

'If you were struggling with things, why come here?' she asked. 'I understand that it's working for you but there are lots of other places too.'

'It's the house, the location, the people. It's Moses and

the way he talks to you. He wants you to be a better person, which makes you want to be better yourself. Don't you feel that?'

'Moses certainly has something about him . . .'

'Exactly. I realise I shamed my family with the drink and the drugs but it's being here that has helped me to change things.'

So vague, so little detail.

'Is there something specific though?'

Ali glanced away from her, his face half-lit by the moon, which had reappeared and was shining brightly again. He was biting on the inside of his mouth. 'There was a particular moment that changed things for me.'

'What?'

'It's awkward . . . I don't know if I should talk about it. I don't know if he would appreciate it.'

'Moses?'

'Glenn.'

Jessica felt a flurry in her chest, knowing she needed to hear what he had to say. She tried to sound as cool as she could. 'He seems like a decent guy.'

She didn't believe her own words but Ali seemed to be warming to her, smiling crookedly as he ran a hand through his dark hair. 'He is. I know you're new and sometimes he can seem a bit abrupt but he does other things too. Like tonight – helpful things.'

'Like with you?'

'Yes . . .'

Jessica knew she had him.

'It was late one evening. I hadn't been here for too long

but I was feeling a bit of withdrawal. You get used to certain things. Mine was living on the streets and drinking. I had been waking up sweating in the middle of the night, and it was probably clear to everyone that I was struggling.'

'What happened?'

'Glenn took me out of the house one evening. I thought he was going to take me off-site entirely, perhaps even expel me, but he led me across the gardens, through this gate and into these woods.'

He stopped, pointing over a copse in the distance where Jessica couldn't see.

'We sat on the edge of this small lake and he simply asked why I was here.'

Jessica knew she somehow had to get a look at the lake, if only to see what was around it. She couldn't risk asking Ali if there was a greenhouse nearby but now it was clear that the area wasn't just a patch of overgrown land left to its own devices. She wondered if she could get away to take a look.

'What did you say?'

'Everything I had said before about wanting to get clean and being a better person.'

'That was what enforced your opinion about everything?'

Ali shuffled uncomfortably. 'We were only out here for a short time. Glenn told me that if I was committed then I had to prove it, then he started walking back to the house. I didn't know what he meant until I returned to my room. On my pillow were bottles of vodka and whisky. I knew straight away that it was a test. I sat there for ages just staring at them, remembering the taste and the feeling. Later that night, I went to find Glenn and asked him to take them away. After that, there was never another problem.'

Jessica thought that explained the alcohol and drugs she had found in Moses's office at least to a degree. Their way of deciding who was worthy of staying in the community was apparently by offering people their vices and seeing who gave in. It also explained how Wayne had got his hands on alcohol ahead of his own breakdown – someone had given it to him. That either meant Glenn's outrage at seeing him drunk was an act, or he genuinely didn't know.

With the tests, like the one she had just been through, some like Ali passed, others like Wayne and perhaps Liam failed. With them both dead, that left Jessica with the obvious question: was their murder the punishment for failing?

'Why all of this, though?' Jessica asked. 'The bag, the kick, the shoves, the ties. You could have just asked me to come out here and I would have done.'

Ali shrugged. 'I don't make the rules. We all have to go through it, though. It questions our motives, making us ask what we're hoping to achieve.'

Jessica doubted that. They might not be Ali's rules but the only thing Glenn or Moses were hoping to achieve was to find out what she had told the police.

For the first time in what seemed like a long while, Jessica could feel the tips of her fingers again. She pressed her hands onto the bark and pushed herself upwards, swaying slightly on her wobbly legs but still keeping balance.

'I want to go inside,' she said, unable to stop herself shivering.

Ali stood, placing an arm on Jessica's shoulder, which only made her colder as it pressed the damp material onto her skin.

As he led her through the woods, Jessica turned from side to side, trying to take everything in. If she could somehow get out of the house, she wanted to remember the route back to the clearing and then the lake beyond. She pinpointed the taller, spikier trees, memorising the twists and turns in the absence of any path. Ali knew the woods so well he must have been out here a few times before.

Glenn was waiting by the gate, as he had said. 'Are you done?' he asked Ali.

'Yes.'

'Good.' He turned to Jessica. 'You should know that both Moses and Zip are very pleased to have you here. Hopefully you will become a large part of our community in times to come.'

Jessica hoped not.

'Of course, we all hope you will fully embrace the lifestyle,' he added.

Before giving her a chance to respond, Glenn turned, unclipping the gate and holding it open for Ali and her to pass through.

Jessica wondered exactly what he meant, hoping he wasn't referring to Moses's advances.

They started to walk back to the house but Jessica found it slow going, her legs cramping and unsteady across the uneven lawn.

As they began to descend a slope, Jessica stumbled, tripping over a loose twig and collapsing to her knees. Glenn turned, a look that was largely annoyance on his face. She couldn't work out if he had any genuine concern for her, or if he simply enjoyed taking people to the woods and scaring them. He took a few steps backwards, offering his hand.

'Come on,' he muttered.

Jessica took his hand with her left, placing her right on his belt and hauling herself up with a grunt.

'Sorry,' she said. 'It was sitting on that log, my legs went to sleep.'

Glenn turned, shaking his head. 'Whatever.'

Luckily for Jessica, he was so concerned at wiping his hands on his top that he didn't notice her slippery fingers sliding across his belt. She flicked the carabiner clip and tugged away the basement key she had seen him putting there – the one two-thirds of the way around that wasn't on a big loop. She slipped it into her sleeve, a trick she had been taught by Hugo, and then followed him the rest of the way back to the house, knowing tonight was the night she would find out what was in the basement.

SIX MONTHS AGO

The doctor might as well have been speaking Swahili for all Jessica cared. She peered over his thinning grey hair at the chart on the wall, reading the letters from the top in silence, making sure she nodded when he paused.

As a child, she'd loved being able to read every line of the sight chart, starting at the bottom right with the smallest letter, moving up to the biggest one at the top just to show off. Now she could read the top three lines clearly, make out the one after that if she squinted and have an educated guess about the contents of the fifth line because of the shapes. The bottom two were a blur of zigzags and swirls.

Around the rest of the room was a variety of charts and posters, a map of the world split into zones showing what jabs you needed where and a multitude of other things Jessica skimmed across so that she didn't have to pay attention.

'. . . How does that sound, Miss Daniel?'

Jessica focused back on the doctor as he addressed her. His face was tired, showing a lifetime of giving people bad news. She wondered how you ever got used to it. She certainly hadn't, though it was rarely down to her to do the death knocks in the early hours of the morning any longer. The man in front of her had spent his career telling people they had any number of problems in their lives that he either couldn't fix, or would spend a long time attempting to do so with no guarantee he would ever succeed.

When she was young, Jessica's father always told her she could be anything she wanted to be, pointing up at the planes that flew over and saying she could fly one if she tried hard enough. He'd say there was a big wide world out there and that she had to find her own place in it. Her mother had always been quieter, almost with an expectation that she would find a nice man, settle down nearby and give them lots of grandchildren. If she ever got bored, there was still the post office they ran which could be handed down. When Jessica had gone to the hospital after tripping and cutting the inside of her knee, the doctors and nurses had been so kind that she had asked her father if she could be a doctor when she grew up. He told her that of course she could – except that it wasn't all about giving little girls a lollipop to make them feel better.

Now Jessica stared at the doctor's desk, wondering if there was a tub of sweets in one of the drawers. She felt weary, unable to look at him properly, glancing back above him at the eye chart.

'I can't see the bottom two lines properly,' she said.

There was a pause. Jessica felt Adam shuffle in the chair next to her. The doctor's eyes flitted towards him and then back to her.

'I'm sorry, Miss Daniel, I—'

'It's Jessica. I don't like the formality.'

The doctor sounded flustered. 'Jessica. I apologise. I was asking if you—'

'I know what you were asking. I'm just saying that I think my eyesight is starting to go. I used to be able to read the bottom line, no problem. Now it could say anything.'

'I, erm . . .'

Adam tried to cut in. 'Jess, we can always get you to an optician if you want but you need to make a decision about what he's asking you.'

'E, K, J, that's the top two lines. Then it's I, L, P, then M, J, E, B. Although that last one might be a P.' Jessica scraped her chair forward, squinting as much as she could. 'I think the next line starts with a G, but it might be a C. Then it's I, U, D and I think the last one is a V. After that, I have no idea.'

'Jess . . .'

Jessica snapped, turning to face Adam. 'What?'

'He's trying to help. He said there was a very small likelihood of things working. A small hope is better than no hope.'

Jessica waved a hand in his face, turning her attention to the map. 'That's utter bollocks. It's the type of bullshit we come out with when someone's gone missing. It's always: "We're hopeful he'll return", "We're following up a number of promising leads", "We're narrowing down the search parameters", and then two days later we find the poor fucker in a ditch where we knew he was going to be the whole time.'

She flashed a hand towards the doctor, not looking at

him. '"Small likelihood", you might as well just say, "You've got no fucking hope, love", and show me the door.'

The venom of her language silenced the room. Even the people in the waiting area outside seemed to have gone quiet, the birds that had been chirping outside scared away too.

'I'm sorry, Miss . . . Jessica,' the doctor said. 'I know it's hard for you. There is no easy way to say it. I am simply trying to lay out a few options for you.'

Jessica didn't reply. The fact he was still being polite after she had needlessly torn him off a strip annoyed her even more.

'Perhaps it would be better if we took some information away,' Adam said. 'We can have a look through everything and then come back at another time.'

The doctor spun his chair around until he was facing the computer. He started typing and then a printer whirred to life at the back of the room.

Jessica continued staring at the map, thinking of how few places she had actually visited. Aside from a year backpacking around south-east Asia, something which opened her eyes to how big the world was, she'd done nothing other than visit a couple of places in Europe and have a week in Las Vegas that left her with nothing but bad memories.

'Seven billion people,' she said.

The doctor spun back to face her. 'Sorry?'

Jessica nodded towards the map. 'Seven billion people live here. All different shapes, sizes and skin colours. Most nice, some not.'

She was waiting for Adam to correct her, to say there was only six point nine, or seven point one. Usually, he would be putting her straight before he'd even known he was doing it. This time he stayed silent. The doctor clearly didn't know what to say either. Across the room, the printer went quiet.

'Seven billion people and I'll never be able to add a one to the end of it.'

She wanted someone to say something, even if it was a lie. None of this 'We've had a small degree of success in clinical testing' nonsense, not a vague 'You can keep trying'. She wanted the doctor to tell her that her body wasn't a complete mess, that he'd somehow mixed up her results with somebody else's and that she could have children after all.

He couldn't even meet her eye.

Jessica didn't wait for either him or Adam, opening the door and bounding through the hallways, ignoring the gum-chewing bored-looking receptionist and hurrying towards the exit. She couldn't bear to look at the clean walls or read the stupid slogans of the posters any longer.

Adam caught her as she pushed through the supposedly automatic door, which was taking its time to register she was actually there. She ignored the way it groaned as she shoved her way out, striding to the edge of the car park.

'Jess,' Adam said.

'What?'

'Are we going to talk about this?'

'What is there to talk about?'

She had no idea where they had parked, heading up a

set of steps and emerging into a garden that she didn't know existed. Not wanting to admit she had gone the wrong way, she went left, cutting across a flower bed and stepping over a low wall into the actual car park, as if she had meant to go that way in the first place.

She still couldn't remember where the car was, turning right and walking quickly past a row of vehicles before glancing up and seeing the 'Staff Car Park' sign. Adam was at the top of a set of steps at the far end.

'It's this way,' he called, one hand on his hip, waiting patiently.

The smug prick.

If there's one thing she hated, it was people who were always right.

Jessica followed him, pretending that she wasn't. When he cut in between two parked cars, she made sure she went between two different cars, just to make it clear she was finding her own route and definitely not tracking him.

Regardless of how clever he was, she still had one up on him because she had the car keys. As he reached the vehicle, she slowed her pace, stopping to tie her shoes, taking a slightly longer way around, making him wait.

She wanted him to say something, even to tap his foot anxiously. Instead he did nothing.

In the car, he placed the pile of papers on the back seat, still not speaking as Jessica pulled away carefully.

She had only reached the end of the road when the rain began. At first it was a series of tip-taps on the roof but before long it was smashing down onto the metal. She put the windscreen wipers on full, watching them crash the water away from her vision as she moved onto the main road.

Unsurprisingly, people were still driving like idiots, some tearing around as if it was a perfectly dry and sunny day, others creeping along fifteen miles under the speed limit and making things worse. Jessica couldn't be bothered to complain, tucking in behind someone going too slowly and following them.

Around her, the storm swirled, wind buffeting the car from side to side, rain hammering from the bonnet, the roof, the road, the pavement, everywhere.

In front, the driver of the car which had been going so slowly decided he didn't want to sit at the traffic lights, speeding up unexpectedly and blazing through them just as they ticked over to red.

Jessica pulled up the handbrake and waited, staring straight ahead as the windscreen wipers feebly tried to clear the glass.

Thump, thump, thump.

Someone pulled up in the lane next to her, revving their engine, waiting for the light to go green. Some dickhead who no doubt had a loud exhaust to make up for his minuscule genitals.

Thump, thump, thump.

A woman dashed across the pelican crossing, thrusting a pushchair out in front of her, as if it was a shield. She didn't have an umbrella and was getting soaked. She probably had half-a-dozen kids at home, each screaming louder than the last. She'd probably never worked a day in her life.

Thump, thump, thump.

A car flew across the four-way junction, brakes screech-ing, turning without indicating and making a cyclist swerve out of its way. Whoever was driving beeped his horn, as if the poor person on the bicycle should have telepathically known he was going to turn. Some selfish idiot who thought they were always right, probably driving home to his children to eat pizza and crisps and sit in front of the television all night watching utter shite.

Thump, thump, thump.

In the sky, a plane soared upwards, disappearing into the clouds, its red lights disappearing in a flash. Hundreds of people off to sit in the sun; to drink, to laugh, to do nothing for a fortnight. Men, women, families, children.

Thump, thump, thump.

The orange traffic light came on and the car outside her screeched away, exhaust blurting a thick cloud into the air. The light turned green but she didn't move, eyes fixed firmly ahead. Car after car pulled past her. Behind, someone beeped their horn, then someone else.

'Jess.'

Thump, thump, thump.

A man in the vehicle behind pulled around her, acceler-ating away with an angry pump of his horn. Three more cars did the same until the lights flickered back to red.

Thump, thump, thump.

Across the junction, someone on a moped tried to swerve around a car, misjudging the lights as they changed to green. The car pulled away at the same time, stalling as the moped moved in front of him. More beeps, an angry gesture.

Thump.

Thump.

Thump.

Jessica unclipped her seatbelt and opened the door, stepping around the front of the car and walking straight ahead. Someone beeped their horn, possibly at her, but she wasn't paying attention enough to know where it came from.

In a matter of seconds, the rain had drenched Jessica, her clothes sticking to her, hair flailing in the wind, matting together from the spray. It felt like the best shower ever; as if God, nature, or whatever else people chose to believe in was showing his displeasure.

Good.

Whoever was in charge should be angry because she was. All these people around her could go home and make babies and she couldn't.

She walked into the middle of the junction, standing in the centre of the criss-crosses on the road, arms out, letting the rain pound her. Cars zipped past on either side, the drivers either beeping their horns or staring in disbelief.

Jessica didn't care. Let them look, let them drive into her for all she cared. More than any of that, let it rain.

She tilted her head back, staring into the silver skies, blinking the water away from her eyes, before closing them. 'Come on,' she yelled. 'Come on!'

Thump, thump, thump.

'Jess.'

'Go away.'

'Jess, we're in the middle of a junction. It's dangerous.'

'Go back to the car then.'

She was shouting to make herself heard. All she wanted was to be on her own.

'Jess.'

'Just. Fuck. Off.'

'Jess, don't talk to me like that, please.'

Christ, he even said please.

'Leave me alone then.'

The cars stopped and for a few seconds there was nothing but the sound of the rain, then they started again from the opposite direction. More beeps.

'You know I'm not going to do that, Jess.'

'Why?'

'Because we're in this together.'

Jessica opened her eyes, blinking away the stream of water. Still it rained. She could feel the drops pulsing against her skin. She turned to face Adam, knowing that on any other day she would be grinning at how ridiculous he looked. His long hair had been blown in all directions, his skinny T-shirt now looked more like a wetsuit. His pasty arms looked so frail wrapped around himself.

'Why?'

'Because I love you and you love me and we shouldn't let this beat us.'

Jessica sighed, droplets of rain running from her top lip and then sliding into her nose as she breathed. 'I'm sorry.'

He smiled. 'No matter, we can always get dry at home.'

The cars stopped again, the lights temporarily all on

red, as if everything in the world had halted except for the rain.

Thump, thump, thump.

'Not for that,' Jessica replied. 'I'm sorry for being broken.'

FRIDAY

28

Jessica had towelled herself dry in the bathroom, telling Heather she was fine and ignoring anything she had to ask about how the evening had gone. She might not blame her roommate for telling other people about her interest in what was going on around the house but she certainly wasn't going to give her anything else to work with. Heather at least appeared to know why Jessica was being short with her and stopped talking, getting changed for bed and clicking off her side lamp.

Jessica lay in bed wearing a fresh set of clothes, waiting, listening, just as she had on the night she made the first call to Charley. This time, the paranoia about not knowing the time got to her and she slipped the phone out from underneath the mattress, turning it on to check and then returning it.

It was only half-past-one – too early – so Jessica continued to wait, counting to sixty over and over until ten minutes had passed and then giving up.

Even though everything except for her hair was dry, Jessica could still feel the clammy dampness on her skin. The rain had become the darkest of friends in recent times: with Adam in the centre of the junction, outside this house, in the woods. It followed her, hunting her, waiting until she was at her most vulnerable and then soaked her. Each time it felt like a test and each time she had come through it. This evening, more than any other point in the past six months, she wanted to see Adam, to talk to him. She had been the one to ask him for a break. She didn't want to break up, but she needed time to herself, not just away from him but away from everyone.

Someone he knew at the university had put him up for a while, then he had spent a week at his sister Georgia's house down south. Jessica found it easier to communicate with him in text messages than she did in person, or on the phone.

Each Friday, she would send him one word: 'Sorry', letting him know she wasn't ready.

In under sixty seconds, her phone would beep with the response: 'I'll wait.'

Jessica lay staring at the ceiling wondering what she had done to deserve him. She wondered if he was still out there, waiting for her. She had messaged him to say she was off to do a job for the force, returning to work as he kept telling her she should. She said they should talk afterwards but that she didn't know how long it would take.

The reply came, the same as ever: 'I'll wait.'

She wished she had her own phone now so she could open her messages and stare at the long list of the ones she'd kept. Twenty-three consecutive weeks of identical 'I'll wait' messages that she wanted to look through, one after the other, each a tiny reminder that someone out there cared for her more than she cared for herself.

Jessica checked the time again, amazed that almost two

hours had passed as she lay thinking about Adam and the baby they had lost.

She had lost.

Wondering what he would have looked like. Would he have had her hazel eyes, or Adam's brown ones? Her lighter hair, or the darker, thicker strands that Adam had?

They had both joked – hoped – that their son was going to take after his father in the temper stakes. The last thing they needed was two of them throwing things, kicking things, and generally getting annoyed when things didn't go their way.

She had spent so many years telling herself she didn't want children, that she wasn't mature enough, that she wanted to do things with her life, but when it had simply happened, she hadn't felt any of that. Instead, things felt right, as if everything had been building up to the moment and that her life would be better, not worse, from now on.

And then it had all come tumbling down.

Jessica gently pulled the covers away, struggling not to shiver from the coolness of the air and the after-effects of the drenching. She turned the phone back off, tucking it under her mattress, before pausing and standing still as Heather rolled over. Jessica counted to ten silently and then crept across to her wardrobe, putting on the softest pair of shoes she had and creeping into the hallway.

The clouds and rain had cleared, leaving the crisp white moon in its place again. Jessica could have spent the evening watching it but knew she had work to do.

Remembering the creak of the banister from earlier, she kept to the centre of the staircase, moving one step at a time until she was at the bottom, and then heading directly towards the games room.

Each noisy floorboard made her stop and wait until she was certain there was no one around. Then she continued, moving past Moses's office and the games room until she reached the stairs that led only to a platform, rather than another floor. She had thought it was strange on the tour with Heather but assumed it was some sort of storage cupboard. It wasn't as if it was the only piece of odd decoration in the house.

The key pilfered from Glenn was old-fashioned, with a long stem and a small square of teeth at the end. Jessica slipped it into the lock, twisting it one way unsuccessfully and then the other. The only time she'd ever had to use a key like this in the past was for her parents' back door before they had everything redone. That was equally old and unforgiving if you didn't have the key in the exact sweet spot. Trying again, Jessica lifted it slightly, feeling it slot into place, and then turned it slowly until she heard the satisfying click.

Inside, it was dark but Jessica could see from the moonlight in the hallway that the door opened directly onto stone steps. She pushed it closed, blocking out the light, and then slowly made her way down, using the wall to guide her. She stumbled as she reached the bottom, only just managing to keep her balance by stretching out and grabbing onto something that felt like a filing cabinet. Her legs were unsteady, the crack to the back of her knees a memory all too vivid. She still didn't know if it was Glenn or Ali who had kicked her.

Jessica felt around the wall, until her fingers touched upon a light switch.

Overhead, there was a ding as the strip lights fired into action and then Jessica found herself blinking rapidly, trying to adjust to flickering white lights as a low humming sound enveloped the room.

As everything came into focus, Jessica realised she was in a sort of reception area, a narrow room that led into another.

She made her way into the next area, taken aback by the lack of size. Jessica suspected the basement would be as large as the house but it was only twice the space of the bedroom she shared with Heather. Off to one side was a mirror the entire width and height of the wall. Jessica moved towards the centre of the room, staring at herself, concerned by how thin she had become. The clothes she was wearing were the smallest in the store that Zipporah and Heather had shown her, yet the trousers still hung limply around her waist, the shirt making it look as if she had no curves left.

She looked horrible.

Jessica lifted her shirt, eyes fixed on her abdomen, wondering what might have been.

Only a clunk from the lights made her remember what she was supposed to be doing. Although she had been in the room for a few minutes, it had taken until that moment for Jessica to realise what surrounded her. Aside from the mirror, the other three walls were covered with padding. She stepped across, pressing her hand into it, which felt like the fake leather on cheap sofas. It was squishy, with button-sized indents at regular intervals. Even the inside of the door she had entered through was covered in the material, while, above her, in between the lights, there was more padding.

Jessica moved back to the centre of the room, running her hand across two pillars, both of which were also covered. She stared at herself in the mirror again before taking a risk.

'Hello,' she called out.

There was a slight echo but nothing like as loud as she'd have expected. The floor was hard and smelled of disinfectant.

Jessica headed back to the room at the bottom of the stairs, where there was a wooden cabinet built into the wall.

She gasped as she opened it; the insides contained a toolkit utterly different to the ones in the cupboard on the floor above. Jessica ran her fingers across the instruments, pressing the metal of each to see if it was real.

There was a row of three saws: a thin-bladed hacksaw, a solid-looking tenon saw and a full panel saw. Next to those, there were three types of hammer, then different-sized sets of pliers, hand drills, a crowbar, thick masking tape, small scissors and large bolt cutters with thick, curved jaws.

At the far end was a set of handcuffs with two keys on separate hooks next to it.

Everything was meticulously organised; clean, gleaming

in the overhead light and smelling of detergent, rather than any work they might have been used for.

Jessica breathed in sharply, closing the cupboard doors, knowing exactly what she was looking at. This was a custom-built torture chamber, put together by someone intent only on hurting others. Kevin had been brought here but allowed to leave. She assumed Wayne had not been given that luxury. Perhaps even Liam had been brought here before being drowned.

Returning to the main room, Jessica knew she still didn't have enough to call Charley in. Everything had been cleaned by someone who knew what they were doing, leaving no trace that Wayne or Liam had ever been here. Yes, it was strange, but Jessica had heard of odder things. Who could prove beyond doubt that this wasn't simply a weird-looking workshop?

Jessica continued to peer around the walls before realising she had missed something obvious. The walls and ceiling weren't just padded, the padding was entirely made of a dim green material. When Moses had asked Glenn if he needed anything else for the greenhouse, he hadn't been talking about some glass structure outside, he had been talking about this place.

Jessica knew there had to be something else, approaching the mirror until she was close enough to see the dark bags under her eyes. Her skin was whiter than she had ever seen it and she looked so unlike herself that even if Ali, Moses or anyone else had a photo of her from a few years ago, then they probably wouldn't be able to say for sure it was her.

Turning to the side, she noticed there was a crease in between two sets of padding on the wall. Jessica dug her fingers into the space, running them down until she found a hidden mechanism. The door clicked open with barely a sound, opening into another darkened corridor. Jessica turned until she was facing the direction of the mirror, following a dim glow until she found herself directly behind it in a hidden room.

Suddenly, the receipts made sense.

The mirror only worked one way and Jessica could see through to the other side, into the greenhouse. On a tripod was a video camera facing the space too, a cable running from the back along the floor, connecting to a computer on a desk.

Jessica sat in a leather swivel chair, watching the lights blink on the front of the computer case, before leaning forward and turning on the flatscreen monitor.

The artificial light from the monitor felt like an old friend. She couldn't remember the last time she had been on a computer. She hadn't used the laptop in months, let alone her PC at work. Looking at the list of icons along the bottom of the screen felt like a reminder of something in her past. She glanced at the bottom right-hand corner for the time – twelve minutes past four in the morning. She knew she should be tired but this discovery was keeping her alert.

Next to the time was a spinning globe, indicating there was an Internet connection.

Jessica clicked to open a browser window, waiting as

the cursor spun, considering whether to respond to her request.

Everything about this place was so planned that Jessica wondered how long it had been going on for. Perhaps Wayne and Liam were only the start? In the same way that Wayne had apparently been a fraction away from ending up in landfill, perhaps that was what had happened to others? Maybe they were buried in the woods she had been taken to?

That was something for Charley and her team to deal with. For now, Jessica had to give her enough of a lead to get her here.

The browser window finally appeared, showing the homepage for a news site. Jessica had an urge to check all her old favourite websites, which she hadn't done in months. She could only guess how many emails there were waiting for her; probably the usual set of advertisements for casinos, plus various enlargement surgeries and pills she used to forward to Adam for a laugh.

She didn't know how the house had an active Internet connection considering Charley didn't know about it and there was no apparent phone line but she guessed there must be a bank account somewhere set up to pay for it.

Not knowing what she was looking for, Jessica continued to hunt the home screen for any programs that could provide clues but there was nothing except for the browser.

Jessica flicked back to it, opening up the history, which was empty except for two items: the news homepage and a site she had never heard of.

Holding her breath, Jessica clicked to open it, the screen turning black before asking for a username and password. The username was already typed in, with a row of asterisks in the password field. Clearly whoever used the terminal wasn't very good at remembering pieces of information.

As the site loaded, Jessica could barely bring herself to look at the screen. There was a long list of video clips, each promising various degrees of torment and degradation.

She left the cursor hovering over one from the day Wayne had been assaulted in the garden, knowing she had to press it but not wanting to. When she finally composed herself, Jessica covered her eyes, listening to the terrifying sound of a drill before finding the strength to open one eye and watch as Wayne was tortured in the room in front of her.

29

Jessica removed any trace from the history of what she had done and closed the browser window. She felt sick, barely able to peer through the window into the room ahead, knowing what had gone on in there. She could have continued hunting through the website's contents but that would be the job of some poor investigator from Charley's team. Jessica turned the monitor back off and then moved around the side of the mirror towards the door.

She was about to exit into the greenhouse when she noticed another door ahead of her. She felt drained, unable to believe that she had been upstairs at a time when a masked, hooded figure was inflicting such pain on another human being for their own amusement. They weren't too tall, with Glenn the only real candidate Jessica could think of. The other option was that it was being done for the money. The website likely had some sort of pay system, so it could be making a fortune, offering a service to viewers for whom a Hollywood movie was not enough.

Jessica approached the door, opening it to see what appeared to be a cleaning cupboard. The light was dim, but she could see a mop and bucket, a sink built into the wall, and two large containers of cleaning product underneath. She was about to turn to leave when she noticed a light switch. She wanted to get out of this place, feeling the weight of everything that had happened here upon her.

But knowing that it must be there for a reason, Jessica flicked the switch, turning to see the room was much bigger than she had first thought. Stacked floor to ceiling were rows of tightly packed bags. Jessica walked towards them, realising that they didn't just run the full length of the room but that the bags were at least four deep too. Hundreds, perhaps thousands, of compacted bags of ammonium nitrate.

They were all living on top of a bomb big enough to bring down the entire building and kill every person inside.

30

Jessica knew she had two things to do: call Charley and then get out.

But could she leave so many innocent people here on top of something that in the wrong hands could do so much destruction? Whether it was Glenn or Moses who had set it up, Jessica had to assume they knew what they were doing. If she was going to go around the bedrooms getting people out, who should she trust? She knew Heather had betrayed her, but that didn't mean it was right to leave her here. The same could be true of Ali. And what about Naomi or Zipporah? How could she get them away without alerting their husbands?

Jessica stood staring at the fertiliser bags, not knowing what it took to make a bomb from one. The only reason she knew the danger of what she was looking at was because they had all been on a two-day anti-terrorism training course. At the time, she'd thought it was a complete over-reaction; now she was relieved she had paid a modicum of attention.

Wires ran from the bags but she didn't know if that signified some sort of trigger. Slowly Jessica turned, almost tripping over the cleaning bucket. She flicked the lights off and closed the door, entering the greenhouse and pulling the padded door into place.

Each step she took across the hard floor felt like she was trampling on somebody's grave in the way she had as a child in the cemetery close to her home. Then she was oblivious to it, now she was sickened.

She closed the other door, checking the tool cabinet one final time, and then headed up the stairs, locking the basement door as quietly as she could.

Jessica didn't want to leave anyone behind but figured if she could get hold of Charley, a police team could be sent along before anyone woke up. She remembered what Cole had told her, knowing he was right – 'Sometimes you have to help yourself'. Could she really walk away from the house and leave Heather and everyone else behind? Perhaps she had to?

Keeping to the centre, Jessica raced as softly as she could up the stairs, taking two at a time even though the backs of her knees still hurt.

Without seeing or hearing anyone, she reached the bedroom door, out of breath, heart pounding. Tentatively, she pushed it open, glancing across to where Heather lay facing away on her side, asleep. Jessica tiptoed across to her bed, slipping her hand in between the mattress and the bed frame, feeling the panic growing inside her as she realised the phone wasn't there.

31

Jessica ran her hand along the full length of the mattress and then climbed on top, lifting it up and peering under the area where her pillow was. She crouched, running her hand along the floor underneath in case the phone had somehow dropped.

It hadn't and it was nowhere to be found. Someone had taken it – perhaps even Heather, who may have seen the light when Jessica had checked the time, waiting until she had left the room and then hurrying across to hunt for it.

Jessica sat on the edge of her bed, peering across the room in the dim glow towards where Heather was still facing away, her side gently rising and falling. Could she be awake right now, faking it? Could she have the phone with her now, or had she already passed it on to someone else? Jessica knew her roommate's feelings for Moses and he would surely have been her first point of call.

There was now only one thing she could do: get out of the house unnoticed and get to the town centre to alert Charley and everyone else.

Jessica didn't know if whoever had taken her phone might be waiting in the hall, so she went to the window, pressing as hard as she dared on the unmoving handle. Escaping that way was always going to be unlikely seeing as it was locked before and even if it had opened, it would have been a long drop to the ground.

Knowing she had no choice other than to go back the way she had come, Jessica changed into shoes she could run in and headed into the still-silent hallway. She looked both ways, edging slowly across the carpet and listening for any sense of movement.

It was such a cliché that it sounded too quiet, but Jessica couldn't think of any other way to describe it. The house was old and she expected pipes and the antique wooden furnishings to be creaking and squeaking but they weren't.

Jessica headed down the stairs one step at a time, crouching to peer through the banisters to the first floor. She continued to the bottom only when she was certain there was no one below. Jessica had never been great with maps, let alone ones in her head. She tried to picture from above where all of the corridors led, knowing the most direct route to the front door would take her past Moses's office, the games room and the work room. If anyone was around, that was surely the route they'd expect her to take.

Heading in the opposite direction, Jessica used the paintings to guide her, remembering what she had been shown by Zipporah and Heather on her first day. Twice, she ended up in a dead end and another time, she stumbled into the kitchen, almost knocking a pile of metal pans from the counter top just inside the door.

Eventually, she figured out where she was, doubling back until she found the passage she had been looking for.

Jessica checked around the corners, moving efficiently until she entered the main hallway at the front. The enormous painting of Moses stared down upon her, as imposing as the real person.

Jessica crept across the floor, trying not to make a noise. When she reached the front door, she stopped to catch her breath, reaching for the first bolt as Glenn's voice sounded behind her.

'Where are you going?'

She pulled across the bolt but heard the rush of footsteps, knowing she'd never be able to wrench it open before he got to her.

Jessica moved quickly to the side, turning to see Glenn reach the door, spreading his arms as if guarding something. There were two doorways that would take her into the rest of the house but Jessica didn't fancy her chances at out-running Glenn, not to mention that there could be other people in the corridors. She still hadn't seen Moses.

'I was going to go for a walk,' Jessica said, her voice echoing around the high walls.

Glenn wasn't dressed for bed and must have been up for a little while. He was staring at her, more daring her to make a move than being surprised or angry.

'It's a bit late for a walk, isn't it?'

'I don't know, there aren't any clocks around. It feels like it's early.'

He poked out his bottom lip, nodding in acknowledgement. 'Right you are. It's around five o'clock, if you're wondering.'

Jessica yawned unexpectedly, having not felt it coming. 'It still feels like a nice time for a wander,' she said. 'Everyone keeps saying that we can leave at any time. I'm not even leaving, I just fancy a stroll.'

'Is that right?'

Jessica shrugged, holding her hands up. 'I'm not sure what to tell you.'

'So why don't you come and let yourself out?'

Glenn stepped to one side, leaving the door invitingly free but not taking his eyes from her. She took a pace forward, wondering whether he had her phone. Heather could have taken and kept hold of it, with Glenn simply making his early-morning rounds. She had never been up at this time to know if this was a regular occurrence. Somebody in the house had to be up to set off the morning alarm.

Slowly, she walked forward, glancing from the door to Glenn and back again. He took another step backwards, giving her more space.

Jessica laid one hand on the door, half-turning towards it when she felt Glenn moving towards her. Despite his strength and presence, he couldn't do anything about his short legs. Moses might have been able to get to her in two strides but Glenn was slower.

He reached for her, a snarl of triumph on his face, but Jessica saw him coming. Her knees were sore and they buckled under her weight when she tried to kneel. The natural momentum sent her lunging forward but Glenn had grasped too high. Jessica reeled back and punched him as hard as she could in the groin, feeling the satisfying crunch of flesh followed by the gratifying groan. Glenn doubled over in pain and Jessica punched him in the same area before driving up with her shoulder, catching him under the chin and sending him flailing to the ground.

As she tried to stand, her knees almost gave way but she kept her balance and rushed to one of the exits. There was little point in going for the main door as Glenn was capable of crawling the metre or so it would take to grab her.

She dashed back the way she had come, heading towards Moses's office, hoping the window wouldn't be locked. Behind her she could hear movement, not knowing if it was Glenn or someone else, but she darted through the passageways until she got to the office. Jessica slammed her palm down on the handle but it didn't give way, locked as she knew it would be. Just to be sure she reared back, kicking the area next to the handle as hard as she could, but only succeeding in making the pain spread from her knee to her hip.

As she heard the footsteps getting louder behind, Jessica set off again, running past the basement entrance and the stairs which went nowhere and rounding the corner.

It was only as she dashed away from the games room that Jessica felt a sense of déjà vu from when she'd stood there looking for a way into Moses's office. She had overheard the cooks talking, being nice about everyone but giving her the one piece of information she should have remembered – 'I'll get the back door unlocked last thing Thursday so we can get straight onto it'.

There was a delivery due later in the morning and one

of the cooks would have left the back door unlocked to help with the loading. If she had only remembered that in the kitchen a few minutes ago, she would have been out of the house now.

Now the kitchen was behind her, the only way back was the long way around, which would take her past the front door, or the shorter route, meaning she had to face whoever was following her. If it was Glenn, he might have left the main door unguarded but she didn't know how many people were involved. Moses had to be somewhere, directing everything from the shadows, not wanting to get his hands dirty.

Jessica headed for the stairs, reaching the landing and lying flat on her front, knowing she could see the scene below her but that anyone on the ground floor wouldn't be able to see her unless they climbed a few steps. Outside, it looked as if the early vestiges of daylight were beginning to appear. She knew she was vulnerable if anyone was coming down the stairs but if Glenn or Moses started to come up then she might be able to lunge at them, knocking them backwards and leaving her free to run.

She waited until Glenn finally hobbled into view. He was moving relatively quickly considering the way he was clutching the inside of his thigh but there was a dribble of blood on his chin. He stood at the bottom of the stairs looking both ways as Jessica waited, unmoving, holding her breath.

Glenn stood, waiting, pulling out a watch from his pocket and checking the time. Just as she thought he wasn't going to move, he shrugged his shoulders, grunting in annoyance, and started walking back the way he had come. Jessica shuffled forward slowly, forearms burning against the carpet as she peered through the banisters, trying to see if Glenn had left the corridor.

He was heading towards the kitchen, blocking that way out. Ultimately he could end up back at the front door but he was moving slowly enough that Jessica knew she could run the long way around and make it to the front door before he got there.

Managing a fluid movement which surprised her, Jessica sprung to her feet like a frog, bounding down the steps. She only realised her mistake when she heard a roar of outrage behind her. Glenn had been going more slowly than she had thought, not even reaching the end of the corridor. Not fancying her chances of getting past him, Jessica dashed in the opposite direction for the second time.

She wanted to drive on but the backs of her knees were aching and she couldn't get the image out of her mind of how she'd looked in the mirror, her arms and legs like twigs.

She glanced over her shoulder to see Glenn struggling too but there was no way she could outrun him back to the door.

Jessica flung herself around the corner, unsure of what to do, only looking up at the last moment to see someone standing in front of her.

32

Zipporah's eyes were full of surprise as she stepped back at the last second to stop Jessica colliding with her. Around the corner, Glenn's footsteps were echoing as he picked up speed.

Whether something like this had happened before, Jessica didn't know, but Zipporah acted quickly, whispering, 'In here', holding the door open.

Jessica had never been in the room before, mistaking the door for a plain wooden panel when she'd passed it on previous occasions. She had no time to think but the bruise around Zipporah's eye swung it for her. This was someone who had seen the type of violence she was hoping to escape. She dived into the room as Zipporah clicked the door silently into place.

Jessica lay on the floor, trying to catch her breath as she heard Glenn race past outside. She was overcome by the tiredness from not sleeping and the exhaustion of the chase. She rolled onto her front, allowing Zipporah to pull her to her feet.

The woman's face looked worse than it had the last time Jessica had seen her, a rainbow of colour stretching from her eye socket all the way down to the base of her neck, set off against her dark brown eyes.

She noticed Jessica staring at her and turned away, whispering: 'It's nothing.'

'It looks sore.'

'I've had worse.'

Jessica finally had a chance to look around the rest of the windowless room, taking in the long rows of bookcases filled with leather-bound hardback books. The spines alternated between red and green, creating something Jessica thought would probably look impressive through an old pair of 3D glasses.

'What is this place?' she asked.

'It was my father's library. You might not know this but this was my house before I married Moses. Every title you see was bound specifically for my father. Sometimes when I can't sleep, I come downstairs and sit. I don't even read the books but it feels nice to have them around. It reminds me of my dad.'

Zipporah sat on the edge of a solid wooden table. The room was taller than it was wide, a cubby hole hidden away behind a panel.

She peered up at Jessica, looking a broken woman, tired. 'Do you know, I've been married to Moses for all these years and I've never told him about this room? This has always been my little corner where I can get away. In the early days, before people started coming to stay at the house, sometimes I'd spend a few hours here. I'd hear Moses – or Jan as he was then – in the corridors, calling my name. When I eventually came out, I'd tell him I'd been on the top floor or something like that.'

It was the first time Jessica had heard anyone other

than Charley call Moses by his real name. Zipporah yawned, making Jessica follow, until they both smiled. Jessica couldn't help herself.

'What was going on out there?' Zipporah asked, nodding towards the closed door.

Jessica pressed against one of the bookcases, wondering what she could say. She didn't want to mention what went on in the basement, figuring that if Zipporah was this protective of her father's hidden library, then she probably wouldn't want to know what was happening underneath the house. The poor woman was going out onto the streets once a week to recruit people, not knowing that those who didn't pass her husband's tests were ending up in the basement of the place where she had grown up, being tortured for either fun or money. Or both.

'I want to leave,' Jessica said.

'What happened?'

'They took me out to the woods.'

'Who did?'

'Glenn and Ali.'

Zipporah nodded knowingly. 'I've heard from others about what goes on. My husband . . .'

She didn't finish the sentence but she didn't need to.

'I think it was just to scare me.' Jessica held up her wrists to show the marks.

Zipporah winced. 'That looks nasty.'

'They had these plastic tie things which dug in. They asked all sorts of questions about who I was and had this really large knife. I didn't know what they were going to do with it but they eventually cut me loose and brought me back.'

'My husband likes his way of controlling people. He thinks that if he can break them down, then he gets to build them back up in whichever way he chooses. Glenn is his right-hand man. Ali . . . I'm not so sure.'

From what Glenn had said, Ali was the next in line – assuming he continued to do whatever Glenn told him. Jessica had looked into his eyes though, seeing how scared he was of the knife when he held it. She doubted he had it in him.

'So have you had enough?' Zipporah added.

Jessica couldn't stop herself from yawning again. 'I want to go back to my old life.'

'Even after everything with your father?'

'Yes.'

'And the baby that you lost?'

Jessica reached for her stomach, running her fingers across the area underneath.

'The doctor said there might be a chance it could still happen. It might only be slim but a small hope is better than no hope.'

It was exactly what Adam had told her in the doctor's office all those months ago. If only she had listened to him then.

'So you might still be able to have children?'

Jessica shrugged. 'I have no idea.'

'If you go, you will be much missed.'

Jessica bit her lip, not knowing how to respond. She might be missed by Moses having one less person to grope, or Glenn as someone who wasn't going to end up in his torture room. One less person to be crushed if the fertiliser bomb went off.

'I'm sorry,' Jessica replied, not feeling it at all. She nodded towards Zipporah's face and her arms. 'Perhaps you should think about—'

Zipporah didn't let her finish, pushing her long black hair back behind her ears defiantly. 'You forget whose house this ultimately is.'

Jessica was about to reply when she heard footsteps in the corridor. She closed her mouth, staring at the door, wondering if it was about to be pushed inwards. Zipporah was silent too, understanding what was going on.

When the person passed, Jessica whispered: 'Why do you let him run it if it's your house?'

Zipporah rubbed above her eyes, blinking away the tiredness. 'It wasn't always like this. He always had his beliefs but things grew and grew. If it had been one spur, you could have turned around and said "stop". When things happen over a long period, you don't even realise until it's too late.'

'What does he do?'

Jessica knew she had to go but wanted to hear what Moses was like to his wife. It felt important.

Zipporah sighed. 'Are you married?'

'No.'

'I'm not sure I am any more, either. It's not as if our vows have meant anything for a long time – "loving and faithful as long as you both shall live" hasn't been true in a while.'

'Katie?'

'Not just her. It isn't her fault either, not really. At first, he had the idea of using this great big house to help others. We could create a haven for runaways or other people who had problems in their lives. Before I realised what was happening, everyone here was female. You must have noticed that all the girls are younger and most of the males older?'

'But aren't you the one who recruits them?'

Zipporah nodded. 'If you know someone is going to be rejected and sent away, then what would be the point of bringing back a person who was unsuitable? There are the odd younger males but mostly this is the balance we've had for some time. With the girls, they see what I saw all those years ago. Moses is a captivating figure – you must have seen it?'

Jessica thought of the way his uninvited hands moved across her. 'He speaks well but I don't see it.'

There was a flash of confusion on Zipporah's face which disappeared as instantly as it arrived. 'You've not been tempted?'

'No. I have someone.'

'Perhaps it's because you're a little less naive than some of the others? Is it the father of . . . ?'

'Yes it is.'

A thin smile spread on Zipporah's face. 'At least you have something to return to. Some of the others would simply have the streets.'

Jessica knew that was the other reason some of the residents were so willing to believe in Moses. He gave them an alternative to the lives they had lost. Jessica still had something to go back to.

'I need to go,' Jessica said.

'You never really said what you discovered. You just said you'd been taken to the woods.'

'It's Glenn – he doesn't want to let me go.'

'Why?'

'I don't know. I suspect he's worried about what I'll say about the woods when I'm out.'

'He didn't actually do anything to you, did he?'

'No, it was just a scare.'

'So what are you going to say?'

Jessica knew this was her opportunity to let everything out. She could admit she was a police officer, tell Zipporah that if she gave evidence against her husband and Glenn that this could all be over with. She could keep using her house as a refuge if she so chose, or keep it for herself as somewhere to live.

'Nothing,' Jessica replied. 'I'm just ready to leave. You said I could go any time I wanted to, so I'm not sure why he's trying to stop me. If it's your house, perhaps you can tell him to let me go?'

Zipporah's smile was weary. 'I'm not sure that would be for the best.'

'He's not going to let me go otherwise.'

'I've lived in this house for my entire life. You probably know by now that the windows are secured. That wasn't done by Moses or me. When this was my grandfather's house, there was a burglary. My father was a child at the time. He never forgot and was obsessed by security. That only leaves two doors out – the main one at the front and the delivery one in the kitchen.'

'The front door is still bolted. I don't know where Glenn is, or if there's anyone else in the corridors.'

'Do you know where the kitchen is?' Zipporah asked.

'Yes.'

'If I go to the front, I can keep Glenn occupied there while you do whatever you have to.'

For the first time since realising her phone had gone, Jessica felt a sense of relief. Zipporah would head one way, she would go the other and within a few minutes, she would be out. Glenn would not realise she had gone until she was out of the grounds and on her way towards the town.

'Thank you,' Jessica replied.

Zipporah pushed herself up, ready to move.

'Can I ask you one more thing?' Jessica said.

'Of course.'

'When we first met, in the city centre, you didn't hesitate in inviting me here. Was that because I'm a woman and I'm not too old and you thought I'd be the right type, or . . . ?'

Zipporah licked her lips, her eyes flicking across Jessica. 'Oh, my dear, I thought you knew. I thought that's why you came here. Regardless of anything else that goes on, the principle of this house is the same – that we try to help people. The reason I invited you is because you're as broken as anyone I've ever met.'

Jessica gulped, glancing away from Zipporah, unable to meet her gaze. She had always hoped that wasn't the reason, even though it had been so clear the entire time that it was.

'Okay,' Jessica replied, stepping towards the door, keener than ever to leave.

From the inside, the opening looked the same as the outside – a wooden panel. Jessica reached for a handle that wasn't there, running her palm along the grain of the wood before realising she simply had to push. As she emerged into the corridor, Jessica looked in one direction, feeling so close to freedom that she was already planning what she would say to Adam.

In the fraction of a second it took her to check the other way, the blow clattered across the back of her head, sending her slumping to the ground as thoughts of home slipped from her mind.

33

Home.

Jessica thought of walking through the front door of the house she and Adam had bought, throwing her keys towards the basket he had picked up because she was always losing them. He knew her so well. Annoyingly well.

She breathed in, but it didn't smell the way their house did, instead it was cleaner. The faint whiff of bleach drifted through her, meaning she definitely wasn't at home. Jessica didn't think she had ever cleaned a room with disinfectant in her life. It was always someone else, mainly Caroline, who did that type of thing and now Adam. He'd get on and do it without complaining, allowing her to put her feet up after a long week. As if she ever had any other kind.

Her head felt heavy, her legs tired. Jessica realised she was standing but it felt like too much of an effort to open her eyes. She had been so tired for such a long time that sometimes it was nice to rest with her eyes closed, stare into the darkness and relax. Perhaps if you spent long enough thinking about sleeping, then it would actually count as sleep and you wouldn't feel so tired any longer?

Except that Jessica couldn't sleep because of the smell. She wondered why she was standing with her eyes closed and tried to move before finding her hands were behind her, locked together. There was something digging into her back too, square and pointy, her hands tied behind it.

Still with her eyes closed, Jessica remembered what had happened: Glenn and then the library with Zipporah. She had tried to leave the room but something had prevented her. She tried listening to see if she could pick up anything that would give her a clue as to where she was but then she remembered the rest too. In the torture chamber in the basement, there were two pillars, both covered with the green padding. She could feel that now, brushing against her skin. The corners hadn't quite been covered and were cutting into her shoulders. Her wrists were still sore from the ties but they were secure again, this time with the handcuffs she had seen in the cabinet at the bottom of the stairs.

Eyes clamped shut, Jessica realised she was in more danger now than she'd ever been. All she could do was stall. If she could keep pretending to be unconscious, she might be able to buy more time, to think of a way . . .

Jessica's eyes flew open instinctively as water was thrown into her face. She had been breathing in through her nose as it hit her and coughed painfully, trying to free the liquid from her lungs. She blinked rapidly, eyes focusing on herself as she realised she was facing the large mirror in the basement.

'Wakey, wakey,' Glenn said, stepping into her eye line. He had an empty glass jug in his hand but put it on the floor. Behind him was a table with a row of tools neatly laid out. Jessica could see two of the saws, a hammer, a pair of pliers, the bolt cutters and a drill.

Glenn must have seen her eyes flicker towards the table because his smile grew. 'Nice, aren't they?' he said.

Water was still dripping from Jessica's face into a puddle on the floor, although she could breathe again. 'I just want to go,' she whimpered.

'I know you do. Unfortunately, I did warn you in the woods about asking questions and then you went and broke the rules again.'

Glenn reached into his pocket, pulling out Jessica's phone and dropping it to the floor, stamping on it three times until the casing was flat.

'How did you get that?' Jessica asked.

'A little birdie . . .'

Heather.

'This time there's no Ali to speak up for you,' Glenn continued. 'He's a good lad but far too soft. In the woods, I said there was something not quite right about you but he insisted you were fine. I shouldn't have listened but perhaps I'm getting lenient in my old age too. It's been a busy few weeks and I'm tired of cleaning up, so there was that as well. He's got a thing about that girl you share a room with. Perhaps I'd be better finding someone else to train up?'

Glenn crossed to the table, picking up the hand drill. He rotated the handle, creating a gentle whirring noise and purring with pleasure himself. After wiping away a speck of dust, he returned it to the table, lining it up with the other tools, and then picked up the hammer. Gently at first, he tapped it on the table, the metal clang being absorbed unnaturally by the room.

353

'Do you hear that?' he asked, turning to Jessica. She couldn't look at him directly, staring into his back via the mirror, not replying. 'I love that sound,' he added. 'The padding gives everything that extra little touch if you ask me. Wait until the screams come later, it's unbelievable.'

He put the hammer back down, turning to the side as the door that led behind the mirror opened. When the person emerged, hood hanging limply around the shoulders, mask in hand, Jessica realised how naive she had been not to see it before.

Zip's keen on getting her involved a little down the line.

When she had heard Moses say that, Jessica had assumed he meant that his wife wanted her to be part of the recruitment team. As Zipporah walked into the room with a smile on her face, Jessica understood that this room was hers all along. What Moses had actually meant was that his wife was keen to bring her here at some point. He might not have been involved with the green-house directly but he knew enough about it.

Zipporah hadn't taken Jessica into the library to help hide her from Glenn; she had been in the halls with him, trying to find her.

Zipporah nodded to Glenn, who disappeared through the door that led behind the mirror.

'Hello, Jessica,' Zipporah purred. 'Thank you for the chat upstairs. I know you want to leave but it was useful to find out how much you knew about everything before we brought you here. As it turns out, you know practically nothing.'

Jessica didn't know how much worse things could have

been if she had admitted to knowing about the basement, let alone if she'd said she was from the police, but she felt some relief anyway at what she had held back.

'Welcome to my greenhouse,' Zipporah said. 'We used to call it a basement, or a dungeon, but that's a bit dull, I think.'

'What are you going to do to me?'

Zipporah was standing directly in front of Jessica, blocking her view of the mirror but she half-turned, motioning towards the table. 'What do you think?'

'Why?'

Zipporah shrugged. 'This place is expensive to run and my father only left the house in his will. You can't think we're able to keep going by simply selling some clothes and crafts every week?'

She's the one always talking about money anyway, especially with things the way they are with the house.

Without knowing she was in the cupboard, Moses had let slip everything Jessica needed, but she hadn't realised the significance.

'I don't understand,' Jessica said.

'Why would you? All you need to know is that people always pay more to see the girls suffer.' She stepped forward, running her gloved hand across Jessica's cheek. 'Especially the pretty ones. You should feel flattered. The men are for fun, for practising on with the tools: the girls for profit.'

'Moses?'

Zipporah didn't react at first, peering intently at Jessica before bursting out laughing. 'This is my house. What I

355

told you upstairs about my marriage is true – but he can have his women if that's what he wants. Keeping this place in my family is far more important than what he gets up to. I just keep an eye on the type of people he's associating with.'

'Heather?'

Zipporah shrugged. 'Well, yes. It's always useful to have someone who'll come running. That's the benefit to deciding who he gets to spend his time with.'

Jessica wouldn't have guessed it before but that was why all of the girls seemed to think of Zipporah as a motherly figure. If they wanted to be with Moses, and so many of them seemed to, then they had to win her approval. That way, she got to control Moses and all of the girls in the house too. It was no wonder she opted for young, pretty females to recruit. They needed the odd man to do the dirtier jobs but the vulnerable women were the ones Zipporah could really use – not to mention the ones who made the most 'profit' if they were no longer needed.

Heather must have seen the light from Jessica's phone, found it and then taken it to Zipporah, hoping it would win back her approval. When she was fishing for information about how Jessica's police interview had gone, Jessica's replies would have been fed back to Zipporah.

Sometimes words can be dangerous, Jessica. We have to be careful about what we say and who we say it to.

Zipporah had said that to Jessica on the stairs but it was only ever to win her trust, which it ultimately did. If she had fallen for it before, saying who she really was, she would have found herself in this room a lot earlier.

Glenn had queried with Moses whether it was wise to let her work outdoors. Jessica had thought it was strange he was showing concern for her, but really he was worried it might mess up her appearance in front of the camera in this dungeon. It had always been planned that she would end up here eventually, with Moses admitting that she 'looked the right type'.

The three of them were in it together: Moses letting someone else do the dirty work but living off the money and girls it brought; Zipporah was in it for the money, to help keep her father's house going; Glenn was someone who enjoyed watching. She had seen it in him as he fingered the tools from the table. She wondered which of them was going to be used on her.

'What was the phone about?' Zipporah asked, brushing the broken pieces to the side with her foot.

Jessica could feel the cuffs resting against the cuts on her wrists. They weren't as tight as the plastic ties and she could at least rotate her wrists and wriggle her fingers.

'You use them to call people,' Jessica replied. 'It's a bit like magic. You type in numbers and press "call", then someone answers at the other end and you have a conversation. It's amazing really. You should try it.'

Zipporah didn't smile, her lips tight. 'Is this really the best time for you to be making jokes?'

'When's there a bad time?'

'Perhaps after you miscarried? Was that particularly funny for you?' Zipporah's sneer said all it needed to. Jessica felt a stabbing in her chest, even though the other woman was nowhere near her. Whatever implements

Glenn or Zipporah used on her would not hurt as much as her words.

Jessica had been so desperate to see that Zipporah was like her, damaged, hurting, that she had missed the obvious. The bruises on her face and neck had not come from being beaten by her husband or Glenn. Jessica had noticed them the day after Wayne had gone missing. Whatever Zipporah had done to him, he had fought back, trying to escape, battling for his life. He had at least caused her a few injuries in the process.

Zipporah turned, walking towards the table. She raised a hand to the mirror, signalling for Glenn to start the camera and possibly the computer too. Jessica didn't know if what was going to happen was going to be broadcast live, or recorded.

The end result would be the same.

'Are we ready?' Zipporah called out.

The reply was muffled but clear. 'It's show time.'

Zipporah pulled the hood up and then clipped her mask into place. It was almost entirely white with faint grey lines around the cheeks. She was dressed entirely in black, a long cape trailing theatrically behind her. The only part of her skin still visible was a hint around the eyes and mouth of the mask. For the people who would be watching, she could be anyone.

Slowly, she picked up one of the saws, posing for the camera as she ran her gloved fingers along the blade, before returning it to the table.

Jessica tensed, her body tingling with fear as Zipporah reached for the drill. She turned the handle in the same way Glenn had, holding it up for the camera before facing Jessica. She spoke quietly, her lips apparently still because of the mask, the soft whirr of the drill almost drowning her out.

'I think we'll start with this today.'

34

Zipporah stepped forward, pressing the tip of the drill bit to Jessica's bicep. She was so close that Jessica could see the smirk through the thin mouth slot of the mask, her eyes narrowing in concentration.

As her fingers tensed on the handle, she froze, peering towards the ceiling as the alarm blared through the house above. For a fraction of a second, their eyes locked. In a flash, Zipporah lowered the drill, spinning towards the mirror.

'What's going on, Glenn?' she shouted.

The alarm was stifled by the padding but Jessica could still hear a clear wail; the same sound from when the group of locals had been outside throwing stones.

Glenn burst in through the door next to the mirror, eyes staring above.

'I have no idea,' he replied as Zipporah crossed to the table, dropping the drill, not bothering to line it up with the other tools this time.

They leant in, whispering something to each other and then Glenn ran through the second door towards the stairs.

Jessica continued to rotate her wrists, contorting her fingers up and stretching into her sleeve. The cuts from the ties were burning but she ignored the pain, wriggling furiously.

Zipporah unclipped the mask, putting it on the table before dropping the hood next to it and turning to face Jessica. Her expression was difficult to read; angry but hesitant. She seemed curious too, looking at Jessica in a different way, not as a plaything, now as an opponent.

She stepped closer, her footsteps clip-clopping across the hard floor, the echo dying almost as quickly as it started.

When she was a metre away from Jessica, she stopped, staring into her eyes. 'What did you do?'

'What can I possibly have done? I'm tied to a pillar in a basement. I have no phone, no contact with the outside world.'

'But you've done something, haven't you?'

Jessica could not stop a grin from sliding onto her face. 'Maybe.'

'What?'

'That'd be telling.'

Zipporah turned, striding back to the table and grabbing the hammer. 'How about we see how smug you are when you're missing a few teeth?'

'Try it. My dentist keeps going on about how he can give me a good deal on some veneers anyway.'

Zipporah hesitated, stepping backwards and then forward. 'Who are you?'

'Detective Sergeant Jessica Daniel, Manchester Metropolitan CID at your service.'

'You're police?'

'Unless CID stands for Central Idiot Division, which

admittedly it could sometimes.' Jessica didn't feel as confident as she sounded but she needed to play for time.

Zipporah seemed frozen to the spot, her arrogance gone as she glanced towards the door that led to the stairs. There was no sign of Glenn and the alarm was still raging.

She turned back to Jessica, angry. 'How did it feel when your dead child flopped out of you?'

This time, Jessica was braced for the comment. 'How does it feel being so haggard that your husband has to prey on girls half your age?'

Zipporah lunged, a cry of incoherent rage erupting from her lungs. Overhead, the lights flickered off, before humming back to life. In the half a second they were gone, Jessica leapt forward, the handcuffs hanging limply from one wrist. Zipporah was so shocked that she had no time to move as Jessica's forehead smashed upwards into her nose.

Jessica felt the satisfying splat as Zipporah's nose fractured. She reached up to wipe the blood from her face as Zipporah fell backwards, the hammer bouncing across the floor with a metallic clatter. Jessica gave her no time to recover, reeling back and punching her hard in the face three times, grunting in effort and anger, before heaving herself to her feet and using the key to undo the cuffs.

When she had seen two sets of keys hanging next to the handcuffs in the cabinet on her first visit to the basement, Jessica had thought they might be useful at some point, burying one deep in her back pocket. It had taken a bit of work to get it out while being tied to the pillar, not to mention twisting her wrist enough to unclip the cuffs – but then she had learned the basics of palming and escapism from Hugo. He might be an unconventional teacher, tying Jessica and himself to a bench in the middle of St John's Gardens in winter, but he certainly knew his stuff.

Zipporah was unconscious on the floor, blood drenching her face. Jessica peered towards the table of tools, a horrific thought flashing into her mind before she dismissed it. Her heart was racing as she turned to the mirror, trying to clear the rest of Zipporah's blood from her forehead but only succeeding in smearing it across her skin. She stared at the haunted stranger in the mirror: emaciated, drying blood on her hands and face, in her hair, feeling dazed and weary, as if the last minute had happened to someone else.

Jessica clicked back to the present as a large bang sounded above, followed by someone shouting. She took one final look at Zipporah's unmoving body, plucked the hammer from the floor, and then headed for the stairs.

When the alarm had gone off because of the youths throwing stones, everyone had moved calmly towards the bedrooms but this felt different. The electricity was flickering on and off, the strobe lights overhead mixing with the fading moon and rising sun to create a menacing and disorientating atmosphere. Jessica could hear footsteps on the floor above but the corridor outside the entrance to the basement was empty.

Jessica dashed through the passages, heading towards the front door, hearing Glenn's voice shouting as she got near. Blue flashing lights spilled through the windows at the front, tingeing the corridor where Jessica waited, back pressed to the wall.

'Police!' Glenn yelled, stating the obvious as someone charged past Jessica.

She could hear Moses too but his voice lacked the gravitas of before and was being drowned out by the din as Glenn shouted over the top of him.

The noise was building; the alarm, the screeching of tyres outside, the clatter of footsteps around the hallway, people shouting and calling to each other in confusion. Jessica turned, racing through the passages towards the kitchen. As she rounded the final corner, she almost ran into Ali, confused and panicked in a pair of striped pyjamas. He stepped away from her quickly, eyes flickering to the hammer in her hand and the blood on her face.

'What's going on?'

Jessica had to shout to make herself heard over the alarm. 'Everyone has to get out. Use the kitchen door if you have to.'

He yelled a reply but Jessica couldn't hear him, shaking her head and bellowing, 'Go'.

Ali still seemed unsure, setting off in the opposite direction, peering back over his shoulder. Jessica couldn't wait, running for the kitchen and the back door. Even as she pulled down the handle, she still had a twinge in her stomach that she was trapped, only believing she was free as she gulped in the cool morning air. She stopped, crouching to touch the dewy grass, the freshness clearing her mind.

The alarm was faint now she was outside but Jessica

heard someone running, looking around as Charley dashed towards her, a dozen uniformed officers trailing behind.

'I got your email,' she said, breathlessly.

Jessica stood, clutching the hammer.

'What's going on?' Charley added, glancing nervously towards the weapon.

'Zipporah and Glenn are part of some torture website thing. When I emailed you from their machine, I didn't realise it was her.'

'Zipporah?'

'She's the main one.'

'What about Moses?'

'He knows but I'm not sure how involved he is.'

Overhead, a cloud drifted slightly, flooding the area with the eerie mix of moon and sunlight, allowing Charley to notice the blood on Jessica's face. 'What happened to your—'

'It doesn't matter. I'm fine.'

'What's going on in there now?'

'I got away from Zipporah but—' Jessica tailed off, suddenly aware of what she had done. 'Oh no – I've left her in there with a giant bomb.'

35

In her confusion and desperation to get away, Jessica had left Zipporah unconscious, forgetting she was a few metres away from a potential bomb big enough to destroy everything in the immediate vicinity.

'Bomb?' Charley queried.

'I emailed you before I found it. I wanted to call but they took my phone. There's an area in the basement packed with ammonium nitrate.'

Charley's eyes widened. 'Is it rigged?'

'I'm not sure. There were wires running away from it but I don't know enough to say. We've got to get everyone out.'

Charley stepped backwards, holding her arms out to stop anyone passing. 'I can't let any of my men enter if there's a chance it could blow up.'

'But there are innocent people in there!'

'People who chose to be there.'

'If you retreat now, they could go into lockdown. Everyone will be used as hostages.'

Charley took two more steps backwards, pushing the closest officer away. 'We'll have to call the bomb squad anyway. This goes way above either of us.'

'But they're real people! They have families; parents and kids looking out for them. They're not numbers.'

'We have to call—'

'Bollocks to that. You know what they're like; they'll spend three hours talking about what they're going to do, by which time everyone will be locked inside. There'll be news helicopters over the top and we'll each spend three months giving evidence to some prick in a suit about what went wrong – even though what actually went wrong was the sheer number of pricks in suits sticking their oars in.'

Charley shook her head. 'We've got to go.' She turned to the officers, shooing them away and telling them to get off the grounds.

Jessica heard a clatter of footsteps behind her, stepping out of the way just in time to avoid being trampled by Ali and two others. They all stopped as they saw the police officers retreating, afraid of the outsiders.

Jessica couldn't remember the name of the person nearest to her but she grabbed his arm anyway, pointing towards the far side of the grounds and telling him to run.

'What's happening?' Ali asked. 'Glenn's at the front door stopping people leaving. He says the police are here to take us all.'

'There's a bomb in the basement. The police are here to get us all to safety.'

'How do you know?'

'I just do.'

Ali seemed torn between following the other two or running back into the house to be by Glenn's side.

'Heather's still in there,' Jessica said, knowing the effect it would have.

Ali glanced behind him, then back to Jessica.

'There's definitely a bomb in the basement?'

'I think so. We need to get everyone out.'

'Fine.'

Ali turned, running back into the house. Jessica started to follow but Charley had hold of her top.

'You don't have to do any more,' she said, tugging Jessica backwards.

'I want to get Heather and everyone else out.'

'What about Glenn? Zipporah? Moses?'

Jessica raised the hammer. 'What about them?'

'Are you really going to use that?'

'I hope not.'

Charley sighed, signalling towards her officers who were disappearing over the top of the ridge. 'Let's get to safety first. When I was talking to your DCI about using you after our first meeting, I told him no because I could see this rash streak. He assured me your instincts were good and that you wouldn't do anything stupid. Why are you so reckless?'

Jessica pulled herself free. 'What else have I got to lose?'

The need to escape had been driven largely by fear of being trapped in the basement, but now that dread had gone Jessica was ready to finish what she started. She ran back inside, bounding through the kitchen into the main part of the house. Ali was in the corridor, shouting at Katie and two more people to get out through the back door.

'Can you get people out?' Jessica called to him.

She couldn't hear his reply over the racket going on around him but it wasn't difficult to lip-read his one-word reply: 'Yes.'

Jessica gripped the hammer tighter, heading for the basement. She didn't just want to get everyone out, she wanted to stop Zipporah entirely.

The corridors now felt familiar, even with the overhead lights still flickering. Jessica took the most direct route to the basement, skidding to a halt as Moses hurried down the stairs. He was tugging at his beard, eyes wide, knowing the game was up.

'It's Glenn,' he shouted. 'He's at the front door shouting about a bomb. He's trying to keep us all in.'

Jessica took him at his word that he didn't know about the potential explosives. There was no reason for him to be faking it. 'That's because your mad wife has fertiliser packed into the basement.'

'It's true? How do you know?'

Jessica raised the hammer slightly, making Moses take a step backwards. Realising she must have been down there – and escaped – he didn't bother waiting for a reply, pushing past her and running for the front door, no doubt to get himself to safety.

A coward to the end.

Jessica started to call after him that the back door was unlocked but stopped herself – he could find his own way out.

She continued on, past the games room and Moses's office, through the unlocked door down to the basement. Before she turned into the main room, Jessica could see in the mirror that Zipporah was no longer on the floor. She dashed around the corner, taking one look at the pool of blood before racing through the opening on the far side into the area with the fertiliser.

Zipporah had gone. The lights were still off, the only sign of life the cleaning bucket which had toppled onto its side. In the computer room, the monitor was still on, illuminating the darkened space with a hazy blue glow, but otherwise everything was as it was when she had last been here.

Determined not to let her get away, Jessica ran out of the basement, heading through the empty corridors up the stairs towards the bedroom with the wide double doors. One of them was open a crack and Jessica pushed her way in. A huge oval-shaped window was at the far end of the room, allowing a perfect view of the sun rising in the distance. Opposite was a four-poster bed next to a smaller double bed. The covers were tossed to the side, clothes strewn across the floor.

At the other end of the room, a chest had three drawers hanging open, with an empty jewellery box upside down on the ground. In the corner, a safe had been opened and was bare except for two cleared-out metal cash boxes.

Jessica went to the window, looking out over the front of the property as the blue lights of the police vehicles continued to whirl. A few of them were pulling away, with other uniformed officers waiting in the distance close to the gates. There were fewer officers than she had first thought but her email to Charley had clearly caused some sort of panic, as an early-morning warrant would have been essential to make all of this happen.

With no sign of Zipporah, Jessica went back down the

stairs, following the sounds of raised voices towards the front door. The hallways were empty but the alarm was still going off. She pressed against the wall, peering around the corner to see a scene of pure relief.

In the main entrance, the front door was open, Glenn and Moses both on their knees, hands cuffed behind their backs as Charley stood over them, half-a-dozen officers at her shoulder.

Charley waved Jessica across, not taking her eyes from the two men in front of her.

'I thought you were retreating and calling for help?' Jessica said quietly enough that only Charley would hear, even though the alarm would have drowned it out to listening ears.

'What can I say? We didn't want to leave anyone behind. People are people.'

Jessica couldn't stop a small grin from creeping onto her face. 'Did you stop Zipporah? She's not in the basement and she isn't upstairs.'

Charley pulled a radio from her back pocket, checking with the person they had at the back door, before shaking her head. 'She must still be in here. We'll check the basement first and then send a team through. There are only two doors, right?'

'Shite.'

Jessica turned, running as fast as she could until she reached Moses's office. The door was ajar, the window wide open. She approached it anyway, peering out towards the woods and the orange sky, knowing Zipporah was gone for good.

36

Jessica cradled the mug between her fingers, using it to warm her hands. 'How come we get tea from a machine that tastes of washing-up liquid and you get proper hot drinks up here?'

Charley leant back in the chair, yawning, before turning to DCI Cole. 'I'm not the person to take it up with.'

Cole had a drink himself. 'Luckily I keep a kettle in my office, so I don't go near the machine anyway.' He winked at Jessica. 'Perk of the job.'

Jessica pulled the blanket around herself that she had been cradling since it was given to her by an officer as she left the house. 'This incident room is quite nice too,' she said. 'Your tables don't wobble, the lights don't flicker, the walls aren't crumbling.'

'Our toilets flooded while you've been off,' Cole added.

Jessica shook her head, unsurprised. 'Let's hear it then,' she said, turning to Charley. 'I've been here most of the day giving statements and I want to go home. Your lot can visit if you want to hear any more.'

Charley put down her mug, stifling another yawn. 'There's no sign of Zipporah – Sophie. We found a few spots of blood on the grass leading towards the woods but lost them pretty quickly. We assume she slipped away as we were dealing with everyone else coming out of the house. Her photo has gone to all of the local forces and the media but she had a big head start. We can't be sure because it's such a big place to search but it also looks like she took a large amount of cash. We found a few loose twenty-pound notes at the bottom of a drawer in the office she left through and we suspect she took some from the bedroom too. She could have thousands of pounds on her.'

'What about the bomb?' Cole asked, looking disapprovingly at Jessica.

'We've got a team at the house removing the fertiliser now. It wasn't primed and was quite basic. Without being able to ask her, we suspect Zipporah didn't try to set it off either because she didn't know how, or because she wanted to make sure she got away.'

'I think it was to do with the house,' Jessica replied. 'Moses said something about money being awkward and I reckon it all came down to that. It was the one thing she actually seemed to care about.'

Charley shrugged. 'You might be right. We're trying to get warrants for the off-shore bank accounts, so we're not sure what sort of a state they might be in.'

'Is Moses speaking?' Jessica asked.

'He's denying all knowledge, saying it must have been Glenn in it with his wife. Glenn's doing the same, saying it was down to Moses and Zipporah. Her involvement is the only thing they agree on. When we've finished going over your statements, we'll go back to them, but we've taken the computer equipment and our guy says there are still videos on that. There are IP addresses of the users, plus we're doing some work to trace the credit cards people used for access. This could end up being massive. The videos weren't just produced at the house, there was a whole underground network thing.'

'All creating these torture videos?' Jessica asked, staring into the remnants of what was left in her mug, trying not to think about it too much.

Charley nodded. 'I've not seen them but we've had someone on it all day in case there was any clue to where Zipporah might have headed. They found something of Liam being drowned and another of Wayne being beaten to death.'

Jessica shivered involuntarily, knowing it had happened to Wayne as she slept upstairs; knowing it could have been her.

'Anything else?' she asked.

'Glenn's wife . . .'

'Naomi.'

'Yes, she's been very helpful. It sounds as if she's been trapped in there for a fair while wanting to get away. She's been giving statements most of the day too. With that, the videos and everything else, there should be enough to charge Glenn at the very least. In the next day or two, we're going to sweep the woods to see if there are any bodies there. It's very unlikely these were the only two.'

'What about Moses?'

'Charging him might be harder because we don't have Naomi's direct evidence and, from what you say, he wasn't necessarily a part of what went on in the basement – even

374

if he knew about it. You know what the CPS are like – they'd rather have a single nailed-on charge for Glenn than something against him and Moses if there's anything flimsy. None of the residents seem to have anything bad to say about Moses – that's if they are talking at all.'

Jessica put her mug down a little forcefully, the clang betraying how annoyed she was. 'He sent Kevin down to the basement – he knew something went on down there.'

'We'll have to see. It's looking a little circumstantial at the moment. Glenn's statement probably won't be enough because he's trying to get himself off.'

'So let's do him for sexual assault then.'

Charley and Cole froze, both staring at Jessica, waiting for the other to speak. Unable to make eye contact with either of them, Jessica explained the occasions he had touched her, insisting she would go to court and do whatever was necessary to make sure he was charged with something.

They each asked if she was okay, pointing out there were specially trained officers to deal with these types of cases, but Jessica said she would sort things in her own way.

Feigning resilience even after everything she had been through.

Charley led Jessica and Cole into the hall of the police station, halting in reception to say goodbye. The area was buzzing with activity, with some of the house's former residents sitting in chairs, staring uncomfortably at the floor and other officers hurrying in and out. Jessica

375

wondered what would happen to them. Despite everything that had gone on at the house, it was their home. Now they only had the lives they had run away from.

'Hey!'

Jessica looked up to see Heather standing and pushing past an officer towards her. Jessica started to ask if she was all right but Heather took her by surprise, shoving her hard in the chest and then, as she was pulled back by two officers, pursing her lips and spitting in Jessica's face.

Charley reacted furiously, ordering the officers to take her to the cells, but Jessica wiped the saliva away with her sleeve, saying she should let it go. Heather was shouting hysterically, her words vicious but uncomfortably close to the truth for Jessica.

'You might be able to fool your mates but I know how fucked up you are.'

Cole and Charley each had a hand on Jessica's shoulder, telling her things were fine. Jessica felt more sorry for Heather than annoyed. Whatever had been going on at the house was based around the egos of Zipporah, Moses and Glenn, with everyone else drawn into it.

It wasn't unfamiliar now but Jessica had no idea what time it was, only realising it was night as they moved towards the glass front door where it was dark. She felt tired, trying to remember the last time she had slept.

As Cole was about to lead her outside, Charley cut in, asking if she could have a moment. Cole nodded, saying he would wait outside, leaving them alone in the porch between two glass doors.

'Thanks for your help,' Charley said.

Jessica shrugged, too tired to accept any praise. 'I just want to go home.'

'Country life not for you?'

'Maybe . . . No . . . Perhaps. I don't know. How did you do it?'

'What?'

'Leaving everything and going somewhere completely new.'

Charley bit her bottom lip, thinking. 'I suppose it's easy when you have nothing to regret leaving behind.'

'I suppose . . .'

'What about you? Do you have something to go back home to?'

'I don't know.'

Charley reached into a pocket inside her suit jacket, taking out a business card and passing it over. 'If you ever want to try something new, I know a few places you could have a look at. It'd be good to work together again at some point.'

Jessica read Charley's name on the card and then pocketed it.

'We'll be in touch about Moses and everything. I don't want you to feel you have to do something you don't want to. I'll know a lot more tomorrow, so we'll talk then.'

'Okay.'

Jessica was never sure how to say goodbye at the best of times, especially with someone she didn't really know. The two women hugged briefly and then Jessica went through the main door into the car park.

The breeze was chilly, the night cloudy. Jessica pulled

the blanket around her, realising no one had asked for it back. On the far side of the car park, she could see three figures waiting for her under a street lamp, leaning against Cole's 4x4. Even though the only thing she wanted to do was sleep, she couldn't resist grinning as she trudged across the tarmac.

Initially, no one spoke as Jessica rested against the bonnet watching them. 'How long have you been here?' she asked eventually.

DC Izzy Diamond stepped forward, putting an arm around Jessica's shoulders. 'About six hours. It's bloody cold out here and Dave's spent five hours fifty-nine minutes talking shite.'

'What happened to your hair?'

Izzy pulled at a long strand, letting it catch the light. 'What's wrong with it?'

'It's brown. I've only ever seen it red or purple.'

'This is the natural colour. I fancied something different.'

Jessica held out her free arm, inviting DC Dave Rowlands towards her and giving him a squeeze. 'It's good to see you both.'

'Are you okay?' Dave asked.

'Been better, been worse.'

They stepped away, ready to climb into the vehicle when Dave asked the question Jessica had been anticipating: 'When are you coming back?'

SATURDAY

37

Jessica sat on the sofa staring at the floor. She remembered the day she and Adam had chosen the sofa, oblivious to the fact that her first choice would have been too big to get through the door and only settling for this one when he pointed that out.

'Welcome home,' she said.

She could feel Adam watching her in silence, waiting for her to acknowledge him. When she peered up, he was sitting cross-legged in the armchair, hands on his knees. He was wearing tight dark jeans and a T-shirt that showed how skinny he was. It wasn't just her who had lost weight over the past few months.

'Is this still home?' he asked.

'If you want it to be.'

He tucked a strand of hair behind his ear. 'I told you I would wait – but there's no point if you have nothing to wait for.'

'I don't want you to wait any longer. I want you to stay here for good.'

Adam puffed out his cheeks, breathing out slowly. He sounded so tired. 'We can't keep doing this every time something goes wrong.'

'I know.'

'What do you want, Jess?'

'I want you to come home.'

'That's not what I'm talking about.'

Jessica looked away again, unable to continue looking at him. It hadn't been long ago that she had been here by herself, hiding under the window to stop Cole seeing her. It felt like such a long time had passed.

'I don't know what I want.'

'Do you want to go back to work?'

'Not right now but yes. I'd have to talk to a few people.'

'What about us?'

'I want you to forgive me.'

'What about everything the doctor said?'

'If you forgive me, we can see him again. I'll listen this time.'

Adam uncrossed his legs, moving to sit next to Jessica on the sofa and putting an arm around her. She rested her head on his shoulder.

'I'm sorry,' she said. She felt like she wanted to cry but had such a feeling of emptiness that there was nothing left.

'Stop saying that.'

'But I am.'

'I know and you've said it enough times. There's no manual to cope with everything you've been through.'

Jessica closed her eyes. 'Why are you always so nice to me?'

'You shouldn't have to ask that. When you love someone, you're nice to them.'

'But I've been horrible to you.'

Adam gripped her tighter. 'You've coped with things

the only way you know how – relying on yourself. We just have to train you to turn to others. To turn to me.'

'I can do that.'

Jessica pulled away slightly, peering closely at Adam's face.

'What are you doing?' he asked.

'Looking at you.'

'Why?'

'Because you're good to look at. And I couldn't see you properly when you were sat over there. My eyes are going, remember?'

'I remember.'

'How is Georgia?'

'It looks like she's going to be moving up this way. She's waiting on a couple of things. We'll find out later this week.'

'That's great . . .'

There was a short silence as Adam waited for her to finally ask the question she had brought him here for. She swallowed hard, before finally whispering it. 'Are you going to move back in?'

Adam didn't hesitate. 'Yes – but I need you to understand one thing. Not just say you do, but really appreciate what I'm saying.'

'What?'

Adam took a breath, composing himself. 'It was my baby too, Jess.'

A few moments earlier, Jessica had felt unable to cry any more but as she grabbed Adam tighter, clutching and clawing at him, breathing him in, she had one final sob for the child they had lost.

Adam held her back, leaning in and whispering in her ear. 'Remember what you said when we found out you were pregnant? Let's do that.'

ALMOST A YEAR AGO

Jessica could feel her heart pounding as she reached forward and picked up the pregnancy-testing stick, deliberately holding the indicator bar downwards.

'Well?' Adam asked.

'Well what?'

'What does it say?'

'What do you want it to say?'

Adam grinned. 'I'm not sure the world's ready for another mini-you.'

Jessica smiled back. 'But . . . ?'

'. . . But, it would be pretty fun inflicting another you on everyone.'

Jessica took a deep breath and could feel her hand trembling. She knew her life could change based on what was on the other side of the stick. A lifetime of being scared of children had suddenly been replaced by a feeling of being comfortable with one of her own, surprising her more than anyone.

She pressed her thumb across the result and turned it over. 'Are you ready?'

Adam grinned. 'For you? Always.'

Jessica smiled back, removing her thumb to show two blue bars, holding them up into the light to make certain there wasn't just one.

'What does two mean?' Adam asked.

Jessica turned the stick over, peering at the back and making an hmming sound. 'I have no idea.'

'Aren't women supposed to know this stuff?'

'I don't know, we were never taught about pregnancy tests at school.' Jessica peered over Adam's head towards the kitchen of the flat they were staying in that belonged to her friend Caroline. 'I threw the box and instructions in the bin,' she added, handing the stick to Adam and standing up.

He took it from her, before holding it in the air between his thumb and forefinger. 'Ugh, you've had a wee on this!'

Jessica went to the kitchen, hunting through the bin without looking over her shoulder. 'You'll be fine. Stop being a baby.'

Finding the leaflet she wanted, she pulled it out of the crumpled box and returned to the sofa, where Adam was holding the stick at arm's length. She unfolded the instructions, running her finger down the page until she found what she needed.

'How many lines are there?' she asked, deliberately teasing.

'Two.'

'Hmm, two lines . . . let me see.'

'It can't be that hard to read. How about you hold your own wee stick and I'll check the page.'

Jessica snatched the paper away before Adam could move, standing in front of him and holding it behind her back.

'Guess what?'

'What?'

'We're going to have a baby.'

Adam dropped the stick as Jessica dropped the paper. He knelt in front of her, lifting her shirt and rubbing the area below her stomach. When he spoke, his voice cracked. 'Really?'

'Really.'

'Wow.'

'Can we make a pact?' Jessica asked.

Adam hadn't taken his eyes from her skin, running his fingers along gently. 'What?'

Jessica rested a hand on the back of his head, stroking his hair. 'Regardless of whether it's a boy or a girl, whether they're straight or gay, beautiful or annoying, shouty like me or calm like you. Whatever we've made, let's make sure we never forget this feeling. Deal?'

His reply was instant. 'Deal.'

APRIL

A Jessica Daniel interlude*

by Kerry Wilkinson

It's every parent's worst nightmare.

April Willis is walking to school when someone in a white van tries to snatch her from the street.

It's the second attack in less than a week, and, with parents and students beginning to panic, it's down to Detective Sergeant Jessica Daniel to find the culprit.

* This story occurs between *Playing with Fire* and *Thicker Than Water*.

Detective Sergeant Jessica Daniel used a hand to shield her eyes from the glare, spotted no one, and so rapped on the glass door.

The problem with being a police officer was that something was always happening. There was never a time where the criminals, ne'er-do-wells and general pains-in-the-backsides put their collective feet up, sat down to watch Jeremy Kyle, and thought, 'Nah, I can't be bothered today'.

Sod having a national holiday for St George's Day, forget May Day, let's not worry about the weather on Easter Monday. Could everyone just get together, find one Monday a year, and declare it a stop-acting-like-an-arse day. It'd be bliss. No early morning call-outs; no late nights in interview rooms; no ever-increasing pile of paperwork. Just a nice, peaceful few hours at work.

Lovely.

Still, if it *was* a national holiday, everyone would go out on the lash, want to kick off, and then the whole stop-acting-like-an-arse thing would become like every other bank holiday, riddled with tales of boozy assaults and people vomiting all over themselves, before they collapsed into a gutter and had a stranger call an ambulance.

What a rubbish idea.

Jessica stepped backwards, peering up at the banner across the top of the doors. She had at least turned up to the correct school, which showed more ability than above half of Manchester Central's CID division. Turning up at the wrong place would've been a tough one to live down.

She tapped on the glass again, smiling towards a woman who emerged from a door that Jessica had assumed was a cupboard. Either it wasn't, or school budgets really had been slashed beyond all recognition. The woman motioned towards the side of the door, where there was an intercom and buzzer that Jessica had somehow missed. That would have definitely been simpler . . .

Jessica took out her identification card and pressed it to the window as the woman peered at it closely, before offering a satisfied nod and pushing something on the wall to unlock the door.

She wasted no time, relocking the door behind Jessica and turning. 'You'll have to sign in, then I'll take you through to Mrs Marsh's office.'

There was a small table next to the door with two clipboards and pens. One was marked 'Late List', the other 'Visitors'. Jessica scrawled her name on the visitors' sheet and then followed the woman.

Being marched through the school corridors reminded her of being a young girl. There were posters and certificates pinned to every wall: sign-up sheets; reminders about school trips and clubs, plus an array of paintings and drawings. The problem with school was that it was wasted on the young. In your twenties, it would be fabulous to go on regular trips to various places and be encouraged to be creative on a daily basis. After being jammed in call-centres, offices and shops, adults would actually appreciate school. Kids simply wanted to play in the park and pick on the smallest kid, not waste time in a classroom.

The woman led Jessica up a small flight of stairs, through a set of double doors, and into an office that smelled like it had been cleaned with instant coffee.

Mrs Marsh was tall and officious, with greying hair tightened into a bun, a crisp white blouse and a grey skirt. Very head-teachery, which was perhaps largely why the governors had appointed her. You had to look the part, if nothing else. Jessica introduced herself and then they did the whole tea/coffee, yes/no, are you sure thing, before Mrs Marsh pointed at a door, lowering her voice.

'April's next door,' she said. 'I figured it was best if we pulled her out of classes temporarily.'

'Are either of her parents here?'

Mrs Marsh shook her head. 'When April got to school and told us what happened, we called you, of course, but she said she wanted to be the one to contact her mum. She made the call but said her mother couldn't make it in – I assume she's stuck at work, or something similar. She's aware of what occurred.'

'How old is April?'

The head teacher understood the implication. 'Thirteen – I'll be happy to sit in.'

'Is there anything else I need to know?'

Mrs Marsh glanced towards the door, lowering her voice further. 'Just that she's been through a lot. She'll finish year eight in a few weeks but she's not had a good time since coming here. She was one of the stars in year seven but her father died around a year ago, just before the summer break. She came back in September but her grades have fallen away, she's missed days and there's a problem with her time-keeping. I've spoken to her mother on the phone a few times and her aunt came in for parents' evening but it's not had much effect.' She glanced at the door again, dropping her voice to a whisper. 'It's such a shame – she's clearly a smart cookie but thirteen is when some of the students start to . . . *change* and she's had to cope with her father's passing too.'

'How did her father die?'

'Cancer, I believe. I don't know all the details but I think it was sudden. We offered support when she came back but April wanted to do her own thing. Her form tutor says she won't talk about it, which is – of course – up to her. There's only so much we can do. We used to have a student counsellor who worked for three secondary schools and spent two days a week here. He was made redundant a year ago.' She shrugged and sighed, checking her watch. 'Cutbacks.'

April Willis was sipping from a can of Coke Zero, not looking up from the floor. When Jessica introduced herself, she received a grunted 'hi' in return, which was quite animated for a thirteen-year-old. April was wearing a pleated grey skirt with a maroon sweatshirt. A striped tie poked out from the top and her greasy dark hair was wrenched back into a ponytail. Unlike the puberty-affected thirteen-year-old girls Jessica remembered from her own time at school, April wore no make-up and had no jewellery other than a small stud in her ear. Her bag was underneath her feet, a black canvas backpack, covered in small round badges for various bands that Jessica had never heard of.

'Are you okay to talk to me, April?' Jessica asked.

The girl nodded but didn't speak.

'Can you tell me what happened on your way to school?'

April nodded at Mrs Marsh. 'I already told her.'

'I understand that but it'd be nice if you could tell me too.'

A sigh.

'I was on my way to school when a van pulled up—'

'Whereabouts were you?' Jessica asked.

'On that road behind the church, just before you get to Bold Street.'

'Were you walking by yourself?'

A shrug, presumably meaning yes.

'Do you often walk on your own?'

'So what?'

'I'm not trying to catch you out,' Jessica said. 'But the more detail you can give me, the more chance we have of catching the person responsible. I'm asking to try to find out if you could have been specifically targeted. For instance, if you're usually with a friend but were on your own today, that's a change to your routine. If you always walk on your own, then it's more random.'

'Oh . . .' April finally peered up, putting her can of Coke on a nearby table and tucking a loose strand of hair behind her ear. She didn't meet Jessica's eye, instead staring through the window towards the car park, but it was an improvement. 'I usually walk on my own.'

Jessica asked where she lived and then added: 'How long had you been walking?'

'Five or ten minutes.'

'Did you notice anyone following you, or paying particular attention?'

'No.'

'Okay, so tell me what happened.'

'There's this road behind the church which is a bit of a cut-through. I was walking along when this white van pulled in next to me. I kept walking but the door opened and this man grabbed me, trying to pull me inside.'

'Did he say anything to you?'

April was biting her nails. 'He asked what the time was but I kept walking.'

'So did he grab you from behind?'

'I s'pose.'

'Did he say anything while he was grabbing you?'

April's eyes darted towards the clock on the wall, then back to the floor. She pulled her knees up to her chest and started to hug herself. 'No.'

'How would you describe him?'

'Just a man.'

'We can have you speak to an artist but what colour hair did he have?'

'Dunno, dark, I suppose.'

'How tall was he?'

'Dunno, taller than me.'

'What was he wearing?'

'Dunno.'

They went back and forth but April couldn't remember much about either the van or the man who'd tried to snatch her. He was white, not old but not young, she hadn't spotted an accent when he'd asked the time, plus there'd been no markings on the van. After he grabbed her, she swung her elbows, screamed, and then ran for it. It wasn't a lot to go on.

'You called us at eight forty,' Jessica said. 'Was that straight after it happened, or when you got to school?'

'At school.'

'This might sound like a stupid question, but was there anyone else around when it happened – students, adults, people on their way to work?'

'I dunno – I didn't see anyone.'

Both Jessica and Mrs Marsh said they could find someone for her to talk to, or take her home, or contact her mother again, but April said she wanted to get on with her day. Jessica offered a small shrug to Mrs Marsh, who dismissed the girl. With her freedom granted, April grabbed her bag and scuttled out of the room.

'That's what a lot of thirteen-year-olds are like, I'm afraid,' Mrs Marsh said. 'They hit puberty and then you can't get anything out of them – even when it's something like this.'

'Probably shock, too,' Jessica added.

The head teacher sighed, rubbing the bridge of her

nose. 'That's two attempted abductions in two weeks – Lucy last week, April this. The parents were angry after the first one and the students are obviously frightened. We've put out letters and had assemblies, urging them to walk in twos, but it's not something we can force – not that I'm saying we should.'

'We're doing all we can,' Jessica replied.

Mrs Marsh yawned, waving her arm. 'Oh, I know, I know . . . it wasn't a dig at you. When I heard you'd arrested that man last week, I assumed that was it but then you let him go.'

'He had an alibi – he was on CCTV at his work on the other side of the city ten minutes after the first abduction attempt. We only brought him in for questioning because there was a partial match from the number plate on his white van to an ANPR camera two streets over from where it happened. He was never arrested. Somebody tweeted that we'd got him and then we spent two days trying to play it down.'

'Right . . . I know . . . sorry, I'm not having a go.' She smiled weakly. 'It's just that it's two girls in the same year. You feel protective of them, well, I do. I just want you to catch the person responsible.'

'We're still working on various leads – vehicles and potential drivers, plus his van wouldn't have disappeared this morning. He'll be on a traffic cam somewhere. We'll find him.'

Mrs Marsh nodded. 'All of the girls are in morning assembly if you want a quick tour of Lucy and April's form room. I'm not sure there'll be anything there, but . . .'

Jessica didn't think it would provide much but there were already people trying to track down the white van and its owner, with others going door-to-door in the area around the church. There wasn't a lot she could add by joining them. She called the station, passed on the few details that April had given her, even though there was little new to add to those from the 999 call, and then followed Mrs Marsh up a set of stairs.

Compared to Jessica's time at school, the biggest difference was the computers. When she'd been a student, there was a dedicated IT room with a few fat-backed monitors, a constant hum, and a general sense that only the weird kids spent much time there. April's classroom had a row of flat screens and thin brushed-metal keyboards on a long table at the back. There was a triple-locked cabinet next to the desk at the front, where Mrs Marsh said they kept the iPads. The whiteboard was covered in titles of Shakespeare plays, with posters around the walls depicting the characters and historical figures about whom he'd written.

'As well as being April's form room, this is an English classroom,' Mrs Marsh said.

Jessica continued peering around the walls, focusing on the poster for *Macbeth*, with a man in a crown and a map of Scotland. She read the text around the edge, trying to remember the plot.

'I hated Shakespeare at school,' Mrs Marsh said out of the blue. When Jessica turned, the other woman was sitting on the corner of a table, smoothing her skirt. 'I just didn't get it. Plus, it gets rammed down their throats sometimes, when there's no context of who Shakespeare was and the times in which he lived.'

The classroom was eerily quiet. There were school bags littering the floor, with jackets across the backs of the chairs. Early summer sun was beaming through the windows, casting its light across already faded posters. It felt like a space that needed to be occupied.

Jessica continued her loop of the room, stopping in front of an A3 poster. 'HOUSE OF PORTIA' was written across the top, with 'This week's star: Kim Lever, 8 merits', underneath.

'What's the House of Portia?' Jessica asked.

'Each year is separated into four houses,' Mrs Marsh replied. 'Macbeth, Hamlet, Portia and Katherina. The students get points for good work, high marks, reaching certain attendance criteria – that sort of thing. There are also inter-house competitions, some sporting, others like our annual literary quiz, and the debating cup. At the end of the year, there's a winner.'

'What do they win?'

Mrs Marsh snorted, not seeming so officious. 'Pride.'

Jessica laughed too. 'Right . . . that old chestnut. That's how they try to get us to do unpaid overtime.'

The head teacher smiled more widely. 'It's not just teachers who get screwed then? Either way, some of the students take it very seriously. There's a house cup, upon which each year's winner's name is engraved. It's been running for over fifty years. It does work but there's an obvious problem—'

Jessica cut her off: 'The kids who are bothered are the ones who'd be keen to do well anyway. The ones who don't care about getting high marks also don't care about their house winning the cup.'

Mrs Marsh held up both of her palms, a half-smile on her face.

'I didn't really care about high marks at school,' Jessica added.

'Not just that – Portia's romped away with it this year. Unless something disastrous happens, they'll win, so even the students who *are* interested start getting bored around this time.'

'What do you mean by disastrous?'

'They can lose points for bad behaviour – not doing their homework, being late, even things like running in the hallways.' She smiled. 'That's a recent rule update – you'd be surprised by how many kids start walking when they know running will lose them merits. It polices itself because nobody wants to be the one who costs their house points.'

Sneaky.

Jessica thought they should definitely bring in a similar house system at the station, only with a better prize: a massive packet of chocolate Hobnobs, something like that.

Despite the computers and iPads, Jessica was happy to hear that the sound of the school bell hadn't changed. There was a shrill *ding-ding-ding* and then voices in the distance.

Jessica pointed a thumb towards the door. 'I should probably go.' She was almost out of the door when she peered up to see the clock and turned back to Mrs Marsh. 'What time does school start?'

'Eight thirty.'

The head teacher held the door open for Jessica and they passed into the corridor. From the far end, a chattering buzz of excitement was building until it erupted as a chorus of girls emerged from around the corner. She noted they were all walking, keeping their heads down, with the din quieting as they spotted Mrs Marsh – aside from a few brave souls who offered the customary 'Good morning, Miss' as they passed.

Among the crowd, Jessica spotted April, head angled to the floor, following the other young people in an orderly line. The girl glanced up briefly, catching Jessica's eye, and then instantly looked away again as she heaved her bag higher on her shoulder and disappeared into her form room.

Jessica hurried to her car, phone clamped to her ear. Cars streamed past on the main road outside of the school, howling into the distance as they openly ignored the 20 mph limit.

'So, in short, nobody's found anything,' she said.

DC Rowlands sounded distracted as he replied, not that that was unusual. He'd probably spotted something shiny on the wall. 'Not only that, someone tipped off the *Herald* and they've been asking questions. Plus that bloke we spoke to last week with the matching van has been on at us because someone showed up at his work again.'

'Not again . . . what is it with idiots on the Internet jumping to conclusions? What did Cole say?'

'He's been in meetings all morning. The Chief Constable is in the house.'

'"*In the house*"? You sound like a granddad trying to be down with the kids by showing them his vinyl collection.'

'Whatevvvvvver.'

Even though nobody could see her, Jessica rolled her eyes. DC Izzy Diamond was due back from maternity leave soon and she couldn't wait to have a normal conversation again. It was typical: DCI Cole seemed to spend half his life holed up in his office and there was no point in asking about anyone else, seeing as DI Reynolds had recently been suspended and there was nobody incoming any time soon. The Chief Constable showing up was worse than policing a royal visit. At least a royal appearance meant someone would put on a buffet – usually a sodding good one. Victoria sponge, Earl Grey: the lot.

'What *has* been done?' Jessica asked.

'We've got some people going through the traffic cameras, uniforms going door-to-door looking for witnesses, the usual.'

'And nothing's come back?'

'It's like last week – white van, white male. The guv said the e-fit artist is stuck in Paris because of a Eurostar strike.'

'Isn't there anyone else who can do it?'

'Someone's phoning around. There's a guy in Lancashire but he's freelance and there was a problem over who pays him.'

Another eye roll. It was a good job most people didn't

get to see the inner workings of the police force. The people were great but the internal politics were a joke. Someone had tried to snatch a teenager from the street as she walked to school and they couldn't even get someone to put together an artist's impression. April had been shown the e-fit sketch of the apparent abductor from the previous week but the teenager had shaken her head, unsure, saying it might be the same person. It was anything but conclusive.

'Can you do me a favour?' Jessica asked.

'I'm not cleaning your car again. You told me there was a sponsored clean for Red Nose Day.'

'I was teaching you a life lesson, David: don't be so gullible. Anyway, the girl's name is April Willis. She lives somewhere around Alexandra Park. Can you get me an exact address? There can't be too many Willises around there. Text me when you have it.'

'Fine – but I'm still not cleaning your car.'

The front door would have once been white UPVC but was now speckled with a browny-grey crust of dirt. The thin frosted glass panels of the top half were equally dirty, making it impossible to see inside. There was a red and white wire poking out of the wall where there should have been a doorbell, with a strip of white paper taped to the letterbox, a simple message scrawled in felt-tip: 'NO FREE PAPERS'.

Jessica could hear a television inside – *Bargain Hunt*, unless she was very much mistaken. It was so loud, she could make out individual voices, so she knocked hard, stepping back onto the pavement and peering both ways along the long row of terraced houses. Cars were parked here and there, half on the pavement, with brown and blue bins scattered along the kerbside. A few streets over, there was the unmistakeable *beep-beep-beep* of a dustbin lorry reversing.

Nobody answered, so Jessica tried knocking on the window, pressing her forehead to the glass in an attempt to see inside. She could see the flickering light of the television but no other movement.

Not wanting to be beaten, Jessica walked to the far end of the terrace, heading into the thin alley that ran along the back, separating it from the identical row of houses behind. The cobbles were uneven, with chocolate wrappers, chip papers and a pile of pizza boxes dumped along the edges. She counted the houses until she was behind the correct one. There was a gate but it was rickety, wooden, and wide open. An invite, if ever she'd had one.

She stepped onto the crumbling patio, feet crunching across the loose stones. There were overgrown bushes along the sides, with an upturned barbeque underneath the kitchen window. Shoots of green poked through the gaps between the slabs and there was the general smell of grubbiness, like when you were underage and hung around by the bins at the back of Morrisons, drinking illicit cider out of sight of the rest of the world. Which Jessica *definitely* hadn't done. Well, not recently.

After pressing herself against the kitchen window and

spying the draining board full of crockery, she knocked hard on the back door.

'Hello?'

No answer.

'Mrs Willis?'

Jessica tried the window again. The television was still blaring and she could see the outline of someone's knee through a pair of open doors. As she knocked on the glass again, the knee twitched and then disappeared. Moments later, a woman appeared in the doorway, worry lines etched across her forehead. Her hair was thinning and she was wearing a giant tartan blanket. Even through the murky glass, there was an obvious resemblance: she shared April's brown eyes.

There was a clunk and the back door sprung open. Mrs Willis leant against it, scowling, though her unfocused eyes never met Jessica's, instead concentrating on the upturned barbeque. She didn't appear concerned that there was someone at her back door. 'I don't buy anything door-to-door,' she mumbled. 'My daughter has my card anyway.'

'Mrs Willis, I'm Detective Sergeant Jessica Daniel, and I'm here because of what happened with your daughter earlier.'

The woman shrugged, wobbling slightly as she tried to stand. 'What about her?'

'Um . . . I believe she phoned you . . . ?'

April's mother's pupils shrunk as she focused on Jessica before turning away again. 'Oh, right, that . . . it's all sorted, isn't it? No need for the police to get involved.'

Jessica watched her for a moment: the clothes, the overly loud TV, the filthy front and back of the house, the draining board. She nodded slowly.

'You're right,' Jessica said. 'No need to get involved. I'm just making sure you're all right. I tried the front but there was no answer.'

'I'm fine, love. Is that everything?'

Jessica said goodbye, returning to the front of the house. The dustbin lorry was at the far end of the road, the swarm of fluorescent-jacketed figures hurrying around, dragging the bins onto the street. The television was still blaring inside. Jessica checked behind her before approaching the blue bin outside April's house. She flipped the lid, peering inside to see exactly what she'd suspected: a cluttered pile of empty vodka bottles.

Jessica watched from the driver's seat of her car as the succession of women berated the uniformed officers in front of the school. There was a row of police cars stopped on the yellow zigzags as students streamed out, some jumping into nearby vehicles, others heading along the road in twos and threes. Jessica knew exactly what the women were angry about – 'it's a bit late for the police cars now, isn't it?' They were right, of course, though Jessica wasn't quite sure what they expected. It wasn't as if they could park marked cars outside every school in the area on the off chance somebody was trying to snatch children. Besides, neither April nor Lucy had said they'd been approached outside the school anyway. Apart from escorting each of the children home, there wasn't much they could do.

It was hard to tell that to concerned parents, though.

Jessica watched as April exited the school gates alongside another girl, button-clad bag slung over her shoulder. As soon as they reached the zebra crossing, the other girl headed one way, with April ducking into an alley that would eventually lead to Bold Street and her route home. Jessica waited for a few seconds, then reversed the car, did a U-turn, and sped along the street, taking two rights until she was parked at the far end of the alley, just in time to see April emerging, fiddling with an earphone that was dangling from the V of her sweatshirt. As Jessica opened the car door and clambered out, April peered up, spotting her, before quickly shifting her gaze to the road ahead.

'April.'

The girl turned to face Jessica, tugging at the earphone cable. 'What?'

'Can we go for a walk?'

'Why?'

'You know why.'

April shuddered, glancing quickly away from Jessica and starting to stumble along the path. 'I need to get home . . . my mum . . .'

'I went to see your mother.'

The girl spun, mouth open. 'Oh . . .'

Jessica nodded to the play park on the far side of the road. Someone had graffitied the word 'bum' across the climbing frame but the equipment was intact, which was more than could be said for most of the play parks in the area.

'When was the last time you played on the swings?' Jessica asked.

'Huh?'

'The swings – I can't remember the last time I went on.' Jessica checked both ways and started to cross the road. 'Come on.'

She didn't turn back but could hear April's trudging footsteps behind. Jessica headed through the low metal gate, stepping across the springy black stuff on the ground. There was none of that in her day – if you fell off, you cracked your head open on the rough concrete and learned a lesson. Now you'd land on the rubbery stuff and, five minutes later, be straight back on the roundabout. It felt like cheating.

Jessica sat on a swing and pushed herself gently with her feet until it started to rock. Without a word, April sat next to her, sitting and swaying her legs. With the gentle June sunshine and breezeless atmosphere, it was wonderfully relaxing. Doctors should prescribe this – balls to conventional medicine, go and play on the swings for a bit instead.

'How many times have you been late for school?' Jessica asked.

'What?'

'House points mean a lot to some people. You're in the House of Portia and you're going to win this year – unless something disastrous happens, like certain students losing merits for poor time-keeping. So how many times have you been late?'

Jessica turned sideways to see April shrugging. She was rocking gently, her bag abandoned on the floor in front of her.

'I know there was no white van man,' Jessica said.

For a moment, there was no reply. Jessica turned her gaze from April to the road ahead, where a police car zipped past, going too fast without its lights on. Tut, tut.

'Do you want to say anything?' Jessica added.

No reply.

Jessica planted her feet on the rubberised matting, stopping the swing and climbing off. She spun around, sitting the opposite way so that she could see April properly. When she'd been a teenager, she'd done this with her friend, Caroline, chatting about boys and their dreams for the future. Funnily enough, this had never been one of her ambitions.

'There might have been a white van with Lucy last week but not with you.'

April met her stare and, for the first time, Jessica saw the vulnerable thirteen-year-old. She was tiny, the weight of the world on her shoulders. There was no brightness to her gaze, no expectation of what life might hold for her.

'What do you mean?' April said, maintaining eye contact, trying to be sincere. Jessica had spotted too many liars in the past to be taken in.

'It was because you couldn't be late again. You phoned us at eight forty from school when you were supposed to be in registration for half past.'

'So?'

'When you realised you were going to be late again, you

panicked, until you remembered what Lucy had told people the previous week. No one's going to mark you down as being late if someone tried to snatch you from the street. That's why there were no other kids around, too. No witnesses, because they were already at school. Plus your description of the white van and the man was too similar to last week's.' She took out her phone, scrolling down the screen, and reading the account Lucy had given them. 'People see different things – even when they're looking at something identical,' Jessica went on. 'Witnesses will contradict one another over everything. One person will say the speeding car was grey, the person next to them that it was light blue. Someone will tell you they were assaulted by a man with brown hair, the witness across the road will insist the attacker was blonde. That's just the way it is – except that you and Lucy had identical stories.'

April continued swinging, her knees clamped together, feet kicking forward and back. She couldn't meet Jessica's eyes.

The girl spoke so softly that the words were almost lost. 'Are you going to tell anyone?'

Jessica looked away, staring towards the green on the far side of the park, where half-a-dozen lads had emerged through a hedge. They dropped their bags on the grass, creating goalposts, as one of them booted a football into the air.

'I have to tell some people where I work . . .' Jessica replied, pausing, wanting April to know it was serious. '. . . but not everyone.'

'Am I going to be in trouble?'

Jessica sucked on her bottom lip. This was the part of the job she hated: the grey areas. Bad guys were easy to deal with – find them, give them a metaphorical boot up the arse, then let the courts sort them out. What did you do with kids like April?

'What's it like at home?' Jessica asked.

April answered too quickly: 'It's fine.'

'Really?'

'It's brilliant.'

'So why not tell your mum that someone tried to snatch you from the street? Even if you'd made it up, it's surely the type of thing you'd tell her? You told Mrs Marsh you'd called.'

April stopped her swing. 'You didn't tell her, did you?'

Jessica planted her feet on the floor again, turning sideways until she and the girl were staring at each other.

'Are you caring full-time for your mum and then coming to school?'

April glared back for a moment, before standing abruptly and grabbing her bag. 'Of course not!'

Jessica stood too, manoeuvring in front of the girl and then keeping pace as April tried to walk away. 'You're only thirteen, April. You shouldn't have to do this.'

'Do what? Everything's fine.'

'I saw the vodka bottles in the recycling bin – besides, Mrs Marsh clearly thinks your mum's working somewhere, which isn't true. Your aunt came in for the last parents' evening and your teachers have only ever talked to your mum on the phone. Your mum even told me you have her debit card – does that mean you're doing the food shopping?'

April continued walking, reaching out to open the park gate, before Jessica rested against it, blocking the exit.

'It's only a few things on the way home,' April said.

Jessica sat on the top of the gate, wishing she could be better at this. *Thirteen?!* She'd grown up in a two-parent home with a mother and father who rarely fought and did everything they could for her.

'How often do you have to pick up a few things?' Jessica asked.

'I dunno . . .'

'If you're doing the shopping, where does the vodka come from?'

A shrug. April stared at her shoes. 'Are you going to tell social services?'

Jessica scratched at her head, wondering if she should lie. She could say 'no', and get more from the girl, but it wasn't fair. 'I've got to,' she whispered.

April barged her shoulder forward, trying to push past, but Jessica held the girl's upper arms as gently as she could. From nowhere, there were tears streaming down April's face. Her voice was a teary mix of sobs and furious anger.

'You don't know what it's like!'

Jessica leant forward, cupping her hand around the back of the girl's head and pulling her onto her shoulder.

'I know I don't,' she breathed softly.

April fought momentarily and then pressed her eyes into the base of Jessica's neck, rocking back and forth as she continued to cry. Jessica had no idea what to do, other than to hold her. Somewhere, there'd be guidelines about this, with a long list of things she'd probably done wrong.

The girl sniffed, hugging Jessica, before pushing herself away, wiping her eyes with her sleeve. Her cheeks were puffy and red, eyes swollen, hair ruffled and messy. Somehow, she was both a terrified thirteen-year-old and a world-weary grown-up.

'My dad died a year ago,' she croaked.

'I know.'

'It's not her fault. She's been sad ever since.'

'You're still only thirteen,' Jessica said.

April shrugged. 'If you tell people, they'll take me away.'

'How much do you do at home? The cooking? Cleaning? Do you pay the bills? Open the letters?'

Another shrug. 'It's fine.'

April's bottom lip was wobbling again.

Jessica took a deep breath, staring towards the boys on the far side of the park again. There were ten of them now, with two sets of schoolbags for goalposts. They were racing back and forth, shouting and laughing. Enjoying being young.

'I know someone,' Jessica said. 'She's called Esther and works for the police. She specialises in family issues but isn't social services. I'll have a word with her and ask her to visit you. If she's satisfied, then that'll be good enough for me. I can't simply forget all of this. You deserve better.'

April rubbed her sleeve across her eyes, sniffing and dabbing at her nose. 'What's Esther like?'

'She's fair,' Jessica held the girl's gaze, 'but you're the priority.'

April nodded slowly, straightening herself, trying to be confident again, as if the hug and sob had never happened. She took a breath, lifting her bag onto her shoulders, but nothing could hide the crack in her voice.

'Everything's going to be all right, isn't it?' she asked.

Jessica closed her eyes momentarily, listening to the boys playing football. To lie, or not to lie?

She opened her eyes, stepping away from the gate and opening it. 'Everything will be just fine,' she whispered.

COMING SOON

CROSSING THE LINE

Jessica Daniel Book 8

Nitric acid, baseball bats and HIV-filled syringes: people are being attacked publicly by a masked figure in the centre of Manchester, and Jessica Daniel doesn't know how to catch the person responsible.

Not that she'll get much help from the media – it's been twenty-five years since the notorious Stretford Slasher was caught, and those who can remember are feeling nostalgic.

With the city held in a wintry grip, Jessica has a case-load stacking up and an old friend to look after – and all while she's wilting under the shadow of secrets a quarter-of-a-century old.

COMING SOON

SOMETHING WICKED

The first book featuring
Private Investigator Andrew Hunter

Nicholas Carr disappeared on his eighteenth birthday and the world has since moved on. His girlfriend has gone to university, his friends have got jobs and the police have other cases to investigate.

But his father, Richard, is still hung up on the three fingers the police dug up from a sodden Manchester wood. What happened to Nicholas on the night he disappeared and why did he never come home?

Private Investigator Andrew Hunter is Nicholas's last hope – but Andrew has his own problems. There's something about his assistant that isn't quite right. Jenny's brilliant but reckless and he can't work out what she stands to gain from their working relationship. By the time he figures out who's a danger and who's not, it might all be too late . . .

extracts reading groups
competitions books new
books discounts extracts extracts reading groups discounts events
competitions extracts events
books reading groups
new discounts reading groups
events books extracts
reading groups books new extracts titles reading groups interviews new reading groups
interviews events extracts extracts reading groups books
books discounts events interviews new
new books events books extracts
events new events new extracts
discounts extracts discounts books
www.panmacmillan.com
extracts events reading groups
competitions books extracts new